To
TW

If ever thou shalt love,
In the sweet pangs of it, remember me.
For such as I am, all true lovers are;
Unstaid and skittish in all motions else,
Save in the constant image of the creature
That is beloved.

Twelfth Night, II, iv.

Lesbian Novels by Sarah Aldridge:

The Latecomer	1974
Tottie	1975
Cytherea's Breath	1976
All True Lovers	1978
The Nesting Place	1982
Madame Aurora	1983
Misfortune's Friend	1985
Magdalena	1987
Keep to Me Stranger	1989
A Flight of Angels	January, 1992

ALL TRUE LOVERS

Sarah Aldridge

the
Naiad
Press
inc.
1991

Printed in the United States of America on acid-free paper
First Edition
Second Printing, 1982
Third Printing, 1985
Fourth Printing, 1991

Cover design by Tee A. Corinne

ISBN: 0-930044-10-X
Library of Congress Catalog Card Number 78-59626

I
1932

She didn't know why she didn't tell her mother about it. It happened so unexpectedly. Because it was Wednesday she was later going home from school. Wednesday was the day she stayed for an extra hour with Miss Fitch, the English teacher. That meant that she did not travel in the streetcar that gathered up the whole mass of chattering, yelling, shoving adolescents who left the high school at three o'clock.

The streetcar she was on was half empty. None of the seats at the back were occupied and with a sense of luxury she picked out one several back from the stout woman who sat majestically in the middle of hers. In her usual dreaminess she gazed out of the window at the leaf-strewn pavements of Wisconsin Avenue. Miss Fitch's class was in the midst of Malory's *Morte d'Arthur*. A few of them had accepted Miss Fitch's suggestion that they study it as a drama. What a difference it made, thought Andrea, studying something like this in high school. She was still excited, half bold and half timid, at this rush into a quasi-adult world, away from the childishness of grade school.

Some other feeling intruded into her day-dreaming. To identify its source she looked around, into the back of the car. A man was standing in the middle of the aisle, close to her, just behind the stout woman's seat, facing her. At first she did not know what she was looking at — a shriveled, hairless, naked, pink thing, hanging limp against wrinkled white skin. It showed in the middle of the man's trousers, peeping out from what she suddenly realized must be his fly. Panic seized her, a deep-going fear. Automatically her eyes traveled up to his face. He was a slight man in a thread-bare suit and he was smiling at her in a grimace, his eyes glassy. She was too frightened to make a sound, but she looked wildly behind her to where the conductor stood near the rear door of the car, his back turned. As she looked away she half-saw the man hurriedly close his fly and move quickly to the front of the car. Still too shocked to feel relief, she saw him ring for the next stop and watched as he jumped off, almost running away along the street.

Half an hour later, when the car reached her own stop, where she changed to the Fourteenth Street car, she was still trembling. She had not been able to analyze her feelings. She had never been

1

told anything about a man's organ. Even as a little girl she had never joined schoolmates in whispered sessions of sexual discussion and exploration. Yet she knew the moment it was presented to her what she had been shown and what the gesture meant and it had aroused in her a profound, unarticulated fear.

It was only when she reached the front door of her parents' house that she began to realize that she was not going to tell her mother. Going up the steps she found in herself a mixture of feelings. As she came into the white wainscoted entry, her mother called to her from the kitchen. It was the commonplace thing for her mother to greet her this way as she got back from school and for her to go where her mother was and tell her immediately the incidents of the day.

The first half-hour of their talk passed and she had said nothing about the man. Once or twice her mother had glanced at her, as if about to comment on her quietness, her pallor. Finally her mother said, "It's time for your period, isn't it, Andrea?" She had only begun to menstruate a few months before and her mother was still preoccupied with the subject.

She nodded and still was silent about what had happened.

When she thought about it that night in bed, she realized why she had said nothing. Six months ago her mother had been reluctant for her to go to high school. She was too young, her mother said, a full year younger than the other children graduating from grade school. And then to go to Western High School, which her parents preferred to the other Washington high schools, half way across the city, transferring from one streetcar to another. For the first month or so she had been timid, often wishing that her mother had insisted and had held her back, safe at home. Her new schoolmates had frightened her with their greater sophistication. But she had fended off the aggressive attempts of both girls and boys to force her acquaintance, inwardly afraid of their inquisitiveness, their boldness, though striving to maintain a show of self-possession. They were curious, she guessed, sometimes antagonistic, because she was younger and yet resisted their bullying. They wanted to shock or perhaps they thought her innocence deceptive. She even overheard two of the teachers talking about her — "that pretty little blonde girl with the big innocent blue eyes. It's a pity she has to wear glasses."

But she had got over all that. She had established her own place in the eyes of everyone. The novelty wore off and she was largely left alone, ignored in the skirmishing between the defensively seductive girls and the predatory boys. When her mother asked her how things were going, she was able to say that everything was fine. She had no more trouble. Her mother now and then mentioned the fact that she did not seem to make friends, she never brought anyone home with her. But for the time being she wanted to be on the outside and watch.

2

It was the long car ride that had become precious to her. She was used to being always closely within her mother's surveillance. In this trip back and forth from school each day she began to savor a life of her own, a chance to see things for herself.

So she did not tell her mother about the man. After a few days the vividness of the encounter faded, the memory of it buried at the bottom of her mind, occasionally coming to the surface. At such times the episode unrolled in its own sequence — the sight of the man's penis, the sudden fear that overwhelmed her, the man's flight from the streetcar. The last remnant of the scene always lingered a little longer — the strange, shamed, pitiful appeal in his eyes and puckered face as he saw she had seen him and he turned to run away. Even if she had told her mother about what had happened, this last remembrance, something that stood out in sharp reality in the midst of her emotional reaction, was something she could never have explained to anyone, not even to her mother.

* * *

April came. She would be fourteen in two weeks. The first warmth had come too and the car windows were open to it. It made the crowd of boys and girls who always got on with her even more noisy and restless than they had been through the winter months.

It was then she first noticed the girl. The girl sat there, still, unspeaking in the midst of the noisy crowd. She got on at the stop at Q Street, with a group of girls from the Convent. Sometimes she got a seat near the front, on the long side bench behind the driver. Sometimes she stood, a little taller than the girls around her. In either case she seemed oblivious of her surroundings, her eyes on the distance, her face immobile. It was a long face, unsmiling, with a firmly closed mouth. A Catholic girl, thought Andrea, taught by the nuns, brainy, aloof. Once, when the girl had pushed her way down the aisle, her eyes had met Andrea's in a fleeting glance. They were grey, penetrating eyes, under long lashes. Andrea had waited, breathless, for the quick, casual nod that most of the girls gave you, acknowledging the fact that they saw you every day. But the girl's eyes had moved on, as if she had seen nothing.

After that Andrea waited, each day, for the moment when the girl boarded the streetcar. And she became aware that the girl was not as inattentive as she seemed. Her eyes would move quickly, glancing here and there. She was not, after all, wrapped in a disdainful daydream. But she sat there in the midst of the noisy pushing and shoving abstracted and wary. She did not act like the few grown people on the car — annoyed, impatient. But she was as little a part of the crowd as they were.

One afternoon the streetcar was so crowded that Andrea caught just a glimpse of her in the group of girls waiting at the Q Street stop. Then she was lost to view until the streetcar came to the stop in front of Stohlmann's ice-cream parlor, which always

3

acted as a signal for renewed uproar. A sudden shrieking filled the car and a mass of long-legged girls and hefty boys jostled each other to be the first out. Andrea could not see the girl for a while, hidden behind the struggling bodies. Then the car became half-empty and most of the passengers were middle-aged people, silent except for two women in the back intent on a whispered conversation. Andrea saw the girl alone in a seat halfway down the aisle. She was gazing out of the window, a truly abstracted expression on her face now. Andrea stared at her profile, seeing the long nose, the decided mouth, the sharply cut brows. That wasn't exactly a frown on her face. It was more a stern look, serious, absorbing, and left no place for frivolous thoughts.

The girl turned her head suddenly and the grey eyes met Andrea's. Andrea, in a panic, looked down at the pile of books on her lap. When she looked up again the girl had a book open and was reading.

* * *

It was Wednesday again and Andrea stayed for the extra hour with Miss Fitch's class.

It was almost May. The bright spring sunshine made the brick of the old houses rosy. The quiet of the street, which usually was thronged with her classmates all headed for Wisconsin Avenue, seemed to change its character. I like this a lot better, thought Andrea. She noticed roses blooming in the small front gardens, the curious pattern of the brick-paved roadway, the small birds taking dustbaths in the gutters — all sorts of things unseen in the usual afternoon rush.

The streetcar when she boarded it held only a few people, mutely absorbed in their own concerns. The trip home on Wednesdays was always the same, the long car ride through desultory traffic, in the lull after the schoolchildren had gone and before the bustle of people coming home from the government offices downtown. Andrea sat dreaming in the serene sunlight. At the stop at Q Street she automatically looked toward the pavement. She did not expect to see the girl

But there she was, climbing into the car, the only passenger waiting at that stop. She handed her ticket to the conductor and glanced up the aisle. Each seat held one person, next to the window. An impulse seized Andrea to gesture towards the seat by herself and the next moment she was paralyzed by the mere thought of having done so. The girl paused. Then she came down the aisle and dropped into the seat beside her.

"Hello," she said, offhandedly, and settled the burden of books on her lap.

"Hello," said Andrea, and after a silence, "You're late today, aren't you?"

The grey eyes came round to study her. "And so are you."

"Oh, no —! I mean, I'm not late for Wednesday."

4

The girl's eyebrows went up. "For Wednesday?"

"I take an extra English period on Wednesday."

After another silence Andrea said, her mind racing ahead in search of a bridge of words, "Do you go to Annunciation?"

As the girl nodded the little golden cross on the thin golden chain around her neck stirred.

As she said nothing, Andrea offered — here I am babbling, she thought distractedly as she spoke — "I go to Western."

The girl nodded again. That was stupid, thought Andrea. She would assume that. Still unable to restrain herself, she added, "I expect you guessed that."

Again the girl glanced round at her. "You could have been going to the National Cathedral School. They have day students, don't they?"

"Why, I think they do."

The streetcar reached M Street. The girl's attention seemed taken by the shops they passed. Soon she will be getting off, thought Andrea. She always gets off at Washington Circle. I've seen her walk across and go up New Hampshire Avenue. Why don't I just ask her what her name is? She said aloud, "My name is Andrea — Andrea Hollingsworth."

"Mine's Isabel — Isabel Essory."

After the next stop Andrea said, "You get off soon, don't you?"

"Ordinarily I would. But today I've got to go downtown. Sister Mary Joseph has sent me to Muth's for some supplies for the art class."

"Do you draw and paint?"

"Oh, no."

"Then, why —?"

"Oh, Sister Mary Joseph is our bursar. She often sends me on errands to buy supplies when we need things. I like going to the bookstores best. But last time she sent me to Kann's to price sheets and pillow cases." Isabel paused for a moment and then added thoughtfully, "It's all interesting."

The streetcar was passing the White House. Andrea said hastily, "I have to get off at Fourteenth Street, too. I live on Rittenhouse Street."

They got off the car together and stood for a moment on the street corner. A sense of politeness seemed to hold both of them. Then Isabel said, shifting her burden of books into a more comfortable angle, "Well, goodbye." And Andrea, clutching her armful nervously, replied daringly, "See you tomorrow."

* * *

Thursday afternoon was like every other day — the streetcar filled to capacity with chattering, restless girls and boys. Andrea pushed her way on, anxious to find a place in the car from which she could see Isabel get on at the Q Street stop. But Isabel was not one of the small crowd of girls boarding. Andrea went the rest of the way home in dejection. She was absentminded through the evening when her mother spoke to her and went to her room early to do her homework.

Friday Isabel was there, one of the first to board the streetcar, with the patient, resolute movement that was characteristic of her. She doesn't act, thought Andrea, as if any of those girls are friends of hers. The Annunciation Convent girls were easy to spot. Their clothes had a certain elegance in contrast to those of most of the girls from the public high school. They all had an air of greater assurance, a touch of aloofness in their manner even when they eyed the boys covertly, under cover of uninterrupted conversation among themselves. Isabel was different. She gave the air of being by herself, not a part of the throng of girls surrounding her. And her clothes — yes, her serge skirts, her plain white blouses were shabby.

Andrea held her breath as Isabel pushed her way down the aisle to stand beside her seat. Wildly Andrea thought of getting up to let Isabel sit down or at least to stand with her. But the impulse died under the eyes of the boys pressing around them. Instead she said, "Do you want me to hold your books for you?"

Silently Isabel helped her pile the books on top of those already balanced on her knees.

"I didn't see you yesterday," Andrea said timidly.

Isabel looked down into her eyes, her gaze as calm and aloof as ever. "I had to help Sister Agnes grade papers for the junior girls."

"Do you do that a lot?" What a silly question! Andrea exclaimed to herself in despair.

"Oh, quite a lot. It's good practice."

"Are you going to be a teacher?"

An ironical look came into Isabel's eyes. "I'm going to be anything I can earn a living at." There was a little flicker of anger in her face as she spoke.

Andrea, chagrined, dropped her eyes and was silent.

She spent the weekend dreamy, inattentive, impatient for Monday. But Monday she had to stay behind, held by the algebra teacher. She could make no sense of algebra. But Mr. Compton, the algebra teacher, was patient and friendly. He insisted on going over her test paper to point out her basic misunderstanding. There were certain principles, he said, that she would have to clarify in her own mind before she could solve the simplest problem. As he talked on, Andrea, striving to pay attention to him, looked out of the wide classroom window and watched the stream of students passing down the steps of the school and down the walk that led to the street. The afternoon was warm and breezy. Most of the girls wore their thin blouses, with only sweaters over them. She remembered that Isabel's sweater was always the same one — pale yellow with the sleeves pulled up a little on her firm round arms.

6

"Andrea, you're going to have to buckle down and study if you expect to pass algebra this year." The exasperated male voice penetrated the fog of her dreaming. Guiltily she looked back at the teacher, aware now that he had observed her gazing out of the window. From the expression on his face she guessed at his thoughts — "these girls, wrapped up in adolescent yearning for boys' attentions." A little smile blossomed in her heart. Boys. She set herself to concentrate on what he was saying about binomial theorems and integral indices.

He gave her extra homework to do and said to bring it back next day and stay after class for half an hour so that he could go over it with her. Andrea's heart sank. The time after supper, when she should have been thinking only of the exercises she had to master, she spent instead seeking some means of avoiding the delay in catching the streetcar. If she stayed after school, she would inevitably miss Isabel again.

When the class ended she thought desperately of gathering up her books and running out of the building before she could be stopped. But she lacked the courage. Her heart leaden within her, she walked up to Mr. Compton's desk and laid her work paper on it.

Mr. Compton glanced at it and at her. "Oh, Andrea, we're going to have to postpone this. I've got a teachers' meeting to attend. Here, do these pages —" he caught up her algebra book and indicated them — "and bring everything back to me tomorrow."

Joy was behind the brilliant smile she gave him as she snatched up the book and ran down the hall.

She did not get a seat in the streetcar. But she was standing near the door when Isabel got in and stood next to her.

"I missed this car yesterday," Andrea said, with eager happiness.

Isabel's calm face was turned towards her. "I thought I didn't see you yesterday. But there is always such a mob on here."

Andrea giggled nervously. Isabel had looked for her. "I had to stay behind and see Mr. Compton. He teaches algebra. I'm not very good at algebra."

Isabel accepted this confession with a nod. It was not indifference. Perhaps she took such incompetence for granted but with sympathy.

"Do you like algebra?" What an idiotic question, Andrea thought as soon as it was out of her mouth.

"Not especially. But if I go into science, I've got to have it."

"Science?"

"Physics, chemistry, medicine —"

"Do you want to be a doctor?"

Isabel's calm eyes met hers. "At this point I couldn't say."

"I should think that would be wonderful — to be a doctor."

"Do you want to be one?"

"Oh, no! I don't think I could. I haven't — the — the — Well, I

7

just couldn't. But I think you would be wonderful as a doctor."

The faintest smile came into Isabel's eyes. "There's a lot more to it than that." She seemed to have guessed what Andrea left unsaid. "It takes a lot of time and a lot of money."

"But you could get scholarships and things."

"Could I?" Isabel's smile became more definite.

Why do I have to sound such a fool? despaired Andrea, looking out of the window to hide her vexation.

But Isabel seemed to guess that, too, and said soberly, "It's not so easy to get scholarships when you're a girl — I mean, the kind I would have to have. Girls don't usually choose science."

Restored, Andrea said earnestly, "I meant, you're so brainy and all —"

"How to you know that?" Isabel's voice was sharp.

Andrea blushed with confusion. "I just guessed it. You look that way." She waited fearfully for Isabel's cutting reply, but Isabel said nothing and presently she stole a glance at her face. Isabel was frowning but at something in her own thoughts. They were both silent as the car clattered across the M Street bridge.

Presently Andrea asked, "Are you going downtown today?"

"No, I've got to be home early. My mother has to go to the doctor."

"Do you have to go with her?"

"Oh, no, but somebody has to mind the boys — keep them quiet while my stepfather's sleeping."

"Oh." Andrea strove to fit this information into her picture of Isabel. Up till now Isabel had appeared in her consciousness as Isabel alone, a clever girl, surrounded by sympathetic nuns who relied upon her good sense. Now Isabel was a daughter, a step-daughter, a sister. She said impulsively, "I wish we could talk some more," as Isabel reached up to press the button.

Isabel looked down at her. But all she said was, "See you tomorrow."

But tomorrow was Wednesday and there was no Isabel at the Q Street stop when Andrea reached there. The afternoon seemed an utter waste. She fretted through the hours at home, dimly aware, through her preoccupation, that her mother noticed her self-absorption. She sat up late in her room, school books spread around her as a shield, until her mother, coming to her door for the third time, commanded her to turn out her light and go to bed. But even then she did not sleep and spent the dark hours wondering about Isabel, remembering Isabel's mannerisms, seeing Isabel's self-possessed gestures, Isabel's aloof face. It was almost morning when the brilliant thought came to her and she fell asleep.

But the next day was Thursday and she was not able to get near enough to Isabel to talk, only to nod at her in the distance. Thursdays the car was filled not only with school children but with many black women who worked as maids in the neighborhood of the high school. Then the car was always full beyond the stop at Washington Circle. She saw Isabel step down, waving to her as she waited on the curb to cross the street.

The next day, Friday, she felt desperate. The weekend loomed and she could not face having no glimpse of Isabel till Monday. She would put her plan into action. She escaped from the classroom a few minutes ahead of the bell, intent on catching the streetcar that preceded the one she usually boarded. Breathless she climbed into it and stood fidgeting at the back door until it reached Q Street and she could jump off. Impatiently she waited, eagerly watching the pavement down which the girls from the Convent must come. Her heart leaped at the sight of Isabel, taller than most of the others and a little behind them, walking with her confident, unhurried step, certain that she would reach the carstop in time.

The group of girls filled the narrow, brick-paved sidewalk. Their voices, mingled, punctuated by sudden laughs and little cries, flowed towards Andrea. To get past them she stepped over the thick, upraised roots of an old maple tree that had heaved up the bricks and cobbles in the street. Isabel, whose long gaze had shifted suddenly to focus on her, stopped in surprise as she reached her.

"Isabel, can you wait for another car?"

Isabel looked at the backs of the other girls, running now and screaming, and at the streetcar pulling to a stop at the corner and then turned her eyes on Andrea. She said nothing.

Andrea persevered. "Can you come with me to Stohlman's and have an ice-cream soda?"

Isabel, reordering her thoughts, nodded and they walked slowly side by side down the still shady street to Wisconsin Avenue. At Stohlman's they sat at one of the little tables in a far back corner, away from the big mirrors behind the soda fountain. Isabel had said nothing when Andrea had paid for the sodas. They had scarcely sat down when the parlor filled up abruptly with girls and boys stopping by for ice-cream cones and within a few minutes as quickly emptied.

Andrea said, "I haven't seen you to talk to since Tuesday."

"Well, you're always late on Wednesday. I was late, too, but I didn't see you."

With an acute sense of loss, Andrea protested, "But why weren't you on the same car, then?"

Isabel pondered for a moment. "It was Miss Bosanquet's fault."

"Who's she?"

"The new lay French teacher. Reverend Mother wanted some of the older girls to stay and meet her — those that are going to be in her class."

"Are you one of them?"

Isabel's tone was crisp. "I'm not. But Reverend Mother thought it would be a good thing, because I can speak French. At

9

least, I can speak more than the others."

Andrea's tone was fervent. "I'll bet you're a whizz at it."

Isabel looked directly at her over her straw. "Why do you suppose that?"

Hot with embarrassment Andrea retorted. "Didn't you say you were at the Convent on a scholarship? You have to be good at things to get a scholarship."

Isabel was gazing pensively at the big ceiling fan hanging motionless over their heads. "I don't know how she's going to work out."

"Who?"

"Miss Bosanquet."

"Do you like her?"

Isabel shrugged. "It's more important for her to like me."

"Why?"

"Because I'm supposed to get lessons in advanced French from her. It's Reverend Mother's idea." Isabel paused for the tiniest second before adding, "I think Reverend Mother thinks it will be good for Miss Bosanquet's soul."

Andrea was mystified, watching the secret smile on Isabel's face. "What do you mean, Isabel? Doesn't Miss Bosanquet want to?"

"She won't get paid for it. But she has to do it if Reverend Mother says so."

"Oh." Andrea drained the last drops in her glass through the straw. "What is she like?"

Isabel drained her glass. "Bossy -talky — knows all about everything — French. She has stirred things up. She says anything she likes. Some of the Sisters are shocked. They say she isn't even respectful, much less devout. She made a joke about a religious painting that hangs in the hall. They were scandalized, though it's not great art. But she is witty. She makes everybody laugh in spite of themselves. Reverend Mother says she knows everything there is to know about French literature. She's fascinating, really."

A dart of jealousy went though Andrea. "How old is she? Is she pretty?"

"No, she's middle-aged and she has big black eyebrows. But she's got a sort of elegance and she can think as fast as lightning."

"Do you think she likes you?"

Isabel contemplated her in silence. Finally she said, "I don't think liking people is important to her. I think she feels hemmed in with a lot of schoolgirls and nuns. She wants to have some men around to show off in front of. What a man thinks is more important to her than what a woman thinks." Isabel paused. "Most women feel that way. They think men are more rational, that they're wiser. They've got the key to things."

"Oh." Inwardly Andrea looked fearfully into that dark unknown she had been aware of and yet had ignored ever since she

10

had realized that there was a difference between men and women. Her mother had instructed her about menstruation and childbirth. But the instructions had stopped there. Her mother had also made clear that no self-respecting girl had anything to do with a man until she was married, but her mother had not elucidated what having anything to do with a man consisted of. Obviously her mother depended on the force of nature to lead her to the right conclusion and in fact she did guess what men and women did together, in a general way. But something further lay beyond all this. Isabel's words seemed to lead in the same direction. Why was a man's opinion more valuable than a woman's? Her mother had the habit of deferring any important decision until she had consulted Andrea's father. I shall have to see what your father says, she would say, though obviously she had already made up her mind.

Andrea asked, "Then why does she teach in a Convent school?"

"Because she can't get a good job just now anywhere else. She knows Reverend Mother treats her better than anybody else would. She really respects Reverend Mother."

"Then she ought to be thankful."

"Thankful?" Isabel's tone was derisive. "I don't think Mademoiselle wastes much time being thankful for anything." She got up. "I guess we'd better go now."

* * *

The car today was full and they were getting close to Washington Circle, where Isabel got off when she was going straight home. They had not been able to sit together or even stand side by side in the press of bodies. In fact, it did not seem to Andrea that Isabel had made any effort to come towards her. There was a strange look on Isabel's face — a set look around her mouth, as if her teeth were clenched, and her eyebrows were drawn down. Andrea had seen that look on her mother's face sometimes, when her parents had had one of their disagreements or her mother was displeased about something else. But she had not seen it on the face of a girl before.

On an impulse Andrea followed Isabel off the streetcar when it stopped at the Circle. They were separated by the jostling of the little girls from the nearby parochial school who were crowding on board. Isabel did not know that she had got off behind her until she caught up to her at the curb, about to cross Pennsylvania Avenue.

"Isabel!" Isabel!"

Startled, Isabel turned to look at her with wide eyes. "What is it? Why did you get off here."

"I wanted to talk to you. You were 'way up front. My transfer is good for half an hour."

Isabel did not reply and they crossed the street to the Circle and, in a tacit understanding, walked to an empty bench under one

11

of the big elm trees and sat down. George Washington on his horse had his back to them, looking down the Avenue to the White House. The other benches were chiefly filled with women minding small children and babies or old men with canes. Occasionally there were younger men, sitting with their arms flung out along the bench-back or hunched forward with their heads hanging down. The two girls recognized them — unemployed men, resting for a while in the endless search for jobs or waiting hopelessly for the afternoon to pass so that they could return home or go and look for somewhere to spend the night. The bonus marchers had begun to arrive in Washington, bands of unkempt, hungry-looking men who set up camp in the parks, in empty buildings, in vacant lots. The newspapers, Andrea knew, alarmed her mother. A million marchers, they said, were converging on Washington from all over the country. Her father talked about the groups of idle, truculent men he saw on his way to and from work, standing about on the street corners or coming up to accost him when he parked his car, asking for money. The economic condition of the country, he said, was getting daily worse.

Isabel said, looking away from the man sitting opposite them, "Your mother's going to be uneasy about you being late."

"I'll tell her I had to talk to one of my teachers about my grades."

"Are you having trouble with your grades?"

"I'm not doing as well in school as I usually do."

"Why aren't you?"

"I guess I don't pay attention the way I should." She glanced timidly at Isabel. Can't you tell, she thought, that I can't pay attention to anybody or anything when I get to thinking about you? Can't you tell that my life is in upheaval, that all at once that placid, smooth, childish life I used to lead, so empty, so nothing, is now filled with you? That I can't study, I can't listen sensibly to people? Don't you know?

She glanced at Isabel. Isabel sat looking across the park.

To fill up the silence she said, "It's all so silly."

"What's silly?"

"Oh, all the things I'm supposed to learn. I guess it's just —" She could not find the words to express her feelings and stopped. She had lived in books ever since she had learned to read. Books had aroused in her vivid emotions — the howling of winter winds across barren wastes, the poet Horace's delightful languor sitting by a fountain eating grapes in the Roman sunshine, the tempest of Jane Eyre's unrequited love, Juliet's despair. All these things had been far more alive in her than the incidents of her own life. How could she explain to Isabel now that books seemed dead things, remote things, far-off, inconsequent? Her mind, her heart now was so filled with this all-encompassing splendor, something so personal, so glorious, so entirely hers — How could what she read in

12

books compare with it?

She glanced up to see that Isabel was looking at her. But Isabel did not press her for an explanation. Instead she said, "I get tired of reading sometimes. Even if it isn't something I have to study. But usually I have plenty of other things to do."

"I like to play tennis," said Andrea, eagerly. "Do you have courts at your school?"

"I've learned how. But I don't have much time to practice. It takes a lot of practice — like learning the piano."

"Do you do that, too?"

"Sister Mary Cecilia is teaching me, whenever she has some time and I do. The trouble is, I don't have a piano. I have to practice at school, after hours. Even if I had a piano, I couldn't practice at home."

"Why not?"

"Too much noise, too much interference."

Something in her manner stilled Andrea's tongue but presently she asked, "You live near here, don't you?"

"On New Hampshire Avenue — up there." She pointed.

"In a house?"

"No, an apartment. I wish it was a house."

"Why?"

"There'd have to be more room. But I bet I know what would happen if we lived in a house. We'd have roomers. That would be worse."

Still held back by shyness Andrea nevertheless found her voice to ask, "How many brothers and sisters do you have?" Catholics usually had large families.

Isabel's eyes, ironic and yet half-angry, were turned directly on her, as if she understood the implication. "I've got two half-brothers, little kids, brats. They fight all the time. My mother can't manage them worth beans."

"Oh."

"We've got two bedrooms. I sleep on the couch in the living room. My stepfather works at night. He's a mechanic. He works at the Navy Yard. He gets mad if he's waked up."

She stopped abruptly. Andrea, aware of a different Isabel from the cool, indifferent girl who sat so composed among the noisy crowd on the streetcar, said nothing.

It became a habit for Andrea to step off the streetcar at Washington Circle, whenever Isabel was headed home. With tacit understanding they spent the half hour her car transfer permitted sitting on a bench, talking. It was the second Isabel, made talkative by a consoling sense of drama, sometimes brooding and resentful, that came to the surface.

"I guess I'd have left home and gone to the dogs by now, if it hadn't been for Aunt Gertrude."

"What did she do?"

13

"She's paying for my education. That is, she persuaded Reverend Mother to take me into the school at half-rates. She's paying the difference."

"Why, that's wonderful!"

"Wonderful? Well —" Isabel's gaze was on her, speculative, as if she was considering some other, deeper, larger, more remote problem that Andrea could not be expected to understand.

"I mean, it's wonderful for her to think so much of you — of your brains — that is she is willing to pay for your schooling."

The expression on Isabel's face changed to ironic amusement. "Aunt Gertrude doesn't give a hoot about my brains. She's only interested in my immortal soul — and getting back at my mother."

Andrea was bewildered and embarrassed. "Is she your father's sister?"

"She's not really my aunt. She's my great-aunt — my father's aunt." As Andrea still looked bewildered, she explained, "My father's side of the family are Catholics — well, I suppose I should say that Aunt Gertrude is. There isn't anybody else left. She didn't like it when my father married my mother. My mother is not a Catholic. She doesn't care, really, what I am. But Aunt Gertrude thinks if she sends me to Catholic schools, the Sisters will turn me into a good Catholic. She's snatching me away from the Devil."

Andrea's embarrassment deepened. "Don't you care, Isabel?"

The frown returned to Isabel's face, the cool hardness to her voice. "That's the least of my worries. I'd do anything for an education."

Andrea said nothing. Isabel gathered up her books and said, "Your half hour is up. You'd better catch the next streetcar."

The next day they got off the streetcar together and crossed to the park and found a bench. Isabel was silent. The May day was warm. The man on the bench opposite them had taken off his coat and rolled up his shirt sleeves. The fat woman sitting next to him was fanning herself with a folded newspaper. Some sparrows hopped about near them, watching to see if any crumbs would fall.

Andrea glanced at Isabel. She wanted to talk to her, to cut through the brooding silence in which Isabel was wrapped, but she felt timid. It was a relief when Isabel suddenly said,

"Miss Bosanquet is making things lively."

"Is she giving you lessons?"

"Yes. That is, she always talks to me in French and sometimes she gives me a book to read and assigns a review." She stopped and after a pause, went on, "She is not a bad sort. She just doesn't like to work for nothing. Well, I wouldn't either. She gets annoyed at me, but I don't think she really holds it against me personally."

"How does she makes things lively?"

"She speaks her mind. She has a lot of modern ideas about Catholic doctrine. She belongs to some advanced philosophical society. I don't understand it all. And she's very sophisticated. She

14

doesn't think girls should be so sheltered from the world. She has a wicked sense of humor."

"Do the Sisters approve of that?"

"Some of them are shocked. She's not even respectful, they say. I told you she made some pretty scathing remarks about a painting of the Virgin Mary that hangs in the hall outside the refectory — said it was worse than a child's daub and how could we form any sort of appreciation of painting if we looked at that every day. Then she went on to say that it was enough to take her appetite away, but that maybe that was just as well because obviously our cook had never learned the rudiments of the culinary art."

Andrea giggled and Isabel grinned at her.

"Of course, some people don't like her. They're not used to someone who talks like that. But she doesn't seem to care if people don't like her."

"What else does she do?"

"Well, sometimes I hear her speaking French to one of the other lay teachers when none of the innocents are around and then you can really hear something!"

'What do you mean?"

Isabel's eyes, watching the sparrows, gleamed under her lowered eyelids. "She has a lot of pretty racy things to say — about the men she's known. She hasn't spent all her life in convent schools. This is sort of a comedown for her." Andrea, watching her face, saw it cloud again with some remembered resentment. "But she doesn't have to act as if I was a dummy. She caught me listening today and she told me off — not because she cares whether she's saying things I shouldn't hear — that wouldn't bother her in the least. She just doesn't want me going and telling Reverend Mother. Damn her!"

The injustice that had created the mood Andrea had first noticed had boiled to the surface. Isabel suddenly stood up. "You'd better go. It's silly to sit here jawing about it."

But Andrea, also getting up, caught at her arm. "Isabel, don't go! Talk to me some more. Oh, I don't want you to go!"

Isabel's frown was now furious. She was stiff with resentment, disgust — at what? thought Andrea, in despair.

Isabel said harshly, contemptuously. "What do you want me to do? I've got to get home and look after the brats. You don't know what my life is. You don't have any responsibilities. You can do just what you like, you little mamma's darling!"

Andrea, stunned, watched her walk quickly to the outer pavement of the Circle. She ran after her and clutched at her arm. They reached the other side of the roadway together and stood at the corner from which New Hampshire Avenue led off under the arch of great elm trees. Isabel turned round angrily and told her to go home.

Andrea said stubbornly, "Why can't I walk with you to your apartment building? It's only three blocks. I can get another streetcar."

"I don't want you to! For Pete's sake, go on home! I don't want you tagging along after me!"

"I just want to be with you a few minutes longer!" Andrea's eyes, in spite of herself, filled with tears.

"Well, for God's sake, don't stand there crying!" Isabel glanced nervously around. There was no one near them except a red-eyed old man in a ragged coat, watching them. Andrea saw his leer but still she could not bring herself to leave Isabel.

Isabel, reacting to the old man's grin, began walking as fast as she could. Andrea, wavering for a moment, slowly turned back and walked dejectedly towards the streetcar.

She felt the familiar self-loathing, self-contempt. Why had she acted that way to Andy? Loving, unthreatening Andy, who gazed at her with such adoration. Andy's stricken eyes stared at her all the way up New Hampshire Avenue. Of course, Andy was not the cause of her sudden rage. It was her own thoughts, sparked off by Andy's innocent questions. She could never explain all this to Andy. She didn't want to. Andy dwelt in a special place in her heart, in that secret place inside herself. But Andy did not know that. Andy had seen only her bad temper, heard her angry words. She had trampled roughshod over Andy's feelings. Perhaps this was the end of their friendship. She could scarcely blame Andy, if it were. What a damn fool she was when it came to dealing with people.

She began to mourn in her heart. Why couldn't she keep her dealings with people on an even level, a normal plateau of dignity and good feeling? Other people seemed to be able to do this without effort, with no special thought. They could exchange opinions, recollections, even opposed views without feeling a threat to themselves, without a later shame for being intemperate, self-revealing, giving offense. There seemed to be in them no inner spot of fire, like a mine set off by a careless foot.

It was the after-thoughts that were so painful. Did anyone else examine and re-examine their own feelings, the impression they might have made? After any encounter that had any meaning, she could remember with the greatest clarity the words she used, the expression on the other person's face. Then she would be led to wonder, had they understood just what she meant, had she given herself away irreparably, to ridicule or condescension? Even when, in the first flush of recall, she looked back on a certain half-hour or even an encounter of a few minutes with happy self-confidence, cheerful friendliness, in a little time these self-doubts came up and after a while she no longer wanted to remember the episode or savor the pleasure, fearful that her good showing had been made only in her own mind, that in fact there had been fatal flaws in her

16

behavior that had been instantly apparent to the other person.

Mademoiselle kept her off-balance especially. Mademoiselle's manner was insidious. Most of the time she treated Isabel as a semi-confidante, someone in whose common sense and superior intelligence she relied, someone whose natural gifts of mind and heart made it possible for her to single her out as a sympathetic peer. There was flattery in this, to be so singled out. But mademoiselle was capricious and at the times when she railed against her fâte or savagely criticized the students, the nuns and even Reverend Mother, she lashed out also at Isabel. Some instinct seemed to tell her of Isabel's shaky self-esteem, and a devilish pleasure entered into her quick tongue in saying things that would demolish Isabel's brief moments of self-assurance.

I shouldn't let her upset me, Isabel told herself. Even if I'm not a whizz at everything, I'm quicker than the others. Her common-sense told her that at such times mademoiselle was only venting her own frustrations. After all, she should not really place so much value on the praise given by someone whose good opinion was based on such a shallow estimate, whose character had such obvious flaws. But mademoiselle was the only person who saw her whole, close-to, who treated her on the basis of intimacy, who most of the time, at least, did not discount her as a mere fifteen-year-old girl with no acquaintance with life.

Intimacy. Real intimacy of mind, emotions. Even — and Isabel looked fearfully at this from the corner of her mind's eye — physical intimacy. She longed for that all-encompassing intimacy, was so filled with longing, in fact, that she thought sometimes she would be consumed by it. That was when she was most vulnerable to mademoiselle. And then was when mademoiselle seemed most aware of her vulnerability. Or did her own awareness give mademoiselle a discernment she did not really have? Was it only her own knowledge of herself that caused her to endow mademoiselle with prescience?

She was studying Moliere with mademoiselle and mademoiselle, under cover of the satire and the puns of the seventeenth century French playwright, maintained a running fire of comments with double meanings. Mademoiselle liked an audience, so she chose to give Isabel her lessons in the corner of the refectory, where they were more or less in the midst of the comings and goings of Convent daily business. Isabel, catching the spirit of the thing, played up to her, enjoying in spite of herself the wondering, frowning, admiring glances of the nuns, the other students, the Convent servants, even the occasional, sparkling, knowing surveillance of Reverend Mother herself. She knew that she did well, remarkably well, in keeping up with mademoiselle. She knew that the better she did, the faster, the more elaborate mademoiselle's speech and innuendoes became.

At the end of these sessions she was exhilarated, keyed-up to a pitch of excitement that took her completely out of herself. Life at this level was glorious, endowed with a splendid future, full of open doors to magnificence. The only equal moments were those when she was able to lose herself in music, in Beethoven especially, when her spirit was carried along from the meanness of everyday life into something dazzling, many-colored, pregnant with a brilliant future. Those moments were solitary. You needed to be alone, uninterrupted, almost disembodied, to soar away on the emotions aroused by the music. And when the music ended, life seemed to reclaim her so instantly, so completely. Whereas the euphoria that followed mademoiselle's lessons lingered — lingered until her self-doubts reasserted themselves, until the self-analysis, the painstaking recollection of each phrase she had uttered, each mistake she had surely made, deflated it. Mademoiselle nearly always left her with a brisk, "Bon! A bientôt. Tu dois recapituler les significations caracteristiques de Moliere, ses humeurs, les perspectives de son âge." It was mademoiselle's way of conferring praise.

But today mademoiselle had been in a temper. Something had happened beyond Isabel's ken that had set ablaze her uneasy spirits. And Isabel had been her whipping boy, her scapegoat.

I know that, said Isabel to herself, as she reached the apartment. Why do I give her so much importance. And I've lost Andy.

She went up the stairs to the apartment and fetched the little boys. She could take them to the grocery store. There was no way she could keep them quiet at home.

* * *

When her mother returned, she set out to visit Aunt Gertrude. She did not mention where she was going, because it always irritated her mother for her to mention the old lady. But her mother knew and said sharply, "I'm not going to wait dinner."

Isabel did not answer. The misery of her thoughts still held her. It would be impossible for her to explain to anyone the grinding demand that her life seemed to make on her spirit. To whom would she explain it? Reverend Mother? Reverend Mother would have some inkling, no doubt, would try to understand, try to soothe, but most surely she would give a gentle lecture on moral values and the importance of faith in turning one's thoughts away from worldly frustrations.

Aunt Gertrude? How very far away Aunt Gertrude seemed from the realities of her life. Dutifully she paid a visit to Aunt Gertrude at least once a week. Aunt Gertrude lived in a tall apartment house with an elevator, overlooking Washington Circle, its back to the slum where the black people lived closer to the river. She was the widow of a judge and though everyone said she had means, for years she had supplemented her income by giving piano lessons to children. Her family had come from Germany in the 1850s and music was a tradition with them. Isabel wondered, when she thought of the matter, whether the lessons were a means of keeping the practice of music in her life, rather than a source of money.

Whenever she visited Aunt Gertrude she stepped into a world far from the chaos of her mother's. The judge had served in the administration of the United States occupation of the Philippines after the Spanish American war. Her apartment was cluttered with oriental furniture and ornaments. These came originally, she had once explained to Isabel, from China, carried away during the upheaval of the Boxer Rebellion at the beginning of the nineteenth century and offered for sale in Manila while she and her husband lived there. A huge black-enamelled screen stood just inside the front door, so that when you came into the apartment you could not see at once into the livingroom. Only by turning around could you see its inset panels painted in brilliant colors, showing landscapes with tiny figures climbing mountain trails, gazing across lakes from airy pagodas, dallying on bridges with fellow travellers in palanquins.

In Aunt Gertrude's apartment there was a resolute sense of preserving privacy, hindering clear views of anything, in the Victorian stuffiness. From the windows you looked down on Washington Circle. Isabel wondered if Aunt Gertrude had ever observed her sitting down there on a bench with Andy. But the big trees hid most of the park. In the distance was the flat landscape of Washington, red-roofed four and five story houses amid the green of lofty trees, reaching to the ridge of the Maryland hills on the northern horizon. Further away, down towards Georgetown, were the huge gas tanks, close to the river, surrounded by lumber yards and coal yards, amid streets lined with small, untidy brick houses. But she doubted if Aunt Gertrude ever looked out. The windows were always swathed in heavy lace glass curtains and velvet drapes.

Aunt Gertrude was a tall, bulky woman who wore voluminous dresses trimmed in jet beads. Her manner was always ceremonious — a gentle, firm, punctilious ceremony. Isabel, whether she came from the decorous cheerfulness of the Convent or the rackety disorder of her mother's apartment, felt at once a big soft hand take hold of her, wipe out whatever mood she arrived in, stifle any sense of rebelliousness. An hour was as long as she could stand the airless formality. Then she began to fidget so that she could not hide her restiveness from Aunt Gertrude. If only Aunt Gertrude would talk about music, instead of catechizing her about the Convent, Reverend Mother, the nuns, what religious reading she had been assigned. A constant anxiety underlay these visits — Aunt Gertrude's unspoken anxiety about her devoutness, her own anxiety about hiding from Aunt Gertrude the confusion in her own mind and spirit.

Aunt Gertrude never spoke of Isabel's mother. The two women

19

almost never met. Isabel's father's mother had been Aunt Gertude's younger sister — a wilful, pretty girl who had defied her German martinet father and risked her religious faith by marrying a Protestant. Isabel knew her only in the small, handpainted photograph that stood among the jumble of silverframed family portraits on the mantel over the false fireplace.

Isabel's father was there, too, as an eighteen-year-old boy, fairhaired, handsome, childish, and as a man in dark civilian clothes — not the army officer's uniform he wore in the photograph of him that her mother kept in her bedroom, mounted in a double frame with one of herself in bangs and painted cupid's bow mouth. He had been brought up a Catholic. It was one requirement his mother's family had been able to make. But Isabel sensed from Aunt Gertrude's manner when she referred to him that he had vacillated throughout his life between the sentimental romanticism of his Bavarian forebears and the race-proud touchiness of his Virginian father's family.

Was that why he had married her mother, Isabel wondered? Had marriage to the pert, pretty, careless, poorly-educated daughter of a rootless tribe of Southern backwoodsmen been a sort of escape from the ambivalence of his own family background? Aunt Gertrude had never used the phrase to describe Isabel's mother, but it came up in Isabel's mind when she thought of her one recollection of her mother's people — a rundown house in a mountain town and a tall, gaunt woman old enough to be her grandmother, who was her mother's oldest sister. It was the merest glimpse of a memory. She must have been a very young child when that visit was made — after her father's death and before her mother had married Mac. But it was a vivid glimpse, clearer than any photograph.

She had grown up with the sense of her mother's resentment permeating everything. At first, from the time she could begin remembering, she had felt the force of that resentment, had felt in answer an unquestioning loyalty. She had come to adopt that resentment as her own — her mother's grudge against the fate that had made her marry into a family that rejected her. Her mother never spoke of her father's parents and sisters except with angry malice. The Virginian family had never acknowledged her mother. The German had ungraciously tolerated her presence at family gatherings — for Isabel's own sake, Isabel later realized.

Isabel never doubted whose side she was on, who was the injured victim. Her mother held and deserved her undivided allegiance. Her father, whom she did not remember, was an appealing but unreliable ally. Vaguely she thought he could have done more to make his people accept his wife. But he had not and he died very young, of typhoid fever in an army camp before he was mustered out after the end of the war.

It was only when Isabel had reached her teens, only a couple of years ago, in fact, that she had realized that she was almost illegitimate. It had been her conception that had forced her parents to marry, when her father was already eager to escape from the tug-of-war between her mother's attractions and his family's censure, when her mother had already lost respect and fondness for him. Her mother did not say this. But whenever she spoke of him there was an extra edge of bitterness, a more than usually virulent drop of acid on her tongue when she mentioned her in-laws and their influence on the man she had finally married.

Aunt Gertrude never got near this subject. Partly Isabel supposed that this was because the question of illegitimacy, of birth outside of marriage, was one she would never willingly discuss, certainly not with an adolescent girl. Behind Aunt Gertrude hung the heavy impenetrable curtain of Catholic doctrine. Lust was one of the seven deadly sins. Only marriage in accordance with the Church's sacrament could save from the sin of lust those who commited the sexual act, which was to be performed only for the procreation of children. This also Aunt Gertrude did not say to her in so many words. But she cast out unmistakable hints, which grew more frequent as Isabel entered puberty. Girls must preserve their freshness, their innocence, their sexual ignorance. Aunt Gertrude deplored the sight of women's breasts, prominent under their dresses, even great paintings that depicted the temptations of women's round, soft, naked bodies.

Isabel stood in the middle of this conflict of attitudes, but she felt no division from her mother, no separation between her mother's view of right and wrong, until her mother met Mac. When as an eight-year-old she had protested the invasion of their privacy by this man — this loud-voiced, insolent creature who ordered her out of the way — her mother had ignored her indignation, had for the first time pushed her away, smiling in a preoccupied way, acted as if she was scarcely aware of her existence. Then when her mother married him there had been a complete estrangement. The coquettish subterfuges her mother had used before became more definitely defensive maneuvers to outwit his demands, to extract money from him.

And Mac dropped all pretense of considering Isabel's feelings. He tried but could not get rid of her her. She was too much of a child to be sent away somewhere. Isabel realized later that he had tried to get her mother to send her to her father's people. Her great grandfather had still been alive then, a very old man in a wheelchair, very German still in his way of speaking and ordering Aunt Gertrude around. But her mother had refused — not entirely for her own sake but because her mother would not give Aunt Gertrude the satisfaction of taking over her child. Aunt Gertrude had been the one to insist that her nephew's child be baptised a Catholic. Isabel's mother had no coherent religious faith to interpose. It was Aunt Gertrude who supplied all the luxuries in her life — the

21

toys at Christmas, the pretty dresses for her birthdays, the occasional treat in an ice-cream parlor. Isabel remembered the Christmas tree that Aunt Gertrude, with true German sentimentality, had loaded each year with the elaborate ornaments that came originally from Bavaria, the ornate Christmas cards with many panels, each to be opened a day at a time through Advent until the whole scene was complete — lighted candles, the waits, the heralding angels, on Christmas Day.

Only now that she was fifteen had Isabel begun to wonder about her father. He had always seemed nebulous before, someone whose existence she had taken on hearsay. Why had he wanted her mother? Aunt Gertrude had referred to it as a wartime marriage — an unfortunate infatuation that had come about in the stress of the Great War. As people of decidedly German ancestry and manners — they always spoke German among themselves and Isabel had seen letters her father wrote to Aunt Gertrude in the old-style script he had been carefully taught — Aunt Gertrude and her sisters had suffered the indignities visited on German-Americans in 1916 and 1917. Yet her father had joined up voluntarily. And he had married her mother, whose origin was as remote from his as could be.

Isabel could not imagine a love affair between her parents. Aunt Gertrude said, "a wartime marriage." She did not speak of a "wartime romance." She meant, Isabel knew she meant, the entrapment of an innocent, well-brought-up young man by a scheming young woman of no background, aided by the irresponsible emotions generated by the menace of death in battle. Isabel looked at this image as bravely, as forthrightly as she could. She could not believe it true. She could not see her mother as so steadfastly calculating, so capable of carrying out a campaign of seduction. Her mother was too volatile. Her lack of persistence would be fatal to any scheme. In spite of herself, Isabel had learned that her mother was untruthful, unreliable, slipshod in her daily habits, ready to use any dishonest means to get a little money, if she was certain she would not be found out.

It was the incident in the Piggly Wiggly, when she was still a little girl, that had made her see this side of her mother, in spite of herself. She remembered following her mother down the aisle of the self-service grocery store, watching as she picked up cans and packages. Once or twice she had handed one to Isabel, saying, "Carry this for me." Then she had pushed a small can or a package into the big pockets of the pinafore Isabel wore. By the time they reached the cashier Isabel had forgotten the things in her pockets. Her mother was in a gay mood and chattered as they ranged around the store. And for a while it seemed that they were just going to walk out by paying for the things her mother put down on the counter. But the weight in her pockets suddenly reminded her and as they were about to go through the turnstile, she had pulled

22

her mother's arm, anxious. Something warned her not to talk out loud. But her sudden distress had called the attention of the store manager, a thin, harassed man who stood nearby with a deep frown on his face. He had stopped her mother peremptorily.

"What's that your little girl has in her pockets?" he demanded.

Her mother must have forgotten the things, too, she thought, because her mother gazed at him in surprise, her eyes wide open. Then she looked down at Isabel and said, "Why, Baby, what did you pick up? You know you mustn't pick things up and put them in your pocket that way!"

Isabel was stunned. She tried to protest but the words died before she could speak. She listened aghast while her mother, talking eagerly to the manager, snatched the things out of her pockets and handed them to him.

The man loomed over her, turning the things about in his hands.

"Funny things for a kid to pick up," he said, his voice full of disbelief. "These are luxury items for grown people. Kids usually try to steal candy and chewing gum."

Isabel felt hot with indignation at the word "steal" and tried to say something, but her mother's fingers squeezed her arm tightly enough to make it hurt. Her mother talked even faster to the man. Isabel could tell that his suspicions had turned into certainty, but his frown had lightened as he looked at her mother. Her mother was a very pretty woman. People did not like to quarrel with her. Only Aunt Gertrude succeeded in being severe with her.

Her mother had kept up the stream of reproach as they finally left the store and walked down the street. How could she be such a bad girl? "Don't you ever do such a thing again!" For the first few minutes, ready to sink into the pavement at the stares of passersby, Isabel had been silent in shame. When she finally found her voice to protest, her mother told her to shut up. "And don't you ever tell anybody about this," she warned.

Isabel never had. Until a year or so ago she had pondered over the unhappy memory, wondering how her mother could have so twisted the incident, how she could really have forgotten that she herself had put the things in Isabel's pockets, and how she could have blamed her to a stranger as a thief. Then at last the truth of the matter became too apparent to her for her to deny it. Her mother was a liar and a cheat.

This was something Aunt Gertrude knew. Now and then Aunt Gertrude made some small hint, inviting Isabel to join her in an unspoken league against this pretty, flighty, unreliable young woman who had stolen her handsome, worthy young nephew. Her father's death, Isabel knew, was the great tragedy of Aunt Gertrude's life. As long as he lived she had hoped that he would be won from his amiable vacillation to a firmer faith, her faith. But he was gone and his child had taken his place in the focus of her interest.

Her mother said, "But Andrea, I just don't understand this. You've never had any trouble with any of your subjects in school. This report card is very disappointing."

"I can make up my grade with Miss Fitch. She says I can write a paper on Tennyson — all about what he said about the education of women in *The Princess*. And history is not hard and I haven't any trouble with civics —"

"C is not your usual grade in anything. Seriously, Andrea, I don't understand why you've let everything slide like this. I thought you were studying hard every night. What have you been doing, with your light on so late?"

Andrea did not look at her mother. She picked nervously at the buttonhole of her sweater where a thread was loose.

Her mother said, "Mooning, I suppose. It must be your age — the phase you are going through. These days you don't answer me until I've spoken to you three times. I can't imagine what has got into you. I'm really disappointed in you, Andrea. Deedee was never interested in books, so I didn't expect anything from her in that line. But I did think you really wanted a good education. You were so eager to get into high school."

"I know, Mother —" Andrea started to speak but found her throat closing up. She had been able to sleep very little the night before. The image of Isabel walking away from her, angry and contemptuous, had been with her even in her fitful dreams. How could she regain Isabel's sympathy and attention? She did not really understand why Isabel had become so angry. She realized now that there was a fire burning fiercely under the cool, calm surface that Isabel presented to the world. How she wished she could comfort her when she felt so upset. But how could she, if she did not know really what it was that upset her?"

Her mother's voice interrupted. "Andrea! You are not listening to me even now! Has something happened in school that you haven't told me about? Has something distressed you?"

In alarm Andrea looked up at her mother. Her mother had taken off the glasses she wore for reading or sewing and was frowning at her through sharp blue eyes. Everyone said she looked like her mother and now that she was growing taller they were almost of a height. She denied hastily, "Oh, no!" And immediately her mind went back to herself. If only she had been able to see Isabel again today, but they had not met in the streetcar and the burden of yesterday's quarrel lay so heavy.

"Well, I must say, you are acting very strangely. What is worrying you? If you don't get better, I shall have to take you to the doctor. Your periods are regular, aren't they? Sometimes girls your age have trouble settling down to a regular routine."

"Oh, Mother, there isn't anything the matter with me! I'll do better in everything except —"

"You really want to go to college, don't you? If you don't do well in high school, you won't be able to. Your father expects to send you to college. He will be very disappointed otherwise. He is counting on it. You've always said you wanted to go."

As her mother's voice flowed on, Andrea thought, "How am I going to tell her about Mr. Compton?" Aloud she said, "It's algebra that's really bothering me, Mother. I just don't seem to make any headway with it."

"No, I can see from this report card that you don't. I know you have no head for figures, darling, but you did well enough in arithmetic. You can't graduate from high school without algebra."

"Mr. Compton says that I have to have a tutor, that I'll never master it unless I have special instruction."

"A tutor?"

"Yes. He says it is too late now. I won't be able to make up enough before the end of school this year. But he says that he won't fail me if I have special instruction this summer so that he can give me a test before school opens next autumn."

Andrea, studying the floor at her feet, felt the weight of her mother's scrutiny. Finally her mother said, "That's pretty bad, Andrea. I'll have to talk to your father about it. If you have to have special teaching, you will have to have it. But you must give up this mooning about and get down to work in earnest. I've thought all along that when you've been late getting home from school you were spending extra time studying with Mr. Compton."

"He — he has given me extra exercises to do after class." Still Andrea did not look at her mother. Then she burst out desperately, "But it doesn't do any good. I just can't understand him."

Her mother sighed. "He can't be such a bad teacher. It must be that you just don't pay attention to him when he is explaining things." Then, seeing the tears in Andrea's eyes, she put her arm around her daughter and said, soothingly, "Now, now, don't cry about it. That won't make matters any better. We'll just have to arrange for some special lessons."

Her mother turned her attention to something else then and she relapsed again into her own morass. For twenty-four hours she had suffered the pain of rejection. How easy it seemed to be for Isabel to walk away from her like that, to spurn the love she offered up to her in two upraised hands. Over and over in her mind she saw again the broad, tree-lined avenue, empty to her eye except for Isabel's stiff, proud back going away from her. She re-lived her longing for Isabel to turn and glance back just once. She was overwhelmed again by the feeling of desolation when she realized that Isabel was not going to turn back and look at her.

Her mother's voice came out of the cloud of misery. "Andrea, eat your dinner. Are you sure you feel well?"

"Yes — yes. I'm just not hungry."

"Well, you're losing weight. That's not good at your age. If you

25

don't do better, I shall have to take you to the doctor."

Inwardly Andrea shuddered. She was perfectly well. Only, food did not interest her and the time seemed to go by and she hadn't done the things she was supposed to do. Even tennis — the weather had remained so mild that her tennis team had played every day. Her game had got very bad. Her partners complained that she did not pay attention, that she just stood there and watched the ball go past her. They did not want to play with her any more and she was happier just sitting on the bench wrapped in her own thoughts. Well, she could not call them really thoughts. They were not coherent thoughts. It was better to call them feelings — vague but all-enveloping feelings. They all centered on Isabel. But usually these feelings glowed. Now they were mired in despair. What did Isabel's withdrawal mean? Had she really thrown her over, got tired of her adoration? Yes, she adored 'Bel. That's what she called her in her own mind. Isabel called her Andy. Nobody else had ever called her Andy. Her mother disapproved of nicknames except for Deedee and Bob, who had always been Deedee and Bob.

She couldn't help it. 'Bel filled her heart, her world. But 'Bel was impatient, 'Bel grew restless at repetition of anything, even something she very much liked.

Andrea yearned for the time to pass, for the morning to come, for the afternoon to arrive, for school to be over. As the time drew near for dismissal her anxiety rose to a fever pitch. She had missed breakfast — all she could choke down was a glass of milk. Her lunchtime sandwich had stuck in her throat. Now, waiting for the streetcar, she felt sick at her stomach. She trembled with anticipation. How would 'Bel act? Would she ignore her, turn that cool distant side to her, greet her in that smooth, impersonal manner, as if politeness alone prompted her to act?

As the streetcar came to the Q Street stop Andrea strained for a sight of Isabel among the girls waiting. The car today was not crowded. A practice baseball game at the high school had held a good number of students back. Andrea sat by the window, the seat beside her empty. There was 'Bel! She almost cried out when she saw her. Hurriedly she shifted in the seat so as to discourage anyone else from sitting beside her. She held her breath as she watched 'Bel get on and drop her ticket into the fare box. She searched 'Bel's face for some clue as 'Bel walked slowly down the aisle.

'Bel said "Hi!" casually as she dropped into the seat and rested her pile of books on her lap. They sat together silently for a while. Andrea felt the fluttering of her stomach subside, the tautness in her muscles relax. She glanced shyly at 'Bel's profile. The deep-set eyes, the sharply-cut nose, the firm, sensitive mouth gave no hint of anything but a calm indifference. But something else seemed to come to her from 'Bel with the slight warmth of 'Bel's body. The

26

nightmare of the last twenty-four hours began to dissolve. Perhaps 'Bel was sorry she had been so harsh.

But all 'Bel said was, "Can you get off at the Circle?"

Andrea's thankfulness came up in a rush to overwhelm her. "Oh, yes! 'Bel —" She did not really know what she wanted to say.

'Bel gave her a quick sidelong look. They were silent again. The warm spring afternoon was quiet without the usual clamor of the crowd of schoolchildren. They both got up without a word as the car came to the Circle. They said nothing as they walked into the park and sat down on a bench.

A slow sense of grievance dawned in Andrea, replacing the anguish that had held her for so many hours. She demanded, " 'Bel, why did you act that way? Why did you get mad at me?"

'Bel did not answer promptly. "I wasn't mad at you. I just — you can't just come tagging after me. When I say I've got to go home, just leave me alone." Her voice and manner were sullen.

"Well, I think you ought to say you're sorry. I've been very unhappy ever since."

"Unhappy! I don't make you unhappy. Nobody gets unhappy unless they want to be."

Andrea's anger flooded her face with color. "You did make me unhappy! You know you did! You didn't have to talk to me like that!"

'Bel jumped up. Furiously she retorted, "If you don't like how I act, I don't have to stay here! You can find somebody else to tag around after —"

Andrea was on her feet beside her, her hand on 'Bel's arm. " 'Bel! Don't go away like this! What are we fighting about?"

'Bel sat down so suddenly that Andrea was left standing in front of her for a moment. She sank back on the bench again and leaned down to pick up the books they had dropped. 'Bel sat mute, staring at the ground. After a while she managed to say, "Nothing, I suppose."

Andrea recognized the phrase for what it was. This was as close as 'Bel could come to an apology. They sat primly together for a while, conscious of the attention they had attracted from the woman on the bench opposite and the idle men sitting further away. The scent of the big straggly lilac bush in bloom behind them filled the air. It wasn't going to be long now, thought Andrea, before the school term would end. And then there would be an end to these daily meetings with 'Bel. She hesitated for a while to mention the fact, uneasy at 'Bel's possible response.

"When is your school out, 'Bel? Mine ends in the middle of June."

"Earlier — at the end of May. A lot of the girls go away for the summer or else they don't live in Washington."

"What are you going to do?"

"Get a job. Or earn some money, anyway. I've got to."

"What kind of a job?"

"I don't know. Perhaps I can get some tutoring to do."

"Oh!" A brilliant idea came to Andrea. "Could you tutor me?"

"What in?"

"Algebra. I have to make up algebra this summer. Mr. Compton says he'll pass me if I take special lessons and pass a test he'll give me next fall. 'Bel, could you give me lessons?"

The surprise in 'Bel's eyes turned to speculation, but she did not say anything.

"Oh, 'Bel, you could do it, couldn't you? My mother is upset. She thinks I haven't been studying. She has told my father that I need extra lessons. Why can't you teach me? Than we could see each other all summer!"

'Bel looked at her and then nodded. "Algebra isn't a subject I'm particularly good at. But I guess I could do it."

Andrea's face lit up. "Oh, 'Bel, I'll tell my mother as soon as I get home!"

"Wait a minute, Andy. I'm going to have to talk to Reverend Mother about it and see if she'll let me do it. What is your father's name and what does he do?"

"He's a biologist with the Department of Agriculture. Oh, 'Bel, this is wonderful!"

* * *

"A girl? From Annunciation Convent? How did you meet her, Andrea?"

Under her mother's scrutiny Andrea's nervousness increased. "On the streetcar, coming home from Western. She gets on the same car I do."

"Do you know anything about her family? What does her father do?"

"I don't know. I think he's dead. She has a stepfather."

"Oh. Well, what does he do?"

"I don't know." Miserably, Andrea tried to think she was not lying. She did not really know what 'Bel's stepfather did. Vaguely she remembered that 'Bel had said that he was a skilled mechanic. But she did know that her own parents would not think well of the daughter of a mechanic. Especially since 'Bel herself was so contemptuous of her stepfather, for reasons Andrea did not understand.

Her mother said, "You certainly don't seem to know much about her."

"Oh, 'Bel's an awfully nice girl! You'd like her a lot!"

Her mother saw the sudden bright glow that lit up Andrea's blue eyes. Vaguely troubled by it, she said, "But what sort of background does she have? Her parents must be fairly well off for her to go to Annunciation."

"No, they're not. She's on a scholarship. She's very brainy."

28

"She must be, to be at a school like that on a scholarship. I never heard of girls getting scholarships to Annunciation. But the Sisters there are famous as teachers. They would not neglect the chance to educate a bright girl who couldn't afford it otherwise." Catching the skepticism in her mother's voice, Andrea said with eager uncertainty, "It's not exactly a scholarship. But she doesn't have to pay full tuition. Everybody knows how brainy she is and Reverend Mother helps her get tutoring."

At "Reverend Mother" Mrs. Hollingsworth gave her daughter another sharp glance. Andrea hurried on. "She's writing a letter to Dad. 'Bel will bring it with her tomorrow and I can bring it home."

Next evening, anxiously eavesdropping, Andrea heard her mother say to her father, "She's well recommended, according to the Mother Superior's letter. She is a year older than Andrea. Read this letter."

There was a brief silence and then her father said, "She must be competent. The girl probably has a gift for mathematics. Perhaps she can hold Andrea's attention enough to get some algebra into her head."

"It seems a safe enough association," said her mother.

* * *

It was Friday. Tomorrow was Saturday. Two more Saturdays and then school was out. This was 'Bel's last schoolday. How relieved she was that her mother had consented to 'Bel's being her tutor. The nightmare of a long summer without seeing 'Bel every day had been dissipated. But tomorrow — She did not want to spend all day Saturday without 'Bel.

They sat on the park bench and Andrea could not tell from looking at her face what kind of thoughts were absorbing 'Bel. 'Bel sat with one hand steadying the books on her lap, pursing her lips now and then.

"What are you going to do tomorrow, 'Bel?"

"I've got a lot of things to do. I've got a job in a bakery in the morning. Their regular saleswoman is sick. That's till one o'clock and then I have to go and see Aunt Gertrude." She looked up involuntarily at the apartment house across the park.

"Could I meet you here after that?"

'Bel hesitated. She seemed to be weighing things in her mind.

"I usually go and read in the reading room at the Library of Congress," Andrea said urgently, "My mother lets me do that on Saturdays. I can leave early and meet you here."

'Bel looked at her with half-absent eyes. "Three o'clock? When do you have to be home?"

"Before five o'clock."

"All right. If I'm not here, wait for me."

The next morning Andrea arrived at the reading room when it opened and tried to work concentratedly on her assignments.

These Saturdays had always been a magical part of her life. For the hours she spent there she was far away from the everyday life of her home and school. She dwelt in a world entirely her own, absorbed in the books she read, freed for a few hours to think about things on her own, without the interference of her mother, her teachers, anyone. In the books she read she found things she knew nothing about, strange attitudes to familiar things. She had slowly realized that she was growing out of the tight, simple, well-defined world in which her mother had brought her up. Occasionally she had been troubled by the discoveries she made, especially when it came to the dealings between men and women, troubled enough to try and talk to her mother about them. But the instant wariness in her mother's response gave her warning. Not on any account would she jeopardize the glorious freedom of her Saturdays at the Library. Whatever the answers she needed she would have to find them out for herself.

But now there was 'Bel and 'Bel had taken over this favorite terrain of hers. She could not exclude her as she excluded everyone else. 'Bel came between her and the books she tried to read. She had to find out what 'Bel was. Her heart beat faster as she thought about 'Bel. 'Bel's gestures, the funny faces she made when she mocked someone, the quick frown when a sudden suspicion of someone's motives assailed her. 'Bel. If she could just understand her.

It was scarcely past two o'clock when she reached Washington Circle. She got off the streetcar a couple of blocks too soon so that she could spend a few minutes among the desultory Saturday crowd, going in and out of the small shops along the Avenue. She stood for a while examining the objects displayed in a second hand furniture store. There was a massive carved lampstand in the doorway and a set of English dinnerware in the window. They must once have been very expensive. A middle-aged woman came out of the door, counting some bills in her hand, a grim look on her face. The thought suddenly occurred to Andrea that the woman had just sold something to the storekeeper, and hadn't got as much for it as she had expected. Andrea remembered that the evening before her mother had been telling her father that she had recognized a neighbor's heirloom silver in a shop in Georgetown. Would the depression never end? her mother had asked. Was there no bottom? Couldn't the government do anything about so many people out of work, forced to sell their possessions, their family valuables? Her father had muttered something behind the evening paper. Andrea, watching the woman walk hurriedly down the street, turned away in sudden shame and ran on to the park.

She had brought a book along and she tried to read it, waiting for 'Bel. But continually she lost the thread of the story, looking up every minute to glance across at the apartment house. It was past three o'clock when she finally saw 'Bel come down the short flight of steps and cross the roadway.

They greeted each other in the almost wordless way they had fallen into and for a while had nothing to say. Andrea's happiness ebbed away. Until then her day had been filled with joyous anticipation, flights of fancy, happy soundless voices, her own and 'Bel's, a great rich treasure of nameless delight. Now it was suddenly empty. The imagined, nebulous splendor in which she had been swimming vanished. The world shrank to the park, the prosaic streets, the indifferent people who sat near them. 'Bel's brooding quiet enveloped her.

'Bel sighed and Andrea looked at her in surprise.

"What is the matter, 'Bel?"

"I can't tell her anything and she knows something is wrong."

"Who do you mean? What is wrong?"

"Aunt Gertrude. I'm just not as religious as she thinks I should be. She thinks she has a stake in me. She is helping me with my education so that I can become devout, like herself. I guess it isn't honest for me not to tell her."

"Tell her what?"

"That I've got all sorts of doubts. She thinks I ought to spend more time reading about the saints and trying to be more like them. I suppose what she really would like would be for me to say I want to be a nun. She tells me how wonderful it is to have religious teachers and how they do so much good in the world and yet don't get involved in worldly things. Their minds are always set on heaven. I can't be a nun. I haven't the vocation. Even Reverend Mother understands that. I know a lot of girls at my age go through a stage of wanting to be a nun. But not I. It just isn't part of me. I can't go through life putting off everything here because I'm waiting for heaven."

She was silent for a while and Andrea, at sea, did not interrupt her. All at once 'Bel said, "I'm not even sure sometimes that I believe in God. Do you?"

The sudden question dumbfounded Andrea. She had never heard anyone ask the question. Her parents did not go to church. At least, now they did not, though they had been married in church and she and her brother and sister had all been baptized. She could remember going to Sunday school when she was little. Her mother had at that time read her Bible stories. Later her mother had said that she wasn't against believing in the Gospels as an historical record. She believed — yes, she believed — in Jesus in a vague, undefined way, as the Sum of Goodness, as an ideal of brotherly love unattainable by ordinary men. But Andrea had never heard anyone raise the question of God's existence. In fact, she was sure that if anyone in her parents' world started to talk about God, everyone present would be very much embarrassed. Her father sometimes said something satirical to her mother about people who believed in a fundamentalist interpretation of the Bible. Usually this happened because of something he read in the newspaper. She wondered now whether her mother in fact took God for granted; her mother had been brought up an Episcopalian. Or whether there was a deepseated doubt in her mother that accounted for her attitude. Otherwise, the only times when religion entered into her life were when there were weddings and funerals. Deedee, of course, had been married in St. Margaret's on Connecticut Avenue. Andrea remembered that her grandparents' graves were in Rock Creek Cemetery. Her mother occasionally visited them. Her grandmother had been a churchgoer. Probably that was why Andrea had been sent to Sunday school.

'Bel was still looking at her. "Does it make any difference to you, if you don't? I mean, do you do things because you think you ought to or because you think God expects you to, or will punish you if you don't"

Andrea looked bewildered. She realized that 'Bel was asking these questions chiefly of herself.

'Bel went on. "Reverend Mother suspects I have doubts. She keeps suggesting books for me to read. She must have said something about me to mademoiselle, because mademoiselle sometimes brings her talk around to theology and gives me all sorts of clever answers, just in case I've been asking myself that sort of question. But Aunt Gertrude doesn't believe in questions. You just believe blindly."

"Would it make a great deal of difference to *you* if you didn't believe in God?"

For a long time 'Bel did not answer. While they sat silent Andrea struggled with the question she herself had raised. The newness of it stumped her. She began to suspect that it *was* something that had lain far in the back of her mind. Not the question of whether God existed. She didn't think she really questioned that. Something existed, something had to explain the universe to her. When she studied astronomy and evolution and the history of the earth in school, she realized that she had to take a lot of it on faith. It was not demonstrated in a way that she could really grasp. Any more than she could really grasp the idea of a divine will. But she didn't doubt that it was all true.

'Bel said, "Sometimes I think it would make a difference and sometimes I think it wouldn't. Some days it seems to me that God makes no difference in my life. That God has nothing to do with what happens to me."

"Then it wouldn't matter what you did."

"No, it wouldn't, if you don't believe in divine punishment for sin. A lot of people don't do things they shouldn't simply because they're afraid of what will happen to them when they die. They believe in divine retribution."

"But you don't."

'Bel retorted hotly, "Who says I don't?" Then she said more

quietly, "I don't really think I can believe in a God of vengeance."

"There are a lot of people who don't care. Otherwise they wouldn't do the things they do."

"And sometimes they pay for what they do while they're alive on this earth. But nobody lives their whole life without sin. You can't do that — unless you are a saint."

Andrea, whose acquaintance with Roman Catholic dogma was confined to what she had read in novels, especially those laid in mediaeval times where the characters spoke of having been shriven of their sins, said uncertainly, "But that means nobody would go to heaven."

'Bel looked at her with a half-indulgent, half-disdainful expression. "That's what purgatory is for. You work off your sins there and how long you stay depends on how many sins you commit here. Aunt Gertrude reminds me of that all the time."

"I think it's a horrible idea!"

'Bel shrugged. "It's logical. It's not supposed to be attractive." She seemed to shake herself. "Oh, well, let's talk about something else. I won't be seeing you next week. Next week I'm going to help the Sisters get things ready for Commencement. I expect I'll be pretty busy."

"Oh, 'Bel!"

They looked at each other and were aware that they both felt the menace in the coming separation. They sat silently yearning, longing to cling to each other in an open embrace. They sat paralyzed by the enormous strength of this pull towards each other. The park, the people around them receded into a hazy distance from them.

As the moment ebbed 'Bel moved slightly and said quietly, "I expect you'd better be going home. Your mother will be looking for you."

"Where are you going? Are you going home?"

"It's Saturday. I've got to go to confession."

Bravely Andrea plunged on. "Where do you go?"

"Usually I go to Father Greeley, at the Convent. But that's a long way off. I can go to Saint Matthew's. That's just a few blocks away, on Connecticut Avenue. Everybody goes there who doesn't have a regular confessor."

"Can I come with you — I mean, can I walk there with you and wait for you?"

'Bel stared at her. "Your mother wouldn't like it."

"I won't tell her."

'Bel nodded and they got up together and walked out of the park and along K Street. They said very little as they walked along, yet there seemed to be a dialogue going on between them nevertheless. At the side door of the big red brick church 'Bel said, "You can come in and sit in the back here."

As they entered 'Bel automatically dipped her finger in the

33

holy water basin and crossed herself. Andrea, breathless with the novelty of the situation, stood near her until 'Bel pointed to the back pew and walked away from her to the curtained booths in the corner of the shadowy vestibule.

Andrea sat there nervously, frequently touching the scarf 'Bel had tied around her head as they paused on the steps outside. 'Bel herself wore a lace square that she had taken out of her purse and put on her head. There was a scarcely audible murmur of voices in the big church, just sound enough to tell Andrea that there were people moving about in the dim light punctuated by the flickering candle flames ranged in banks before the images in the side altars. She had never been in a Catholic church before and had never experienced the weight of tradition and of a dogmatic faith which seemed now to enwreath her like the incense that filled every cranny. She was greatly relieved when 'Bel came back and touched her on the arm and they walked out into the clear light of the long evening.

She looked at 'Bel, expecting 'Bel to be back with her as they had been sitting on the park bench. But 'Bel's eyes were remote and hooded, as if whatever happened in the brief moments in the confessional had changed her mood, had blocked the free flow of her thoughts. Andrea reached for 'Bel's hand, impelled to try and draw her back. For a moment 'Bel's hand lay in hers, lax and then 'Bel's fingers closed on hers.

* * *

Andrea, radiant, watched 'Bel across the dinnertable. Three afternoons a week she came to give her an algebra lesson and they sat in her room upstairs, in the soft warmth of early summer. This was the first time that 'Bel had agreed to stay for supper. Mrs. Hollingsworth had invited her several times before, but 'Bel had said, No, she had to be home to help her mother with the younger children.

Mrs. Hollingsworth had said to Andrea, "Her people probably don't want her to go home alone late at night. But they need not worry about that. Your father will see that she gets home safely. You should tell her that."

But Andrea had made excuses for 'Bel. "Oh, I don't think she wants him to do that. I think she'd rather we didn't interfere."

"Interfere? I wouldn't call it interfering. We can't let a girl of fifteen go all that distance alone after dark. I'm sure her people would object to that. They'd appreciate our concern for her."

"She can — she can make some arrangement — to meet her mother somewhere."

"I thought her mother couldn't leave the younger children unless Isabel is home to look after them."

Andrea had no answer to that. Then her mother said, "What about her stepfather? Can he come and get her?"

34

"Oh, no! He works at night. Besides, she wouldn't want him to."

"Wouldn't want him to!"

Andrea flushed with embarrassment. "Bel doesn't like him. Besides, I don't think he would do it."

Mrs. Hollingsworth said thoughtfully, "She doesn't like him. Has she said why?"

Andrea said distractedly, "I don't know. She hasn't told me."

Her mother said doubtfully, "It's very strange. I must ask Isabel about this. But in any case, we should let her people know that she will be safe going from here home. It would be nice to have her stay for supper."

The next time she was asked 'Bel said Yes, she would stay for supper. Andrea announced that fact to her mother, who said at once, "Then I must tell your father that he will have to take her home."

"Oh, no! No, Mother, please don't. 'Bel won't like it. She says she often goes home alone in the evening. She is not afraid."

Mrs. Hollingsworth's voice was sharp with disapproval. "Andrea, that is ridiculous. I am responsible for any young girl who comes here to our house. I wouldn't think of letting her go home alone. Your father would certainly agree with me."

But Andrea was relieved that her mother did not raise the question with 'Bel at the end of the afternoon, when the two of them went down to the kitchen to help her mother with the evening meal. 'Bel sat at the kitchen table, cheerful but not talkative. She was deft in everything she did with her hands, peeling potatoes, shelling peas, wiping water glasses. Andrea knew that her mother noticed this deftness and approved it.

When they sat at the dinnertable 'Bel was ready to talk, brightly, eagerly. She was not sulky, touchy, suddenly abrupt — as Andrea had sometimes seen her to be in stressful situations. Andrea's father looked at 'Bel whenever he spoke, as if he was interested in how she would respond to what he was saying. He listened attentively when she replied. Her father liked 'Bel, Andrea exulted to herself.

He said to 'Bel now as he passed her plate laden with slices of potroast, "And how did you learn that about Voltaire?"

"From Mlle. Bosanquet. She has many stories about the famous French writers."

"I would not have supposed Voltaire to be much quoted in a convent. Mlle. Bosanquet must have a pretty broad view of what's suitable for young ladies in a convent school."

There was a note of teasing in her father's voice that Andrea recognized. She glanced uneasily at 'Bel. The slight flicker of 'Bel's eyelids told her 'Bel had also sensed it. "I learn a lot from her out of class. She is giving me lessons in advanced French literature."

"I see. And how about mathematics? Is it your specialty?"

"Oh, no. I like both. I'm not sure what I'm going to major in yet — the humanities or science."

Andrea saw the amusement in her father's face grow. He was always on the edge of joking whenever someone younger than himself took themselves, as he thought, too seriously. "Well, you're not letting any grass grow under your feet. Now, I wish that Bob, there, had as clear an idea where he was headed." He looked over his glasses down the table at his son and Andrea saw that lightness had gone out of his mood. His narrow, lined face had grown serious.

Her brother looked up briefly from his plate of food, roused by the sound of his father's voice speaking his name. But the quick glance seemed to tell him that his father's attention was not really directed to him and he went back to his dinner without saying anything. Bob was twenty and would be a junior when he went back to college in the fall. He was a big young man, burly for his age, perpetually lost in his own concerns, which were confined to sports and the odd jobs that brought him pocket money. All through his adolescence his father had watched for evidence of a bent for science, if not his own field, biology, then something related. But there had been no sign that Bob had any aptitude or any interest in that direction. Whatever held the key to Bob's future was locked up in the silence he maintained about himself. Andrea, from old familiarity with Bob's habits, saw him focus for a moment on what his father said, consider it, and then, realizing that the comparison was with a girl, dismiss it from his mind.

Afterwards, helping her mother in the kitchen with the dishes, Andrea listened intently to the sound of 'Bel's and her father's voices in the living room. Dad sounds just the way he does when he has his own friends here, she thought — people he likes to talk to, like Professor Gerardi or Dr. Fineman. Her heart swelled with a bursting pride that nullified her mother's scolding when she dropped a glass.

She had forgotten about the question of how 'Bel was to get home. Then she noticed that her parents were casting glances at the clock and at each other. 'Bel, wrapped up in the warmth of the acceptance she felt, was oblivious to the passage of time.

Andrea, hoping to forestall what she feared would happen, said hesitantly, " 'Bel, shall I walk down to the corner with you?"

She saw 'Bel's mood change instantly, like a bird's flight checked in mid-air. The blankness of disappointment appeared in her face and then she frowned as she looked at the clock on the mantel.

Mr. Hollingsworth said, getting up from his chair, "I'll take you home. It is too late for you to go on the streetcar. They don't run very often at this time of night."

Andrea waited in dread. But 'Bel said, meekly, "Oh, I can get home all right. I'm used to going home alone at night."

Andrea saw the glance her parents exchanged. Her mother

said, a familiar note of firmness in her voice, "It's so far from here. We'll all feel better if we know you are home safely."

'Bel recognized the firmness. So, after a certain awkwardness in saying goodnight, Andrea was left standing in the hallway with her mother as 'Bel and her father went out of the front door. They stood together listening to the Ford car starting up and driving away. Andrea waited for her mother to say something but she was silent.

Andrea burst out, "She is used to having to take care of herself, Mother. She has to."

"I don't think very highly of her parents, then."

"I've told you, Mother, she doesn't have a father — just a stepfather."

"What about her mother? Doesn't she care about her daughter?"

"She can't do anything. She has to look after the little kids."

"That's hardly an excuse. I'd not let any daughter of mine go about alone after dark that way. You know I wouldn't think of letting you, Andrea."

Andrea did not reply. Presently her mother said, "Well, I expect you'd better go to bed. It's almost eleven o'clock."

Andrea went unhappily upstairs. She had felt how every fiber of 'Bel's body was vibrating with rejection of the idea that the Hollingsworths should know where she lived and how. But 'Bel's normal combativeness seemed suddenly in abeyance, as if her will to resist what she would not accept had temporarily deserted her. She did not want to upset me, thought Andrea, by being rude to Mother and Dad. A certain sense of guilt crept into her feelings about the evening, as if she had contributed to 'Bel's defeat.

Her father came home before she had got into bed and she listened intently to what he and her mother said to each other as they closed the house and turned off the lights and came upstairs.

She heard her father say, "They live in one of those small walk-up apartments on New Hampshire Avenue just north of Washington Circle. The neighborhood is quiet enough but there are a lot of alleys where the colored people live. It's not the sort of place for a young girl to be out alone at night."

"Well, no place is, really," her mother replied. "What are her people like?"

"I didn't see any of them. She insisted it would be better if she just went upstairs by herself. I waited for a while downstairs, till I was sure she had got up to her own door."

Her mother's voice dropped to a murmur as she closed the bedroom door. Andrea could hear only a few words: "— we've got to be careful —, a very bright girl, really, — but I must know something about her mother, — Andrea is at the impressionable age —". Her father's voice was a mere mumble as he tried to follow her mother's instruction to speak softly.

37

Eventually she gave up listening and got into bed.

For a day or two Andrea noticed that her mother was absentminded, with the special sort of abstraction that meant that her attention was fixed on Andrea. One afternoon, when Andrea came into the house from a trip to the Public Library, she saw her mother smiling, that secret, scarcely visible smile that always baffled her.

"Andrea, is your white linen dress ironed? And look and see if your good strap shoes are polished. We're going visiting tomorrow afternoon."

"Visiting?" Slowly Andrea lowered her armful of books to the seat of the chair by the telephone stand.

Her mother's smile broke out frankly. "I've told you before. We're going to a tea party at Annunciation Convent. Reverend Mother has sent me an invitation. It's quite an affair, I understand. You must look your best."

Andrea was silent with surprise. 'Bel had told her about these tea parties at Annunciation. Most of the girls who went there came from well-to-do families. They were the daughters of foreign diplomats, of members of Congress, of high government officials. The tea parties, 'Bel explained, served a number of purposes. They gave the girls an opportunity to show off the social training they had received at the Convent. They also were Reverend Mother's subtle way of making the special quality of the school known to the new members of the ever-changing world of Washington society.

Surely 'Bel would be there. All sorts of vague uneasy feelings took possession of Andrea throughout the rest of the day into the night and through the next morning, before she set out with her mother on the familiar streetcar trip. Real anxiety beset her as they walked from the carstop along the uneven brick sidewalk to the door of the Convent. She fought off panic as they passed into the sudden shadow and still coolness of the entrance hall. The indistinct shape of a white stone figure glimmered in the subdued light. 'Bel had told her something about it. It was the work of a French sculptor. French nuns, refugees from the French Revolution, had established a school here in the beginning, and a French nobleman had given the money to build the chapel. The French influence, 'Bel said, was still very strong. It was cultivated, in fact, for its appeal to the parents of the girls sent there for their grooming for the world of high society.

Andrea clung to these thoughts, impersonal, measured, as a lifebelt in the treacherous sea in which she found herself. She tried to keep up the appearance of poise. The best she could do was sit close to her mother and ignore the curious glances of the other girls, some of whom undoubtedly recognized her. Before this she had only seen them in glimpses, surrounding 'Bel as she got on the streetcar, purposefully chattering among themselves as a sort of concerted defense against the boys who eyed and jostled them.

They wore their hair in a long bob and swung it disdainfully off their shoulders with a practiced awareness. Invariably they wore rings with small but genuine precious stones and the religious medals around their soft necks hung on gold chains. Their hands were slender-fingered, with carefully manicured nails, ladies' hands. Only 'Bel seemed to have broad-palmed, capable hands, ready for any duty.

Now she saw them close to, in party dresses, attentive to the older women, their faces schooled to shallow smiles, their voices modulated to polite murmurs. Only when their eyes looked up briefly at her from under their eyelashes did she see anything of the bold, provocative, half-disdainful glances she was used to seeing them cast over the boys and other girls in the streetcar.

After a while she caught sight of 'Bel in a far corner, talking to one of the nuns. Obviously 'Bel had duties here and when she came close enough to speak, only said Hello to her mother and Hi to herself before going on to another part of the big room. She was glad when the chance came for her to mingle with some of the girls, prospective pupils and therefore not so frighteningly suave, who had come with their mothers to be shown the school. They, also, were intimidated by the glittering polish of the graduating students and stood in a little crowd near the refreshment table to sample the French pastries and ice-cream.

It was only when the time finally came for them to leave that she discovered that her mother had spent a considerable part of the hour chatting with Reverend Mother. Every so often there were occasions when Andrea was nonplussed by a facet of her mother that she did jot recognize. Now her mother was worldly-wise, voluble, animated, not at all the quiet, positive, serious woman she was used to. Her mother had obviously been discussing the history of the Convent, its art treasures, the value of a cultural education for girls as future wives and mothers, the upbringing of daughters as a safeguard of civilization.

The tall woman in the nun's habit looked down at her and said, "This is your daughter, Andrea. She is a very pretty child." She paused and Andrea looked into the bright clear eyes gazing down at her from under the white band of the coif across her forehead. "Isabel has spoken to me of you, Andrea. She is tutoring you in algebra, I believe."

Andrea, staring up at her hypnotized, tried to speak but her mouth was too dry. The tall figure in the black robe rose before her like a wall. Not in her mind but in her bones she felt that here was something that separated her from 'Bel, something that lay like a dark shadow behind 'Bel even when they were alone together, a vague something that 'Bel sometimes fled from, sometimes succumbed to.

Reverend Mother smiled. Her eyes, she seemed to say, had told her all she needed to know about 'Bel and Andrea. She turned away to say goodbye to Andrea's mother.

* * *

Though school was not in session, 'Bel went several times a week to Annunciation. It was expected of her, she explained to Andrea. There were various things that the Sisters liked her to do. And then Reverend Mother had seen to it that Mlle. Bosanquet continued to give 'Bel French lessons. The Frenchwoman remained at the Convent for the summer. She had not the money to live elsewhere and, besides, 'Bel suspected that she was saving as much as she could so that she could seek employment in another school later.

"She's pretty shrewd. She's real French, you know. She knows what she wants to do and she is going to do it. But she isn't going to tell anybody about it until she's good and ready to."

Andrea watched the slight, remote smile in 'Bel's face as she contemplated Mlle. Bosanquet in her mind's eye. After a moment 'Bel went on, "I think she and Reverend Mother like to spar with each other. She knows that in the end she has to do what Reverend Mother says, but she puts off agreeing until the last moment."

"Does she still act mean to you, 'Bel?"

'Bel hesitated. "She never did really act mean to me — just impatient. But she's French, you know, and they're always impatient, especially with foreigners learning their language."

"But you know a lot of French and you sound like a French person when you talk."

'Bel turned her slight smile, indulgent now, on Andrea. "Yes, I do, but that just makes mademoiselle more impatient. I'm thwarting her. She talks faster and faster, just to try to trip me up. She wants to rattle me."

"She *is* mean, then!"

"Oh, she isn't exactly easy to get along with. But I'm learning an awful lot. When she gets really bad tempered, I just let her go on. I pick up all kinds of words and expressions then. I think Reverend Mother would be surprised."

"You ought to tell her."

"Tell who?"

"Reverend Mother."

"Oh no. That wouldn't work. Besides, I don't really want to get mademoiselle in trouble. She — we —" 'Bel's sentence trailed off. Andrea, watching her, felt her own disapproval and jealousy increase.

"Do you really like her, 'Bel?"

'Bel glanced at her, briefly hearing the disapproval. "I think she likes me, really. At least, I think she likes to talk to me, she likes to have me around. I'm different, you know. She doesn't have to be so much on her guard. She still shocks the Sisters sometimes, the way she says things, but she never really speaks her mind to them. She — she — she — isn't a virgin."

"Oh!" The word spoken so slowly hung between them. "Did she tell you that?"

'Bel nodded. She was trying to act as if what she had said was a commonplace, a casual remark. But Andrea noticed a telltale tightness around her mouth.

"But how —?"

When she did not finish 'Bel said, with a laugh, "Oh, she didn't give me the details!"

Andrea blushed in spite of herself. "I didn't mean that. What I meant was, how did she come to tell you that?"

"She just said she got so tired of remembering to be demure, of minding her ps and qs. She says she finds the Sisters' company very insipid. They know nothing of life — she means men. They're such innocents, fit for the kingdom of heaven but very dull company."

"Well, that doesn't mean that she —"

As she floundered, 'Bel supplied, "That she has gone to bed with a man. No, but she also said that a woman never knows anything about men unless she has slept with at least one man. She says it does something to your mind."

Andrea stared at her. She had read such phrases in books and their exact meaning had caused her long hours of solitary conjecture. But she had never heard anybody say them.

'Bel went on, "I think she talks too much about how brilliant and experienced and popular she has been. If she is sought-after, why has she come to Annunciation? Why is she so anxious to stay in well with Reverend Mother? Why isn't she more 'out in the world', as she is always saying?"

"Maybe she can't find another job. She is a foreigner."

'Bel was impatient. "Of course it is hard to get a job just now. Don't I know it! But mademoiselle always talks as if people were lined up waiting for her to say she would work for them." 'Bel's smile was suddenly sly. "Why doesn't she use her wiles on men, not women?"

Andrea, too bewildered to answer, was silent.

They talked often about the Frenchwoman. Though 'Bel did not say so and though Andrea was too shy to ask, she somehow knew that mademoiselle was a large part of Bel's daily life. 'Bel, telling of her own hour-by-hour activities, mentioned her a dozen times. Mademoiselle said this to Reverend Mother and Reverend Mother said that to mademoiselle, the Sisters complained of her, mademoiselle sought every opportunity to talk privately with 'Bel, seeking her sympathy. 'Bel reported all this with a tone of criticism, of dislike. But Andrea wondered. It was flattering for a girl like 'Bel to be made the confidante of a worldly, witty woman. 'Bel could not be impervious to that flattery.

One day, when she came for the algebra lesson, 'Bel was short-tempered. The moment they were alone in her room, Andrea knew something was wrong. 'Bel tossed her books down with a small extra jerk. But Andrea knew better than to ask outright. There were reticences in 'Bel, and 'Bel angry, unhappy, was full of thorns.

'Bel sat down in the armchair by the window and impatiently opened the algebra book.

"I've done all of those," said Andrea, seeing the book open at the wrong page.

'Bel dropped the book onto her lap and stared out of the window.

'Bel, what is the matter?"

The grey eyes came around to her. But they were not stormy, as Andrea had expected them to be. She saw instead hurt, uncertainty, fear.

"Why, 'Bel —!"

"I don't know what to do."

Andrea had never heard 'Bel's voice like that — a sort of cry that reached to her heart. "About what? What is it?" Wild, half-formed fears took possession of her. 'Bel lived in a much more dangerous world than she did, full of menace that she sensed but could not formulate. Was it a man — had something happened to 'Bel, like —. The buried memory of the man who had exposed himself to her on the streetcar came back to her in a vivid flash. Sometimes 'Bel talked about her stepfather. She hated him. She rebelled at having to live in the same place with him. She despised her mother for putting up with his drunkenness, his foul language, the occasional blows he aimed at her and at the younger children. But 'Bel had never said she was afraid of him.

"It's mademoiselle. I don't know what she is going to say about me."

Andrea, watching her face closely, saw the nervous movements of her lips, the restlessness of her downcast eyes.

"Why is she going to say anything?"

"It's something she's been doing right along now, for quite a while. When she is giving me a French lesson, she's always patting me, giving me little shoves to emphasize a point. She makes me act out a character, while she makes the responses. It was fun to begin with. It's more alive to study a novel or a play that way. I just thought she was a wonderful teacher. But I began to get uncomfortable. It wasn't what she did. It was the way she has. She gets as close to me as she can and her eyes shine. It bothered me at first but I got used to it. She uses some sort of French perfume — the Sisters talk about that. It's a tantalizing sort of scent. I didn't like it in the beginning but I got so that I thought about it as being part of her."

Andrea was astonished at the sudden flash of understanding that came to her as she listened to 'Bel's words. So mademoiselle was enticing 'Bel. This was the sort of thing her mother had talked to her about, in roundabout terms — not letting boys put their hands on her, not listening to boys who might try to tempt her into kissing them. She had never found that idea the least bit attractive. But now it was mademoiselle and she recognized her quite clearly — a woman she had never seen. She saw her smiling at 'Bel, cajoling, teasing, flattering, finding out the vulnerable spots in 'Bel, making 'Bel's eyes grow bright with the stimulation of attention, making 'Bel laugh with delight at being singled out as a special friend, treated as an equal. Oh, 'Bel, she thought, how easy it is to get under your defenses, how easy to demolish the wall you try to build around yourself to hide behind.

Andrea could not keep the anger out of her voice. "What did she do?"

"She said let us go to her room. She has a great big corner room on the second floor and she gives little parties there sometimes — she calls it her salon. I've been there before, when there have been other people. But this time we were by ourselves. Usually she gives me a lesson in the corner of the refectory, where there are a lot of people coming and going. This afternoon the refectory was all arranged for something else. Mademoiselle said it would be better if we had the lesson in her room. We could be freer in declaiming. She loves to declaim. She loves the sound of French poetry, French drama. She can go on in it for hours. And she can hold your attention, Andy."

"Well, go on."

'Bel, her inward eye fixed on what she was recounting, merely nodded.

"Well?"

'Bel, looked up at her briefly. "Well, we went up to her room. She was telling me about the Comedie Francaise. She knows some of the famous actors and actresses — I don't know, perhaps she talks as if she knows them better than she really does. But she makes it all interesting — exciting, sometimes. I didn't notice what she was doing until she stopped talking. Then I saw she was just looking at me. She wasn't going on with the lesson. She said, "Ma petite, que tues belle! Et si intelligente! Que j'ai du arriver ici dans ce pays sauvage pour decouvrir ma petite reine!"

'Bel was speaking very fast now, not in her own voice. It must be mademoiselle's, thought Andrea, with the familiar feeling that her feet were slipping out from under her in the avalanche of foreign words. She broke in, "Bel, I can't keep up with you when you talk French so fast."

'Bel came to an abrupt halt. "It doesn't matter, really, what she said. The words, I mean. I was flabbergasted. I suppose I just stood there with my mouth open. Anyway, she came close to me and put her arms around me and kissed me, on the lips."

"What did you do?"

"I tell you, I was so surprised, I just stood there. And then she began to stroke the back of my neck. I could just feel her hand going around here in front —" 'Bel's own hands went to her breasts, holding them up, cupped,

Andrea, her eyes fixed on her in fascination, murmured, " 'Bel, why didn't you push her away, tell her to leave you alone?"

'Bel's seriousness broke for a moment into a little laugh. "I couldn't. I was too — interested. I was beginning to shiver all over. Mademoiselle felt it. She began to hold me tighter, kissing me with her mouth open, putting her tongue in mine."

" 'Bel!" the revulsion in Andrea's voice was clear.

"I couldn't move. I wanted her to stop but at the same time I didn't. She put her arm around my waist and pulled me down on the chaise lounge she has in her room. I felt as if I was drowning. She was holding me as if I was a baby and saying all kinds of baby talk to me."

Furious, Andrea demanded, "Why didn't you hit her? Why didn't you get away from her?"

'Bel was a long time answering. "You know how it is sometimes when you're having a nightmare — you want to scream and you can't make a sound — you want to move and you can't? Besides —" 'Bel's voice trailed off.

"Besides what?"

"I didn't want her to go on. I wanted to stop her. I hated having her fondle me that way. But there was another part of me that wanted her to go on. I wanted to find out. I wanted to know what she was going to do. I wanted to see how it felt."

"How what felt?"

'Bel looked directly at her. A different expression had come into her face. Instead of the troubled dismay there was a brooding calculation. Without putting it in words to herself, Andrea recognized what 'Bel meant. 'Bel had been on the verge of that unformulated something that grown people seemed to know so much about and said little of. There was some sort of passionate feeling that gripped people, even staid, solidly based people who gave no sign of romantic feelings. There it was, in novels, in poetry, in plays, hinted at but not described. She knew that in the most private place in her own body there was a spot that could throb under her own stimulation and even in response to things she read. She searched out clues in what she read. Occasionally an overheard statement lit up the dark places. But her mother had created a wall around her that she could not breach, even with her mother. It was something that fascinated her. It was terribly near at night in bed when in the midst of fantastic dreams her fingers found that throbbing spot, eager to respond.

Now, watching 'Bel's face, she quaked. How bold 'Bel was, how reckless she seemed in daring to look over that wall that surrounded all obedient, well-guarded girls. But 'Bel was not so well-guarded. 'Bel was halfway out into the edge of that unknown terrain.

'Bel was answering her question. "What it's like to have some-one make love to you."

"But mademoiselle isn't a man!"

Dark red color flooded 'Bel's face. "I wouldn't stand for a man handling me like that. I think mademoiselle knows that. She wanted to see what I would do if she did."

"Well, what happened?"

"I finally pushed her away. I told her not to touch me. She fell over on the floor when I shoved her."

"And then what did she do?"

"She was furious. She used some very bad French words. But then after a bit she laughed at me and called me a silly little fool."

For a while they were both silent. Then 'Bel said, "I'm afraid of her now, Andy."

"Afraid of her? Why? You should tell Reverend Mother —"

She stopped at the sight of the pure horror in 'Bel's eyes. "Andy! I couldn't do that. Don't you see, she would tell Reverend Mother that it was me who started it all."

"But Reverend Mother would know you were telling the truth!"

"Would she? Oh no, she wouldn't. Mademoiselle would know how to tell her about it, so that it would sound like my fault. She would say it was just something a girl my age would do — that it was something she understood, growing pains. She'd be very sweet about it all, saying that she was only telling Reverend Mother about it for my own good — that I wasn't to be judged, that I was to be pitied, not punished. And I'd have to go to confession and do hours of penance and the Sisters would all treat me as if I had some terrible disease and had to be chided and corrected."

So vividly did 'Bel's words create the situation that Andrea stared at her wonderingly. How was it that 'Bel knew all these things, could fathom ahead of time the reactions of other people? How did she know that this was the way mademoiselle would act and Reverend Mother?

'Bel started to say something. "Besides —", and stopped.

Andrea waited till she could wait no longer. " 'Bel, she is wicked! She shouldn't do things like that!"

"You mean, egg me on?"

"She shouldn't try to touch you and then lie and say you were the one!"

As they had been talking 'Bel's tension had vanished. She was almost goodhumored now. "Oh, Andy! She's not wicked! She's just — sophisticated. She is bored with living in the Convent and not having anybody to fool around with. I expect I looked like a little dummy — following her around and admiring her."

But though she tried to speak indulgently, Andrea saw the goad underneath, the self-contempt in which 'Bel writhed. 'Bel had turned away from her and was standing by the window, staring out into the green shade of the pin oak tree that broke the sun's rays. Andrea came close to her.

" 'Bel, what are you going to do? What do you think mademoiselle will do now?"

"I'm not going to do anything. I just hope mademoiselle won't say anything to Reverend Mother. Perhaps she won't if I just lie low. But she might anyway, just to get revenge, because I pushed her away. Or maybe she'll just let me go on worrying about whether she will do that — enjoying the hold she has over me — until something else comes along to distract her."

They stood facing each other. 'Bel seemed about to say something else. Andrea waited. They stood so close that they could feel the warmth of each other's body. And then the moment passed.

* * *

The afternoon was warm and fragrant with wild honeysuckle. It grew all over the fence that shut off the garden from the broad cobbled alley that ran down the middle of the block. Andrea's father swore that some day he would pull it all out, that it was damaging the fence and always getting into the vegetable patch he planted in that sunny spot. Perhaps, thought Andrea, he did not really want to get rid of all of it, that in spite of the nuisance he enjoyed the scent as much as anyone. In any case, every summer it was there, growing into great thick ropes hidden in sheets of green leaves and clusters of yellow and white blossoms that filled the air with perfume, blowing in through the kitchen windows.

The house was silent. Andrea and 'Bel came into the cool quiet from the hot sun of the street. They both stopped at once in the dim hallway and by common consent stood listening. The quiet of the house became conspiratorial. No sound came to them from the upper floor. There was no rustle or clink of china or metal from the darkness underneath the stairs where the door to the kitchen stood open.

"Mother is out," Andrea said, almost in a whisper.

A common feeling of license, of release from supervision flooded them, held them while the surge of a joyful freedom welled up in their bodies. After a moment Andrea roused herself to walk to the foot of the stairs and 'Bel followed her. About to take the first step Andrea stopped and faced around.

"Shall we go up to my room or shall we stay down here?"

She was voicing the hesitation they both felt, the wariness that had suddenly gripped them, as if they were in a trackless jungle full of unknown dangers. They were alone in the house. The fact loomed large in their consciousnesses. Simultaneously they recognized it and with it the further fact that were faced with a choice. They could choose to abide by the prohibitions and commandments by which they lived, in this unsupervised moment, or they could choose to strike out on their own.

46

'Bel said quickly, "Let's go upstairs."

In Andrea's room they dropped their books on the little desk by the window. Dozens of times now they had spent the afternoon in this room, part of the time working diligently at algebraic equations, part of the time talking — talking about the things that happened to them when they were separated, about the books they read, about the people they encountered, about the things they liked and disliked, always, in the end, about themselves, what they felt, what they thought, what they guessed themselves to be, what they would become when a few more years gave them independence.

To Andrea, this was a vague realm, this realm of independence. It consisted chiefly of freedom, a freedom she understood in the terms of freedom from the present routine of her days, freedom from the need to do and be what her mother and father and teachers seemed to expect her to be. Yet within this realm her parents still figured, the main lines of her life remained unchanged. She was still cared for, sheltered. The difference seemed to be in her being able to escape from the limits set for her by others. Her parents would still be there, loving, but acquiescent in her choice of opinions, actions, occupations. She did not want her mother's disapproval, or in any way to disappoint her father, for that would mean sorrow. She shrank from sorrow.

She was aware that 'Bel also sought freedom. But 'Bel was eager to seize it, to rush into independence, reckless about any loss it might bring. Of course, 'Bel had much less to lose, because she had already lost so much. 'Bel did not seem to fear sorrow. There was a fierce sort of fire that burned in 'Bel. Its heat sometimes reached Andrea. It would consume any sorrow, any regret.

"What do you want to be, what do you want to do, 'Bel?"

"I want to make money." 'Bel's tone was defiant. "I want to make enough money so that I can live the way I want to. I want to have enough money so that nobody can make me do things I don't want to do. And I want enough money —"

She stopped, finding it difficult to convey even to Andrea the demand for freedom that welled in her. She tried but could not say aloud, that she wanted enough money to ensure that her mother, that anyone who had any claim on her, could be bought off, enough so that she could feel free of these claims, that she could pay to solace anyone else's longings that might otherwise be sought through her.

Andrea, who rarely thought of money, reproached her. "Oh, 'Bel, you want something more than that!"

'Bel shot back at her, "It's the basis of everything else. You can't do what you want to without money. Money is the first thing. There's no use wasting time on anything else to begin with. I want to live properly, to have my own place, so that I can have things right and some peace and quiet — not to have to look after squal-

47

ling kids and to put up with my mother's whining. Not to have to be there all the time, watching her push Mac away because she's afraid of having another baby."

The familiar shock went through Andrea's nerves, as it always did when the subject of men and women, so wrapped in mystery in her own life, came so suddenly to the surface as 'Bel flung out these violent words about her home circumstances. 'Bel seemed to know all the unspoken things about the dealings of men and women that her mother knew and never mentioned to her, except in cryptic phrases of comment on people of her acquaintance. Andrea had been eight years old when her sister Deedee had married and moved out to Ohio six years ago. The ten years in age between them made her seem to Andrea almost a contemporary of her mother's, partly because they were so unlike in temperament. Whenever Deedee visited, she and her mother at once fell into a close alliance, their conversation full of half phrases and allusions only understood by each other. Whenever Andrea asked for enlightment, her mother would say, When she was older, when she was more experienced.

Experienced. It was a convenient word, never clearly defined. It certainly seemed to apply to her brother Bob. His life was even more mysterious to her than Deedee's. His friends were all, like himself, engrossed in sports. The only girls he seemed to know were the daughters of her parents' friends, whom he saw only in family gatherings. Or if he knew any others, he did not bring them to the house. Andrea was aware that her mother sometimes had long, anxious conversations with her father about Bob. But she had the impression that her father dismissed her mother's anxieties with a phrase or two. Bob was just a boy. He'd outgrow these things, whatever they were.

On the surface, it all seemed normal, serene, not fraught with any danger or threat, this placid, secure life her parents provided. She knew there were dreadful things that happened to other people. She read about such things in the newspapers. Her mother's friends sometimes had tragedies to relate. She realized that some of the children she went to school with were the victims of homes not as fortunate as her own. But the reality of life seemed to reach her only now, when she heard 'Bel lash out at her own troubles.

'Bel sometimes railed at her. "You haven't got anything to be unhappy about. Your parents give you everything you want. You're little miss prim with your own room and civilized people to live with. What do you know what it's like, to have to take care of yourself, not to be able to trust anybody?"

At first, these tirades hurt Andrea deeply. Then she learned that under this anger, under the bravado, there was a sorely wounded 'Bel, a 'Bel who for the moment needed to hurt, to wound, to draw blood, in order to diminish her own pain. And then Andrea, pushed to defend herself so as not to show the compassion that would only infuriate 'Bel the more, retaliated, and they would quarrel, briefly, violently, stopping suddenly, the rush of angry words stilled by the remembrance that the sound of their upraised voices would carry downstairs to Andrea's mother.

But now they were alone in the drowsy quiet of the house. The only sound was the trilling of the canary in the cage that hung on the back porch of the neighbor's house. The sweet song came in through the window with the mild air that stirred the white curtain. Without words they sat down together on the edge of the bed. They often sat this way, side by side, to pour over the algebra book. But now there was another, half-understood motive. They were alone in an unexpectedly empty world and the fact, which they did not articulate, even separately, each to herself, paralyzed them for a few moments of awe. In the quiet a promise brooded.

Andrea sat inwardly trembling on the brink of a revelation she could not grasp. The two of them had often sat this way together but aware of the normal sounds of the house or, if there were none, nevertheless of the felt presence of Andrea's mother. Andrea had often felt that she wanted to touch 'Bel, something more than the casual contact when they shared a seat or handed each other something. But how touch her she had never visualized. It was something that hung behind a curtain in her mind. They never kissed. 'Bel had a way of drawing back involuntarily when someone made any casual motion to embrace her. The first time Andrea's mother, with automatic kindness, sought to kiss her in saying goodbye, Andrea had seen 'Bel shrink, and then, suprisingly, respond. After that she had seemed to accept without question the quick peck of Mrs. Hollingsworth's kiss.

It was 'Bel who was the first to rouse, to confront the moment. She put out her hand and laid it on Andrea's arm. "Andy —". What she wanted to say escaped her. Andrea sat immobile. 'Bel's hand went around her waist. They sat for a while with their faces very close, so close that Andrea felt 'Bel's warm breath on her cheek, was acutely aware of the quick rise and fall of 'Bel's breast against her own shoulder. Her own body was caught in an inescapable tension. It had become a vibrant prison.

All at once 'Bel thrust her face against Andrea's throat. She felt 'Bel's kisses, the moist, eager movement of 'Bel's lips on the tender skin under her chin. A thrill traveled through her body, a strong, involuntary inward shiver. Fascinated by the sensation, she felt it pass through the nerve-ends in her skin down into her depths, till it centered in that spot between her legs, the very crux of her being that so often at night she was driven to excite with her fingers till the climax came, a bursting of tension. This was something she tried not to do, and once she had done it, tried not to acknowledge even to herself. And yet inevitably she was drawn into doing it again. She knew this was something she must never

49

admit to. She must keep it hidden, her longing for this building up of tension, the ecstasy of release, hidden from everybody. It had been worse lately, when she realized that this longing arose in her while her thoughts dwelt on 'Bel, or when eagerly anticipating being with 'Bel, she caught an unexpected glimpse of her.

And now 'Bel was here pressed close against her, drawing out of her all this yearning. She could stand it no longer. Breathless she responded to 'Bel's embrace. Together they fell backwards across the bed. 'Bel's face hovered over her own, so close she could not focus on 'Bel's eyes. Their hands sought each other's body. Andrea clung desperately to Bel's. It was as if they were trying by sheer pressure to merge with each other. Andrea's own drive was undirected, forcing against 'Bel's stomach. Desperately she wondered if 'Bel knew what to do, if 'Bel knew what she needed. 'Bel's hands, frantic, reached under her skirt and pulled at the elastic of her panties, shoving them down. She felt 'Bel's fingers reach the hot, wet cleft between her legs. She felt 'Bel's forefinger rubbing up and down in that smooth little trench between the opening into her body and that throbbing button at the top. Within an instant the world was filled with herself, bursting into a cascade of intense feeling. She shuddered and lay limp.

But 'Bel was still on top her, taut as Andrea had been, moving in little uncontrollable jerks as she clutched at Andrea. Knowing her own ignorance, clumsy with excitement, Andrea fumbled at 'Bel's clothes. At last she found her way in, felt 'Bel's vigorous muscles under the satin skin, scarcely reached the warm pulsing spot before 'Bel's body arched against her with an almost intolerable pressure, going from climax to climax till slowly they relaxed their grip on each other and lay still, clinging together.

For a while they lay on the bed side by side in a kind of daze. Gradually the mist of feelings and wandering thoughts cleared in Andrea's mind. She turned her head to see the back of 'Bel's, the long golden brown hair tumbled on the bedspread. 'Bel lay on her stomach, her face half-buried.

" 'Bel —" Andrea started to speak and fell silent, her fingers in 'Bel's hair.

'Bel stirred and then turned over and looked up at her. Andrea saw that her eyes were full of tears. For a moment they stared into each other's eyes, wondering, questioning. Then 'Bel reached up and seized her in a grip so hard it hurt her.

After a while they sat up as if by agreement. Andrea brushed away the traces of tears on 'Bel's face. They sat together wordless on the edge of the bed as they had before, the time flowing past them unheeded. They knew, each of them, that they had crossed a bridge together. They were in a new and unknown country.

The sound of the front door closing downstairs came up to them. Together they jumped up automatically, pulling at their clothes to straighten them. They stood for a moment without mov-

50

ing, every nerve on a stretch. Then, simultaneously, silently, they threw themselves into each other's arms and clung desperately.

* * *

"But I still don't understand," said Mrs. Hollingsworth, "why she is so reluctant to say anything about her parents? She has been coming here every Tuesday and Friday for four weeks to tutor you and I still know very little about her background. Oh, I've been to see Reverend Mother. Apparently Isabel is able to drive some algebra into your head. They obviously think a lot of her there at the Convent. But what about her home?"

"I've told you, Mother, she doesn't have a father. Mac is only her stepfather. And her mother is not a Catholic. She doesn't like 'Bel being a Catholic."

Andrea saw her mother's mouth tighten a little in disapproval at "Mac". "Well, that is all very unfortunate. But her mother must have consented to her being brought up as one, so that cannot be any new thing for her to get upset about. How old was she when her mother married this man? I gather he is a skilled mechanic."

"I don't know," Andrea said helplessly.

Her mother looked at her keenly. "Doesn't Isabel tell you anything about her home life?"

"She doesn't like to talk about it."

"Then she can't be happy at home. That is too bad. Does her stepfather resent her? Some men do resent their stepchildren."

"I think — so."

"I'll just have to talk to her about it myself."

"Oh, Mother! Please don't! It'll upset her. She hates being asked questions about her family."

"Well, I can understand that she is sensitive. Girls your age usually are. But after all I'm not being merely curious. I'd like to help Isabel. She is a remarkable girl. Your father is very much impressed by her intelligence. Reverend Mother said some elderly relative is paying for her education."

"Her Aunt Gertrude. She is not really her aunt. She's her father's aunt. 'Bel goes to see her a lot. She is quite an old lady."

Her mother glanced at her sharply. "Have you met her?"

Andrea knew she was flushing. " 'Bel took me with her one day, after we had been playing tennis. She lives in an apartment on Washington Circle, you know, the big tall building. Oh, Mother, Aunt Gertrude has all sorts of things. They're very valuable, I think."

"What kind of things?"

"Chinese things. Great big vases with dragons all around them and porcelain figures, ladies with fans and silk scrolls with paintings of mountains and lakes with sail boats on them and men in straw hats carrying sedan chairs on poles — oh, all kinds of things! You can hardly move without touching something."

51

Andrea talked on, immersed in the recollection of the stately old lady in the black dress, who with such graciousness had welcomed her grandniece's young friend. Andrea remembered the gnarled, wrinkled old hands touching the Chinese figurines on the black carved whatnot, the deep voice talking about Beethoven and illustrating an anecdote with a few bars of music on the great black piano. The savor of a bygone age with its special elegance and romantic, foreign outlook had come to her through Aunt Gertrude and she longed to transmit something of this to her mother.

Mrs. Hollingsworth, smiling a little at the unusual animation in Andrea's face, said, "How did she get all these things?"

"She brought them from the Philippines. Her husband was a judge out there. When he was alive they used to live in a big house on I Street near Pennsylvania Avenue. But she has lived in that apartment ever since she became a widow. She is worried because she says the people who own the apartment house want to sell it and she is afraid that it will be torn down and she'll have to move. She doesn't know what she is going to do with all her antiques."

"I've heard that they're going to put a hospital on that site. Does she have any children or other relatives except Isabel?"

"I don't know. I don't think so."

"So perhaps Isabel will inherit something from her. That is probably why Isabel's mother wants her to do what the aunt wants."

"Oh, Mother!"

"Well, it would be foolish of her not to do what she can to make things easier for Isabel. Otherwise, I gather they are dependent on the stepfather."

" 'Bel's mother works. She has a job."

"As a shop clerk, I gather, and she doesn't seem to be able to keep any particular job for any length of time." Andrea wondered how her mother had learned this. 'Bel must have said something that her shrewd mother had at once understood. "Have you ever met her mother, Andrea?"

"No, 'Bel never takes me to her place."

"Well, I'm just as glad for that. I don't like the sound of that home situation. I'd rather you didn't get too intimate with her. I've nothing against Isabel but her ways are not yours. It's all right for you to play tennis with her. But you shouldn't let her monopolize all your time and attention. I'd like you to make friends with some other girls."

* * *

It was almost ten o'clock and the brief freshness of the early morning was already gone. It was going to be a hot day for tennis. But she and Andy could sit a lot of the time on one of the benches in the shade of the big oak trees of the Cathedral grounds that overlooked the courts. She had not expected to have been able to spend

52

so much time playing tennis this summer. But Andy paid for the tickets.

An enormous sense of luxury took possession of her. Seldom, very seldom, did she have a day like this, when she had no commitments, a day that wasn't chopped up by appointments to do this and do that. Her mother had left on the bus at eight o'clock, taking the kids to visit somebody in Front Royal. Mademoiselle had gone to New York for a week. Sister Mary Cecilia had gone to take a seminar in musical theory at the music summer school in the Berkshires. And it was not one of the days she worked as a part time clerk in the bakery.

She sat on the bench furthest away from the tennis courts, her back to the players. She thought about idleness. Idleness was a luxury when you didn't have much opportunity for it. She supposed she would never really want too much of it. There was a nagging pull at the back of her mind that she did not have much time in which to accomplish all she wanted to do. But sometimes there were moments, like this, when she rebelled, when emptiness seemed about to engulf her, when she luxuriated in the feeling of wasting time, when idleness seemed to be a great drifting stream that held her motionless as it flowed imperceptibly but inexorably on to some unknown end. Or perhaps it did not end. Perhaps it was eternal and her most active efforts were as twigs carried along in its flow.

Reverend Mother once or twice had noticed these moments of spiritual inertia, when she stubbornly drifted along, sometimes from day to day, refusing to give any more of herself to the task at hand then was absolutely necessary, when she seemed to herself hollow and empty and refused to rouse herself to a more normal energy. It was natural at her age, said Reverend Mother, sometimes to lack energy and purpose. She was leaving childhood behind. Coming womanhood put a great strain on her body. Still, this lassitude, this emptiness of spirit was something she must fight against, strive to overcome. It was here that her religious faith must be most important, when it would justify her greatest reliance on it.

Of course Reverend Mother said that because she knew. She knows, thought 'Bel, idly drawing the toe of her tennis shoe across a trail of ants in the dust, that I'm losing my faith. Or that is how she sees it. At least, she thinks that I may be in danger of that, even though I may not myself be aware of it. But I wonder if I ever had it, at least, the kind of faith she has, and the Sisters?

There was a time, when she was little, when she knew that everything would eventually be all right, that she was safe from unknown dangers because of the angels that stood guard over her. That sort of trust had been worn away, by what had happened to her, by her mother's ways of doing things, and also, as she grew older, by the realization that this faith, this expectation of good, was not universally held. The books she read — Reverend Mother knew nothing about these and her own mother was indifferent to whether she read or not — introduced her to a good many contradictory opinions about God, goodness, evil, the existence of one's soul, the nature of a possible hereafter, what a moral life really was. So that, in the end, she was often ready to adopt the idea that a divine power was a figment of some people's imagination and that there was no point to her looking for divine intervention, whether good or bad, in her own affairs.

But it wasn't such a simple thing, to dismiss all that. A moment always came when some statement, some expressed idea, some emotional appeal nullified all this rationalization, and she found herself caught up in the most exquisite sense of a live faith. Very often such moments came when she was listening to music. Sacred music, especially, human voices soaring up out of the darkness of the world into the pure light of heaven, borne on the wings of the poignant words of the New Testament drama, bodying forth the passion of Christ, the sorrow of the Holy Mother, the yearning of worldlings for the Infinite. A moment such as that could carry her back into the very bosom of the faith she had thought gone forever. Even when the emotion of the moment faded, the savor of the feeling it had aroused lingered to color the cool thoughts that returned to her.

Perhaps, she thought, I'm more like mademoiselle. Because what she had learned — and had not been able to tell even Andy — was that mademoiselle was not entirely the mercenary, self-seeking, cynical woman she appeared. Mademoiselle was also subject to these sudden sweeping storms of an emotional faith, when the tears she wept as she prayed before the image of the Holy Mother were hot and genuine. 'Bel had found her in such an ecstasy not long after the episode between them in mademoiselle's room. Something had told her that mademoiselle's despair was not connected with that episode. This was something deeper in mademoiselle's own consciousness. She had gone away as quietly as possible, not letting mademoiselle know she had observed her. That, to mademoiselle, would have been the last straw.

Her mind slid off to the Frenchwoman. For days after the episode she had described to Andy she had lived in dread of the consequences. But nothing had happened. Obviously mademoiselle had said nothing to Reverend Mother. And mademoiselle herself had scarcely altered her own manner. In their sessions together she had sometimes made sly remarks, asides to the lesson, that were ironic or sarcastic comments on 'Bel's behavior. Or do I just imagine that is what they are? she wondered. She knew her own self-consciousness, her own embarrassment was so great that mademoiselle could not fail to see it, must feel it, and therefore was prompted to make these sly little digs.

But chiefly, she thought, mademoiselle's attention must have been distracted to something else, something more important to her. Her whole bearing had changed, to everyone, as if something more far-reaching then baiting the Sisters or seducing a schoolgirl had come to occupy her thoughts. Perhaps she has had an offer from another school, a college, or at least the chance at an opening of that sort, and she is absorbed in the possibility. Gradually 'Bel's uneasiness had subsided, in a sense of thankfulness, even though the change meant that mademoiselle was less attentive in teaching her, that their sessions together became more and more perfunctory.

A little breeze stirred the warm air. 'Bel felt its breath on her skin with sensuous pleasure. A redbird moved in the tall straggling bush behind her and his movement caused a rustle that added to her feeling of idle luxury, swimming in the summer air, subdued light under the trees, the brilliant blue sky seen through the tree-tops. She was living now altogether in the moment. The past, the future was suspended. Even the ants, in the dust at her feet, orderly again after her disturbance of them, were part of this timeless moment.

She leaned back on the bench and looked over her shoulder. Andy was entering the gate in the high wire fence around the tennis courts. They waved to each other.

* * *

Andrea, getting off the bus at the corner, walked quickly along the pavement to the gate of the tennis courts. A couple of young men were playing on one court. The rest were empty. Her eyes sought over on the shady side, at the boundary of the wild park at the bottom of the wooded hill sloping down from the Cathedral. Of course 'Bel was there. She was always early to their rendezvous. She sat with her back turned, lost in some reverie, some thoughtful consideration. Andrea was used now to this metamorphosis in 'Bel's manner. When she was with people she was always watchfully alert, warily intent on what they were doing, saying. But at times when she was alone or with her, this tenseness relaxed and her mind seemed at once to wander off to some private concern of her own.

Very often when they were alone together they spoke in half phrases, understanding each other's intent before they had framed the words to say. Andrea's mother had noticed this. And she doesn't like it, Andrea thought. Lately her mother seemed very much aware of their closeness. She commented on it more and more often, with an undertone of disapproval.

"I don't want you to cut yourself off so from your other friends, Andrea. You'll regret it later on. After all, Isabel's circumstances are different from yours. She's a Catholic and she has been brought up to see things differently. You have always been truthful. I don't

55

want you to lose that. And I don't altogether like the idea of girls going to a religious school. Girls of your age are very impressionable and sometimes they become too much affected by the nuns."

Andrea, mystified by the apparent lack of coherence in these statements, knew there were further thoughts in her mother's mind that she had not expressed. Was that because she feared them and therefore did not want to give them the life that came with sound?

It wasn't because she didn't like 'Bel. She did. It was obvious that she was attracted by 'Bel's quickness of mind, 'Bel's air of maturity beyond her years, that charm of manner that 'Bel could display when she wanted to or felt there was some reason to. In fact, thought Andrea, if Mother knew 'Bel as a grownup woman, she wouldn't have any reservations about liking her. But it is me she doesn't trust with 'Bel. She thinks 'Bel is too sophisticated. She thinks 'Bel will teach me things she doesn't want me to know. That is why she wants me to make friends with other girls, girls I won't particularly like. She knows I've never made real friends with anybody. I've never met anybody that thinks the way I do, except 'Bel. They are not interested in the things I'm interested in. And the things they talk about she would not like, either.

Her mind went back to the afternoon in her bedroom. It shone there with a brilliance beyond anything that had ever happened to her. The very remembrance was a touchstone, reactivated every time she and 'Bel were together, though they had not again had a moment thus to themselves. Could it be that something of what had happened that afternoon showed in her own manner, in 'Bel's, when they were together? Did some hint of it reach her mother and was this the reason why her mother so constantly tried to bring about a separation between them, suggesting other companions, objecting to her being daily with 'Bel, to their semi-articulated communication? It could not be. This must be her awareness of the event, her own overwhelming feeling of its importance.

Very often, when the three of them were together, in the kitchen while her mother prepared dinner, on the porch when her mother sat sewing, Andrea felt that her mother and 'Bel were adults, speaking to each other as equals, while Andrea herself was relegated to the status of child, to be indulged but at the same time guarded from an understanding of adults' talk. I'm not supposed to know about what happens between grown people, men and women. But Mother takes it for granted that 'Bel does. 'Bel tells her things, about her own mother, about Mac, that Mother puts together and understands. She thinks I don't. And that is what she is afraid 'Bel will tell me. Her mother had deliberately tried to keep her a child, innocent, ignorant, her baby. She knew now that her mother had even warned Deedee, married and expecting her first child, not to be careless in talking in front of Andrea. It had not been hard for her to keep a distance between Andrea and Deedee. The ten years

56

difference in age had always been an effective barrier to intimacy between her two daughters. And also the difference in their temperaments. Her mother often contrasted them. Deedee as an adolescent girl had been lively, unbookish, always eager for play of some kind. She had, her mother said, had quite a problem with Deedee and boys. Deedee had gathered boys around her like the proverbial flies around the honeypot. When her mother talked this way about Deedee there was a tone of indulgence in her voice, now that Deedee was safely married.

But with Andrea her manner was different. How many times had Andrea heard her say to a friend or acquaintance that, yes, Andrea was her youngest, and oh, how she wished she could keep her little, her baby? Andrea had always been aware that there was a difference in the way her mother treated her and the way she treated Deedee. It was as if Andrea was more closely her own child, more completely a part of herself.

But there was also an ambiguity in the way she talked. She often said that she was thankful that with Andrea she had not to go through the anxieties she had suffered over Deedee. Andrea, she said, seemed unaware of boys and not even curious about them. But then there were times when she talked to Andrea, in that curious, roundabout way she had, about the importance of boys, the significance of boys in an adolescent girl's life, as if she was worried about the very absence of the menace she rejoiced in not observing.

Just this morning, for instance, as she and her mother had stood in the kitchen, the early morning sunlight touching on the breakfast dishes, washed and left to drain, her mother had asked, with false unconcern, "How long are you and Isabel going to play tennis today?"

"Oh, I don't know. I expect it depends on how many people want the courts. There is not such a crowd just now. Maybe it is too hot."

She stood uneasily, with the brown paper bag of sandwiches in her hand, barely restraining her eager feet from carrying her out of the door to the freedom of the day.

Her mother, standing with the jam jar in her hand, said, "There must be some boys who go there to play. You never mention them."

"Oh, yes! There're some kids from St. Albans! They are all going to be champions."

"I mean, young men."

"Yes, I guess so."

She knew that her mother noted her vagueness. She did not want to say that she and 'Bel were the only girls who played there regularly during the working hours of the day. She wondered if her mother had doubts about 'Bel's reactions to these vague young men, whether she suspected that 'Bel might be too free in making

57

friends with strangers and involving Andrea.

Her mother sighed and turned away to put the jam on the shelf. "I just wanted to know whom you are associating with, Andrea. Do be careful about strangers. Does 'Bel ever bring someone else with her to play?"

"Oh, no. We just play together."

"Well, I want you to meet new friends. But if you make friends, bring them here to the house. I want to know who they are."

"Oh, yes, Mother!" Andrea seized the moment's tacit consent to run to the door and pick up her tennis racket from the porch.

She put all that behind her as she ran down the shady street to the car stop. She hoped to goodness she had not missed the car she usually caught. There was a long wait between steeetcars out here, once the morning office rush hour had passed. On the car she switched her thoughts to 'Bel. In these long, lazy summer days 'Bel had dropped that harassed manner of hers, always full of responsibilities and duties. She was a different 'Bel. She was ready to be lazy through the hot still hours, as they sat on a grassy bank among the big trees, aware only of the woodland sounds, the distant thud of tennis balls, the disassociated voices of the players. Often she had the impression that 'Bel was ranging off in some far world of her own. The feeling gave her a little pang of jealousy, of being deserted, forgotten. But 'Bel came back to her at once with the slightest reminder of her presence.

Tacitly, without trying to put it in words, they had reached a world of their own, a still oasis inhabited only by themselves, in the midst of the greater, noisier, dangerous world in which their lives were embedded. They had reached their own terms of a dual existence. 'Bel had dropped her truculent manner when money became the price of their freedom together. She let her bring the sandwiches and thermos for their lunch, let her pay for the tennis tickets, for her carfare. This release of a small portion of her independence, Andrea knew, was the price 'Bel was willing to pay for their joint hours.

Andrea had reached the narrow path that led up through the trees and shrubs to the bench where 'Bel sat. At the sound of Andrea's tennis shoes on the stony ground she looked up and smiled.

* * *

The rainy night enveloped the house in a curtain of steamy quiet. The rain had come in a series of thunderstorms, the lightning revealing the empty street and front gardens of the houses in blinding flashes. Andrea, sitting by the window of her bedroom watching it, thought thankfully that this was not one of the days 'Bel came to coach her, because she would have been caught in the first of the showers as she returned to the streetcar. The nearest car stop was two long blocks away on Fourteenth Street.

58

At least, she hoped that 'Bel wasn't out in that teeming rain. A sudden thought had come to her that she did not know for certain whether 'Bel would be safely home. 'Bel's mother was away. 'Bel had said she had taken the two boys and gone to North Carolina to visit her sister.

"I think she is fed up with Mac," 'Bel had said. "He's out of work again. He got drunk on the job and was fired. He thinks he's such a good mechanic that he can do as he likes. But there're too many fellows out looking for jobs."

"He doesn't sound very nice."

'Bel had given her an amused smile. "No, I wouldn't say he is."

"You didn't like it for your mother to marry him, did you?"

"No."

"Why did she?"

'Bel had flared up. "Do you mean, did she have to? Did she get pregnant and have to marry him? No, she didn't. Not this time."

Daunted by 'Bel's sudden anger, as she always was, Andrea was silent. 'Bel, aware of the little drawing away, had said, "That's what happened with me. That's why my father's people didn't want to accept my mother. They said they weren't sure he was my father. But my mother says he was."

"Oh!"

"Yes —oh!" 'Bel was angry again.

" 'Bel don't get mad. I mean, why did your mother marry Mac? How could she like him?"

"He flashed a lot of money around and she was tired of working at the five and ten and not having a good time. She didn't find out about — the other things — till later."

Under Andrea's gaze 'Bel had looked away. The anger in her face changed to sullenness. She had said, as if compelled, "He likes to go to taverns and pick up women and get drunk. And when he comes home, he beats her up, because she calls him names. He was going to beat me once, when I tried to stop him. He took his belt off and was going to use the buckle end. But my mother told him if he did, she'd call the police. He said he'd kill her if she did. But she managed to get out and take me to the police station and we stayed there all the rest of the night. He never tried to beat me again."

" 'Bel, why doesn't your mother just leave him — go away somewhere?"

Bitterness had filled 'Bel's voice. "Because she's got the kids and she'd have to support them herself. He wouldn't help. He's not going to keep a woman he can't sleep with, he says. And she says they're his kids and he's going to keep them. Well, she's gone to North Carolina now, to see Aunt Pearl. She says she might as well, since he is out of a job and broke. If he gets any money, he spends it on booze."

"Didn't she want you to go with her?"

"I don't think she really did. And anyway I didn't want to go. I couldn't have gone. I have things I'm committed to do. She got mad when I told her that. She doesn't understand that I've got a sense of responsibility that she doesn't. If she wants to go away, she just throws up whatever she's doing. She gets mad when I don't do that. She says I don't act like a daughter at all. I think this time she is just as glad I'm not with her. She gets sorry for herself and tells me I make her unhappy. That means she thinks I don't give her all of my money. I have to keep a little for myself. She says I pay more attention to other people than I do to her, that I think more of Aunt Gertrude and Reverend Mother and the Sisters than I do of her. And when she gets that far she begins to harp on how wicked pious people can be, stealing the affections of a child from her mother."

She and 'Bel had both been quiet for a while after that, the algebra book laid aside and their arms around each other, gradually losing in the soft warmth of each other's body the psychic chill that 'Bel's words had brought to them.

A flash of lightning and another roll of thunder startled Andrea. A second storm was approaching. The rain, which had dwindled to a steady patter, began to drum again against the window. Andrea pulled the curtain aside and looked out. She could see the front steps of the house, sheltered only by a small overhang. This had been Deedee's room and when Deedee married it had become hers. Andrea could remember her six-year-old self covertly aware, in the tiny room at the back of the house that was her own at the time, of Deedee's excited giggling as she had watched from this window when the boys came to take her out.

As if echoing that memory, the doorbell rang and again Andrea looked down at the front steps. Somebody was standing there, somebody in a lightcolored summer dress. She heard her parents' voices exclaiming in the livingroom downstairs and then the sound of her father's steps across the hall. He switched on the outside light and the beam fell directly on 'Bel's upturned face. Too surprised to move at once, Andrea stared down until 'Bel stepped out of sight into the house and the light went off.

When she ran down the stairs she saw 'Bel standing just inside the door, conscious of the puddles of rainwater gathering at her feet. She wore no hat and her hair was plastered to her head. Rain drops dripped from the end of her nose.

Mr. and Mrs. Hollingsworth stood beside her, perplexed by this sudden intrusion into what was usually the final sleepy moments before they left the livingroom and climbed the stairs to their bedroom. She could see that their disconcertion had destroyed all of 'Bel's self-possession. 'Bel stood stammering, half ready to flee out of the front door again at the idea that they did not welcome her. The sight of Andrea seemed to steady her.

"It's raining so hard — I was late starting to go home — the streetcars —" 'Bel was babbling, eagerly watching Mrs. Hollingsworth's face.

Andrea rushed into the breach. "Oh, 'Bel, you'll just have to stay here!"

"Why, of course!" Mrs. Hollingsworth regained her voice. "It is storming so. You can't be out in all that rain!"

'Bel said, "I thought, maybe, I could stay here till it lets up."

Mrs. Hollingsworth said, doubt in her voice, "It has gone ten already. I'm afraid it will be pretty late by the time this storm passes, and I think the weatherman said it is going to storm all night." Andrea could see that she was weighing several things in her mind. Her mother was always vigilant when it came to her father's wellbeing, his dislike of having a routine disturbed. On the other hand, obviously she would not agree to 'Bel going home alone at whatever hour the storm ceased.

Andrea said eagerly, "She can stay here all night, Mother!"

Her mother said slowly, "I'm afraid she'll have to." She spoke to 'Bel, "Won't your mother be upset?"

"My mother is away," said 'Bel.

"Well, then, you must stay here. You'll have to get out of those wet things. Why don't you take her to your room, Andrea, and give her something of yours to put on? We can hang her things in the basement to dry."

The two girls were silent under her bustling talk. 'Bel followed Andrea obediently up to her room.

In the bathroom they worked together to strip the soaked dress off 'Bel, her garter belt, her slip. She stood looking down dismayed at her sodden shoes. Andrea was aware of a strange passivity in 'Bel's manner.

She sought to comfort her. "Never mind, 'Bel. Don't worry about them. You can wear a pair of mine."

But 'Bel looked up at her with eyes full of anguish. It's not the shoes, thought Andrea as she put a bathrobe around 'Bel's shivering body. Before she could say anything her mother opened the door.

"Andrea, I've put sheets and a pillowcase on the bed in the little room. You can make up the bed there for Isabel. Would you like something to eat or drink, Isabel, before we go to bed?"

'Bel gazed at her for so long in silence that Andrea said, "I'll go and get her some milk and cookies, Mother,." The sound of her voice seemed to awaken 'Bel from her trance and she said, "Oh, yes, please!"

Mrs. Hollingsworth looked at her for a moment thoughtfully but went out of the woom with only a "Good night".

Andrea held the bathrobe tightly around 'Bel and they went down the hall to the little room. 'Bel's body still trembled under Andrea's hands. "Andy, I can't tell your mother, but I can't go home tonight."

"Well, you're not going to. Don't you see, Mother has put the bed clothes here for you? She doesn't want Dad to have to take you

61

home, so she's decided you're to stay here. Oh, 'Bel!" She gave 'Bel an extra squeeze.

But 'Bel did not respond. She stood passive in the middle of the room, the bathrobe hanging loosely around her. Andrea said, "I'll go and get the cookies."

When she got downstairs, her father was still checking the doors and windows as he did every night before going to bed. Her mother was still in the kitchen.

Her mother said, "Isabel is upset about something."

"She's scared of the storm." Andrea spoke glibly, the first thing that came into her head. She did not think it was true. If 'Bel was afraid of thunder and lightning, she would never admit it. That sort of fear would never unnerve her. No, there was something else the matter and some deep instinct told Andrea that it was something that she and 'Bel must keep to themselves.

Her mother said, "Well, I suppose it can be terrifying to be out alone at night in a violent storm like this." A sudden last bolt of lightning lit the kitchen window. "But a girl like that shouldn't be out alone at this time of night."

Andrea, reaching into the refrigerator for milk, did not answer. She put the glasses and the plate of cookies on a tray and said goodnight again to her parents.

"Don't wake Bob up," said her mother. "He was pretty tired."

Bob was not likely to wake for any reason, thought Andrea. Bob had a job for the summer with one of the few builders in town still in business. He left the house at six in the morning and came home in the evening too tired to do more than eat and go to bed. He was saving his money. His goal was a car of his own.

When she got back to the little room she found 'Bel sitting on the edge of the unmade bed. She was staring at the floor, now and then rubbing her hand over her face.

Andrea put the tray down and handed her a glass of milk. They ate and drank in silence and then Andrea said, "I guess we had better make the bed. My mother will come and check on you."

They had only just finished putting the cover on the bed when Mrs. Hollingsworth appeared in the doorway. She said she hoped Isabel would be comfortable. There was no reason to be afraid any more. The last of the thunder and lightning had gone off across the city and down the river and there was now only a steady rain. It was bringing cooler weather.

'Bel said meekly, "Goodnight."

Mrs. Hollingsworth said, "Andrea, it's time you went to bed. I expect Isabel needs to rest."

Andrea followed her out of the door, looking at 'Bel over her shoulder. 'Bel stood again in the middle of the room, the borrowed bathrobe reaching only part way down her long legs. Her eyes still had the half-fixed, half-preoccupied expression. It was obvious that she did not want to stay where she was, that she felt a powerful urge to follow Andrea. But enough of her sense of caution remained so that she held herself still.

Andrea sat on the edge of the bed in her own room and waited restlessly for the usual sounds of her parents going to bed. Her mother was a light sleeper. Any unusual noise could wake her. She called out softly to Andrea to put out her light. Andrea did so promptly, annoyed with herself that she had not remembered that her mother, returning from the bathroom, could see the streak of light under her door. If only her mother would drop off to sleep quickly.

Several times in the next couple of hours she tiptoed to her door and carefully opened it, with the idea that she could creep softly past her parents' door to the little room and 'Bel. But each time her courage failed and she shut herself back into her bedroom. The steady drumming of the rain on the hatch over the front door made it hard for her to hear sounds inside the house. She could not afford to have her mother find her with 'Bel. Ordinarily she could always count on 'Bel's quick wits to save a situation when they were taken by surprise. But she knew now that tonight 'Bel would not be able to respond. Some heavy weight lay on 'Bel's spirit.

The rain gradually grew less and the softer sound lulled her to sleep. She was not aware that she had fallen asleep until she was awakened by a gentle tug at the bedclothes.

"Andy." 'Bel's voice came into her consciousness naturally, insinuatingly. 'Bel's pajama-clad body slipped under the covers and lay against hers. Drowsily she roused enough to roll over so that there was room for her. They lay straight, touching at breast, stomach, hip, thigh, knee.

'Bel's voice said in her ear, "You were too scared to come and see me."

There was an overtone of reproach but underneath there was the echo of 'Bel's usual self-confidence. Awareness of the fact brought Andrea fully awake. "I fell asleep," she whispered. "I was waiting for Mother to go to asleep."

"You were too scared."

"Sh-h. She wakes up very easily."

'Bel's murmur dropped in pitch. "You mustn't tell her."

"Tell her what?"

"Why I had to come here tonight."

"What is it, 'Bel?" Andrea sat up and in the dark searched for 'Bel's face. Her finger touched lightly on 'Bel's eyelids, mouth. There was a faint tremble in her chin. "What has happened?"

"It's Mac. He tried to grab me. He almost caught me. He would have, if I hadn't been expecting it. He's been watching me, ever since my mother left."

'Bel's murmur ceased. Andrea sank down again in the bed and they lay clasped in each other's arms.

"What was he going to do?"

'Bel's breath tickled her ear. "He was going to force me. He was all big in front and he was trying to get his pants unbuttoned. He tried to catch hold of me with his other hand. He was between me and the door — I didn't hear him till he'd got into my room. I've been using the boys' room. I always lock myself in. But this time he fooled me. He was lying on the sofa in the livingroom when I came in. I thought he was asleep drunk. He must have been pretending so he could catch me."

"Well, what happened?"

"His pants finally fell down." 'Bel's murmur ceased again and a strong shudder went through her body.

Andrea thought involuntarily of the classical statues she had seen in museums and reproduced in histories of art. But 'Bel had told her that in live men the flesh was wrinkled and ugly and bluish and an erect penis was hard, a weapon, a tool of destruction. She answered 'Bel's shudder with one of her own.

Bel said, "He tripped over his pants. He was too drunk to get free of them fast enough to hold onto me. I got around him and ran out of the apartment. He was yelling and cursing. I could hear him all the way down the street." 'Bel stopped and Andrea felt the wetness of her tears. Then she said, "I didn't even notice the rain to begin with. It was thundering and the whole street was full of branches off those big elms. But I just ran as fast as I could. I just wanted to get away, so he couldn't follow me, wouldn't be able to find me. Than I saw a streetcar coming and I got on. I didn't have any money. But a colored woman sitting on one of the front seats gave me a car ticket. She told me I shouldn't be out alone at night like that. I saw she was looking at my religious medal. She said I didn't look like the kind of girl to be out in the streets late like that. When she got off she was still lecturing me about going straight home. I tried to tell her that if I knew her name and where she lived, I'd come and pay her back. But she just got off the car shaking her head. I didn't even think where I was going, till I got off the streetcar at your street. There was nobody left on the car by then and the conductor was turning the sign for the trip back downtown."

Andrea wiped the tears from 'Bel's cheeks with her fingers. "Oh, 'Bel, I'm so glad you came here!"

"Yes, but what are you going to tell your mother? What am I to say?"

"You've already told her you had to be out later than usual."

"But she is going to want to know the details."

If she does, thought Andrea, we'll just have to rely on 'Bel's inventiveness. She asked aloud, " 'Bel, has he tried to get you before?"

"No."

"You said you always locked the door."

"That's because I didn't trust him. It's been building up, ever since my mother left for North Carolina. He's been watching me. At first he had a few odd jobs and he wasn't home when I got there. But lately he has just been loafing, shooting pool down at the corner poolroom and I guess he's won some money to buy bootleg liquor with. Anyway, he's been lying there on the sofa reading magazines when I came in and he looks at me around the edges." 'Bel was quiet for a few moments. "Once, when I was little, he tried to fool with me, tried to get me to sit in his lap, so that he could get under my dress and stick his finger in me. But I yelled and mamma heard me. She was furious and she said she'd kill him if he tried anything like that again. I think she scared him, because at that time he wasn't used to her temper."

Once again Andrea felt the wetness of 'Bel's tears. This time she did not ask any more questions. They sank closer together in the bed and as drowsiness overcame her, Andrea thought, we're going to have to get up before Mother wakes.

Just as the daylight began to make the room vaguely visible she woke to the sound of the mockingbird outside the window. The delicious warmth of 'Bel's body against her own roused her and she raised herself on her elbow.

" 'Bel, 'Bel."

'Bel jumped awake and they sat for a moment staring at each other.

"It's six o'clock, 'Bel. Mother always gets up at six thirty."

'Bel was already out of bed and Andrea sprang out after her. They stood, eyeing each other, a few inches apart. Then simultaneously they moved to kiss, grasping each other with a violent, frantic reach.

'Bel picked up the bathrobe and threw it around her shoulders. She opened the door carefully and peered into the dim hallway. She turned her head to breathe, scarcely audibly, into Andrea's ear, "If she comes out, I'll say I've been to the bathroom."

But Andrea, watching through a crack in the door, ready to shut it at any sound from her parents' room, saw her white-robed figure edge silently past the stairhead to the door of the small back room, saw the door open enough to let her body pass through and close again.

She remembered, sitting on the edge of the bed, that 'Bel's clothes were down in the basement, hanging near the water heater to dry. A sudden sound in the hall made her jump and then she realized that her brother's alarm clock had gone off and that within a few minutes he would be in the bathroom. In his half-awake state he was always noisy. Within a few more minutes he would be clumping down the stairs and her mother, invariably roused by the sound of his movements, would already be down there getting his breakfast. I'd better wait, thought Andrea, till he's gone.

She waited till she heard the sound of the front door closing. When she reached the kitchen her mother was putting the milk

65

back in the refrigerator. She looked around.

"Why, Andrea, you are early."

"I am going to get 'Bel's clothes."

"Oh, yes. Well, I expect she is going to have to iron them. The ironing board and the iron are in there in the room she slept in."

The first sunlight was coming into the kitchen as Andrea carried the bundle of clothes upstairs. The storm, as such storms in August often did, had brought the temperature down abruptly. 'Bel was going to be chilly in this thin cotton dress.

'Bel took the bundle from her as she entered the room. Andrea set up the ironing board and plugged in the iron. They did not speak until she saw 'Bel looking with dismay at her ruined shoes.

"Never mind, 'Bel. I'll get you a pair of mine. I'm sure you can wear them."

'Bel nodded.

When Andrea returned carrying the shoes, she found 'Bel ironing the dress. They were silent again until Andrea asked, "What are you going to do, 'Bel?"

"I've got to go back there and get my clothes and my books. I wouldn't go back if I didn't have to."

"Maybe he won't be there."

"I'm not going in if he is."

"Where are you going to move to?"

"There is only one place I can go to — Annunciation. I'll have to tell Reverend Mother. Maybe she can find me somewhere to stay."

" 'Bel, can I come with you? I can help you carry things."

'Bel was silent as she took the dress off the ironing board and held it up to see how it looked. Then she said, "I'm going to need help, Andy. But how about your mother? What are you going to tell her?"

Andrea did not answer at once. She had been wondering to herself what she would tell her mother. She would have to think of some excuse to leave the house with 'Bel. They would not be playing tennis. The clay courts would be soaked. Then she remembered. This was Wednesday and Wednesday morning was when her mother went to the Red Cross and did volunteer work. She would leave soon after her husband went to his office. They would have all morning to themselves.

* * *

Following 'Bel into the vestibule of the walk-up, Andrea saw that the building had a rundown look. The tile floor had not been washed recently. The wall along the stairs had a dark smear, left by people's hands steadying themselves as they went up or down. There were four floors. On each was a wide, bare landing onto which four doors opened. She followed 'Bel up to the top. They stood for a while without speaking in the middle of the landing.

66

"You don't have a key," said Andrea.

"He doesn't lock the door because he's lost his key."

"Then how will you know whether he is in there?"

"He's usually down at the corner by now, having a drink — as soon as the place is open." 'Bel stepped over to one of the doors at the back of the landing. She turned around. "You'd better go back to the stairs. If he's in there, I'll have to get out in a hurry."

Reluctantly Andrea went back to the head of the stairs. Her heart was beating fast with the sense of dread that 'Bel's manner had conjured up in her. She watched intently as 'Bel tried the door, opened it and stood for a moment listening and peering into the apartment. She went inside, disappearing from Andrea's sight. Andrea stood staring at the door. There was no sound on the landing except the desultory crying of a sleepy baby in one of the other apartments. Presently 'Bel appeared again in the doorway and beckoned to her.

"He isn't here. Let's hurry."

Andrea, repelled by the frowsty smell of the closed-up apartment, followed gingerly behind her. What, she wondered, would they do if the man came back and found them there? Well, anyway, there were two of them. He could hardly attack two of them at the same time.

'Bel was working furiously, pulling clothes off hangers in a closet and folding them hastily into an old suitcase. The apartment had three square rooms, sparsely furnished with shabby chairs and scuffed tables and disheveled beds. There was an unkempt look to everything, from the littered livingroom to the kitchen cluttered with dirty pots and dishes and empty bottles. Even the screened porch off the livingroom was cluttered with discarded clothes, remnants of food and more bottles.

'Bel had reached the point of picking up the few books that stood on top of a cabinet in one of the bedrooms. Andrea knew she did not have many clothes, Everything she owned was now in the suitcase but the books would not fit in.

"Let's tie some string around them," said Andrea. "I can carry them."

'Bel found a length of laundry line on the porch and they tied the books into a bundle. 'Bel snatched up the suitcase. She was in a fever to leave.

"Aren't you going to leave a message for your mother?"

'Bel's voice was full of scorn, "And tell *him* what I'm doing?"

She led the way out of the apartment. As they came out on the landing they almost collided with a woman coming out of one of the other apartments. She gave them a cool examination, her eyes lingering on the suitcase and the books. Andrea, embarrassed by the bold stare, saw that she was young, heavily made up and smoking a cigarette.

"Going on a trip?" she inquired.

67

'Bel nodded abruptly and started for the stairs.

The woman said, "I haven't seen your mother around."

"She's in North Carolina," 'Bel answered shortly.

"Just visiting?"

"Yes."

"She didn't tell me she was going away."

"You weren't here."

"That's right. I just got back from Atlantic City. Are you going to join her?"

But 'Bel was already going down the stairs as fast as the weight of the suitcase would allow and she pretended not to hear. Andrea said, "Excuse me," and hurried on down after her. They did not stop until they had left the building and had gone down the street to the corner, where, panting, 'Bel put down the suitcase. She was furiously angry.

"Damn her! She's aways poking her nose in. She knows all about mamma and Mac fighting. They make enough noise. And mamma confides in her when she's feeling sorry for herself. Oh, I wish mamma would have some sort of self-respect! She tells everybody everything when she feels like talking. I hate it! I hate it!"

'Bel was half sobbing with rage. Andrea, shifting the bundle of books, said earnestly, "Oh, 'Bel, don't get so upset! Let's go on and get the streetcar." She was still haunted by the feeling that Mac would appear in pursuit of them.

They reached the big front door of the Convent. Andrea, who had walked through it only once before, with her mother on the afternoon of the tea-party, hung back nervously as 'Bel rang the bell. She could not see who opened the door, but 'Bel picked up the suitcase and walked in. Andrea stood hesitating, until the old man who acted as doorkeeper looked out at her and motioned her in.

The big vestibule was cool and quiet. One of the Sisters stood talking to 'Bel. She was a tall slim woman with a calm white face.

"You want to see Reverend Mother? Why, I shall have to see if that can be arranged."

"Oh, yes, I know. I'll wait as long as necessary. Is there somewhere I can put these things?"

The nun gazed at the suitcase and then at the books in Andrea's arms. There was a long moment of silence as she seemed to take in the situation and weigh the circumstances. Then she turned her eyes towards the old man who still stood by the door. "James, no doubt, can keep them for you for a while. James."

The old man came forward to take the suitcase, reaching with his other hand for the books. "They'll be in my porter's room, miss," he said to 'Bel, and walked across the vestibule to a small door under the stairs.

"Wait in the parlor, Isabel," the nun said, glancing at Andrea, "with your friend."

They sat side by side on a hard sofa in the austere parlor, dim

68

from the heavy curtains at the tall windows. The dead silence pressed on Andrea's eardrums. Opposite was a religious statue, white against the dark background. Its immobility seemed to emphasize the suspension of life. There is not even a clock ticking, thought Andrea. She glanced at 'Bel. 'Bel's profile told her that 'Bel's mind was absorbed in the prospect of the interview with Reverend Mother.

She could only guess that they had been sitting there for at least half an hour when another nun, a shorter, stouter woman, appeared in the wide doorway and beckoned to 'Bel, who sprang up to follow her. Andrea sat on alone. The silence, the motionless air, grew more and more oppressive. It seemed to her an age before 'Bel came back and said,

"I'm going to stay here, Andy. I'll walk to the streetcar with you."

They had walked as far as P Street before either of them said anything. Then 'Bel stopped, her hands thrust in the pockets of the jacket she had put on at the apartment, her toe thoughtfully scuffing at the big tree roots that thrust up in the edge of the brick paving.

Andrea asked, "What did you tell her?"

"I told her that my mother had to go and see her sister in North Carolina and I was getting afraid to stay in the apartment alone." 'Bel gave her a fierce look. "That's true! She did leave me alone there with Mac!"

"Did — did she ask you anything else? You didn't tell her what he did?"

"No, I didn't mention him."

Andrea stared at her. "But *why*, 'Bel? Why didn't you tell her?"

'Bel was gnawing her lower lip. "Because I'm a minor. If I said Mac was there, she'd be afraid to let me stay. He could say she was interfering with his parental authority. He *is* my stepfather. He could threaten her with the police."

"Oh, But won't he know you're here?"

"No. I suppose he could guess. But he's just as likely to think I was with Aunt Gertrude. That's one reason I didn't go to her. He'd follow me there and try to get money out of her by threatening her. I've got to let her know right away whère I am, so she won't be upset if he shows up and says I've disappeared."

"But what if he finds out you're not with her? Won't he guess you're here?"

'Bel brooded for a while. "Well, maybe he won't do anything. Maybe he'll just be glad I cleared out."

"Well, then, you had some other reason for coming here instead."

"I guess so," 'Bel admitted. After a moment she added, "I hate to let her know what he did. I hate for her to know that mother would go away and leave me with him. Oh, I suppose she has a pretty low opinion of my mother anyway, but I can't admit to her that I realize how flighty she is."

Andrea put her hand on 'Bel's arm, half expecting it to be violently shrugged off. But 'Bel's touchiness had sunk down. They were both silent for a while. Then 'Bel said, "I think Reverend Mother knows there is something else I haven't told her. She probably can guess what it is."

"How long are you going to be here, 'Bel? What are you going to do?"

"Why, I guess I'll be here till mamma comes back. I'm going to help Sister Mary Ignatius with the office work, to pay for my board and lodging. The woman who works here regularly is on vacation for a couple of weeks."

"Then we won't be able to meet every day."

"I guess not. I can't help it, Andy. I'll call you as often as I can."

Andrea thought at once of her own mother, who would notice these frequent phone calls. But she dismissed the thought. She would have to explain them as well as she could.

When her mother got back, 'Bel moved back to the apartment. On the telephone, when Andrea questioned her, 'Bel was laconic. Yes, she had told her mother why she had gone to stay at the Convent. No, her mother hadn't said anything to Mac. 'Bel knew this, because if her mother had confronted him, there would have been a big fight.

"But, 'Bel, isn't she angry about it? Isn't she going to do anything?"

"Oh, she's mad about it all right. I guess she's just keeping it for some time when she can use it against him. I'm pretty sure that Mac knows she knows about it."

There was a dark cloud in the apartment now all the time, 'Bel said. She knew trouble was brewing. She lay awake sometimes at night, waiting for an explosion.

Hanging up the phone, Andrea saw her mother standing in the hallway.

"Andrea, is there something the matter with Isabel?"

"Why, no, I don't think so."

"She seems to call you very frequently."

Andrea had wondered when her mother would speak of it. "That's because we don't see each other so much now. 'Bel's terribly busy."

"Well, if she is that busy, I don't see how she can have the time to call so often."

When she told 'Bel this, 'Bel nodded. "I've been trying to call you when Sister Mary Ignatius has been busy with something else. But lately she has been watching. She hasn't said anything."

They were standing in the lobby of the Palace Theater on F Street where they had agreed to meet. Andrea's heart contracted as she looked at 'Bel. 'Bel's clothes looked shabbier than ever. The

70

hollowness under her collarbones was more pronounced. Her face was pale and there was a tired sag to her body. In fact, the day before, when 'Bel had come to the house, Andrea's mother had commented on her appearance.

"Isn't Isabel feeling well, Andrea? She is thinner and she looks as if she is coming down with some illness. Do you know whether there is a tendency to tuberculosis in her family?"

"Oh, no, Mother! It's just that she is working so hard."

"You said she is doing office work for the nuns. I should think they'd be careful not to work a girl of that age too hard. But perhaps they don't notice. I suppose they live pretty ascetic lives themselves. Well, maybe it is just the stage she's going through. I wish *you* would put on a little more weight, Andrea. I think you stay up too late at night, reading."

* * *

I can't tell Andy. It's one of the things I can't tell her.

'Bel, sorting index cards for Sister Mary Ignatius' file in the quiet office, kept her eyes on her work and her face expressionless. The small windows high in the wall let in the light of the sky but you could see nothing of the street, the row of narrow brick houses across the way, the big trees whose leaves were rusty from the summer heat and dust.

She was used to Sister Mary Ignatius' oblique method of conveying advice and admonition. You were never left in any doubt in the end about what she meant but you had to listen closely to figure out what it was from what she was saying. She knows about Andy. She knows it is Andy I talk to on the phone. Reverend Mother has said I'm to go on working here even though Mrs. Shannon is back from vacation. So Sister has to put up with me. I don't suppose she minds having all these little niggling jobs done. But somebody has told her about Andy. I guess it could be mademoiselle.

So this is what she means: "You oughtn't to make friends with girls who aren't Catholics. It doesn't matter that your friend is a nice girl — so far as you can tell. But Protestants aren't the same as good Catholics, who go to confession. Why, it used to be a sin to cherish a friendship with a Protestant. Of course, if she becomes a Catholic because of your persuasion, that would be wonderful, but until she does you are putting your own soul in jeopardy. Does your mother know about your friend? I should think she would warn you. You must keep yourself from any taint of corruption, especially when it comes to people and books and art that have an attractive guise but are unwholesome."

'Bel smiled a little secret smile. Sister Mary Cecilia doesn't think about putting my soul in jeopardy when she is teaching me to play Mendelsohn or Beethoven on the piano. Sister Mary Joseph, when she is talking about the Elizabethan poets, likes to point out that there is a case to be made for saying that Shakespeare was a

71

secret Catholic in spite of the Tudors, but she doesn't say that is why we have to think he is the greatest poet in the English language.

And what would Sister Mary Ignatius think if she knew about my mother and Mac? She only knows about Aunt Gertrude and what a devout woman she is. She thinks, I suppose, because Aunt Gertrude is so devout and I'm her niece, the rest of my family are Catholics — good Catholics, her kind of Catholics.

And I don't know what I am. Sometimes I wish I could believe like that, accept things like that, not question. It would be so much easier. I'd have answers for everything — just like Sister Mary Ignatius. But I can't. I wish I could really talk to Reverend Mother. That isn't possible, because she would find out all sorts of things, things she guesses about now but doesn't really know. I would give myself away to her right off. She would know about Andy and me. Nobody is going to make me believe it is wicked for me to love Andy. It just can't be. It's the only thing that has ever happened to me that isn't mixed up with dirt and guilt — what Andy and I feel. I can tell Reverend Mother that I've lost my faith, that I am not honest when I go to confession, I don't tell Father everything, that I try not to go to mass because I don't believe any more in the body and blood of Christ. She would be concerned, she would be severe with me. She would tell me to read the right things and pray to have all these doubts removed from my mind. She would be convinced that this was all just something I will outgrow, something that has resulted from my family mess.

But she would not be understanding about Andy and me. She would tell me that I had to put temptation out of my way, that this is a sort of carnal love that is a temptation of the devil, that I must not see or talk to Andy again. She probably even would tell Father Greeley about it and he would give me a real lecture and threaten me with damnation, tell me that what I am seeking is nothing but the gratification of bodily lust, worse than with a man because it can not lead to children and therefore that God condemns it as unnatural. How can I be damned if I don't believe in God?

But I don't know if that is true. I can say that I don't believe in God and I am convinced that I don't believe in the God I've chiefly been taught about. But I don't *feel* that the world is just what I see and hear and can touch. There's something, there must be something to explain all this. It didn't just happen. *I* didn't just happen. And I can't believe in a God who doesn't know me, me as me. That means a God who would understand about Andy and me — a God that made this possible, something that is pure and good.

Oh, Andy!

* * *

At the end of August Andrea's mother told her that they were going to the Blue Ridge mountains for two weeks. Money was

72

short, her mother said, but her father needed a break from his work as a scientist with the Department of Agriculture. He did a great deal of laboratory work and he was getting stale. He would benefit from the serene freshness of the mountains. Her brother Bob could take care of himself. His summertime job was almost at an end and he would be getting ready to go back to college.

There was no way, Andrea knew, in which she could arrange to stay at home. The thought would never cross her mother's mind that she would not go with them. She longed to say to her mother, Couldn't we take 'Bel with us? But that was impossible. She could easily imagine the suddenly unwelcoming expression that would appear on her mother's face. Her mother always had reservations about bringing strangers into their family group, even though the stranger might be someone they had known and liked for years. For her mother, there was an invisible but impenetrable wall between her family and the world outside.

So she and 'Bel would have to rely on letters.

Write to me at the Convent, 'Bel said. She did not say, but Andrea guessed, that 'Bel's mother opened her mail, if anything aroused her curiosity. 'Bel also did not say but Andrea guessed, that she almost never received personal letters. There was no one to write to her except Aunt Gertrude, who rarely went anywhere, and sometimes girls she knew sent her postcards when they went on vacation. So 'Bel's mother would instantly notice Andrea's letters.

- - - -

"Dear 'Bel: We have a fireplace. Incidentally, mail should be addressed to me at General Delivery at this post office. We're staying at a farmhouse where they take a few boarders during the summer. We have to go down to the village to get mail. We have just had lunch and I'm sitting on the porch, smelling woodsmoke, listening to the wind howling through the trees and practically enveloped in the fog which sifts in and out. Occasionally, it gets quite light and a glimpse of the valley is discernible. This farm cabin is 'way up on the mountainside. They have an apple orchard and it is wood from old apple trees that I smell burning in the fireplace. As a matter of fact, I have mostly been cold. I have a hot water bottle to put in bed with me tonight, I'm still not properly 'checked in' so am not uncomfortable, although I wish I had a warm abutment in the vicinity should the need arise to warm my tummy.

"You would love seeing the mountains. Great dark clouds trailing white mists that cover the tops. It seems so strange for you not to be here with me. It is amazingly pleasant to know, as I usually do, what you are doing and where you are. I say amazingly because when this is so, I accept it without thought so that when I am away now I realize that this is so.

"Later — I went down to the village to get a paper and found your letter. If I get up early, before my parents do, I can go down

73

there and look for mail. Mother always expects to hear from Deedee and Bob, so she wants to know if there are letters for her. There haven't been so far. I don't suppose Bob would even think of writing, really, and Deedee will probably write once just when we're about to go home. So Mother will notice especially if I get a letter from you. Both times I have been able to pick up your letters and read them on the way back to the cabin. Fortunately there've been some things forwarded to Dad from his office, so when she asks if there is any mail, I say Yes and give her those. Oh, 'Bel, if we just could be together without having to hide all the time! I love you very very much."

- - -

"Dear Andy: Well, what do you suppose? It's mademoiselle who brings me your letters. It seems that she is the one nowadays who goes and fetches the mail from the box beside the street door. I guess that is because she is expecting letters for herself. I don't think her plans for the coming school year are definite yet and she is anxious. She has noticed that I get a letter with the Luray, Virginia postmark almost every other day and she has guessed they are from you. Anyway, this morning she brought me your latest and when she handed it to me she said something about how faithful my "petite amie" was. That annoyed me but what is worse is that Sister Mary Ignatius was watching. She doesn't understand French but she could tell from the way mademoiselle acted that there was something funny, especially since mademoiselle looked at her and smiled. I am sure that when I am not present Sister Mary Ignatius is going to ask her questions. And then I am going to get some more disguised lectures from Sister about being careful whom I make friends with.

"Wouldn't it be wonderful, Andy, if we could have a mountain cabin of our own and sit in front of the fire, all wrapped up from the world in a dense fog, where nobody could find us? I think about you all day and when I'm in bed at night. You are my very dear loved sweet darling."

- - - -

"Dear 'Bel: I hope you haven't had any trouble getting my last letter. Mademoiselle wouldn't keep you from getting it, would she? Anyway, this is the last note I'm sending you, because we are going to leave tomorrow. I'll take a chance and call you on the phone when we get home. Oh, 'Bel, your letter was a very 'you' one and it made me feel you right here with me. Goodnight, dear love."

- - - -

"Dear Andy: No, I don't think even mademoiselle would go so far as opening my letters. I've had all of yours. But when you get back to Washington it would be better if we could arrange to meet somewhere. Let me know where when you call me. My little darling, I can't wait."

* * *

They walked together slowly up the steep hill of Wisconsin Avenue in the close warmth of the September afternoon.

"I'm a week late for school," said Andrea. "The principal told my mother I could make it up."

'Bel nodded, shifting her armful of books. "Mademoiselle leaves tomorrow. She has a job teaching French in a girls' school in Connecticut. She'll be able to spend all her weekends in New York. She is so happy about it she got really generous and gave me her old Larousse dictionary. You know, I'm going to miss her. She kept things from getting too boring."

"I'm glad she is going. She won't be spying on us any more."

"Oh, she was a menace all right. Andy, are you going to be riding the same streetcar after school as you used to?"

"I guess so. Anyway, I'll stay and read in the library if I get out earlier. That way I'll catch the same streetcar."

They walked along in silence. It was, they were both aware, a speaking silence. Their separation of two weeks had had an effect they both recognized: it had sharpened the flow of thought and feeling between them, so that words were even less important than they had been.

After a while Andrea said, "Can I go with you all the way to the Convent?"

"I guess so. I'm supposed to help Sister Mary Joseph. She's our English teacher but she also is librarian. We've got new books to catalog. I'll be there till dinnertime."

They reached the door of the Convent. The quiet street was empty and they lingered together on the steps. But presently the door opened and mademoiselle came out, accompanied by one of the Sisters. The two women stopped on the threshold and mademoiselle exclaimed, "Ah, ma petite! We see so little of you these days and I am leaving tomorrow."

As she spoke she examined Andrea, her bright dark eyes traveling over her from head to foot. Andrea saw her glance then, chattering all the while, toward the Sister who stood beside her and saw the Sister smile faintly. It was the same tall, slender one, she remembered, who had greeted 'Bel when 'Bel had come to the Convent to take refuge.

'Bel stood stolidly holding her books in both hands, making attempts to respond in French to mademoiselle's flood of words. At last the Frenchwoman broke off, said an au 'voir to them all with a brilliant smile and ran down the steps.

The nun said pleasantly, "Isabel, I am ready to begin on the new books."

As she spoke she smiled at Andrea. She is not old, thought Andrea, noticing the nun's fresh, smooth skin. She was also conscious of the eyes that gazed down at her, sharp, shrewd, at a variance with the graciousness of the smile.

'Bel, responding to the unspoken demand in the nun's manner, said sedately, "Sister Mary Joseph, this is Andrea."

"How do you do, Andrea? I believe I saw you here at our reception tea this summer. Didn't you come with your mother?" Andrea, wilting under the scrutiny of the keen eyes, murmured, "Yes, ma'am." The scrutiny spoke of more than this moment's encounter. She was remembered, identified, classified as 'Bel's disapproved friend. She was relieved when Sister Mary Joseph glanced briefly at 'Bel and said, "Isabel, I'll be in the library in a few minutes. You might get the books out on the table."

'Bel accepted the dismissal and walked past her into the vestibule without a glance at Andrea. Andrea's gaze stayed fixed on her retreating back until Sister Mary Joseph said, again with that trace of unyielding demand, "Where do you go to school, Andrea?" She continued to question her until 'Bel had disappeared in the darkness of the Convent halls.

Andrea, with an enormous effort of will, answered her without stammering. Yes, she went to the public high school. No, her parents were not Catholics. Yes, 'Bel was the only Catholic girl she knew. Finally overcome by the desire to escape from this relentless interrogation, Andrea stumbled through a leave-taking. She was not helped by the nun's coolly pleasant manner. At the foot of the steps she paused and looked up. Sister Mary Joseph stood motionless, just where she had stopped when she emerged with mademoiselle. Andrea was acutely conscious of the black-robed figure, tall, erect, unbending, and the youthful, adamant face framed by the white coif and black veil. She seemed to stand like a wall, barring her from any further sight of 'Bel. A cold feeling gathered around her heart. It did not dispel as she turned away. She looked back again. The nun's figure had vanished. There was only the closed door of the Convent.

II

1933

Through the winter Andrea's life revolved around the opportunities that she and 'Bel had to be together. Often, when 'Bel had the time, Andrea took her home with her, for an hour or two of listening to music. Her mother always greeted 'Bel affectionately, but Andrea was aware of the reservation that underlay this apparent acceptance. When they were alone, her mother would say that she wished Andrea had more friends, other girls whom she could invite to the house. Andrea would counter with the statement that she did not know anyone else who liked the kind of music she liked. The other girls, she said, just talked about boys. 'Bel had all sorts of things to talk about. When she said this, her mother replied merely with a long speculative look.

Andrea was uncertain about 'Bel herself. Inwardly she had a vision of losing 'Bel, of 'Bel being swallowed up in the mysterious, featureless world of the Convent. 'Bel was back living in the apartment with her mother, but she spent a minimum of time there. Otherwise her days and her energies were occupied with the activities of the Convent. Andrea had the feeling that she was on the periphery of 'Bel's life. 'Bel was dear, loving when they were together. But that was such a small fraction of the hours of the day and night.

The vision arose in her mind, especially in the dark hours of the night, of Sister Mary Joseph's straight, stiff black figure barring the door against her with invisible powers. She never said anything about that to 'Bel, because it seemed so silly. Sister Mary Joseph, she knew from what 'Bel told her, was one of the more agreeable of the nuns, one of those most willing to sympathize with 'Bel and help her. But beneath that graciousness dwelt a steely something, far more threatening than a stone wall. Andrea wondered what was really taking place in 'Bel, about the Convent and the nuns and the faith she had been taught. She sensed an ambivalence in 'Bel, never more strongly than when she went with her to a church and waited while 'Bel said confession or sat with her through evening benediction. At such times 'Bel seemed very remote and she wondered what lay in that remoteness. Was 'Bel retreating from their own little world into the discipline of her

77

religion? Or was she simply struggling with the conflicts within herself — the several conflicts in which she was caught, between her mother and stepfather, between her family's life and that of the Convent, between her mother and Aunt Gertrude, between her instinct to be honorable and independent and her loyalty to her mother in spite of everything?

As the winter went on Andrea was aware that within herself a decided change had taken place. A year ago she had been a child, ignorant, not knowing what the people in the world around her really thought and did. She realized now that someone could be governed by the strength of an indoctrinated idea, how difficult it was for someone to examine such an idea and discover whether it held validity for herself, whether the idea itself was somehow different from the guise in which it had been presented to her. Watching 'Bel struggle, she felt the weight of 'Bel's church. She acknowledged to herself its power and attraction, the feelings it aroused, of yearning for the unassailable assurance it promised, even to herself, who had been brought up to distrust unquestioning obedience.

She also realized that whatever the price required to keep 'Bel, she would pay it. She could not give 'Bel up. If she could have only half of 'Bel, then she must settle for that, take what was left over after 'Bel had finally made up her mind to abide by her upbringing. She watched 'Bel covertly for signs of how things were going. But there was really no clue in 'Bel's moods.

* * *

The cold March wind whipped at them as they left Washington Circle, where they had met this Saturday morning, to walk up New Hampshire Avenue to 'Bel's apartment house.

"I couldn't tell you all the details on the phone. My mother has followed him to Baltimore."

Several weeks ago 'Bel's stepfather had gone to Baltimore. He said he had a better chance to get a job there. 'Bel said that he had quarreled with the man who ran the poolroom and he had borrowed money from all his acquaintances. There was nobody left who would give him any more. He was looking for greener fields. Her mother was angry. She suspected him of looking for more than a job — for women. He had sent her a little money, just to pacify her. But it was the wrong thing for him to have done. For now her mother had thrown up her own job in the five and ten and had followed him to Baltimore with the two kids.

'Bel smiled wrily as she spoke. "Of course, as soon as she gets there, he'll start drinking again, lose his job and she'll have to find one to keep them all, as usual."

"Are you going to stay there in the apartment by yourself, 'Bel?"

"No, I can't stay there. The rent hasn't been paid for two

months, but the landlord can't evict us till the first."

"Then what are you going to do?"

'Bel stopped as they reached the curb and pointed to the large brick house that occupied the point of ground where two streets converged on the Circle. "I'm going to move there. Mrs. Manley owns it. She is a friend of Aunt Gertrude. She's a widow. She takes in boarders, so that she can go on living in her own house. She will let me have a room there without rent, if I wait on the table and help her in the kitchen."

Andrea's first feeling was of dismay, that 'Bel would work as a servant. But then her heart leapt.

"I'm so glad."

"Glad?" 'Bel stopped walking and looked at her in surprise. Then the surprise faded. "What are you glad about?"

"That you are not going to Baltimore — or back to the Convent to live."

"You know I would not go to Baltimore." 'Bel looked into her eyes and saw what the fear had been. She suddenly smiled. "Did you think I was going to desert you, Andy?"

"I didn't know — you seemed to be having such a hard time —"

'Bel started walking again and Andrea fell into step. "I know. I've been doing a lot of thinking. But there is one thing I can't believe — that I have to give you up. Nobody, Andy, can tell me what to believe. That is not right. I must reach my own decision. I've never had any real doubt." She heard Andrea's sigh and glanced sideways at her. "Did you really worry about that, Andy? Well, I suppose you would. I've been pretty wrapped up in myself."

Andrea nodded. They walked on in silence and then Andrea asked, "Do you know Mrs. Manley?"

"I don't *know* her. I've met her at Aunt Gertrude's. Something tells me she is going to make sure she gets her money's worth out of me."

"Oh, 'Bel!"

"I might as well face it. Nobody is going to make an arrangement like this with a girl like me, who isn't looking for a bargain. Otherwise she would just rent the room she is letting me have and hire somebody to do the work. Andy, I don't care what kind of work I do, if it's decent. I don't think it matters what you do for a living. But I want to be properly paid."

They had reached the steps of the apartment house. They walked in and up the stairs in silence. Andrea saw that the landings and stairway were even more unkempt than they had been when she had come with 'Bel to get her things six months before. This time the apartment door was locked and 'Bel opened it with a key. Inside the rooms had a desolate appearance, though most of the furniture Andrea remembered was still in place. But the battered overstuffed chair with the dirty upholstery, the scuffed dining-room chairs and table, the stripped beds with sagging mattres-

79

ses, the torn carpeting — everything had a forlorn, abandoned look. The windows were filmed with grime. The dust on the floor was thick enough to show the paths where feet most often passed.

'Bel divined what was in Andrea's mind. "The furniture belongs to the landlord. And I gave up trying to keep the place clean a long time ago. My mother just took the pots and pans and dishes and the bedclothes. She did leave a couple of sheets and a pillowcase and a blanket."

She led Andrea to the small room off the screened porch where she had slept with the two boys. The bed was made and 'Bel's books were stacked on the floor. The two girls stood in the middle of the room for a moment, til 'Bel suddenly threw her arms around Andrea and Andrea, in instant response, clasped her in her own.

"Andy."

" 'Bel."

Andrea, conscious of 'Bel's warm breath on her neck, buried her face in 'Bel's shoulder. For a long moment they were without words, breathing in each other's warmth, each other's special aroma, each other's essential self. They sat down together on the bed.

"I didn't have time to tell you, 'Bel. My mother has gone to Cincinnati. You know, I did tell you that Deedee is going to have another baby. Well, it is due any minute and Mother has gone to be with her. She left on this morning's train."

Andrea saw 'Bel's eyes light up. "Andy! Could you stay here with me? I can stay here in the apartment until Thursday. Mrs. Manley doesn't expect me until then. Oh, come on, Andy! We'd be all by ourselves!"

The wild sense of sudden freedom flowed to her from 'Bel. Andrea found it hard to resist.

"Dad would be upset. He'd know that Mother wouldn't approve of me not being home at night. She is going to call him by long distance tonight."

'Bel's face turned sullen. "You never will take a chance for me, will you? It's always what your mother wants."

" 'Bel, that's not fair. I can't stay with you. She would be bound to find out that we were here alone. If I did that, she'd say I couldn't have you for a friend. She'd say you were too irresponsible."

"And you'd go right along with that, wouldn't you? You've just got to be mamma's good little girl. If anybody makes any concessions, it always has to be me."

" 'Bel, you can do pretty much what you please. Your mother doesn't care. Anyway, you say you don't have to do what she wants. But that's not true for me. I've got to do what my mother says. And Dad would tell her if I disobeyed her. 'Bel, don't be like this."

'Bel had got up and walked out on the porch, with her back turned. She did not answer. Andrea could see her hands in fists thrust into the pockets of her short jacket, could sense the tension in her thin body. 'Bel was like a tautly tuned string of a musical instrument, ready to snap at too great a strain. She was like a fire that smouldered out of sight, ready to blaze up at a fitful gust of wind. If she could only guess ahead of time what word or phrase of her own would precipitate these sudden outbursts of anger and resentment. 'Bel surely knew as well as she did that they could not stay together there in the apartment. It was the enormous yearning for freedom, the desire for each other that dwelt always within them — it was this that broke forth now at the vision of what might be, something seen in fantasy, like a mirage on a desert.

Andrea got up and followed 'Bel out onto the porch. " 'Bel, don't let's quarrel. We mustn't quarrel when we're by ourselves this way."

'Bel did not answer. Andrea put her arm though 'Bel's. "Come on. Don't be cross at me."

Grudgingly 'Bel responded to her pull and let herself be drawn back into the room. They sat down again on the bed. Andrea kissed her softly on the cheek. 'Bel collapsed against her and Andrea felt the wetness of tears as 'Bel's face was pressed into her neck.

"I'm sorry, Andy. It's just — it's just —" She gave up the struggle to speak.

"Yes, I know. It would be lovely. There's bound to come a day when we can do what we want to."

'Bel sat up straight and wiped her eyes. "This damn business of being a minor!"

Andrea stared at her.

"If I wasn't a minor, I could go and get any kind of job I could find. I'm sixteen now. In another year I'm going to start telling a lie about my age. Then I can really go out and get a job."

"But, 'Bel, you'll still be going to Annunciation!"

"No, I won't. I can finish this June. Reverend Mother said so. She thinks I want to get into college as early as possible. College! How can I go to college, where?"

"Won't Aunt Gertrude help you? And Reverend Mother? They both think so much of you, 'Bel."

After a moment 'Bel said thoughtfully, "Yes. They've both said they'd help, though I think Aunt Gertrude is beginning to feel poor. I think some of the investments she lives on aren't bringing in as big an income as they used to. Reverend Mother is talking about getting me a scholarship at some Catholic school. I'm too young to get a parttime job as an instructor. But I don't think any of that will work."

"Why not?"

"Because of my sainted mother and her brats. She'd never let me go away anywhere where she wouldn't be able to keep track of the money I earned. She can't wait till I get through at Annunciation. Then she can get me a work permit — you know, as a hardshp case, because what I earn is needed at home."

They were both silent after that. Presently 'Bel grew less tense and, turning her head, began to put little kisses on Andrea's ear. Before long they both lay back on the one pillow and held each other close. Within minutes their half-quarrel was forgotten, their mothers, Aunt Gertrude, the Convent, everything receded out of memory and they were alone together. Andrea's fingers trailed over the satin smoothness of 'Bel's young skin, feeling the deep pulse of the artery in her neck. 'Bel's more impatient hands reached under Andrea's clothes, felt gently over the firm softness of Andrea's stomach. Their joint desire mounted, each meeting the other's in successive waves of excitement, until they lay quiet again, breathing evenly in each other's arms.

They neither of them knew how much time had passed when they, reluctantly, became aware again of their surroundings. Andrea, lying on her back, aware of a still drowsy 'Bel beside her, said, with a sudden sense of having thought of something brilliant, " 'Bel, instead of staying in this awful place, why not come and stay with me — at least until you have to go to Mrs. Manley's."

'Bel did not answer at once. Andrea, having broached the idea, withdrew into a consideration of it. Her father, while her mother was gone, would not be home as much as usual. His inner life was chiefly fed by his scientific interests. Even in ordinary times he tended to spend long hours in the Departmental laboratory, pursuing the answers to problems of plant pathology as they applied to farmers and cattle growers. Loco weed was his current preoccupation, the dangerous plant that sometimes invaded cattle lands and dairy farms, giving the cattle the staggers and destroying their economic value. He rarely talked about his research at home. None of his children had ever shone any interest or understanding. But sometimes when his scientific friends came to the house, Andrea had listened with eager curiosity to the conversation.

Whenever her mother was away, and that was rarely the case, he seemed to feel lonely and at loose ends. So he preferred to go to his office earlier than usual in the morning and return later in the evening. Her mother always left explicit instructions about what Andrea should fix for his breakfast and dinner and the sandwiches and thermos he always took for his lunch. Outside of her presence when they ate together, Andrea doubted that he would notice what she was doing. Certainly he would notice if she was not there when he returned home in the evening, and he would raise questions if she said she was going out. Since she never did go out in the evening except with her parents, he would automatically, as her mother's deputy, veto the idea.

But there was no reason why he should complain if she had 'Bel come and stay with her. She turned the idea over in her mind carefully. They could make up the bed in the little spare room. Her father doubtless would think it natural that she wanted company, with her mother away. The only flaw was that he might mention it to her mother, might say to her mother, when she phoned again, that 'Bel was staying in the house. That was a chance they would have to take.

'Bel said, "What about your mother?"

"Don't you remember? I told you she has gone to stay with Deedee in Cincinnati."

"When is she coming back?"

"I don't know. Dad doesn't know. She wants to be there for the baby. 'Bel, we could be alone for days. Dad isn't home very much. My brother is at Duke."

"Your mother would be bound to find out when she gets back."

"Yes, but I can tell her then that you didn't want to be here alone in this apartment. She'd understand that. She'd let me know she didn't like the idea, but that's all there'd be to it."

"I don't want to leave my books and things here. If I go away, the landlord would take over right away. He's just waiting for the place to be vacant."

"All right. We can take your things to my house. We can carry them, can't we?"

"I guess so, if we make a couple of trips."

'Bel looked at her as she said this and Andrea, divining her question, answered, "I've got carfare. We can take your clothes now. I have a knapsack we can use to bring your books in. It used to belong to Bob but he doesn't use it any more."

By three o'clock they had removed from the apartment all of 'Bel's things. As they left for the last time, 'Bel locked the door and put the key in her pocket. "I'll drop it in the mailbox downstairs," she said.

* * *

At first, alone in the house, they had a strange feeling of unreality. They found themselves speaking softly, almost whispering. By mutual, unpremeditated consent, they kept a little distance between them as they moved about, as if they feared someone was spying on them. 'Bel, with only a visitor's acquaintance with the neighborhood, gazed out of the window frequently, wondering if the fact that they were alone in the house had been noted by anyone familiar with the Hollingsworths' habits.

Andrea, knowing the neighbors well, circumspectly observed the house nearest, seeking any sign of the woman who lived there and who often came to converse with her mother over the wire fence that separated the two backyards. But her mother, Andrea knew, disliked too great a familiarity with neighbors. She said sometimes that she preferred to choose her friends with care and that propinquity was not a basis for friendship with her. Nevertheless, Mrs. Schwartz next door would be sure to report, if only by oblique references, anything unusual she noticed during Mrs. Hollingsworth's absence. Andrea said nothing of this to 'Bel. She had

83

already seen that 'Bel was nervous and apprehensive.

By the time her father came home in the evening some of the strangeness had worn off. Andrea, with a casualness she carefully assumed, explained 'Bel's presence. Her father showed a moment's surprise but at once became absorbed in the evening paper, awaiting his dinner. He was a spare, grey man, with a constitutional nervousness that he always sought to quiet with routine habits. After all, thought Andrea, he knows 'Bel. She saw that he had taken in just enough of her explanation, that 'Bel's parents were away and that she did not want to stay in their apartment alone, to satisfy his need for a logical reason for this novelty. She knew her father's outlook on household affairs. He left them in her mother's hands and if he was required to give his attention to them, it was as briefly as was compatible with his sense of responsibility.

At the dinnertable he entered into a long discussion with 'Bel about the economic condition of the country, whether the new President and the Democrats could succeed in bettering it where Hoover and the Republicans had failed, about the social injustice of millions of people without jobs or food and proper housing when others lived in luxury. Andrea's father practiced what he believed, that everyone's opinions should be received with due thought, even those of a very young girl whose enthusiasm was greater than her experience. Andrea knew that few people treated 'Bel with the serious courteousness he used. Occasionally she saw a gleam of amusement in his eyes but it was a kindly amusement. 'Bel, carried away by his attentiveness, plunged into discussion like a swimmer who has been held back too long from diving into the water. She luxuriated in the exercise.

Finally Mr. Hollingsworth said, "There speaks the idealism of youth. Yes, I suppose we'd all like to see a better world. But in all the history of mankind there hasn't been much agreement about how this is to be achieved."

'Bel, wound up, went on talking after she and Andrea were in the kitchen washing up. There it was again, thought Andrea, this chronic state of suppressed rebellion that dwelt in 'Bel. When they were first friends, she had often been astonished and bewildered by the passionate anger with which 'Bel would sometimes attack the opinions of people she scarcely knew or some old social custom that did not merit such frenzied rejection. In these storms 'Bel seemed to go far away from her, into some realm of impersonal things that had nothing to do with their own secret lives. But gradually it had dawned on her that the energy that burst out in these displays was the well of life itself in 'Bel, pent up within the narrow confines of her circumstances. She was like a bird capable of far-ranging flight enclosed in too small a cage.

And then came the usual reaction. 'Bel's euphoria evaporated. She began to see herself as overzealous, too talkative, ridiculous.

"I know, you just think I'm talking a lot of hot air. Your father

84

thinks I'm just a silly girl. He finds it amusing, for me to go on like this, about things that must be changed."

"Oh, 'Bel, don't be so touchy! Dad likes you. You know he does. He has always liked to talk to you."

But 'Bel turned away from her, her face working with angry self-shame. Andrea went to her and put her arms around her.

" 'Bel, please don't be so unhappy."

She could feel 'Bel trembling a little. It was pent-up frustration, she thought, and probably fatigue. Touching 'Bel's cheek she found it wet. Andrea's heart overflowed. 'Bel never cried about the sort of things most girls cried over. With 'Bel it was always some far distant, abstract idea, something that had no immediate, personal meaning.

She took 'Bel's hand and led her upstairs to her bedroom.

There was a special bliss in waking up the next morning to the warmth of each other's body. The pale sunlight filled the room. The house around them was silent. Andrea knew that her father probably was not yet up, unless his wife's absence had made him restless and he had gone downstairs to make himself a cup of coffee. Andrea lay listening for some sound. There was none.

The slight movement of her body roused 'Bel from the final mists of sleep. She rolled over and said sleepily, "What's up?"

"Nothing."

Andrea squirmed down further under the bedclothes. 'Bel lay on her back and Andrea's hand sought lightly over the smooth skin of her stomach for the silky hair at her pubis. 'Bel's arm went under the pillow to lift Andrea's head onto her shoulder. They kissed gently. Neither of them thought of anything except the delicious warmth, the soft invitation of each other's mouth, the yielding pleasure of each other's body. Andrea, pressed close to 'Bel, felt 'Bel's finger seeking in the moist folds of her own private spot. How wonderful, she thought. Till a year ago only her own fingers, surreptitious, half-fearful, had tried to awaken the feeling there, to assuage the hunger, with none of the completeness that 'Bel achieved. Her whole being flowed toward 'Bel. In a moment she would soar away, to collapse, breathless, within the soft, firm embrace of 'Bel's arms.

When it was 'Bel's turn she waited eagerly for the intense fiery climax that she had learned was 'Bel's response to her own coaxing. 'Bel seemed then to take her with her, in a few moments of absolute union.

In the end she lay clasping 'Bel's thin, bony body in her arms. If only her love could provide some sort of shield for 'Bel's exquisitely tender nerves.

A voluptuous drowsiness overtook them finally and it was only the deep note of the grandfather clock in the hall downstairs striking ten that brought Andrea abruptly to the surface. Her father must be up by now. She told 'Bel so.

"You stay here, 'Bel. I'll go downstairs and see if he wants breakfast. You listen and wait till you hear me talking to him before you get up. Remember, he thinks you've been sleeping in the back room."

Her father was downstairs, sitting at the kitchen table, reading the Sunday paper. She noticed the yellow envelope at his elbow.

"Well, young lady, you've got a niece," he said good-humoredly. "Your mother got there just in time. I was going to wake you up but decided it could wait."

Andrea, seized by a cold fear at the thought of this escape, said eagerly, "You mean, the baby is here?"

He held the envelope out to her and she read the telegram's brief message. "Your mother is going to stay for a few more days. She is coming home on Friday, if all goes well."

A sudden joy bloomed in Andrea's heart. Thursday was the end of the month. 'Bel did not have to go to Mrs. Manley's till the first of April. They could be together for four more whole days.

She waited uneasily, as Monday came and went and then Tuesday, to see if her father would say something about 'Bel's presence in the house. But he seemed to accept it as a natural thing. Or perhaps he was not sure whether or not she had given him an explanation that he had not remembered. He had the habit of dismissing from his mind matters that were to him unimportant, as if he begrudged the effort to encumber himself with them.

For 'Bel and herself it was a magical four days. They came home together in the afternoon, to a long session alone before Andrea's father came from his office. For the first time they were free for hours at a time to talk, to play the classical music records that Andrea had collected slowly with her allowance, to sit simply in each other's presence, filled with a sense of peace and companionship neither of them had experienced before. They had entered truly into a world of their own, beyond their bodies, beyond their thoughts, chiefly beyond the intrusion of the world around them.

On Thursday, when they got home from school, Andrea helped 'Bel take her clothes to Mrs. Manley's. They agreed that 'Bel's books should remain in the small bookcase in Andrea's bedroom, from one shelf of which Andrea had evicted a set of the *Book of Knowledge*, which could fit into one of the big bookcases downstairs. Though neither of them spoke the thought, they both had the feeling that by this simple decision they had gathered the first handful of straw which, like the robins appearing with the spring, they would use to build their own future nest.

The first thing Andrea's mother said when they were alone was, "Mrs. Schwartz tells me that you had Isabel to stay here with you while I was gone."

Andrea strove for a casual manner, trying not to evade her mother's amicable but searching gaze. Yes, 'Bel had come to stay because her mother had gone to Baltimore to join her husband and 'Bel did not want to stay in the apartment alone.

Mrs. Hollingsworth nodded, accepting the explanation. "I cannot really understand her mother. She seems to leave Isabel rather to her own devices. She must be a rather careless woman."

"I don't think she had any choice. Her husband was out of work and then he got a job in Baltimore. 'Bel couldn't go with them because she has to finish at Annunciation."

"Yes, I see, It is unfortunate, though, that a girl of Isabel's age is left so much without supervision. Where is she living now — with her aunt?"

"She has a room in the house of a friend of her aunt's. Mrs. Manley lets her have it without rent because she is going to help her."

"Help her?"

"Mrs. Manley takes boarders."

"Oh. Then I don't suppose you'll be seeing much of Isabel."

There it was, thought Andrea, her mother's extreme sense of family privacy. Her mother was repelled by the idea of the invasion of that privacy by strangers, even or perhaps especially strangers who paid for the privilege.

* * *

Mrs. Hollingsworth's nervousness increased and with it her vigilance. It was, she said, dangerous for Andrea to go by herself anywhere with the town full of idle, wandering, sullen men. She still had to go to school, Andrea pointed out. But she must come home promptly, her mother insisted, and always make sure that she wasn't left alone on a streetcar or in a lonely place, waiting for one. She must not go to the public library any more, which was full of unshaven, dirty men reading newspapers or merely sitting, passing the time.

"If I'm five minutes late," Andrea told 'Bel, "she wants to know why. Every time I stop here to see you I have to pretend I missed the streetcar and another didn't come along for a while."

They were in 'Bel's room at Mrs. Manley's. It was a narrow space under the stairs that led to'the second floor and the only window gave onto a small paved areaway where the trashcans stood. It was all very neat. Mrs. Manley had a horror of dirt and vermin. She would allow no clutter of filth in or about her house. But no amount of cleanliness and order could give the outlook any but a grim, bare aspect. Andrea turned her head away from it to look at 'Bel.

'Bel was lying on the bed. She had punched the two pillows up into a backrest. She looked tired but her pale face was beautiful in Andrea's eyes. "She hasn't anyone else to worry about, Andy. Your mother doesn't want to let go of you."

"Oh, she worries about all of us. I wish Deedee lived closer.

Then Mother would have the babies to occupy her."

"How about your brother Bob?"

"What about him?"

"I thought she worried about him — playing football, for instance."

"Oh, she does! But Dad tells her she can't keep him a child forever. Besides, Bob is going to do just what he wants to do. He won't pay any attention to Dad or Mother, unless it suits him."

"Well, since he as got an athletic scholarship, obviously he has to be an athlete. He's in a college where football is important."

"Yes."

"Your father doesn't like that, does he? I mean, about Bob being at college on an athletic scholarship."

"No. Dad thinks boys who get athletic scholarships are just lummoxes who shouldn't be in college anyway. He thinks such scholarships are a disgrace to the academic world. But, you know, Bob isn't stupid. And how could he go to college just now without it? I think it would strain Dad's finances quite a bit. Perhaps that is part of the reason Dad is angry."

Andrea remembered the family arguments of Bob's last year in high school. Even by that time the barrier between her father and brother was fixed. In his early teens, when his father had tried to stimulate intellectual curiosity in him, Bob had grown sullen and disobedient. By the time Bob was seventeen and she eleven, her father and Bob had reached a sort of truce, in which her father had ceased to talk to Bob as to a boy after his own heart and Bob had withdrawn into his own world, lived chiefly outside his home, with boys of his own age and interests. In the family it was acknowledged by then that whatever Bob's concerns were, these did not include a career in science.

But Bob had his mother's shrewdness and he seemed to know what he wanted to do as a man. He was a big boy, strong and self-confident, and sports were what held most of his attention. He was a high school football hero, though his mother worried about the dangers of the game. Whenever there was an item in the newspaper about a high school boy injured in a scrimmage there was a crisis in the family. Her father was more resigned. He dutifully attended the important games in which Bob took part, giving the impression, as he so often did in the commonplace events of life, that he was reserving his opinion.

The question of whether Bob should go to college at all had loomed as a major family crisis in his last year in high school. There were plenty of successful men, Bob said, who had never got beyond high school. He didn't want to be a professor, a doctor or a lawyer. He wanted to make money.

At first the arguments had been between Bob and his mother — or, at least, those that Andrea overheard. Then she realized that there were more private discussions between her parents. Her mother said none of the men in her family had failed to get a college degree. Her father said there was no use trying to impose on Bob the standards of men with a different outlook simply because of family pride. Bob was foolish, said his mother. In the future he would regret it. The stock market was booming and he had the idea that he could make a fortune when he got old enough to act for himself and had learned the ropes. Perhaps he is right, said his father.

At this point, Andrea overheard her mother reply, "John, you don't really think that at all. You're just as anxious as I am that Bob should have a decent education before he goes out into the world. You are being vindictive. You resent him."

Resent him. The idea brought Andrea to a sudden halt in her own thoughts. Did her father resent his own son? She had never thought her father capable of a petty feeling like resentment. He seemed always so judicious, so above sentiment, so immune to the lower motives of other people. But her mother had said it and he had not replied, at least within her hearing.

When she talked to Bob her mother voiced all her father's views. No one amounted to anything, she said, unless he cultivated his mind. However impatient Bob was now at having to spend another four years in school, he would regret his failure to do so later in life.

"Bob," she said, "you must prove to your father that it is worth his while to make sacrifices to put you through college. He thinks you are not interested. He really cannot afford the cost unless you really will do your best."

Andrea remembered Bob, sitting at the kitchen table eating his breakfast, stubbornly silent under his mother's persuasion.

Then Bob surprised them all by announcing, without prior notice, that he had won an athletic scholarship. Andrea had been surprised by her father's total silence. Bob had told them in the middle of dinner, with the casual air of talking about the next football game. But Andrea had seen the gleaming satisfaction in her brother's eyes. This was a moment that Bob had savored in prospect and enjoyed now to the full. It was a moment that revealed to her a facet of her brother's nature that she had only occasionally glimpsed as a child. Bob would have his own way in the world.

Her web of memory was rent by 'Bel's voice. "Where have you gone off to, Andy?"

'Bel's voice brought her back to the little room below the stairs in Mrs. Manley's house. 'Bel's eyes dwelt on her, amused, loving.

"I was remembering something."

"We were talking about Bob and athletic scholarships and what your father thinks about them." But 'Bel made no effort to probe her thoughts. Any important revelation, 'Bel's manner said, would come of itself.

"Yes. My father thinks colleges should not give them because they detract from scholastic standards."

"Colleges give them because there are a lot of alumni who like to see their alma mater win football games. It's the sort of thing men like. It proves how strong and masculine they are — like fighting a war, the more horrible the better."

" 'Bel, I wish you wouldn't talk like that."

"Why not? It's true. That is what all men think about, proving how much stronger they are than somebody else. And women are stupid enough to admire them, egg them on."

Andrea protested, but uneasily she recalled how even her father, the least athletic of men, had commented with undisguised pleasure on the physical excitement generated in him by the thudding of the ground as two groups of powerful young giants collided on the football field. It must be a primal urge, this urge to enter into combat, latent even in disciplined, intellectual men. This was something that must lie at the bottom of the conflict between her father and Bob. 'Bel, who had read a lot of anthropology, said it was the instinct of the old bull driving the young adversary out of the herd, jealous of the rival for the female's possession. Were her father and Bob aware of this atavistic antagonism? Her mother would not acknowledge such a thing. She suffered because her loyalty was divided betwen husband and son. The inner conflict absorbed all her attention, all her energy.

Bob was twenty-two now. Since his twenty-first birthday he had made a point of reminding his parents that he was of age now and that what he did was his own affair. His dreams of sudden riches had vanished with the collapse of the stock market but he had a canny way of earning and saving money. He tended to be secretive and now that he had grown used to being away from home he was less and less inclined to disclose what he did with his days or who his associates were. He had a job this summer that paid well. He was saving money, he said, so that he could get into the securities business, or a bank, or with an insurance company, some line of business that had to do with finance. There were a lot of boys in his college who were the sons of men in such enterprises. That was as far as he would go in discussing his future with his parents. Andrea saw that this baffled her mother, that her mother wished to know more, to enter into the hopes and prospects of Bob's future, to be able to judge and advise. Especially she was anxious about the girls and women in his life, what sort of a daughter-in-law she might expect one day to have.

Bob enjoyed the game of not telling. Thwarting his mother's curiosity seemed to give him a sense of power, of exercising a man's prerogative to keep a woman in the dark about himself. Andrea was indignant when she saw the distress this caused her mother. But there was nothing to be done. Bob had never been accessible to his little sister. He had chiefly ignored her. She could remember the war waged between him and Deedee, when she was very young.

90

They had formed a sort of war alliance, ready to help each other with their separate schemes, hidden from her mother, but also always ready to fight each other for any family advantage.

'Bel's voice interrupted her again. "You're off again somewhere, Andy."

"Bob is graduating from college next month. We're all going up for the commencement exercises. He's coming home to spend the summer, he says. He has a job here in Washington. So Mother will be thinking about him part of the time. She won't concentrate so much on me."

"Well, thank God for that."

"Yes." She had not told 'Bel how much she had been dreading the coming of summer and the end of the school year. It would be much harder to find opportunities to get away from the house. Her mother had no idea how constantly she and 'Bel were together. Her mother could never guess how much of her time was spent waiting for a chance to be alone with 'Bel.

They quickly learned to be wary of Mrs. Manley. She was a small woman, thin, wiry, the same age, probably, as Aunt Gertrude, but far more energetic, with hair still naturally black and sharp, restless eyes behind spectacles. She was rigidly correct in the way she treated everyone, the few friends who came to visit her, her boarders, 'Bel, 'Bel's friend Andrea. Nothing escaped her, however.

"She knows right away if I've put a dish in the wrong place or have forgotten to put the water on to boil for coffee first thing in the morning." said 'Bel. "I don't think she really snoops or wants to meddle in anyone's affairs. She is just watchful, looking out for anything that might go wrong. She wants everything to be proper. She is always watching for something that isn't what it should be — what she thinks it ought to be." 'Bel's eyes suddenly flashed at Andrea. "Like you and me."

They were sitting on a bench in Montrose Park, gazing absently at the old tombstones behind the iron fence of the old graveyard next door. They had learned not to meet too often in 'Bel's room. Mrs. Manley met Aunt Gertrude once a week, at the Friday Morning Club, where the women of Aunt Gertrude's social circle gathered to hear a soloist perform a musical program.

"That means," said 'Bel, "that she tells Aunt Gertrude all about me, how often I go out in the evening and who comes to see me."

"But Aunt Gertrude knows me," Andrea protested. "She wouldn't think I was dangerous."

"But you are not a Catholic. You don't go to Annunciation. The Sisters don't really approve of you. That's the sort of thing Mrs. Manley picks up immediately. She is not kind, like Aunt Gertrude."

'Bel was leaning forward, her elbows on her knees, gazing at the ground. Several sparrows had come and hopped about them, cocking their heads to see if any crumbs would descend on the path.

Andrea burst out, "Oh, 'Bel, when are we going to be able to be together without all this disguising, this maneuvering?"

'Bel laughed a short, mirthless laugh. "Maybe never."

* * *

It was in July that 'Bel's mother came back to Washington from Baltimore. 'Bel called Andrea on the phone one evening, just after the Hollingsworths had finished dinner. Andrea knew by the sound of her voice, before she had said more than, "Andy, it's me," that something was wrong.

"My mother has come back," 'Bel said. "Andy, I've go to talk to you. Can you meet me somewhere?"

Andrea was silent, looking out into the still sunlit evening. The impossibility of going out of the house into it met in her mind with the nearly overwhelming plea in 'Bel's voice. There was panic in 'Bel's voice, mingled with a hopeless grief.

"Andy, did you hear me?"

" 'Bel, I couldn't get out of the house this evening. There isn't any excuse I could give. You've got to come here. I'll think of some reason to tell Mother."

"All right. I'm coming right away."

Slowly hanging up the phone Andrea pondered. She was aware that her mother was standing in the doorway of the livingroom. She looked at her. "It was 'Bel. She is coming over for a little while. She wants to hear that new record of French music I've just bought."

Her mother frowned at her. "You're still seeing a great deal of Isabel."

"Oh, Mother, 'Bel is my best friend!"

The quick anger of her response reached her mother. "That's being childish. I thought you understood that there are some associations one outgrows, when it is obvious that they are no longer suitable."

"But there is nothing wrong about 'Bel!"

"Andrea, I don't want to have to go through all this again. Of course she is a nice girl and quite intelligent. But her background is not ours. She has a very different outlook on things from yours. And her way of life is not yours. The last time I saw her she was wearing lipstick."

"Deedee wears make-up."

"Deedee is a grown woman, married."

"You let her wear lipstick when she was eighteen."

"Andrea, I do not have to justify myself to you. Deedee was well protected when she was Isabel's age. I will not allow you to defy me like this!"

This isn't wise, Andrea thought even as she spoke but she

92

could not stop herself from saying, "I know 'Bel doesn't have a regular family background, Mother, and she has to earn her living. But we like the same things, the same books, the same music. There isn't anybody else I can talk to the way I can to 'Bel."

"I do not approve of that in itself. She has altogether too much influence on you, Andrea. That is my main objection. You do not try to make friends with other girls, girls more like yourself. You've changed since you've been associating with her. You're not my obedient, loving daughter any more." She turned back into the livingroom.

Andrea stared at where she had been standing. It couldn't be and yet she knew it was true now. Her mother was jealous of 'Bel.

She continued to sit on the chair by the telephone, trying to assimilate the fact. It had changed radically, in a twinkling of an eye, the fixed image she had always had of herself. As far back as she could remember and with unthinking loyalty she had always seen herself as her mother's docile, petted appendage. That is what she was meant to believe herself to be, a consolation for her mother's dissatisfactions within the family circle. Andrea saw clearly now how the world looked to her mother: her husband lived in a world of his own, among intellectual pursuits; her elder daughter was an autonomous being, a wife and mother herself; her son had already left home, even though he still lived under the same roof with her, and his inner life was closed to her. But Andrea remained, the sweet virgin daughter, the perpetual child, the justification for every disappointment.

And I'm not, thought Andrea, and mourned for a moment the great gap that had, without her being fully aware of it, till this instant, opened up between her mother and herself.

She hung about the hallway until the doorbell finally rang and she could open it for 'Bel, a distraught 'Bel, whom she had to hold for a moment in the doorway of the livingroom, with a hand on her arm, to greet her parents.

Upstairs, in Andrea's bedroom, 'Bel said immediately, "She's come back and brought the kids. She is staying in a boardinghouse on K Street."

"What about Mac?"

"He's run out on her for good. I told you he would. He's disappeared. And she figured she had better come back here where I am."

'Bel stood in the middle of the room, wringing her hands. Andrea said cautiously, "I suppose that's natural."

"Natural! Don't you see what it means, Andy? I did think I had a chance to live the way I wanted to, to save some money. But she is going to rent a house and take boarders and I'm to help her. That's what she says. I'm doing it for Mrs. Manley, she says. There's no reason why I shouldn't do it for her. It's a lot more natural for me to help her, my own mother, and I'll be a lot better off with her than out among strangers. Better off! A fat lot she thought about that when she went off to Baltimore! Damn, damn, damn! Andy, I won't have a corner to myself anymore. I won't have any money to use for myself. I'll have to stop school. Oh, Mother of God! Help me!"

Andrea, torn between the sight of 'Bel's anguish and alarm that the sound of 'Bel's excited voice would reach her mother's ears, said hastily, "Sh-h! Oh, 'Bel, don't be so upset!"

But 'Bel's only answer was to throw her arms around Andrea's neck and burst into tears. They sat down on the edge of the bed together, their arms around each other in mutual despair.

'Bel stopped crying. "That's not going to help anything. But, Andy, why can't everybody just leave me alone? Somebody is always saying I've got to do this, I've got to do that. I could just run away — like Mac. Go somewhere where nobody knows me."

A cold fear touched Andrea. " 'Bel! We would never see each other!"

'Bel's mood had changed suddenly to resignation. "Yes, I know. And, besides, I'd start worrying about her and the kids. She's no kind of manager. Keep a boarding house! She couldn't keep the place clean. She'd spend the money they'd pay her for all kinds of fancy things and not have enough to buy food for the table."

Andrea sighed with relief. "Maybe it won't be so bad. If your mother rents a house, you can have a room to yourself. She'd have to let you have that."

The glance from 'Bel's red-rimmed eyes was ironic. "She would? Well, anyhow, I've got to go and see her and keep her from doing something silly, like signing a lease for someplace she couldn't afford."

"You haven't seen her yet?"

"No, she called me when she found this place to stay. She called Aunt Gertrude to find out Mrs. Manley's telephone number. So Aunt Gertrude is upset now, and I'll have to go and see her and tell her everything is all right."

They talked on quietly, for a while. Andrea was aware that the time was passing quickly and that her parents' bedtime was near. 'Bel was too preoccupied to notice. Finally, Andrea said, "My mother is going to come in in a minute and say it is getting later."

'Bel's absent gaze came into focus. "I guess so. I guess I'd better go."

"Oh, 'Bel, I wish you could stay here tonight!"

They looked at each other, speculating, testing the idea. But in the end they accepted the inevitable. I can't push Mother too far, thought Andrea. 'Bel said, "Mrs. Manley would be alarmed and she'd tell Aunt Gertrude that I was out all night."

They went down the stairs quietly, Andrea leading the way. Mr. Hollingsworth had already gone upstairs. Mrs. Hollingsworth stood in the hallway, fiddling with the pad and pencil on the telephone stand. Andrea saw that, as she said Goodnight to 'Bel,

94

she stared at her hard, as if seeking some explanation in her still tear-marked face.

* * *

'Bel's mother did not get a boarding house. "I talked her out of it," said 'Bel. "I don't think she wanted to very much anyway. It was just that my being at Mrs. Manley's put the idea in her head. There'd be too much responsibility. She's found an apartment out on Wisconsin Avenue. I guess she can get a job in a store."

"What are you going to do?"

'Bel shrugged impatiently. "Get a job, I suppose. I can't stay with Mrs. Manley. She doesn't pay me anything and I've got to make some money to help out."

"What kind of a job?"

'Bel was silent for a few moments before she answered. "Mrs. Manley is very sympathetic. She told me I ought to apply at the Telephone Company. They're hiring operators. They just hinted — she wouldn't come right out and advise me to lie —" 'Bel's sudden smile was bright and mischievous — "that I could say that I'm older than I am. I don't suppose they are hiring seventeen-year-olds. I don't think I'm going to try."

"Why not?"

"Because I'm not very good at lying — not at that kind of lying, where I'd have to be consistent. Besides, what kind of references would I give? Reverend Mother? Aunt Gertrude? And of course my mother would get into the act somehow. She can never keep out of my affairs, if she can smell money somewhere. I don't mind lying, if I have to. But I can't stand being shown up."

She suddenly looked round, surveying the middle-aged women who surrounded them in the eating place, a bakery that specialized in pies and cakes and a counter and a few tables for customers to sit at. It was a place that had served for more than a generation as a meeting place for matrons patronizing the shops and department stores on downtown F and G Streets. She is looking for Aunt Gertrude or Mrs. Manley or some other friend of her aunt's, thought Andrea.

'Bel turned back to her. "I'm going to look for another kind of job, something I can make good wages at. Don't you realize, Andy, that I'll have no chance of going to college unless I can earn enough money. Even if my mother gets a job, she's going to need help with the kids. She is always in debt."

"How about the scholarship Reverend Mother is getting for you?"

They sat in silence contemplating this idea. This prospect had hung over them since before the end of the school year, Reverend Mother's offer to find a means for 'Bel to go to college. It was a golden dream that enclosed a core of desolation, the threat of

95

separation. Whatever the college might be, it must inevitably be located elsewhere, away from Washington. They had both known this and the knowledge had made them silent on the subject, afraid to explore the pain wrapped in such a glittering hope. Only at a moment like this could Andrea speak of it.

'Bel answered slowly, "That's out. How can I go off somewhere to school? My mother would have a fit. All the money I could earn by odd jobs would be just enough to keep me. I couldn't send her any. She thinks more education just a lot of silly nonsense anyway, especially for a girl. She says, you just go out and get a job, any kind of a job, and that's all there is to it, even if you get married, because you'll have kids to look after when your husband runs out on you."

"Have you told Reverend Mother?"

"No."

The simple negative told Andrea that 'Bel's yearning had not yet died completely. Impulsively she reached out a hand to cover 'Bel's. With a quick but cautious movement 'Bel withdrew hers.

"Watch out," she breathed, and they sat together again in silence, feeling the weight of the women assembled around them. After a few minutes, by tacit agreement, they got up and went out into the street.

'Bel said, as they dawdled in front of the windows of the big jewelers' on the corner, "I haven't told you about Aunt Gertrude."

"What is it?"

"She is going to have to move. They're going to tear down the building where she's living. I think they're going to build a hospital there. The whole block of houses has been bought up."

"What is she going to do?"

"She's in a state. She has lived there ever since the place was built — twenty years, I suppose. She gave up her house when her husband died. She had a house down on I Street, in the Island, below the Avenue. It used to fashionable down there once."

Andrea nodded. "My father's mother lived there, up to the time she died. She had a great big garden and I can remember being there in the evening, with a lot of people and tables and chairs out on the grass. It must have been a party, because there were strings of Japanese lanterns hung all round."

"Aunt Gertrude says that is all disappearing, the big old houses and gardens. Everybody wants to live in an apartment house. Of course, that's what she has been doing. But now she doesn't know what to do. There is a lawyer who looks after her investments. He has told her that she won't have very much money to live on now. Most of the companies her husband invested in aren't making profits or have even gone bankrupt. She is pretty frightened." 'Bel paused while they both gazed inattentively at a set of wedding silver. "She doesn't want my mother to know. I know why. She thinks my mother will gloat and she is right. But my mother will be mad, too, because, according to her, I'm supposed to be Aunt Gertrude's heir and come into a lot of money when she dies. Otherwise, what was the point of my going to Annunciation and being a good Catholic and doing all the other things Aunt Gertrude wanted?"

Andrea put her arm though 'Bel's. "Never mind. It doesn't matter why she played up to Aunt Gertrude. It was much better for you."

She could feel 'Bel's arm stiffen as she said shortly, "Yes, of course. Any means to an end." And they turned away from the window to walk on down the street.

It was more in theory than in fact that Bob lived at home that summer. He had found a job but he did not talk about it much. It seemed to keep him occupied at all sorts of irregular hours. His father wondered privately if he was working for a bootlegger. His mother worried that such a haphazard life, with eating and sleeping at all hours, would ruin his health.

He rarely spoke of what he was doing when he was out till the early morning hours. But one evening, when, as a rare event, he sat at the dinner table with his parents and sister, he said to her, " 'Drea, isn't Isabel Essory a friend of yours?"

Andrea said uneasily, "Why, yes."

"Have you seen her lately?"

Her uneasiness became alarm. "Why, yes, of course."

"Then you know that she is working out at Tommy Rivers' place, in Rockville? I saw her there last night."

Andrea saw her mother's attention instantly caught. Even her father paused in eating to glance at Bob. Tommy Rivers' place was a notorious roadhouse. It frequently made the newspapers as the locale of a raid by the police and the prohibition agents.

Her mother stared sternly at her. "Does she go to such places?"

Andrea said helplessly, "She works there."

"Works there!" Her mother's voice was raised.

Bob intervened. "She is a waitress there. I thought I recognized her."

"Andrea, did you know about this?" Her mother's voice cut into her panic like a knife.

"I know 'Bel has a job as a waitress —"

"But in a *roadhouse* — in a place like Tommy Rivers'!"

Andrea could not answer. Her throat had closed up, the effect of the conflict within her of the need not to lie and the need not to betray 'Bel.

Bob was looking at her with curiosity. He rarely paid any attention to her at all, so that now she felt his scrutiny as a sort of weight.

Her father came to her rescue, demanding of Bob, "What were you doing out there?"

Bob's reply was studiedly casual. "Oh, some people I was with wanted to go, so I went with them."

Her mother's attention was deflected from her. "Bob, I don't like you associating with people who go to such places."

"Well," Bob said coolly, "everybody I know goes out there once in a while. It's one of the few places where you can find any excitement these days."

His father's tone was dry, "More than you'd like, perhaps, if you got caught in a raid."

"Oh, there's nothing much goes on out there. They've got a good jazz band and everybody keeps his bottle out of sight. Sometimes a couple of drunks get into a fight. They've got good bouncers and that sort of thing doesn't last long. And when I see something like that beginning to happen, I leave. I always drive my own car when I go out there, so I don't get stuck when I want to leave."

Andrea was so pained at the look on her mother's face that she looked down at her plate.

Her mother's voice shook a little. "Bob, I hate to hear you talk like that. You could be arrested, if you carry whiskey around with you. It is against the law and you shouldn't do it. I don't like you drinking. It can become a dangerous habit."

Andrea saw the protest, "I'm not a minor," forming in Bob's face, but he did not say it. His sullen silence said as plainly as words, I am self-supporting. I can do what I choose.

His father broke in. :'You say you can hold your liquor. I wonder how many of the young people who are killed in automobile accidents every day said the same thing."

Bob's fair skin flushed. "Probably most of them. But that's where the resemblance ends. I *can* hold my liquor. I don't drink much. I think it's stupid to get drunk. You don't know what you're doing then."

Then nobody said anything and for a while the only sound in the diningroom was that of knives and forks and plates.

But Andrea knew her mother had not permanently forgotten 'Bel. She waited apprehensively through the rest of the meal for her mother to return to the subject and was thankful when she did not. At least her mother had spared her the questioning in front of her father and Bob.

It was when Bob had left the house again and she had finished doing the dishes and was on her way upstairs that her mother said, "Andrea, this is a serious matter. I had no idea that Isabel would work in a place like that. Surely you know what sort of reputation it has. No young girl should be out there for any reason. Any woman seen there must be of questionable character. I thought she was living with a friend of her aunt's and helping run a boarding house."

"She was, Mother. But she had to leave Mrs. Manley because her mother came back from Baltimore and she had to earn more money. She gets a lot of tips out at — at that place."

"She is living with her mother? Surely her mother can't know what she is doing!"

"I don't know. Her mother depends on her."

"Well, where is the stepfather? Surely he would know that is no place for a young girl."

"He's gone away. They don't know where he is."

"I see, he has deserted his family. There are a great many doing that these days. But these are not the sort of people you should be associating with. I will not allow you to go and see them."

"I don't go there, Mother. I've only gone home with 'Bel a few times and I haven't seen her mother. She works, too."

"Then where do you see Isabel?"

"Oh, we meet somewhere sometimes. Sometimes she takes me to see her aunt."

"What does the aunt have to say to this? Does she have any idea what Isabel is doing?"

"I don't think so. Her aunt is pretty upset just now. She has to move out of her apartment house. It is going to be torn down and she doesn't know what to do. 'Bel is trying to help her find somewhere else to live. I think Aunt Gertrude has lost a lot of money. That's another reason 'Bel has to make as much as she can."

She waited while her mother assimilated this information. "Then, I'm quite sure her aunt does not know. Andrea, you must persuade Isabel to leave that place. Don't you realize that she will ruin her reputation? And besides, she is actually in danger there. Any of those men, especially if they are drunk, might —"

She stopped abruptly. She was going to say "Assault her," thought Andrea. But then she'd have to explain to me what she meant, or would think she had to, and she doesn't want to do that.

"In any case, this isn't something a girl like you should be in touch with, even remotely. You must not have anything to do with Isabel while she is in such an environment."

It won't rub off on me, Andrea protested silently. It doesn't rub off on 'Bel. But she was uneasy enough at the atmosphere of menace that had been created that she said, " 'Bel doesn't have anything to do with the people who go out there, Mother."

"I don't see how she can avoid doing so." Her mother was quiet for a few moments and then said, "Doesn't Isabel intend to get an education? I thought you told me that the Mother Superior at the Convent was going to get her a scholarship?"

"She was, but, Mother, 'Bel can't accept it because she has to stay here and work to help support her mother. Her mother can't make enough to keep them all."

Her mother sighed. "What a hopeless situation! However, Isabel must not work in a place like Tommy Rivers' roadhouse. There must be other jobs that she can find. She does not need to be a waitress."

"But, Mother, she makes much more money as a waitress because of the tips."

Mrs. Hollingsworth gave her daughter a long look from under frowning eyebrows. "It is a very small step, Andrea, from tips as a waitress in a place like that to tips for other kinds of services. This is not a subject I want to discuss with you, Andrea. I hope you will never have the slightest sort of contact with the kind of world such people live in. But I do insist, if Isabel continues to be a waitress at that roadhouse, you must stop seeing her altogether."

"Oh, Mother, I can't!"

"Oh, yes, you can and will."

* * *

'Bel played with the religious medal on its gold chain around her neck. Aunt Gertrude had given it to her years ago and this was a habit she had whenever her mind was occupied with a struggle for comprehension and decision.

Of course Andy's mother was right. A job as a waitress at Tommy Rivers' roadhouse was no occupation for a nice girl. It wasn't only Mrs. Hollingsworth, Aunt Gertrude, Reverend Mother who thought so. The other waitresses silently agreed. They were experienced women, used to the battle in that sort of a place, a battle for a livelihood in which indifferent, concupiscent, tyrannical men were the chief adversaries. A girl like Isabel, they silently said, had no business there until, like themselves, she had descended into the arena, tasted the dust and sweat, savored the sexual slavery demanded by the men.

It had been a sort of bravado that had pushed her into applying for the job when she had heard about it from the woman who worked in the same shop with her mother. The woman had said it was such a pity she couldn't go and get it herself. She had worked in roadhouses before and she knew what good money you could make. But the hours were against her. She had to be home nights. Her old man wouldn't put up with her being out till the wee hours.

All the time the woman was talking she was eyeing 'Bel, looking her up and down. And though she had said nothing directly to 'Bel, her thought had carried over to 'Bel.

'Bel had gone out to Rockville the next afternoon, on the trolley that connected with the street car at the end of the line in Tenleytown. In the daylight hours the roadhouse had a closed-up, half-abandoned look. It was after dark that it flourished. It stood on a wooded lot, a one storey, rambling building surrounded by a wide paved area where the weeds came up through the cracks. Its popularity with people who came out there from Washington was based on the fact that the enforcement of the Volstead Act in Maryland was notoriously lax. Occasionally it was raided by federal agents, looking for illegal liquor. But somehow no indictments followed these raids and the local police only visited when the evidence was out of sight.

She knew about all this vaguely and her heart beat quickly

when she rang the bell at the door marked Office. The man sitting inside at a desk was beefy and heavy-browed, his jowls stubbly. But his eyes were bright and keen as he looked her up and down. She managed to say that she knew he wanted waitresses. He answered that maybe he did and maybe he didn't. She knew he was sizing her up, recognizing that fact that she was underage and inexperienced and wondering why she chose to come there to get a job.

"You run away from home?" he had demanded.

She said No. She wanted a summertime job. A speculative gleam came into his eyes. He is wondering what sort of a family I come from, she thought. But again he looked her up and down and a different sort of look came into his eyes. He said, "Your old man's out of work and your mother's taken a powder and the kids have to scratch for themselves. Isn't that it? And what makes you think you can do this kind of work?"

Her heart was beating fast now as she tried to think of answers for his questions. In the end, he said grudgingly that she could try it. He's wondering if I'm ready to make hay out of being young and innocent and if he can make a profit on that, she thought. He'll take a risk on my being a minor.

Her heart was beating even faster when she left to get the trolley back to town. The lack of jobs, the economic desert the country had turned into in the last two years, had given him the answer to his questions why such a girl would come to him for a job as a waitress. But there was something else in his eyes that terrified her, made her sick at her stomach.

When she returned to the roadhouse that evening the scene was quite different. She had tried, in telling her mother about it, to gloss over the fact that it was Tommy Rivers' roadhouse where she was going to work. She called it a restaurant and was shocked when her mother acquiesced in the false image she had created. It make her sick at heart when she realized that the thought of the money she would make more than reconciled her mother to the idea that she would be working in such a place. Because she knew her mother knew perfectly well that her new job was at the roadhouse. She had no trouble closing her eyes to what she knew the world of Tommy Rivers to be.

It was then that 'Bel decided that the larger share of her tips would be her own, would not go into her mother's greedy hands.

One thing she had overlooked entirely was how she was going to get home in the early morning hours. Very often the roadhouse did not close till after three a.m. and at that hour the trolley did not run. Later she supposed that the people at the roadhouse had assumed that she would ride with someone there who had a car or would pick up a ride from a customer. The last thought gave her a shudder. But that first night the cashier, a woman her mother's age, who had kept her eyes on her throughout the evening, had seen her hanging about while the house was being closed up and had

101

asked where she lived. When 'Bel said in Washington, the woman had said she had better ride into town with herself and her husband. The husband turned out to be the doorkeeper — the bouncer, 'Bel soon learned to say — the man who cautiously opened the wicket in the door to see who wanted to come in and who threw out those who became too quarrelsome.

At the time and ever after the month or so she spent at the roadhouse, 'Bel thought of it as being in a bearpit. Her quick wits helped her adjust promptly, so that she learned how to answer the suggestions made to her, how to ward off reaching hands, how to make instant replies to the bawdy jokes about her obvious youth. But though she learned to cope, the sick feeling of being lost in a quagmire stayed with her. She thought sometimes of the Convent, and remembered the sheltered, pampered girls who had been her schoolmates. Thinking about them, it suddenly dawned on her that some of them would have been better prepared to deal with her current life than she was. She remembered how knowing they were, how they lowered their brilliant eyes and suppressed indulgent smiles when they conversed politely with the Sisters, with the matrons who were their mothers' friends, always mouthing the proper phrases, the expected sentiments. She had always felt a barrier between those girls and herself. Up till now she had thought the barrier was made of money and family security. Now she knew it had another ingredient. These girls had been trained from a very early age by their mothers, and grandmothers, by the values of their class of society, to be manipulators of men. They had learned very early to turn their women's servitude into power for themselves. Not as waitresses in a roadhouse. But certainly as the wives and mothers of men of consequence and money. She understood something now that she had only resented in the past.

There was no one she could talk to about all this, except Andy. She just hoped that Reverend Mother did not learn what she was doing. Andy's mother was more likely to. Not from Andy, probably. Andy would try not to give her away. Andy was her rock. Talking to Andy was difficult sometimes, though. Or to begin with it was difficult, because she was so much aware of how far the world of the roadhouse was from Andy's world. But once she started to talk the words poured out, to Andy's distress, Andy's indignation. At the end of such sessions they were left silent together, each of them seeking solace in the touch of each other's hands, in being together.

This time they were sitting in the empty lounge of one of the downtown movie houses. The plush seats around the walls and the thick carpet gave off a slightly musty smell. There were sudden bursts of talking and flashes of light from the screen whenever someone opened the door of the auditorium and came out blinking into the steady lamplight of the lounge. An announcement board on a tripod in the middle of the room advertised the coming attraction, *I Am A Fugitive from a Chain Gang*, with close-ups of Paul

Muni and George Raft.

"Your brother comes out there several times a week," said 'Bel. "He brings girls out there. I guess your mother wouldn't approve of them."

The subtle overtone in her voice reached Andrea. "He doesn't bring the girls he goes with to the house. Mother worries about that. Dad says it is because Bob doesn't intend to get involved with the kind of girl he'd marry. I think Bob intends to make a lot of money first before he thinks about getting married."

"He's pretty careful, isn't he? I've noticed that he never has too much to drink, though some of the fellows he is with do."

Andrea did not answer.

"So your mother says you can't associate with me. She used to like me, Andy."

"She still does! Really she does, 'Bel. It's just that she thinks I'm such an innocent. She thinks you are very intelligent and very attractive. But she thinks you're too sophisticated for me. And she doesn't like your mother. She thinks your mother shouldn't allow you to work at a roadhouse."

'Bel gave a scornful laugh. "I wouldn't allow me to, if I were my mother."

"My mother thinks you're likely to be raped or something."

"It could happen. I keep out of reach as much as I can, Andy."

Andrea nodded and they both silently contemplated the reality of 'Bel's working life. Then 'Bel said, "I don't tell my mother how much money I get in tips, I'd never have a cent of my own if I did. You know I've saved a hundred dollars. I wish I could get an account in a bank. I hate keeping the money hidden in my room, as if I was a crazy old man. The kids could find it. I know they go into my room when I'm not home, just to satisfy their curiosity. I can't keep the door locked. I tried that and my mother raised such a row I gave up."

"Why?"

"I guess she wants to snoop around and see what she can find out, too."

"Why can't you get a bank account?"

"Because I'm a minor. I'd have to have my mother's written consent. Wouldn't that be ducky — a bank account where she'd be able to find out at any time how much I had?"

"I have one — a savings account."

"Yes, but your parents got it for you, didn't they?"

"Yes, but my mother never interferes. She expects me to put some of my allowance into it. Of course, if I take anything out, I have to have her consent, as far as the bank is concerned." Andrea was silent for a moment. A thought had suddenly occurred to her. "Bel, how would it be if you put your money into my account?"

'Bel looked at her in surprise. She did not answer at once, as if she was testing the idea. "That's a good idea, Andy — as long as you could get it out for me if I needed it. The money would be a lot safer than stuck in books in my room. But if I had to have it, you'd have to let your mother know, wouldn't you?"

"We can worry about that later. I don't see why she would object, really."

"She objects now to you seeing me."

"Yes, I know but —" Andrea did not finish and they both relapsed into thoughtful silence.

Then 'Bel said, "If I brought it along tomorrow, Andy, could we meet here?"

Andrea thought quickly of her mother, the day of the week, her mother's usual occupations on Wednesday, her own chances of getting away from the house alone. "It had better be Thursday, 'Bel — at the Library of Congress — you know, in the big hall with all the signs of the zodiac. I'm still working on my summer theme paper. Mother knows it has to be ready in September."

* * *

The accident was reported in the morning paper. Mrs. Hollingsworth never failed to read the details of automobile accidents, especially those involving young people. It was a subject that haunted her. She did not herself know how to drive a car and she worried constantly about the dangers of the road. Andrea knew that she always looked to see if she recognized the names of the victims.

This morning she exclaimed as usual when her eyes found the headline of the stop-press item. Senator's son killed in car crash. Then she fell silent and that fact called Andrea's attention. She and her mother sat alone at the breakfast table after her father had left for his office. He always read the paper first and rarely commented on what he read.

Her mother demanded suddenly, "Andrea, Bob is upstairs in his room, isn't he? I'm sure I heard him come in about five o'clock this morning. He worries me so, coming in at all hours like that. It was almost daylight."

"I don't know," said Andrea.

Her mother had got up from the table and was already climbing the stairs. She heard her tap gently on Bob's door and then quickly open it and go in.

Andrea picked up the paper. It was turned back to the item and Andrea read quickly. The accident had happened at two o'clock in the morning, on Wisconsin Avenue, beyond the District line. The senator's son was the driver of one car. The police said he had been drinking and was speeding, without lights. His two passengers were in Emergency Hospital, with serious injuries. The driver of the other car had been able to avoid the worst of the accident. His passenger was also in Emergency Hospital, with shock and bruises. He was Robert Hollingsworth, the son of an employee of

104

the Department of Agriculture. His passenger, a girl, was Isabel Essory, a waitress at the Tommy Rivers' roadhouse in Rockville, from which all of those involved had been returning to Washington.

For a long moment Andrea stood motionless beside the table, staring down at the newspaper. 'Bel. 'Bel occupied her whole mind. 'Bel in the hospital.

By the time she recovered from the first shock her mother had come back down the stairs, a worried frown on her face.

"He is sound asleep. He does not seem to be hurt anywhere. I am so anxious about him, but I ought not to wake him."

She went on talking for several minutes before Andrea's silence caught her attention. Misunderstanding it, she said, "I'm sure he is all right. There is nothing to worry about. He was not at fault in the accident."

Andrea breathed, " 'Bel. It's 'Bel."

Her mother looked at her in surprise and then noticed that she still held the paper in her hand. "Oh, the girl." She took the paper out of Andrea's grasp and glanced again at the story. "Yes, that is Isabel, isn't it?" She looked at Andrea closely. "I thought you had persuaded her not to go on working at that place. I told you you could not go on associating with her if she did."

"I know. She was going to stop," Andrea lied. "But, Mother, I must go and see her in the hospital!"

She saw her mother hovering on the brink of saying No, and her mind was already racing ahead to find a subterfuge by which she could get out of the house without admitting where she was going. Perhaps her mother read her desperation in her face, because she checked herself and said, "Very well. You may go and see her this afternoon."

"Can't I go now?"

"No. There are no visiting hours in hospitals in the morning. This afternoon. I shall go with you."

To Andrea the intervening hours were interminable. She tried to read but the words on the page had no meaning. She gave up and went into the back yard and lobbed a tennis ball gently against the back fence so that the noise would not carry up to Bob's room. It was a beautiful summer day, rare in Washington in August. The brilliant blue sky was a frame for the heavily leaved trees. A cool breeze from the river kept the sun's heat from concentrating on the shady garden. Andrea thought, this lovely day and 'Bel is in the hospital. But at least she's alive, not banished forever from my life.

Bob slept without stirring until lunchtime. It was only after they had finished their sandwiches that he came downstairs. He yawned as he came into the kitchen.

"Bob!" His mother's voice shook. "Do you feel all right? Do you think you should go to the doctor right away? Your father thinks so. I talked to him this morning. Yes, yes, we saw the account in the paper. Your father did not notice your name. He never reads the accident news."

Bob took the paper from her and glanced at the story. "They've got the details right. I'm sorry about that other fellow, but he was driving like a crazy idiot. He shouldn't have been driving. He was as drunk as an owl. He could have got us all killed."

"But are you all right?"

"I've got an awful stiff neck." He rubbed the back of his head. "Don't worry about it. The police surgeon said there is nothing wrong with me. They wouldn't let me go till he had examined me."

"Bob, you must come with me to Dr. Stansforth. I'll have no peace of mind until you do. Now, don't argue with me. I have no confidence in police surgeons."

Bob was grudgingly agreeing when Andrea burst out, "But, Mother, we are going to see Isabel in the hospital!"

Her mother stared at her nonplussed. "Isabel?"

Bob said, "She's all right, isn't she?" He was looking at Andrea.

Andrea said, "I don't know. She is in the hospital."

Bob said, "Well, why don't you go there and see her by yourself?"

They both looked at their mother. She said, uncertainly, "Yes, perhaps you had better, Andrea."

Andrea left them still arguing, wild to get out of the house before her mother could call her back. Bob was still resisting her mother's intention to go with him. For her peace of mind he would go to see their family doctor. But he was not a child. She did not have to lead him there by the hand. Bob would win the argument, thought Andrea. And if he won, her mother would then remember 'Bel and the visit to the hospital.

It seemed to her that she waited endlessly for the streetcar and when it came the trip downtown seemed to go on forever. At last she jumped off at the corner of the piled up, ugly grey granite mass of the State, War and Navy building next to the White House, and ran for half a block down Seventeenth Street, until the curious glances of the other pedestrians made her slow down to a fast walk.

Once or twice she had been with her mother to visit friends in Emergency Hospital. But going up the steps now she was overwhelmed by a panicky shyness. The smell of hospital disinfectant met her at the door. The big hallway inside was shadowy after the sunlight outside. She walked purposefully up to the desk where the receptionist sat, before her nerve failed. She had to speak twice before the woman understood 'Bel's name and why she was in the hospital. The woman consulted a wide ledger.

"She's in the accident ward, on the second floor," she said, gesturing toward the elevator.

The sight of the long ward with its two rows of white beds gave Andrea another shock. But the nurse seated near the door said 'Bel

106

was halfway down on the left. There was a screen on one side of her and the bed beyond was empty. When Andrea reached the bed she saw 'Bel lying on her back staring at the ceiling. There was a large patch of sticking plaster on her forehead and she looked very pale.

"'Bel." Andrea's voice came out barely as a whisper.

'Bel's grey eyes shifted quickly to look at her. "Andy."

"'Bel, are you hurt badly?"

'Bel turned on her side towards her, grimacing. "I don't think so. I'm just as sore as the dickens. How did you get here, Andy? I didn't think your mother would let you come."

"She is very upset. Especially about Bob. She saw the account of the accident in the paper this morning. Your name was in it."

"Bob wasn't hurt, was he?"

"He says he isn't. He came home last night and went to bed without waking anybody up."

"He saved us, really. The other car sideswiped us on my side. Bob was pretty quick. He was able to turn the car aside so that we didn't get the full impact. The other car hit a tree."

They were both silent for a while. Then Andrea said, "My mother was going to come with me to see you, but she got to arguing with Bob about going to see the doctor."

'Bel smiled wanly. "That was good luck for us."

Andrea smiled back. "Yes. Do you know how long you're going to be here, 'Bel?"

'Bel's jaw set determinedly. "I intend to get out of here tomorrow. I haven't got any broken bones. I'll get over being stiff sooner if I move around." Andrea understood her unspoken feeling: 'Bel felt at too great a disadvantage, helpless in the face of the people who would demand an explanation from her.

"Do you need some of the money you gave me to put in my savings account?"

"No. I'm due my wages for the week." She glanced at the nightstand by the bed, into the drawer of which her belongings had been put. "I did have a night's worth of tips in my handbag, but my mother was here this morning and she said she'd better take the money, before somebody else could steal it here in the hospital. So that's gone. I won't see any of it again."

"You can't go on working there, 'Bel. My mother was angry when she saw your name in the newspaper. She thought I'd talked you out of keeping that job."

'Bel said drily, "I'm sorry I can't do everything your mother wants."

They were silent for a while and then finally the question that had lain buried in Andrea's mind surfaced. " 'Bel, why were you riding with Bob?"

"Because he offered me a lift into town."

"Has he done that before?"

"No."

"Then why did he last night?"

"Because he saved me from a lot of trouble."

"Saved you? What happened?"

"I don't usually finish till after two in the morning and then I come back into town with Violet and her husband. She's the cashier and he is the bouncer. But last night there was a big crowd out there. There were a lot of boys from that military academy out near Olney. They are the ones who really give the waitresses a hard time. They go grabbing at you and trying to pull your clothes. They think they have to prove what big strong men they are — just a bunch of bullies. Five of them cornered me in a pantry. I couldn't get past them to get back into the dining room. That's when your brother turned up. I suppose he was headed for the men's room. Anyway, he knocked one of them down and the rest were too drunk to stand up to him. *He's* certainly a big strong man. But they made such a row that we all got put out of the place. That's a fixed rule there — any brawling and you're out on your ear regardless. It's the way they keep in with the police — no public nuisance. The owner doesn't tolerate fighting. He pays the police to look the other way but he doesn't want the place raided for disturbance of the peace. So there we were, out in the parking lot. Bob said he would take me home and that we'd better get out of there in a hurry. Those boys in the other car were three of those who ganged up on me. They tried to start a fight there in the parking lot, but Bob and I ran and got into his car and he drove away before they could stop us."

"There wasn't anything about that in the paper."

"No, there wouldn't be. The people out at the roadhouse pay to keep stuff like that out of the paper."

"Well, what happened then?"

"When we were coming in on the Rockville Pike we saw that they were following us. They were driving recklessly, faster than Bob wanted to. He thought maybe they'd just go on by us. But when they caught up with us they kept shouting at Bob. The driver tried to crowd us off the road. Bob pretended not to pay any attention. But the drunk who was driving lost control of the car. He sideswiped us and then careened across the road into a tree. There was the most awful crashing noise and screaming. I don't remember what happened after that very clearly. I guess I was stunned."

Andrea saw that she had closed her eyes and she sat silent for a while. Presently 'Bel said, "What else did the paper say?"

"Oh, you know, the police are investigating and all that. I suppose because the boy who was killed was the son of a U.S. Senator."

"That means the roadhouse is going to have trouble. That means I've lost my job there, I'm sure. There's going to be a real stink. They'll have to pretend they didn't know that I was a minor."

Once more they were both silent for a while. Then 'Bel asked,

"Has your brother said anything more about seeing me out at the roadhouse?"

"No. At least, not when I could hear him."

"I told you he goes out there quite a bit. He sometimes takes women out there with him. Sometimes he is alone. He was alone last night. But I've never seen him pick up a woman out there."

"Bob is pretty careful, I guess."

They talked on and off for a long time. At first the ward nurse paid no attention to them beyond an occasional glance. But after a while she stopped by the bed to put a thermometer into 'Bel's mouth.

She said to Andrea, "I think you had better go now."

Andrea, getting up obediently, said, " 'Bel, I'll try and come to see you tomorrow."

"If I'm here," said 'Bel.

The nurse looked down at her dispassionately, the thermometer still in her hand. "I guess you won't have much to say about that."

* * *

When she got home Andrea waited for her mother to speak. There was no sign of Bob and she wondered if he was still at the doctor's.

Her mother was in the kitchen, preparing dinner. She called out as Andrea closed the front door, "You've been quite a while."

Andrea did not reply. She did not want to use once more her standard excuse: the slowness of the streetcar service. She walked back to the kitchen and said, " 'Bel thinks she can get out of the hospital tomorrow."

Her mother said automatically, as she placed the peeled potatoes in a pan, "I'm glad she wasn't badly hurt. It was a very serious accident."

" 'Bel says that it was only because Bob is such a good driver that the two of them weren't badly hurt."

Her mother nodded. It was obvious that her real thoughts were on something else. She is wondering, thought Andrea, why 'Bel was riding with Bob. She wondered what Bob had said about that.

Her mother said, "I don't see why he went out to that place. He has been there before, he says. All sorts of things can happen in a place like that. He could have been caught in a police raid. Sometimes I do agree with your Father. This Prohibition business is ruining the moral fiber of the country. People simply do not accept it. Your father says that all it is doing is teaching people to break the law."

Andrea shot her a surprised glance. Whenever her father got onto the subject of the idiocy of trying to stop people from drinking by legislation, her mother had temporized. She knew her mother had a great suspicion of people who drank regularly, though her

109

father liked beer and sometimes drank a brandy after meals. He remembered with fondness a walking tour of France and Switzerland he had taken as a young student before the Great War.

Andrea watched her mother's deft hands working with the food, her dark shining head bent over her task. Her mother always seemed to her younger than her father, though she knew them to be close in age. Her father was diffuse, dealing with things on general principles, approaching questions obliquely until he had reached the core of the matter, when he drove straight to the heart of it. Her mother, on the other hand, was precise, pragmatic, never deviating from the subject that engrossed her. It was easier for her to deal with her mother. Her mother was predictable. She could foresee how she would think in a certain set of circumstances. Whereas her father sometimes could not be pinned down. She was often at sea in talking to him, aware that it was he who could fathom her thoughts and motives. He often led her astray into intellectual traps, for the fun of watching her extricate herself. He did that with other people, too. It was his idea of enjoyment and she had learned to tolerate it and sometimes even join with him in his pleasure. As she had grown older she had realized that this was the sort of happy relationship he had wanted with his only son and had had in the end to forego. Bob could not and would not respond.

She also saw that Bob was his mother's son in lots of ways. But he was also himself and that self demanded an independence that excluded his family and especially his mother.

Her mother was saying, "Bob will not tell me all the details of what happened last night. What did Isabel tell you? How did she happen to be with him?"

Andrea said blandly, "She was leaving earlier than usual. He offered her a lift. He recognized her, you know. Usually she rides home with the cashier and her husband. But they weren't leaving till later."

"Bob says the boys in the other car were also out at the roadhouse. They followed him. They were drunk and wanted to pick a fight. I think it is dreadful. They're all under age. And so is Isabel. This should certainly lead to an investigation. Minors should not be allowed in such a place. In fact, such places should not be allowed to exist. They are nothing but traps for innocent young people." She paused and gave Andrea a long look. "I wonder if Isabel was the cause of the trouble with the boys — whether the boys were fighting because of her."

Andrea was mute. It was uncanny how her mother could see into a situation like this.

"Andrea, how much do you know about Isabel's way of life?"

Andrea turned cold with dismay. This was the moment she had dreaded, when her mother would abandon her usual oblique approach and go directly to the source of their unease with each other. She temporized, "What do you mean, Mother?"

"She has been working out at that roadhouse for six weeks. It is not possible that she is now as innocent as she was before that. Even with her deplorable family background, she was still a fresh young girl. How has she changed, what has she learned in that awful environment, and what has she told you about it?"

"She hasn't changed. She hates the sort of people who go out there."

"Very well, then. Why does she continue to work there?"

"She has to earn her living. She makes more money there."

"There are other things she could do. What about the women who work there? Most of them, you know, just call themselves waitresses. They are something else, you know. That is what they make money at."

Andrea thought, Poor Mother. She can't bring herself to say the word "prostitute" to me. Andrea spoke gently, "I know, Mother. Some of them do. But 'Bel doesn't have anything to do with that. You know she wouldn't."

"I know she would not willingly — I trust she would not. Andrea, don't you realize that women like that not only destroy their bodies with disease but their minds and hearts also? No woman can make herself a convenience for men without doing so. No daughter of mine can have anything to do with a girl who would bring herself even to mingle with such people!"

I'm my mother's daughter, thought Andrea, feeling her own skin tingle with the sense of revulsion her mother conveyed. But how can I explain to her 'Bel's reckless confidence that she could protect herself in any situation; that 'Bel, beneath the natural trepidation felt by any young creature in a hostile environment, was fascinated by danger, who saw such dangers as a challenge to show that she could vanquish them? Her mother was right. There had been a change in 'Bel lately. She had become arrogant, paraded her disillusionment. Andrea wondered how much of this merely was a cover for the dismay 'Bel felt at the destruction of the half-romantic view she had always had of the world of adults. 'Bel always spoke of men, in the abstract, as an evil force that somehow she would learn to confront. Her mother, thought Andrea, had built her own world on the tacit understanding that men held the balance of power in the world, that only a man could give a woman status. She had received that idea from her own mother and expected to pass it on to her daughters. Only through a man could a woman gain any significance and yet a man always lurked as the threat of a woman's downfall. 'Bel had had another view of life in the world of men. The common denominator between her mother's view and 'Bel's was the fact of the power of men over women.

Andrea became aware that her mother was still looking at her. She stammered, "Mother, 'Bel is just what she has always been. She is always so glad to get away from that place. Of course she tells me some of the things that happen there. She doesn't have

111

anyone else to talk to."

"I'm well aware that you see her much more often then you tell me, Andrea. I realize that you are fond of her. I do feel for her. She is a girl that would be worth a great deal if she were given a good education and background. But she has been spoiled by her experiences. Andrea, you used to be truthful and frank. I brought you up to be so. Now, you are not open with me. I cannot get satisfactory answers when I question you. I am afraid it is Isabel who has made this difference in you."

Andrea looked down to avoid her mother's eyes. Her mother walked away from her.

Her mother did not return to the subject after that but it hung between them whenever they were alone together. The phone rang in the middle of the next morning, while they were in the basement, ranging the shelves in the corner with the dark blue jars of damson plum jam they had finished making.

"You answer it," her mother said, in the midst of pasting a label on the jar in her hand.

It was 'Bel, saying that she was leaving the hospital to go home.

"Can you come and see me at the apartment?" she demanded.

Andrea, conscious that her end of the conversation could be clearly heard by her mother through the door open to the basement, said, "Oh, I'm glad. But do you feel all right? Can you get home all right?"

"No. But I'll feel better when I get out of here. Didn't you hear me? Can you come and see me?"

"I'll try."

"All right," said 'Bel and hung up.

Andrea turned away from the phone to see that her mother had come back upstairs. She volunteered. "That was 'Bel. She is going home from the hospital."

"I hope she is really well enough."

"I think so. She is worried about getting her wages. She is due a week's pay."

Her mother made no reply. Neither of them spoke again of 'Bel while they ate lunch. Afterwards Andrea went up to her own room and sat at her desk in front of a pile of books. She waited, alert for her mother's announcement that she was going out. She remembered that her mother had intended to go downtown to the stores, which were having sales. After a while her mother stopped in the door of her room and said, "Well, I'm going to Kann's, Andrea. We need some new towels. And I may stop by Cornwell's and bring a pie for dinner. I'll be back well before your father gets home."

Andrea listened until the sounds of footsteps going down the stairs reached her and that of the front door closing. 'Bel had no telephone at home. She would simply have to go there.

The streetcar ride seemed abnormally long. There were few

people on it. The dusty end of summer had littered the pavements with a scatter of dry leaves. The neighborhood where 'Bel was living had once been well-to-do and the substantial houses were still in good repair, though beginning to need paint. Andrea had not visited her there before.

She found the address, one of a row of square brick houses with wide, brown-pillared front porches, set back from the sidewalk behind what had once been well-kept, hedge-bordered lawns. The outer door stood open and in the vestibule mailboxes had been installed for four tenants. 'Bel's flat was on the top floor and Andrea climbed the wide, shallow stairs. One of the doors had a white card tacked onto it with the name of 'Bel's mother. She knocked.

It was 'Bel who opened it. The strips of sticking plaster were still on her forehead and she was even paler than she had been in the hospital bed. She had on an old dressing gown tied tightly around her narrow waist.

"Andy!" The half-angry frown with which she had come to the door vanished from her face. "I didn't think you'd be able to come. You sounded so dried up on the phone. I figured your mother was being difficult."

"She was right close by, listening to me. She knew I was talking to you. But she went downtown to the stores, so I came after she left."

They were standing in the short hallway in front of the big room now used as a livingroom. In the dim light they looked at each other, a great deal passing between them without words.

Finally 'Bel said, "Come on in here. This is my room."

She led the way into a room so small Andrea wondered what it had been originally used for. A narrow bed almost filled it and books were piled on the floor for want of anywhere else to put them.

But 'Bel's eyes were gleaming with satisfaction as she turned the key in the door. "At least while I'm here," she said, "I can keep everybody out."

They sat down on the bed and for a long moment were aware only of each other's soft lips and eager arms. Then with a sigh 'Bel straightened up. Andrea stroked her cheek, where a big bruise had darkened.

"Does it hurt a lot, 'Bel?"

"No. I've got a headache. It won't go away. But I'm lucky I don't have a black eye and I didn't lose any teeth. It's my right side that got banged up." She opened the dressinggown to show Andrea the black and blue splotches on the white skin of her ribs and thigh. "It could have been much worse. I could have had broken bones. As it is, my ribs are pretty sore. They may be cracked but there isn't anything to be done about them anyway."

Andrea's fingers delicately touched the big black and blue marks, the smaller ones now beginning to be bordered in yellow.

113

The sight of them brought closer the vision of the dark road, the duel between the cars, the careening swerve of the other car, the rending crash as it smashed into the tree trunk. Her mind drew away from the thought of the dead boy. Bob's car had wound up in the ditch. Neither he nor 'Bel had been thrown out of it. It had not caught fire. The idea of what might easily have happened, the narrow margin by which 'Bel had escaped perhaps even death — Andrea closed her eyes to that.

'Bel saw her. "What's the matter, Andy?"

"You could have been killed."

'Bel shrugged. "Well, I wasn't." She did not really remember the actual crash, she told Andrea, nor the scene of the accident just afterwards. The blow on her head had dazed her. But the moment before the impact, the wild pursuit by the car behind them — that she would remember for a long time.

After a long silence she said, "Reverend Mother came to see me in the hospital."

"Then she knows that you've been working at the roadhouse."

"Yes. She saw the account in the paper."

"What did she say?"

"She is pretty disappointed in me. She didn't say so in so many words. But I could tell. She was kind, as she always is. She told me that she had been concerned about me, because I never came to see her. She had wondered what I was doing."

"What did you tell her?"

"I told her the truth. I told her my mother came back from Baltimore and I had to get some other kind of job, something I could make some money at."

"Did she understand?"

"Yes, she understood. She said she wanted to remind me that she had plans for me. She expected me to make more of an effort to meet those plans. It would be difficult and if I didn't put all my energies into it, she couldn't help me."

"What did you say?"

'Bel did not answer. Andrea put her arm around her. "Did you tell her that you couldn't accept a scholarship because you had to earn money to help your mother?"

'Bel frowned. "How could I tell her that without talking about my mother?"

"Doesn't she know already?" She must know all about your mother from Aunt Gertrude."

"Do you think I don't know that? That's just the reason. You know that, Andy. I can't let anybody talk to me about my mother, especially not anybody that is a friend of Aunt Gertrude's."

"But I don't suppose your aunt really complains about your mother."

"No, of course not. She is too scrupulous. But you can tell somebody a lot without saying anything in so many words. Espe-

114

cially if you're talking to somebody like Reverend Mother."

"Well, if that's so, won't Reverend Mother know why you have to earn extra money, if you are going to college."

"I don't know. I suppose she would like to say that I should cut loose and let mamma take care of herself and the kids without my help. But that's not just what a good religious person should say, is it? You're supposed to honor your father and your mother. You're not supposed to abandon your mother when she needs you."

"Well, you'll have to tell her you can't do it. You'll just have to explain that you've got to stay home and get a job." She saw the tears gather in 'Bel's eyes. " 'Bel, we've got to find some way for you to go to college. Even if you have to wait a while. And, 'Bel, you know, if you don't go away somewhere in September, we won't be separated. Oh, 'Bel, I've tried not to say it, but I couldn't bear it!"

'Bel put both her arms around her. "Andy, I know. I've been dreading it. I've got to get an education, I've just got to. I'm not going to waste my whole life just existing, living off some stupid job or other, that doesn't mean anything. I've made up my mind I'll do anything to achieve a decent life. That's why I got the job at the roadhouse. In the night, when I couldn't sleep, I'd keep reminding myself of that. But, Andy, I kept remembering that if Reverend Mother got me a scholarship in Ohio or New York State or somewhere else, we wouldn't be seeing each other — even though when we do now, we have to talk to each other in front of a million people. Andy —"

She stopped and suddenly hugged Andrea tightly. Andrea heard her little gasp from the pain of the bruises she had forgotten. But she did not relax her hold. Andrea stroked her hair.

"What did you say to Reverend Mother?"

"I said I didn't think I could go away to college and she said, 'How foolish, Isabel! You've never talked like this before.' And I said I hadn't realized that I would need so much money and I didn't think I would be able to pass the entrance exams. Oh, she just listened to me and finally, when she got ready to leave, she said, 'Evidently, I've misjudged the situation. We'll have to think the matter over.' She was quite cool when she left. But she did stop as she was about to go away and said, 'I don't believe you've been keeping up your religious duties. Have you been going to confession?' Of course I couldn't lie to her outright. I said I'd missed a good many times because I didn't have the chance to go. She said that was no excuse and that if I was in earnest I would have found the opportunity. I was pretty miserable, Andy, when she left."

"Never mind, my darling, never mind," said Andrea, hugging her.

* * *

Within a week after she was up and about 'Bel had a new job, again as a waitress, but this time in a big cafeteria that had just opened downtown.

"They pay a lot better wages, Andy, but I don't get any tips. I just serve from the steam table. But is it a good job and good jobs are pretty scarce. In fact, I wouldn't have got this one if it hadn't been for Reverend Mother. The man who owns this cafeteria is a good Catholic, so naturally he was influenced by her. She wanted to get me a job as a clerk in an office — some businessman she has dealings with — but it didn't pay very much. When I balked she reluctantly mentioned this one. I promised her I would spend at least a couple of hours a day studying. I have a lot to make up if I'm going to apply for entrance exams."

" 'Bel, you must! I'm sure she will find a way for you to go to college."

They were sitting in one of the exhibition halls of the Corcoran Art Gallery, surrounded by the frozen forms of plaster-cast models of ancient Greek statues. 'Bel was gazing unseeingly at a reproduction of Lacoon and his sons writhing in the sinuous embrace of the serpent. The grey light from the skylight two stories up shone down on them, emphasizing the dead stillness of the air. One or two people were wandering about looking at the paintings hanging on the walls. A guard stood at the top of the short flight of steps up from the main entrance. Occasionally he gave them a long glance.

"Just now she's concerned with Aunt Gertrude."

"Why?"

"I told you Aunt Gertrude had to move out of her apartment house there at Washington Circle. They are going to tear it down. Aunt Gertrude has to find somewhere else to live. And she has to sell some of her things. Reverend Mother is trying to get some wealthy people to buy them. Otherwise they would go to a dealer for a song. Aunt Gertrude needs the money. She has less and less to live on."

"Does she have any idea where she is going to move to?"

"You remember that old three-story apartment house on Eighteenth Street, between G and F? It's an old brown place. She thinks she will get an apartment on the second floor, which means she has to walk up stairs. Reverend Mother is worried about that, but Aunt Gertrude says she can manage. I am going to help her take some of her things there. I went there with her to look at it the other day." 'Bel fell silent for a while and then said, "Andy, it is hell for an old person like that to have to move and go and live in a dinky little place."

"Is she very unhappy?"

"She doesn't talk to me much about it. I guess she thinks I wouldn't understand." 'Bel's laugh was short and bitter. "Maybe I don't. I've never had the contrast — of stepping down into a slum — that's what it amounts to for her. I've always lived in one. But she is old and has always been sheltered. Having to sell some of her treasures must seem like the end of the world. Reverend Mother tells her she mustn't feel that way, that she must think about it as getting ready to find the real treasure, which is oneness with God in heaven. Father Greeley tells her we leave these temporal things behind. They are of no importance. Aunt Gertrude is very devout. She tries to feel that way — that this is just a prelude to something far better. But it's hard even for her."

Andrea watched, fascinated, the play of emotion in 'Bel's face. In a private moment like this, when they were strictly alone — or at least with no one closer than the mildly curious guard the length of the gallery away — 'Bel's face mirrored the quick, sudden shifts of her thoughts and feelings. This was the real 'Bel, unwary, impulsive, carried to the top of the tree by a generous thought or plunged into the depths of the sea by a stroke of unkindness. Nobody else ever saw 'Bel like this, she was certain, not Reverend Mother, not Aunt Gertrude, none of the Sisters. With them 'Bel was carefully reserved, full of the fear of allowing someone to see too deeply, to understand too plainly her heart and mind.

'Bel startled her by saying, "What are you thinking about, Andy? You're not listening to me."

"Oh, yes I am! I was thinking about us."

'Bel suddenly grinned. "That's a big subject."

But Andrea was stubbornly serious. "Yes, it is. What are we going to do when we're separated?"

"That hasn't happened yet — except for the two weeks you were up on the mountain. Don't worry, Andy. I'm not likely to be going anywhere, and your mother doesn't intend for you to go away to school. You've told me so. She wants to keep her eye on her little ewe lamb."

" 'Bel!" But Andrea could not help smiling in response to the mischief in 'Bel's eyes.

They sat in silence for a while, watching the only other people in sight, a man and a woman moving slowly along the farther wall examining the paintings. The couple stood for a long time in front of the painting just opposite — Sargent's Oyster Gatherers. Andrea could visualize it through the bulk of the two visitors — the long line of the flat Dutch beach, the pale, cloud-flecked sky, the women and children in straw hats, the luminous sea light. The man and woman walked on.

'Bel said, "Andy, your brother came to see me yesterday."

"Bob? Where?"

"At home. My mother was there. It was in the evening."

"Why did he come?"

'Bel gave her a quick, satirical look and said, "Just to see me. My mother got quite excited about it. She thinks he is my first suitor. He said he wanted to inquire how I was. He was very polite."

"He hasn't mentioned you at home since the accident. At least, not in my hearing. I think my mother has asked him some questions, about the roadhouse, about you, what you were doing out

117

there. I think she has the idea that perhaps he went out there because of you."

"Because of me! He never paid any attention to me except to say Hello, until that night."

"It is just Mother's idea. Bob went out there. You were there. Therefore, he went out there because you were there."

"Perfect logic. Except it wasn't so. He nearly always had another girl with him — except the night it happened. I don't think he had a girl with him. If he did, he went off and left her. That doesn't seem the sort of thing he'd do."

"No, but you said that you all got put out because of the fight. Perhaps he thought he couldn't go back for her, whoever she was."

"Well, she didn't come screaming out after him. I don't think he had anyone with him." 'Bel was thoughtful for a moment. "You know, Andy, some men do go out there looking for a woman. Your mother is right. Any woman out there automatically has a dubious reputation. Some of the waitresses were perfectly willing to leave with a man who invited them. And there are cabins there, in the woods behind the place where people disappeared to for a few hours. But I never saw your brother do either. He always came out there with his own girl, when he had one, and left with her. It seemed to me he came for the dancing. They've got a good band. There are people who come out there just for that."

"But there is gambling there, too, isn't there? That's another thing my mother worries about."

"He didn't drink — a whole lot, — that is — and he didn't gamble. He used to watch sometimes, when other people were playing."

"Bob is interested in money. But I don't think he'd really gamble. He'd hate to lose money. He had ideas about playing the stock market, before the crash, when he was still in high school. Even now he studies everything about securities and bonds and business investments. His room is full of books like that. It is the only kind of studying he is good at."

"I'm sure my mother would be delighted to hear that," 'Bel said ironically. "A potential millionaire is just what we need in our family."

Andrea looked at her. "What happened when he came to see you?"

"Well, when I answered the door I was surprised to see him, of course. I had a wild idea for a moment that something had happened to you, but that wouldn't have been the way I'd hear about that. He was very polite, as I said. He had gone to the hospital and they told him I had gone home. They told him where I live. That was several days ago, so you can't say he was exactly in a lather to see me, could you?"

Andrea gave a little laugh. "No!"

"Well, anyway, he said he wanted to see me again. It didn't

take him long to ask me to go out with him."

"What did you say?"

"I said Yes. Andy, I was so anxious to get him away from my mother. She was hovering around, speaking up for me when she thought I wasn't fast enough in answering. Oh, Andy!" 'Bel dropped her face into her hand.

"You are going out with him?"

"He invited me to go and see *The Blue Angel* — you know, that new film with Marlene Dietrich. It's at the Columbia. Tomorrow night. My mother won't let me forget it for one moment. You know, she used to complain about the amount of time I spent with you. I ought to be out attracting boys. I just don't have good sense. If instead of all this nonsense about going to college I'd just find some boy from a nice family, I wouldn't have to worry about earning a living. It's what she did, wasn't it? And look where we are now!"

"Oh, 'Bel, don't get so upset. You know what your mother is like."

"Indeed I do. So she wants me to nail down Bob. Andy, I'm grateful to your brother. He probably saved me from being gang raped." She paused for a moment. "But I don't want to go out with him. Andy, I'm sorry, but I don't even like him. He's not a bit like your father."

"Can you make an excuse?"

"Not now. I'll have to go out with him this time."

"Perhaps he won't want to again."

Again 'Bel gave her a satirical look. "You mean, I've got to act so that he won't be interested? The trouble is that I don't know what he likes about women. I don't know whether he likes them to make themselves available right off or whether he thinks it's more insteresting if they string him along a bit."

Suddenly shy, Andrea looked away. "I don't know, either, 'Bel. I never thought about Bob and girls. My mother worries about him. She's afraid he'll suddenly marry somebody she doesn't approve of."

"Like me, for instance. He probably doesn't want to marry anybody."

Andrea did not answer.

After a few minutes 'Bel asked. "What's the matter, Andy? Where have you gone off to?"

"I was just wondering — 'Bel, would you ever be interested in a boy? If you liked a boy, would you want to go with him instead of with me?"

'Bel stared at her. "Andy, there isn't anybody I want to be with except you. Don't go getting any ideas. I can't imagine wanting anybody to touch me except you."

She had made an impulsive move towards Andrea. "Watch out! I think that guard is still looking at us. Shall we go downstairs?"

They got up from the hard bench and began to walk slowly toward the central hall of the gallery, imitating the man and woman they had been watching. They passed under the long flight of marble steps to the upper floor and found their way to the back exhibition rooms where the huge old tapestries hung on the walls and the small glass cases stood, filled with pieces of ancient pottery. There was no one else here at all and they clasped hands as they strolled about, gazing at the great dark landscapes portrayed in the tapestries, full of wide valleys between forested hillsides, grey castles perched on the mountain tops, tiny figures of people and horses and sheep lost in the vastness. The sterile hush, the muted light of the big room inhibited talk. 'Bel's fingers tightened on Andrea's. In the gloom of a corner between two doors they quickly kissed.

"I expect we'd better go downstairs," said 'Bel.

They walked down a flight of steps to the long corridor under the central gallery. A few small prints were hung there. Otherwise there was nothing to relieve the grey stone stillness except the cold north light coming through the windows that opened onto the side lawn. They sat down on the wide window ledge, 'Bel with her back to the light, Andrea gazing out through the iron grill. The curved drive in front of Emergency Hospital was almost opposite. Seeing it and thinking of 'Bel so recently in there, Andrea sighed.

'Bel, hearing the sigh, gave her a sidelong look. Andy. She tried to tell Andy everything. Otherwise it was all bottled up in her. Andy was the only person she ever wanted to tell anything to about herself. With everybody else there was always this business of choosing words, editing facts, deciding how much it was wise to admit about anything. With Andy she never had to think fast about whether she had given herself away and must cover up, retract.

She wanted to tell Andy everything. She wanted to go through every wall, tear down every veil, so that they could enter into each other's thoughts and feelings. That was the only way you could ever really know someone else. You had to bare your innermost self, reach through all those layers of deception, trivialities, prejudices, that stood betwen people. Only with Andy would this be possible for her.

Andrea felt 'Bel's hand on her bare arm. In the humid warmth of the end of August day the marble and stone around them gave off a dank coolness. 'Bel's hand felt almost cold.

"Let's go in there," 'Bel said. She motioned to the door on which the sign said Women.

They went in. The big stone-floored room with its marble-sided booths was empty. With tacit agreement they both entered one of the booths and closed the polished wood door. In silence they embraced, their mouths together, their eager hands seeking each other's body under thin cotton dresses.

* * *

Sometimes, when they had not been able to make a definite arrangement to meet, they sought each other in certain agreed-upon places — the six blocks of downtown F Street, for instance, where the shops and movie houses were concentrated, giving them the opportunity to stroll along slowly, looking into the shop windows. How familiar, thought Andrea, were the dresses, the women's bras and corsets and stockings, the shoes, the babies' things. The camera shops, the places where they sold fountain pens and gold-leafed diaries, sometimes were more interesting.

On this afternoon she had got as far as the Palace Theater and stood reading in detail the play bills for the next week's attraction. *Red Dust,* with Clark Gable and Mary Astor and Jean Harlow. 'Bel wanted to see it and had said they should try to go together.

"Give your mother some excuse, Andy. She won't know where you've been. Just tell her you are going to the movies."

It was more than that, thought Andrea. Her mother did not like her going to the movies by herself and she did not want to say she was going with 'Bel. Andrea sighed, looking at the silver blondness of Jean Harlow's head. Life seemed to become daily more complicated, more filled with problems of time and place.

"What's the big sigh about, Andy?"

'Bel's voice in her ear made her jump. "Oh, I'm just thinking about us."

"Well, it isn't as hopeless as all that." 'Bel was cheerful.

Together they examined the stills of the movie, silently considering.

"Can you afford it for both of us, Andy?"

Andrea nodded. "It's not that. I'm having trouble thinking of an excuse. You don't get through work till three o'clock. It's got to be Wednesday, doesn't it, the day you're off? If Mother decides she wants me to go shopping with her and I tell her I've got to go to the Library or something like that, it would be just our luck to run into her on the street."

"Andy, you're always looking for disaster. We can keep an eye open and see her coming. And, besides, most of the time we'd be in the movie. Even if your mother decided to go to the movie herself, it's too dark in there for her to recognize us."

"Yes, I know. I guess it's my guilty conscience. She's very touchy these days. She broods quite a lot. I know it is mostly about Bob. But she really resents the fact that I don't tell her all about what I'm doing. I never mention you and that in itself tells her something is wrong."

Andrea was aware, as she spoke, that 'Bel's attention had wandered from her. The expression on 'Bel's face changed. She looked as she did when she was talking to someone she did not know well, with whom she had to be formal and polite. Andrea

121

realized then that someone had come up to them from behind her back.

'Bel said, "Why, hello, Bob. Fancy meeting you here."

Turning Andrea saw her brother standing close to them. He said casually, "Hello, Isabel. Hello, 'Drea. What's on?" He read the poster for the current attraction. "Too bad. I've seen that. Pretty poor stuff. But I'll say it's hot! How about an ice cream soda? I'll stand you both."

There was an ice cream parlor on the corner, next to the movie house. He motioned towards it. Andrea saw 'Bel hesitate and throw her a questioning glance. She said, "That's nice, Bob, if 'Bel has the time."

'Bel, taking the cue, glanced at her watch and said, "I guess I can make it."

The three of them went into the ice cream shop and sat down at one of the small metal-legged tables. By the time the sodas came, 'Bel and Bob were away in a fast moving, bantering conversation that left Andrea a silent third. Watching, she noticed that no matter what they talked about, Bob's attention was not on what 'Bel said but on 'Bel herself, that his eyes stayed on her face nearly the whole time. 'Bel, conscious of the pressure he was putting on her, was nervous. Andrea saw all the signs of it — the too-rapid way of talking, the skipping about in what she was saying, trying to divert his attention by making fun of what he said. But Bob took it as an invitation, as a game to lead him on, and he was in the mood to be led on by someone like 'Bel, eager, lively, different.

He said suddenly, in the midst of a pause, "How about coming out with me tonight? How'd you like to go to Tommy Rivers' roadhouse and have somebody else wait on you?"

'Bel's face flamed. That was Bob's way of doing things, Andrea knew. Never back down, never be frightened away. He had learned boldness as a way of confronting things. And he was offering 'Bel revenge, a chance to get back at the people who had seen her humiliated. But as his woman. 'Bel had seen it faster than she had and she knew the rage that immediately flooded 'Bel.

She was relieved when 'Bel, speaking in a changed voice, merely said, "I'm sorry. I can't go out tonight."

Bob noticed the sudden coolness but he shrugged it off. They got up to leave. Andrea, standing near the door with 'Bel, waiting while he paid the check and talked pleasantly to the middle-aged cashier, thought what a handsome man he was, more than six feet tall, with dark, wavy hair like her mother's, square-shouldered, bulky. He had the assurance of a man older than he was. He had always had that manner of easy-going self-confidence. Women immediately noticed him anywhere, responded warmly to his cheerful good manners, felt the attraction of his bold way of dealing with them. Even the middle-aged cashier, who followed them with her eyes as they went out into the street, was smiling complacently.

On the sidewalk they stood together in a knot in the stream of passersby. Both Andrea and 'Bel were expecting Bob to say Goodbye and to leave them alone as he had found them. But he made no move to go. 'Bel finally said, "Andy, I've got to go home. My mother is expecting me. See you later. Thanks, Bob, for the ice cream."

She looked at Andrea as she spoke and Andrea knew that this was an attempt to shake free. But Bob said easily, "You're going out Wisconsin Avenue? I'll go with you. I have got to see somebody out in Bethesda. So long, 'Drea. Tell Mother I'll probably not be home to dinner."

For the briefest moment Andrea saw her own dismay reflected in 'Bel's face. She watched as they crossed the street to the car stop on the other side. Bob seemed to be doing most of the talking now.

Slowly she turned away and walked down Thirteenth Street to the Avenue to get a streetcar there. She felt both resentful and anxious. 'Bel had told her very little about the only other occasion she had been out with Bob, the time he had come to where she lived and she had gone out with him to escape her mother. They had gone to a movie, 'Bel said, and then somewhere to eat. Bob had acted like a gentleman all through the time they were together. In fact, they had both been formal and polite, so formal and polite that she had wondered why he had bothered to look her up. When he took her back to her mother's flat he had said nothing about going out with him again and she had decided that he was no longer interested.

And now, thought Andrea, I have to tell Mother that I was with 'Bel and that Bob met us and that he has gone somewhere with 'Bel. I'll have to tell her, because I've got to tell her he said he isn't coming to dinner and she will want to know the rest. If I don't, he will.

When she told her mother, Mrs. Hollingsworth said, "What was Isabel doing downtown at that hour? Why wasn't she at work?"

"She had the rest of the afternoon off. I met her downtown. She wanted to see if she could get some shoes at the sale at Hahn's."

Her mother seemed to muse for a moment. "That was a very chivalrous thing he did, rescuing her from that situation out at the roadhouse. He has been brought up to respect women and I am glad that he did so, for her sake. But I must admit I am appalled when I think of the danger involved. He could have been attacked by those other boys and they both had a very narrow escape in the accident."

Andrea listened carefully to what her mother was saying. There was another meaning to her mother's musing. It concerned Bob and 'Bel and had little to do with this recapitulation of the episode at the roadhouse.

Andrea said tentatively, "Bob seems to like 'Bel, even though she is brainy."

Her mother shot her an annoyed glance. "He is not stupid, Andrea. I imagine when he finally marries he'll choose an intelligent woman."

But not 'Bel, thought Andrea. "I didn't mean anything like that, Mother. Bob doesn't go with a lot of girls."

"He doesn't bring them here," her mother snapped. "I'm sure he knows quite a few. And they're not the kind I like to see him involved with." She paused and then said, thoughtfully, "He is too young, really, to marry yet. He'd be bound to make a mistake. I do wish that, if he is attracted to Isabel, she had a better background. I should hate to see him ally himself with the sort of people her mother comes from."

"But her father's people are all right. There's Aunt Gertrude."

"Yes, I realize that she does have a good background there. But her mother has ruined her. I will never understand how a mother can be so careless with a daughter as she has been. It is a great pity, because Isabel is a remarkable girl. I just wish —"

She did not finish what she was going to say and after a while Andrea timidly said, " 'Bel isn't interested in men, Mother. She has a lot of plans for what she wants to do."

Her mother glanced up at her, as if she had interrupted some chain of thought. "That is all the more reason why Bob may become involved with her. Isabel is the sort of girl who can cause a well-meaning young man a great deal of trouble."

* * *

Her mother must be right, thought Andrea. Bob found out quickly that 'Bel worked at the cafeteria and went there for meals and to wait until she finished her shift. She couldn't shake him, 'Bel said. He waited doggedly for her to get off work, he followed her wherever she went, he turned up at the flat in the evening to try and persuade her to go out with him.

Andrea and 'Bel took to meeting in out of the way places — in the newly opened Freer Gallery among Whistler's misty paintings, in the Library of Congress, in the back pews of St. John's church across from Lafayette Square, while the organist practiced and the tourists filed in and out — all places where it seemed unlikely that Bob would find them.

"My mother has all at once got very fussy," 'Bel said, as they sat on the inside steps of the old apartment house where Aunt Gertrude now lived. "She says he can't come to the flat in the evening when I'm alone there with the kids. She says a man's got only one idea where girls are concerned and it is stupid to give yourself away for nothing. As far as she is concerned, he's going to have to pay for his privileges."

"Oh, 'Bel! Bob's not that kind of man!"

"What kind of man? They're all alike basically. Mamma is right there. It just depends on how many layers of good breeding you have to get down through."

Her tone made Andrea defensive. "Well, does he ever act as if —"

124

"As if he expects me to go to bed with him just because he asks me? No, not really. What I'm worried about is —"

"What?"

"He acts as if he really likes me, as if he really wants to be with me, not just any girl. Andy, that really upsets me."

"Why?"

"Because I don't feel that way about him. It makes me feel guilty, as if I am playing my mother's game."

"What do you mean, 'Bel?"

'Bel looked at her thoughtfully, as if weighing what she should tell her. "You know, Andy, you can't say my mother is not sound when it comes to sizing people up for what they're worth to her. She really believes that there is one thing that a woman has that she can put a price on, that she can bargain with. That's herself. She thinks women who sell their bodies to anybody who comes along are stupid, because they are not getting a good deal. They're wasting their stock in trade. And any woman who would let a man trick her into letting him have her for nothing is just beyond anything. If you've got something valuable, why not get the best bid? And the best bid is marrying, so that you have security and respect from people. She says she wishes she had had somebody who could have given her the right advice when she was my age. She tried her best, marrying my father. But she made the mistake of falling for him first and then when she found she was pregnant with me, she had to hook him. By that time she realized that she could have looked for somebody with more to offer. But she was stuck." 'Bel suddenly broke off and burst out in a different tone of voice, "Oh, I hate it when she gets to talking about him. I know he must have been a spineless kind of fellow. Everything anybody says about him — even Aunt Gertrude, when she thinks she is praising him — tells me that. Why couldn't I have had decent parents?"

Andrea, deeply shocked, asked, "What does your mother want you to do?"

"She wants me to play up to Bob."

"Does she want you to marry him?"

"I don't know whether she really does. You see, she can't quite figure out whether he is the best I can do. After all, he is pretty young and though he seems to know a lot about money, she suspects he doesn't have much yet. It's like gambling on how much he will make in the future."

Andrea said soberly, "My mother would be very unhappy if Bob said he was going to marry you."

"She doesn't want my mother. Well, she needn't worry. I'm not going to marry Bob. I'd run away before anything like that happened. I just wish he would leave me alone."

They sat for several minutes in silence. Finally 'Bel said, "I guess we had better go on up to Aunt Gertrude. I told her I was bringing you, so she probably has made some German cookies for

125

you to have with your tea."

"Yes, let's go on up," Andrea agreed, bracing herself for the wave of heartfelt sympathy that always swept over her when 'Bel took her to the old lady's new home. A deep sadness assailed her when she saw Aunt Gertrude in her formal black gown, seated in the featureless room, surrounded by only a few remnants of the treasures that had crowded her former apartment. This room was dark, since the window looked out on the blank wall of a taller building. You were aware of the heavy rug under your feet only by feel, for there was not enough daylight to see its dark patterns. The few pieces of antique furnishings that she had brought with her seemed as shrunken as she did. Her tall figure was stooped. Her hands were bonier and her rings fitted her fingers more loosely.

But she had kept her English bone china tea cups and the massive silver tea service. There was the same gentle ceremoniousness in her manner as she seated the girls and handed them the spice cakes. The world for the moment seemed to settle back into the quieter, changeless atmosphere of a mythical past.

Andrea, watching 'Bel's face, saw it grow calm and assured, as she punctiliously imitated her aunt's stately manners.

But it was after all only a momentary respite. Apparently, thought Andrea, a couple of days later, 'Bel's mother was sticking to her guns. Otherwise Bob would never have been forced to seek her out to intervene with their mother.

It was the middle of the afternoon and upstairs in her own room she heard the front door close as he came into the house. Her door was open so she could hear him coming up the stairs and saw his head and shoulders before he reached the upper landing. Even then she was not prepared for his stopping at her door. She had expected a passing Hi. Instead he stood in the doorway and said,

" 'Drea, Mother's not home, is she?"

"No, she hasn't come home yet."

"Well, there's something I want you to do for me." He stepped into the room and sat down in the armchair, his elbows on his knees. "First of all, why doesn't Isabel come to see you here at the house any more?"

The directness of the question disconcerted Andrea. "Well, she's pretty busy and —"

"You've been friends with her a long time. She used to come here quite a lot, used to have dinner with us. Dad used to like to talk to her."

"Since she has been working she doesn't have so much time to do what she likes. She has to sort of fit things in."

He saw through her temporizing. "It's because of Mother, isn't it? She doesn't like you to be friends with Isabel any more. There is nothing wrong with earning your living. The way things are going you may have to do it yourself before long — if you can find a job."

"It isn't that, Bob. She doesn't like 'Bel's background. She was

126

upset about 'Bel working out at the roadhouse."

Bob was thoughtful. "That wasn't the right kind of job for her, all right. But she isn't doing that now. I thought Mother liked 'Bel."

"I think she still does. It's just that she thinks — she thinks 'Bel is too — 'Bel hasn't had the kind of upbringing she approves of."

"Thinks she is a bad influence, huh? You know, Mother has some pretty old-fashioned ideas. 'Bel's not a tramp, just because of her mother. She's hard to take, I admit. What's this about her father? Lost his job because he drank and ran out on his family?"

"That's her stepfather. Her own father is dead."

"And what was he?"

"He was all right. He had the same kind of ancestors Mother has, from Virginia."

"Ancestors. Well, that's not got anything to do with Isabel and me. I tell you what, 'Drea. How about bringing her home with you to dinner tomorrow? I know she doesn't work on the evening shift at the cafeteria."

"I can't do that unless I ask Mother."

"Well, ask her, then."

Andrea wanted to say No. No, she did not want to play go-between for him with Isabel That was her first and strongest response. But besides that he did not understand how things stood between herself and her mother on the subject of 'Bel and how strong her mother's feelings were. But the hopelessness of explaining all that to Bob prevented her. Weakly, she protested that 'Bel might not be free to come, might not want to. "Bob, she knows Mother does not want her here."

"Well, I want to change that. You call her, 'Drea, and find out and ask Mother. Just tell her you want Isabel to come to dinner."

He had got up and was walking out of the room as if the matter were settled. For him, thought Andrea resentfully, it is. After considering for a while, she decided not to call 'Bel. She would first ask her mother.

After breakfast the next morning she nerved herself to say that she expected to see 'Bel in the course of the day and she wanted to ask her to come to dinner. She could see that her mother was startled. But she also saw that, after her first surprise, her mother seemed to consider something she did not speak of and then her mother said, "All right."

Now it was a question of whether 'Bel would be willing to come. On the way downtown she pondered the situation. Her heart leapt at the thought of a whole evening with 'Bel in the relaxation of her own home, without the nervous apprehension that characterized their usual meetings. But there was Bob. Obviously Bob would expect to monopolize 'Bel's attention. She would have to tell 'Bel that this was Bob's idea.

She went to the cafeteria and got a cup of coffee and a bun. At first there was no sign of 'Bel. The restaurant was almost empty. Breakfast was almost over for most people and lunch was still an hour away. But 'Bel had seen her and presently came over to the table where she sat by the window.

'Bel stood looking down at her, a faint expression of apprehension on her face. "What's up, Andy?"

Andrea smiled reassuringly. "Nothing's wrong, 'Bel. Could you come and have dinner at my house tonight?"

'Bel's eyes widened in surprise. "What for?"

Andrea laughed. "To eat, of course! Mother says I can bring you home to dinner tonight."

'Bel sat down in the chair opposite her. "What's all this about, Andy?"

Andrea was sober. "Yes, there's a hitch to it. It's Bob's idea. He asked me to ask Mother if I could bring you home to dinner."

"So that's it. Why should I want to come?"

"Well, we'd be together all evening."

"With your father and mother — and Bob."

"You always used to like to talk to my father."

"That's a long time ago. Your mother doesn't want me, Andy. She doesn't want me because of you, she certainly doesn't want me because of Bob."

"She didn't raise any objection. She said all right."

'Bel was silent for a thoughtful moment. "I guess she wants to see for herself how things are between me and Bob."

"At least we'd be together for a couple of hours."

"You mean, we'd be under the same roof. You're forgetting Bob. He is going to be pressing me to go out with him afterwards. At least, he is going to insist on seeing me home. How I hate that."

In the end 'Bel consented. The evening was as she had forecast. She tried to start a conversation with Andrea's father, but he was not in the mood or else felt out of it because of his son's talkativeness or his wife's manner. Her mother was her usual gracious self, but there was a watchfulness in her eyes, which flitted frequently over 'Bel and her son. They all sat in the livingroom afterwards and there was a lively discussion of current events in which Andrea and her mother took no part. In the end, Bob insisted on seeing 'Bel home.

This was the first of a series of such occasions. They became more awkward and strained. 'Bel came reluctantly. Sometimes, to relieve the strain, she consented to go out with Bob after dinner, to a movie. Invariably she suggested that Andrea come with them. Andrea, understanding her appeal, agreed and spent the rest of the evening listening, embarrassed, to Bob's disguised, muttered conversation with 'Bel, longing for the minutes to pass. He was always entirely silent on the trip home after they had taken 'Bel to her flat. He never told her on these occasions to stay home and leave 'Bel and him to themselves. She knew this was because 'Bel had told him that she would not go out with him otherwise.

'Bel had been forthright in saying that she did not want any sessions with Bob in the rear seat of his car.

"I've told him that's not for me," she said to Andrea. "I think he believes me. But if I'm alone with him, I know he'll think he can talk me into it. He doesn't really think I'll go that far with him. At least, he wants to find out. He wants to know if I'm the kind of girl who can be talked into necking with him and if so, how far he can coax me into going." She made a sound of disgust. "Andy, I hate it! I hate it! This business of letting somebody poke around you, use his hands and his mouth — it makes me sick at my stomach!"

But Andrea knew that Bob was just biding his time. 'Bel's reluctance egged him on. Perhaps, thought Andrea, he would have forgotten about her, if she had been the usual sort of girl, willing to be persuaded, anxious to please him.

Her mother said nothing to Andrea about the matter. Andrea did not know whether her parents discussed it between themselves. It was typical, she thought, of her family, that some subject that occupied the minds of all its members and created anxiety, dread or distaste in them, should remain unspoken of amongst them. She knew that this sort of anxious restraint grew out of a sort of scrupulousness. You did not talk about something that might embarrass or distress. You avoided confrontations. You denied the existence of a conflict by ignoring it. Andrea wondered at times like this, when this ingrained family habit hid something that festered, whether it would not be better to belong to a family in which accusations were shouted out, recriminations were openly made, people screamed and hit out at each other. But, no, of course not, she herself could not stand such an environment. Violence and bad language solved nothing, led only to more unhappiness.

But she did wish she could say to her mother that it was not 'Bel who pursued Bob. This is what her mother was now convinced of. She seemed to have forgotten the 'Bel she had known two years ago, the clever, talkative girl she had so often invited to eat with them, whose company she enjoyed, whose wittiness had made her laugh, whose determination to better herself she had admired. In those days Bob had ignored 'Bel. She was simply a girl his sister had brought to the house, who talked about things that amused his father but were of no interest to himself.

Obviously Bob saw her in a different light altogether now. 'Bel piqued his interest. The fact that he had rescued her from assault by other males gave her a certain status with him. The whole incident was revived by the police investigation to establish responsibility for the accident. It turned out to be a formality, since everyone involved named the dead boy, the driver of the other car, as having caused the accident. His father was powerful enough to squelch the investigation. Anticipation of the investigation, however, had built up tension in 'Bel, in Mrs. Hollingsworth, even,

Andrea noted, in her father. What its real effect on Bob was she could not judge. He was offhand, acted as if the outcome was foregone. And when it proved to be so, he seemed to forget it. But it left her father disgusted, her mother nervous and short-tempered.

At first she could not get 'Bel to unburden herself on the subject of the police interrogation. When they met the day after on a bench in Washington Circle, 'Bel was mute and downcast. They sat there silently until 'Bel suddenly shook herself, closing her eyes briefly, and said,

"I don't want to talk about it. I don't want to remember it. I told them the truth. I don't remember so much about the crash and what happened right after. I remember somebody screaming — maybe it was me. I remember sitting on the edge of the road and seeing them carry somebody over to the ambulance. And the lights of the police car and the big flashing light in the blackness, shining on the broken glass all over the roadway."

"You don't have to remember it any more."

"Yes, but, you know, that's not so much what they wanted me to tell them about. What they kept asking me about was the boys in the other car, who I thought they were, did I know them, why were they following us. I said I didn't know them. I said they were following us because they had tried to pick a fight when we were leaving the roadhouse. I tried not to tell them any more than I had to, because I didn't know what Bob had said, or the people at the roadhouse.

"They finally stopped asking me questions and said I could leave. The police sergeant did tell me that they wouldn't take a written, signed statement from me because I was a minor and they didn't want to have my name on the police record. I think Reverend Mother had something to do with that. She knows all kinds of people and she knew I was going to be questioned by the police. I think the police had a pretty good idea that something happened out at the roadhouse that started the whole thing. I think they've had other incidents like this, involving those boys. But the senator wanted everything hushed up. Bob said that boy was arrested once before, in another incident when a girl was raped and killed. But that was hushed up, too."

"Dad is furious. He says it is outrageous that somebody should be powerful enough to subvert justice, especially somebody who is in a position of trust, like the senator."

'Bel glanced at her with a wry smile. "Well, in this case, I'm just as glad the senator can and does want to do just that."

For a while they sat in silence, or only exchanging an occasional remark. This time their lack of talkativeness seemed to mean that they had drifted apart. Usually their silences underlined their closeness. That's been happening more and more lately, thought Andrea. She seemed to be out of touch with 'Bel's thoughts. She glanced sideways at 'Bel, to see that 'Bel was far away, her eyes downcast and a little wrinkle in the middle of her brow. She is thinking about Bob, thought Andrea, and felt a chill around her heart. Lately 'Bel almost never said anything about Bob. When she did she did not speak of him openly as she used to, as if taking for granted that Andrea would understand and sympathize, even if she was critical, Also, 'Bel had not come to the house for sometime now. Bob had not raised the question of her being invited to dinner. That must mean that he had been meeting her elsewhere and alone. Yet 'Bel had not said anything about it. Bob had the money to provide the usual sort of opportunities for them to meet — dinners in restaurants, tickets to the theater, admission to places where there was good dancing. At home Bob was even less talkative than he used to be. He seemed rather glum. I expect he really is in love with 'Bel, thought Andrea.

As if anyone wouldn't be. Andrea glanced again surreptitiously at the girl sitting beside her, her heart swelling with love. This time 'Bel suddenly looked up and met her eyes.

"What are you looking at me like that for, Andy?"

Andrea looked away. "Nothing." She felt 'Bel's eyes lingering on her but she did not look back.

The rest of the time they were together, they were mostly silent. Andrea thought unhappily, that's the way we've been lately.

* * *

The newspaper notoriety created by the accident and the police investigation died away. But the gloom that it had generated over the Hollingsworth household did not lift. Andrea noticed that her mother seemed to get more and more nervous and apprehensive. She was preoccupied and quiet when they were alone together. When her father came home in the evening the atmosphere seemed to lighten, but the things they found to talk about were also dismal and unhopeful. The newspapers said that one quarter of the working population of the country was out of employment. The daily paper was filled with stories about the homeless, the wanderers who filled the roads or rode the rails in the search for non-existant jobs, about the mobs of unemployed who besieged any place of business that advertised a vacancy in its work force.

Perhaps all this, thought Andrea, contributed to her mother's pentup anxiety. But the real cause was her worry about Bob. He had finally told his parents that he had a good job with a brokerage firm downtown, a job he had obtained through one of the stockbroker's sons who had been in his class at college. He had opportunities, he said, to make some money on the side, in spite of the dismal state of the stock market, by using tips he picked up and his own natural astuteness. His father made no comment on this. He seemed to accept the fact that Bob had entered upon his own

131

life. But his mother was unsatisfied.

It must be because of 'Bel, thought Andrea. Bob did not talk about 'Bel, but her mother seemed to divine that he was absorbed in her to the exclusion of everything except his working life. There must be much more, she thought, that passed between her mother and Bob than she knew of. Her mother would be careful to keep from her any hint of the disagreements she had with Bob about 'Bel, would take care that she did not overhear anything they said to each other on the subject.

Then one evening Bob came home just before dinnertime, bringing 'Bel with him. He said he had met her just as she was leaving work.

"I told her, Mother," he said boldly, "that you wanted to know why she hasn't been here to have dinner with us lately. I said she had to come now, to please you."

Andrea saw that he was gazing steadily at his mother as he said this. Mrs. Hollingsworth's lips tightened in a fleeting expression of anger. But of course Bob knew his mother's Virginian roots, her innate feeling that hospitality must never be denied.

It was a constrained meal. Nobody seemed to find anything to talk about that would sustain a general conversation. Andrea watched 'Bel covertly. They had had no moment alone since 'Bel had come into the house. She could tell nothing from the studied calm in 'Bel's face. In the kitchen, after dinner Bob came and sat on a stool and kept up a running talk with 'Bel as she and Andrea washed the dishes. Andrea was aware that her mother's attention was focussed on them, from where she sat in the livingroom. When the last pot was put away 'Bel said,

"Andy, let's go upstairs," and they left Bob, who reluctantly went to join his parents.

When they were alone in Andrea's bedroom, 'Bel said, "Of course your mother did not want me here to dinner. That was just Bob's idea. I hope she is not too upset. She seems very nervous."

"She is very unhappy, 'Bel. She is worried about Bob."

"Because of me."

"Well, yes." Andrea hesitated a moment and then plunged on. " 'Bel, I don't know what Bob has told her or what she has said to him. They don't talk about you in front of me."

"No, Bob wouldn't. But I thought perhaps your mother would have said something to you, just to complain, if nothing else."

"No, she hasn't. You know, she thinks I'm too childish to understand anything really important."

'Bel's ear picked up the trace of bitterness in Andrea's voice. "Poor Andy. She's afraid, of course, that I'll get Bob to marry me. I don't suppose I could convince her that I don't want to marry Bob or anyone else. But she won't believe that, especially if I said that he's the one that's been trying to get me to agree. He says it would upset all his plans. He says he intends to make a million dollars first, before he settles down to married life. But he'll change all his plans, if I'll just marry him now. He says he can't do without me. He says — oh, he says a lot of things! And he means them. He thinks he does, at any rate. I guess he has been trying to convince your mother that she ought to help him convince me. She probably thinks this is a game I'm playing. I'm playing hard to get — that's the way to nail a man down." 'Bel paused for a moment and then said in a regretful tone of voice, "I expect he has made her hate me."

"Oh, 'Bel, no!"

"Men can be awfully stupid. He ought to realize that the only thing she can think of is to keep me away from him."

They were quiet for a few minutes, listening to the murmur of voices downstairs.

Andrea gave a little sigh. "I wish things were different." She put her hand on 'Bel's arm. It struck her as she did so that this was the first time they had touched in a long while. The invisible cloud between them seemed to lift a little. 'Bel had not in fact gone so far away. "I wish you and I could live the way we want to, that we didn't have to keep our feelings hidden, just because we're girls. We're not important —"

"Unless we're somebody's woman. Andy, I'm so sick of having to pretend that I'm just like all other girls, that I like boys. I don't like them. Most of them disgust me. All they are interested in is the fact that I'm female, somebody they can — lay."

Andrea blushed a little. 'Bel saw it. She said, "That's on Bob's mind, too, but he's different, at least, he's different to me."

"I think he is really in love with you, 'Bel."

'Bel shrugged. "He thinks he is. He'll get over it. Partly he is provoked because he can't have his way. Oh, he's really nice, Andy. He has some ways that remind me of you. But I wish I could convince your mother that I don't want to marry him." She looked at Andrea, half puzzled, half smiling. "Did you think I did?"

Andrea's blush got deeper. " 'Bel, how could I think that?"

"Well, I think you did. You've been having some doubts about me, haven't you? You've been acting a little funny lately. Perhaps it has been my fault. I've been having a hard time, Andy. After all, he's your brother and I didn't want to get you involved, so that your mother would blame you. And I don't really want to hurt him. He does think more of me than most people do. But I can't give him what he wants. I can't make myself love him the way he wants me to. He's got to find somebody else."

She stopped talking and gently put her arm around Andrea, who leaned against her shoulder.

"Have you been wondering why I came here with him tonight? Well, he's been pressing me hard lately — coming to find me at the cafeteria, dogging my footsteps really. Tonight I couldn't stand it any more. If I came here with him, at least you'd be here."

"He hates it when you make me go along with you when he

takes you home!"

"Well, we'll spare him that tonight, Andy. I'm going to stay here. You're going to have to tell your mother I'm staying."

"You mean, sleep here?"

"Yes. Don't you want me to?"

"Oh, 'Bel, yes! But —"

"You'll just have to find the courage to tell her."

Andrea did not answer. She looked at the little bedside clock. It was already ten o'clock. She looked up to meet 'Bel's eyes and then went out of the room to find her mother.

Bob came to the livingroom door when he heard her coming down the stairs. He turned back into the room when he saw that 'Bel was not with her. Andrea went on into the kitchen. Her mother was there, fiddling around with the last-minute preparations for next morning's breakfast.

Andrea said, "Mother, 'Bel is going to spend the night with me."

Her mother looked up at her. She demanded, "Where is she going to sleep? You know that I have been using the little room to store things. We've taken down the bed."

"She can sleep with me, Mother. There's plenty of room." She waited anxiously for her mother's objection.

Her mother said in a very cold voice, "Is it really necessary for her to stay?"

"She doesn't want Bob to have to take her home. You know, he will insist on doing that."

Her mother's eyes suddenly blazed. It was as if she suspected Andrea of taunting her, of showing a knowledge until then carefully hidden from her. Andrea in confusion looked away. It had been the only reason she could think of at the moment to give.

Her mother's voice was still cold. "I should think that was just what she would have preferred."

"Oh, Mother, no!" But her mother had walked away, into the livingroom and she went back upstairs quickly to escape Bob.

In bed with 'Bel finally asleep beside her, Andrea lay awake. This was the first time, since the night of the storm, that 'Bel had slept beside her in her own bed. She realized that this had been an act of defiance, and she knew her mother had recognized it as such. She had been slipping away, as if under cover of her mother's preoccupation with Bob, from the old, indulged, childish companionship with her mother. Tonight's was a step that could not be retraced. Her leaving childhood behind had been delayed, because she had always been sheltered, petted, babied. So of course this conflict with her mother was more difficult. With 'Bel life had inevitably enlarged for her. She knew things, she felt emotions, through 'Bel that she could not have experienced without her. This was what her mother feared, had tried to prevent. But she was no longer simply her mother's little girl, her mother's darling, a white page of innocence.

She no longer felt empty, blank, which is what she now realized had been her state before. Those amorphous yearnings that arose in her when she read books, absorbed the impressions of others, had a focus now, a living, vivid focus that was at the center of her being — 'Bel.

'Bel stirred beside her in sleep, gritting her teeth as if in a worrisome dream. Andrea rolled over towards her and kissed her bare shoulder. 'Bel was instantly awake.

"Andy."

"Were you having a bad dream?"

"I suppose so. I don't remember it. But it was something unpleasant. I wish I could think of something pleasant for a change."

"Well, there's us."

"Yes, there's us — and what are we going to do about us?"

"What can we?"

"Nothing, I suppose. Not now."

They had turned towards each other and lay clasped in each other's arms. They kissed and fondled each other gently until sleep overtook them both.

* * *

There was something about her mother's manner in the next few days that aroused Andrea's suspicion. She was even more tightlipped than she had been. When Andrea came back into the house from an absence of a few hours, she failed to inquire where she had been. There is something brewing, thought Andrea.

At last, one afternoon, as soon as she entered the front door, her mother called to her and she went into the livingroom to find her. Her mother sat at a small desk in the corner, where she kept her household accounts and paid the household bills. The uneasiness that Andrea had felt reached a climax.

Her mother said, "Andrea, you know that school starts in a week's time."

"Yes, I know. I'm all ready."

Her mother hesitated for a moment, as if to emphasize what she was going to say. "However, you're not going back to Western High School. Your father and I have decided that you will be better off in a private school. I am sending you to Miss Harrington's."

So this was it. Andrea recognized Miss Harrington's. It was an exclusive girls' school at the foot of the Blue Ridge Mountains, a school for wealthy girls and the daughters of old Virginia families. Her mother had gone there for a year or so. Wrily she thought, it was a measure of her mother's state of mind that this decision had been made. It would cost her father quite a lot of money and besides, she did not think he liked the idea. He objected to finishing schools. If a girl was to have an education, he said, it should be a good one, in a school where intelligence counted, not the social graces. Her mother could teach her those. If a girl had a good mind, she should be taught to use it, not fritter away her energy in cultivating snobbishness. Andrea judged that her mother must have had some trouble getting her father to agree to this. Probably he only did so because he could never really refuse her mother anything she greatly wanted.

Her mother went on talking but she did not really hear what she said beyond the first announcement. Her mother, noticing her silence, said sharply, "I know this is short notice, but I have finally made up my mind. You have forced me to do this, Andrea."

"I don't want to go away to school, Mother."

"You have more than a year before college. This will give you a chance to get used to living away from home, to get to know other people. I wrote to Miss Harrington and she has just replied. She remembers me and of course she knows my family. She has agreed to take you for the first half year in any case. I have told her that you are a good student, at the top of your class, and that your father intends that you should go on to college. I know you're a little younger than the girls who will be in your class. But she will make allowance for that. You will be on probation, Andrea. You must work hard to justify her leniency and the outlay your father is making. He cannot really afford this."

"But he doesn't have to! I don't want to go there! I'm doing all right at Western. I'll probably be able to get a scholarship to a college next year!"

She saw her mother's lips close into a tight line. A sense of hopelessness swept over her. When her mother looked like that, nothing would budge her.

"The arrangements are made." Her mother paused for a moment and then burst out, "Andrea, you've forced me to do this. I must take you away from bad associations. If you will not obey me, I have no choice."

Andrea said boldly, "You mean 'Bel. Mother, 'Bel is not a bad girl."

"I've told you many times, I have nothing against Isabel herself. At least, I realize what her problems are. She is a clever girl. I sincerely hope that as she gets older she will be able to overcome her handicaps. But in the meantime I cannot risk the damage she may do you. Her mother is a very dubious character. She would never have allowed Isabel to form the sort of associations she has, if she weren't. By now she is altogether too sophisticated for a girl her age."

" 'Bel is all right. She's not what you think, Mother. She hates that sort of thing as much as you do. Please don't think of her like that."

"And what do *you* know about the sort of thing I mean? Can't you realize, Andrea, that already you're not the sweet daughter you've always been?"

Her mother's appealing glance wrung Andrea's heart. She dropped her eyes, and said, "Oh, Mother! I do love you!"

Her mother turned away from her pleading. "Certainly I've had more experience of life than you have. Girls like Isabel are sometimes forced to adopt a mode of life that sets them beyond the pale of society. I don't say that is the case — yet — with Isabel. But she is under pressure to make what she can of her life, and her mother can lead her only to disaster. You know, one thing I very much resent is that she has attempted to inveigle Bob into a relationship with her —"

"Mother, she has not!"

"Don't interrupt me! I've no doubt this is her mother's doing. She seems like that kind of woman. She wants Isabel to get Bob involved with her daughter so that he can be persuaded to marry her. I do not intend for my son to marry under those circumstances."

"It is not 'Bel's fault. It's Bob who seeks her. She wishes he would leave her alone. 'Bel doesn't want to marry anyone."

"Of course she would tell you so. She would not admit that she is trying to attract him. Any man is intrigued by a woman he must pursue, who makes him think she doesn't want him. She is a clever girl. I've always thought so, and Bob is the answer to her present situation. She can escape from her mother, she will not have to work for her living, if she can marry Bob."

"It's not true, it's not true!" Andrea wailed.

They battled back and forth, until her mother, exasperated, brought their argument to an abrupt end.

"I will not argue with you like this, Andrea. You've no experience of the world. Isabel can deceive you very easily. If she had not been able to pull the wool over your eyes, she would never have been able to establish herself so in the midst of our family. Bob would never have noticed her, if you hadn't had her constantly with you. I've tried to persuade you not to see so much of her, but you've disobeyed me all along. I've no alternative to sending you away to school."

"Mother, I don't want to go!"

Her mother said nothing, as if she were waiting for Andrea to say something more. *She wants me to promise that I won't see 'Bel again, that I won't be in touch with her,* flashed through Andrea's mind.

When she did not say this, her mother said, "It's been decided. I've made the arrangements with Miss Harrington." She paused, as if for a moment her determination failed. "Andrea, I did not want to send you away to school. You're a different kind of girl from Deedee. I know you are not interested in boys. I'm very glad you are not. I don't want you to marry till you are older and more mature.

And you know your father would be very much disappointed if you did not pursue some intellectual interest. He is proud of your intelligence. He will be quite willing for you to go in for a career. Neither of us is anxious for you to saddle yourself with a family too soon."

"I could do just as well getting ready for college at Western, Mother." She did not add that Miss Harrington's was hardly the sort of school that laid emphasis on intellectual brilliance.

Her mother caught her implication and answered it obliquely. "Miss Harrington's has access to all the best colleges. Her school is respected. You have forced me to do this, Andrea, against my inclination. I didn't want to send you away from me." There was the slightest falter in her mother's voice. For a moment they seemed to tremble on the brink of a chasm and then Andrea yielded in her mother's arms.

* * *

And that was it, she told 'Bel when they met the next day. Andrea went to the cafeteria at the end of the breakfast hour and sat, with a cup of coffee before her, at a small table in a dark corner where 'Bel could drop into the seat opposite her. She was uneasy at the resigned quietness with which 'Bel listened to her. Lately she had noticed that 'Bel seemed paler than usual and listless, seldom reacting with her normal fieriness to statements or situations that aroused her indignation. She supposed 'Bel must be pretty tired. 'Bel got free meals in the cafeteria but the amount of rest she got was limited. She still did tutoring in the evenings. Earlier in the summer, while she was still working at the roadhouse at night, she had bought a typewriter and sometimes she typed manuscripts for students working on theses and professors writing books. She complained sometimes that she was always sleepy, yet could not sleep well when she went to bed.

'Bel said now, "You mother is acting according to her lights, Andy. Of course, she thinks it's me who is after Bob. The trouble is he is being chased by several other girls she doesn't know anything about. He gives me a hint about that sometimes. I suppose he wants to let me know that I have some competition. As if I give a hoot. Well, when do you leave for this young ladies' finishing school?"

"In two weeks. I'm going to be late for the opening classes but evidently Miss Harrington is quite willing to overlook that. I suppose she doesn't want to turn anybody down these days who has the money to pay the tuition."

"That means we haven't got much time."

"I know."

"I suppose you'll be incarcerated there. That's the idea, isn't it? You'll be under lock and key, safe from me. I didn't know I was that dangerous — first Bob and then you." 'Bel was grinning.

138

"I don't think Mother thinks you're any more dangerous for me than you've always been. She keeps thinking I'll outgrow you — our schoolgirl crush — or mine. It's Bob. That's serious, because he could marry you.'"

"Doesn't she realize that he is going to do just what he likes? Some day he's going to get married and she'll have to like the girl or else."

"Yes, I know. I think Mother knows that, too. But she can't help putting up a fight as long as she can."

"The maternal instinct."

They sat in silence for a while and then 'Bel asked, "How far away is this place?"

"About eighty miles, I guess. You get there by train."

"Holy Jesus," 'Bel murmured.

Again they were silent, each thinking of the distance, the long train ride, the difficulties of time and circumstance, the miles of countryside that would divide them.

"I suppose I can write to you. They won't open your letters, will they, the way they do in a convent?"

"Why, I don't suppose so. But we'd better be careful. How about your mother?"

'Bel pondered. "You'd better write me in care of Aunt Gertrude. She won't say anything but she will know I'm trying to avoid my mother. She may wonder about your writing so often but she'd never think of opening a letter addressed to me."

"She is a sweet old thing."

There was a leaden quality to the days that followed. Andrea already had acquired her clothes for the new school year, but her mother said that, going to Miss Harrington's, there would be other things she would need. So they went shopping. Her opportunities to meet 'Bel were less. When they did meet they were mostly silent, their yearning, their fears, their grief communicated without words.

The day she left, her father took a couple of hours' leave and he and her mother took her to Union Station. She had never been on a train by herself before and the excitement she could not suppress buoyed her through the long wait on the station platform, making conversation. She kept looking down the platform toward the iron grill where the gates were. That was an idle thing to do. By no stretch of the imagination could she think that 'Bel would come to see her off and encounter her parents. Nevertheless, her yearning was so great that her eyes did stray constantly in search of the familiar figure of a tall thin girl in shabby clothes.

The train conductor came at last, to check her ticket and indicate that he was about to take away the train step. She kissed her parents, she tried to listen to their last minute admonitions. On the train platform she paused to wave them a last goodbye. Once more her eyes sought the length of the open, covered platform. She found what she sought, 'Bel, half-hidden by a pillar far down near the ironwork barrier.

* * *

"There is one fortunate thing. Most of the girls share rooms. But because I was late entering, I have a little left-over room to myself. Miss Harrington says to tell my mother that she'll make better arrangements later, but I'm going to see that she doesn't, if it means having a roommate."

- - -

"I've just seen Bob probably for the last time. He invited me to have dinner with him at Harvey's! You know it is about the most expensive place in town. When I said I couldn't, he said I didn't have to be afraid of him. He said he wasn't going to try to take me somewhere to neck in the backseat of his car. I told him I didn't have the kind of clothes people wear to Harvey's. He said that didn't matter either. So I took a chance. I wore that blue dress. It's wearing out under the arms but I wouldn't have to raise my arms. He was a real gentleman all evening. He ignored what I looked like. He told me that he is going to New York. He has decided that he is not getting anywhere — I suppose he means with me, with his mother — and he has had an offer that he doesn't think he should turn down. He says he is coming back one of these days and maybe then he can make me change my mind. I think he means that, if he isn't around all the time, my heart will grow fonder. I tried to let him know that I'm very glad for his sake. Obviously he is really excited about this chance. He must be pretty shrewd to make his way in that sort of business in these days, when everybody talks about the country falling apart."

- - -

"Here it is a whole month since I saw you last, my darling. I've still got my little room and I think I shall keep it, because I've got the reputation of being a bookworm, a grind. The other girls think I'm some sort of a monster. It isn't the kind of school where you are expected to put study ahead of the social graces. Most of them spend their time primping and *all* of them talk *all* the time about boys. They don't talk about sex. In fact, they never mention it. But they talk all around it — about how many boys they know, who they are (that's very important), how awful it would be if a girl gets the reputation of going too far with a boy. It seems if she does, all the other boys know it and begin to take advantage of her. They really don't know what they're talking about because they're so ignorant. They're just mimicking somebody else. You'd be amazed how ignorant they are and yet all they think about is getting married. I think Mother would be really shocked. It's true that Miss Harrington and the teachers are strict. None of us go anywhere without being chaperoned. That's something the girls are

140

always talking about, too — that they can't wait to get married because then they won't have to be chaperoned. Most of them wear lipstick — they put it on surreptitiously, but Miss Harrington won't stand for make-up.

"That's why I'm being left more or less alone. The girls think I'm a hopeless case. One of them asked me the other day, with real curiosity, why I always had my nose in a book. After all, she said, I'm quite pretty. She's sure I could have any number of boys interested in me, if I didn't make such a show of being bookish. Of course, the girls only see boys on the weekend, when Miss Harrington arranges for a dance or they're taken to a nearby boys' school for football games and that sort of thing.

"Some of the teachers take me more seriously. The English teacher says I have a real gift for writing. Miss Harrington evidently takes it for granted that I'm going to get high grades for college entrance exams at the end of this year. I suppose Mother must have told her that she and Dad want me to go to college before I think of marrying, so she doesn't press me to be a social butterfly."

- - -

"I went to see Aunt Gertrude yesterday to pick up your letter. I'm worried about her. She has never really got over the shock of having to move out of her old apartment and sell most of her treasures. She doesn't seem very well. Her skin is beginning to droop on her arms and face. I know she was always too fat. You remember how much difficulty she had getting up out of that big black leather armchair she used to sit in. But now she's losing too much weight too quickly. I'm afraid she will get sick. Almost nobody comes to see her except Mrs. Manley, who drops in now and then.

"My mother is worrying me, too. She has taken to being mysterious about her private life. She goes out in the evening a lot — leaves me to mind Johnny and Sammy. I think she is going with a man. He must be somebody who has a good job. She has mentioned several times lately, apropos of nothing, that after all she was never really married to Mac, thank God, so she doesn't have to worry if he turns up again and she's interested in somebody else. She can show him the door. The first time she said this, I asked her what she meant. She has always said before this that she was married to Mac. But now she says, Oh, no, she just pretended that because of Aunt Gertrude. He wasn't the sort of man she'd *marry*. And so on. I can't figure it out. Of course, if she wasn't married to Mac and now wants to marry somebody else, that means she doesn't have to bother about a divorce. If she had to get a divorce from Mac, she'd have to prove he deserted her and then, here in the District, she'd have to wait five years before she could be married again. I don't see her doing that. If Mac shows up, things are going to get awkward. She hasn't heard from him since he left her in

Baltimore. I guess that means he is riding the rails or living in a Hooverville somewhere. I'm just uneasy about the whole business."

* * *

At Thanksgiving Andrea came home for the first time. Miss Harrington's was not so far away from Washington that she could not have come every weekend. But she guessed her mother's reason for letting her stay at the school instead. Of course, there was the expense. The train fare was just that much more to be spent on this expensive schooling. But the real reason was 'Bel. Now, she supposed, since Bob was in New York and said he would not be coming home until Christmas, her mother thought the way was clear. *She hopes, I expect, that I've been out of touch with 'Bel and have found new interests in school.*

She was surprised at her own self-possession in dealing with her mother. Neither of them spoke 'Bel's name. She would be home for a week and she discovered that her mother had arranged things so that there was always something to do that left her without a stretch of time in which she could go out and find 'Bel. *It's natural, of course, though Andrea, that she wants me to be with her wherever she goes.* As a child she had always tagged after her mother. And without 'Bel she would have found this interlude happy and congenial. She loved her mother. The old pain at having to deceive her, at having to strive against her domination, returned in full force.

On Saturday she announced she would have to go to the Library of Congress. Miss Finley, the history teacher, had assigned her a work paper for the holiday which she needed references for.

"She expects more from me than from the other girls, Mother."

Her mother did not protest but Andrea saw the familiar tightening of her lips and the quick frown.

She paid a brief visit to the Library and then headed downtown to the cafeteria. It was the lunch hour and 'Bel would be at the steam table. They could exchange a few words, enough to arrange a meeting. But when she got to the cafeteria and passed down the serving line there was no 'Bel. She asked the cashier if she knew where 'Bel was, but the woman said she did not recognize who it was Andrea wanted. Maybe the supervisor — She pointed to a door behind her counter.

Gathering up her courage, Andrea went to the door and knocked. There were several voices on the other side and she opened it. Two or three women in the uniform and aprons of the cafeteria turned to look at her.

"May I speak to the supervisor?"

A broad-bodied woman nodded brusquely and said, "What do you want?"

"I'm looking for Isabel Essory. Isn't she here today?"

142

The woman's expression became wary. "No, she's not working here now. She left a couple of days ago."

Andrea stared in surprise. 'Bel's last letter had reached her just before she had left Miss Harrington's and she had said nothing about leaving the cafeteria. The woman, seeing her surprise, said, "I guess you can find her at home."

Andrea demanded, frightened, "Is she sick?"

But the woman's friendliness evaporated. "I don't know anything about it. All I know is she's not working here now."

Andrea retreated out of the door. For a moment she was too shocked to act. Then she ran to the nearest carstop. Too intent on finding 'Bel to think of the usual impediments, she did not consider if she would encounter 'Bel's mother or the younger children. But when she got to the house there was no sign of activity. Most of the people who lived there either worked or were out looking for a job.

'Bel opened the door of the flat when she knocked and, in relief, without thought of whether they would be seen, she tried to hug her.

But 'Bel resisted and pulled away, holding her head to one side. "I can't kiss you. Don't touch me."

Andrea gaped at her and instinctively glanced around.

'Bel said, "No, there's nobody around. That's not it."

Andrea caught her around the waist in spite of her resistance. 'Bel grew passive in her embrace. "What is it, 'Bel. What's the matter? You haven't said anything in your letters. Why aren't you working at the cafeteria?"

"I didn't want to tell you." 'Bel avoided Andrea's eyes but the look on her face was full of misery.

How thin she is, thought Andrea, and terribly pale. There was a pasty whiteness to 'Bel's skin and her eyes were hollow. "Tell me right away."

"They say I've got TB. I've got to go to a sanatarium."

" 'Bel!" Andrea fell back to stare at her.

'Bel burst out furiously. "I can't help it! I didn't know about it! I wouldn't have gone on working there if I'd known! Even if I couldn't get another job!"

"So that's why that woman acted so funny."

'Bel looked at her with burning eyes. "You go away, Andy. My mother's gone to visit Aunt Pearl in North Carolina. She's taken the kids. I'm just staying here till I go to the sanatarium."

"Where is it?"

"Out in Maryland, near Sykesville."

"Were you going to go off and not tell me?"

"No, I wasn't. I didn't know till after I wrote that last letter that the diagnosis was final. They make you take tests when you work in a food place. That's how they found out. I was going to wait till I got there and then write and tell you. I forgot you'd be here for Thanksgiving."

143

The misery in her face banished Andrea's resentment. She tightened her hold on 'Bel's body. " 'Bel, we've got always to let each other know where we are. Otherwise how can we keep together?"

"I know. I — just forgot. I kept thinking of you at Miss Harrington's, so far away."

"Who is going to pay for sending you to the sanatorium?"

"Nobody. It's where they send people from the District who don't have any money."

"Oh, 'Bel!"

"It's all right. Anyway, there isn't anything I can do about it, except —"

"Except what?"

"Well, I suppose I could run away."

"You can't run away, 'Bel. You've got to have treatment."

They stood together for a moment in silence. Then 'Bel suddenly turned into Andrea's arms and put her head on her shoulder and sobbed.

"Oh, 'Bel, 'Bel. It will be all right."

'Bel drew away from her. She had begun to shake, holding her head in her hands. "It's everything, Andy. I'm always in the middle of a mess. If I could just be a good Catholic, like Aunt Gertrude, and accept what comes to me, rely on God to know what He is doing, even if it means I've got to die. I don't know what to do most of the time. If I could have kept my faith, I could have gone into a convent and forgotten about what goes on in the world."

Andrea gasped. " 'Bel, what would have happened to me, then?"

'Bel did not respond.

When Andrea got home that afternoon she said nothing to her mother about 'Bel. At first her reason to herself had been that it would upset her mother very much to hear that she had spent a couple of hours with someone who had TB. But there was an instinctive feeling that underlay this, one that prompted her to bury, so far as her mother was concerned, any reference to 'Bel. Since her mother's decision to send her to Miss Harrington's, a resolution had hardened in her. She must protect this joint existence of 'Bel and herself since it was in danger of being annihilated by her mother's determination to separate them. Her life and 'Bel's were bound together in a way she could not express to anyone. She would permit nothing to destroy that unity.

And now she knew that 'Bel might die. She would not confess that awful fear to anyone. A superstitious dread kept her from voicing it.

* * *

The first two months of 'Bel's stay in the hospital she was on bedrest and not allowed to read or write letters. She had warned

144

Andrea of this, and Andrea, mailing her letters from the little post office in the village near Miss Harrington's, began to have the feeling that she was launching them into a void.

"Of course, Mother knows nothing about your being in the sanatarium. And whenever I mail a letter to you, I take it down to the village post office so that nobody here will notice I'm writing to somebody in a TB hospital. For all I know, Miss Harrington may have a spy in the post office, but I'll just have to take a chance. Anyway, Mother says she has arranged that she and Dad and I are all going to Cincinnati to spend Christmas with Deedee. I can't help feeling a little amused at the lengths she is going to in order that I won't have an opportunity to get in touch with you. I know that's being mean, but, my darling, what else can I do. I feel in my bones that from now on I mustn't even let her know that we're always together, in spirit if not in body. I've felt that way ever since she decided to send me here to keep me away from you.

"She enjoys being with Deedee. I realize now that I'm older that she loves Deedee in a special way. Well, I suppose she loves all three of us in special ways. But in Deedee's case she feels specially close. Deedee was a trial when she was my age, because she was so pretty and so boycrazy. Mother can't complain about me on that score! Deedee has a natural sort of gaiety. I used to think she was just silly, without any brains. That's not really true. I suppose Mother and Dad couldn't have a really brainless child. She just doesn't have any interest in books and ideas. Now she is Mother's ideal daughter.

"I must say her house is a lot more cheerful than ours. Deedee doesn't have any real troubles. She has beautiful babies. Dan, her husband, is a good natured sort of fellow. I've told you that his family is well-to-do and he works in the family business. Evidently he is quite a shrewd businessman. He and Bob are quite alike. He's big, too — was a football hero in college. Bob used to envy and admire him. But he's not secretive like Bob. He's hearty and open and likes big family gatherings.

"Of course, Dad isn't so happy about the whole thing. He'll last three days, I guess, and then he'll want to go home. He hates to leave his own house, anyway. But he never interferes with Mother. So she and I will stay for the whole time, until I have to go back to school.

"Oh, my darling! This is the blackest night there ever was, not even hearing from you! Sometimes I wonder if I'll ever see you again. Perhaps if I had some of your religious feeling, I could console myself a little. I seem to be lost in a sort of desert. Write to me the very soonest you can. Every now and then I wonder if it would be possible for me to telephone to the sanatarium and inquire how you are. But if I tried, it would create a commotion here, I know, and Miss Harrington would tell my mother.

"Oh, write to me, write to me as soon as you can."

- - -

"This is January and this is the very first day they've allowed me to write a letter. Now, instead of being in bed for eight hours during the day, I can get up and move about except for three hours in the morning and three in the afternoon. I go to the dining hall for my meals and after four o'clock I can read and take a walk. This isn't a bad place at all. It's plain, of course, and it has that bare look of institutions. But the grounds are pretty — at least, I'm sure they will be in the spring. And it is blessedly quiet. Send me some writing paper and envelopes and stamps. I don't have anything here and I haven't any money. I gave you all I had been able to save when I saw you last. I want some books, too. And send me a little money, say, ten dollars."

- - -

"I'm sending a parcel off to you at the same time as this letter. Oh, 'Bel, how wonderful to hear from you! You must be getting well fast. How long will you have to stay there? Do you know? Oh, I long so for us to be together!

"You'll be amused about the parcel. The postmistress has noticed that I write to you — or at any rate, to somebody who is in a sanatarium — and now I'm sending you a parcel. So she couldn't refrain from saying something about it. I thought I'd better give her some explanation or her curiosity whould be whetted. So I told her you were a private charity of mine, somebody I had undertaken to correspond with as a cheerer-upper. She was so taken with the idea I'm afraid she'll talk about it and it will get back to Miss Harrington anyway. Oh, well, that's a story I can stick to. A friendship by correspondence sounds pretty safe."

- - -

"The doctors won't commit themselves about how long I'll be in here, I wasn't an advanced case when I came here, so they expect me to recover. But sometimes, they say, appearances deceive. You think you're going to get well and you don't.

"But this isn't a gloomy place. Everybody seems remarkably cheerful. Maybe that's one of the insidious things about this disease. Probably I've got a reputation for being unsociable. There isn't anybody here I can carry on a conversation with. They're goodhearted, a lot of the women here, but they're not much on reading or thinking about impersonal things. The nurses keep trying to cheer me up. They think my frame of mind isn't helping me get well. Of course, they don't understand. They don't know you exist. One of them, a pretty woman, asked me if I have a sweetheart. She has noticed how often I get letters from you. But she thinks you are a man, and she talks about how faithful you must be and how lucky I am. Most men aren't that attentive, she says. When I get out of here, I'll be reunited with you. She means well. I think about all that, too, and then I wonder whether we'll

146

ever be really united. I don't mean in spirit. In body, so that no one can interfere with us. It can't be wicked to love somebody the way I love you. I don't care what any religious person says about it. It can't be wicked.

"This is later. I couldn't go on writing just then. I get so miserable sometimes.

"I was telling you about the people here. They have the women in one building and the men in another. They seem to think that proximity will cause problems. The ambulatory patients can go to a sort of canteen store they have here and some of the women go there just to meet the men. If I had any inclination to that sort of thing, it would be with one of the women or girls. Some of the girls are very young, which is sad, because the younger they are the less likely it is that they will recover. Anyway, they all think I am a real introvert — only that is not the sort of word they'd use. I do prefer being by myself, to think my own thoughts. As far as that goes, this place is real bliss. I can avoid people to a large extent and there is real peace and quiet. And I'm not working all the time. That is something I can't explain to the nurses either. They think I'm moping. Well, sometimes I do feel pretty hopeless and think I might as well end up here as anywhere. Then I think about you, about us, and I'll be damned if I'm going to die in this place."

- - -

"Of course you're going to get well. Please don't think anything else. Oh, my dearest, what would I do without you? You simply must come back to me."

Andrea's face lifted from the paper. The words were confident. They had to be, going to 'Bel in the hospital. But she had a moment of this sudden fear, this absolute negation of hope. It had come to her once before. 'Bel was gone. She would never see 'Bel again, never hear 'Bel's voice, never again look into those wide grey eyes. She knew that in the future — that future that at this moment seemed a total void — she would always be aware of her physical surroundings at the time, as if she were actually there again — the first time, her bedroom at Miss Harrington's, the while chenille bedspread, the desk beside which she stood, and this time, the school bookroom where she sat writing her letter by the window, the winter-brown grass outside, the still leafless trees, black fingers against the cold sky. She roused herself and began writing again.

"You know, everybody here thinks I'm a very cool customer, all brain and no heart, I believe it is called. Even Miss Harrington herself. My mother has told her, I know, that I'm going on to college and some sort of a career. This rather intrigues Miss H, who is no intellectual slouch herself. But it also disconcerts her a little, I think, because she is used to coping with girls who are social butterflies. I think she also has noticed that I'm not interested in boys. She has a very urbane manner when she deals with men — the fathers of her students, for instance, but I don't think she is a spinster by accident. I've an idea that she never really wanted to marry. You know, my mother says any woman can get married, if she isn't too particular.

"There has been a great commotion here the last few days. Two of the girls were caught smoking cigarettes. As a matter of fact, they got them from one of the teachers — Miss Daugherty, who is pretty lively and reminds me a little of your Mademoiselle Bosanquet. There are all kinds of rumors, that Miss Harrington had her on the carpet, not only because of the cigarettes but for other things. It's hard to tell what really happened because these girls here always giggle and talk so much nonsense. If you believed them, you'd think they all had pretty lurid pasts. They talk about Miss Daugherty, how she makes pets of some of them, so that she has a little coterie always following her around, visiting in her room, etc. Anyway, Miss H called a special assembly to talk about the cigarettes — how smoking was not only bad for a girl, it also made her look hard and unladylike. The two girls who were caught aren't being sent home — that was just somebody's invention. They've been given penalties. Apparently nothing is being done about Miss Daugherty. She is a very competent teacher of dancing and drama.

"I wrote about some of this to Mother. She was amused, as I thought she would be. But she did say that she was glad she didn't have to worry about me, that she could always count on my being a lady."

- - -

"You know, if I ever get out of the sanatarium here, I may wind up teaching in a place like your Miss Harrington's. Being a nurse or a teacher seems to be about the only ways of earning a living there are for women with any sort of training. Sometimes I wonder about trying to be a doctor, but I don't think I could ever make it. It would take years. Oh, Andy, I suppose I shall get out of here sometime or other. Don't worry about me. I have to talk to you. I have to tell you how I feel."

- - -

"I wonder about all this sometimes — about you and me and the world. Miss H has her own private library — some shelves in her office — and she said I was welcome to borrow anything that I wanted to. She realizes that the school library is pretty limited. I think she must have forgotten that she has a copy of the *Well of Loneliness* there. Once my mother made a reference to it, as something that shouldn't be talked about. Naturally, I borrowed Miss H's copy and read it. It upset me for quite a while. Why does the author think that way about girls who love girls? Why does she think she has to pretend to be a man? I'm not abnormal physically,

I know I'm not. And I know you're not. Just because you've got small breasts and long legs and broad shoulders — and a brain — doesn't mean that you aren't as much a girl or a woman as I am. Oh, 'Bel, when I think about your body! Sometimes I think I'll go crazy living this sort of shut-up life."

- - -

"Calm down. I've read the *Well of Loneliness*, a long time ago. It made me pretty unhappy. I was eleven years old and I didn't have anybody to talk to about it. My mother would have been hopeless. For a long time I wondered if there was something wrong with me, whether I had everything a girl ought to have, whether I was partly a boy, especially since I had such strong physical feelings. It wasn't till I met you that I knew of any girl who needed to work off her desire the way I did. I realize now that all girls and women do have some of that sort of urge, unless there really is something wrong with them. I used to read everything I could find that talked about it. But most of the things I found called it self-abuse and said it would drive you crazy or make it impossible for you to be happy if you married and you'd probably not have children, that it would use up your strength, and of course, it was a sin. I never did confess to a priest what I did . There was one priest I went to who used to hint about things like that — sex and sexual feelings. I suppose he thought since I was twelve years old, he ought to warn me ahead of time about the dangers of giving in to your bodily urges. I pretended I hadn't the least idea what he was talking about.

"I've learned a lot since we've been together — chiefly, that what people think is all wrong. You're made the same way I am. Before I met you I didn't know whether I was normal or not. I'd never seen another girl naked. I knew my mother had bigger breasts than I did. But I couldn't think about her and Mac together in bed. The idea of that disgusted me. I hated to think of my mother letting a man do that sort of thing to her.

"Good grief! I hope nobody opens this letter, either here or at your end. We'd be sunk."

- - -

"The German teacher here went to New York for a visit over the weekend and she saw a German film there called *Mädchen in Uniform*. I overheard her talking to a couple of the other teachers. They didn't know I was in earshot. I wouldn't have paid any attention except that they were all so furtive about what they were discussing. The film is about a girl in a German school who is very unhappy because of the Prussian discipline and finally commits suicide by jumping down a stairwell. But the thing is, she is in love with the woman who is assistant to the headmistress. She falls in love with her because she is sweet and kind, not like the dragon

149

who runs the school and who makes the kind woman refuse to be kind anymore.

"I heard Miss Bauer say that not on any account was any of them to mention the film to Miss Harrington or say that she, Miss Bauer, had seen it. Because it might get around to the girls here and if the parents learned about it from their daughters, Miss H would be furious. These little dears here have to be protected from any sort of contamination. If their parents only knew what they talk about! Miss Harrington is no fool. *She* knows but blandly ignores it. I catch her looking at me sometimes as if she was speculating about what goes on in my head. But when she sees I've noticed she looks away again at once.

"Oh, 'Bel dearest, I do miss you so, especially when it is lights out and I can't go to sleep for thinking about you. Don't ever doubt how much I love you. Don't ever think of doing anything except getting well and out of that place."

- - -

"This is the middle of May and what are we going to do about writing to each other when you go home for the summer? Of course, you can go on writing to me, but how am I going to write to you? I saw the doctor yesterday and he said that I'm getting along fine but he can't tell yet when I'd be going home. The way he said it I know that he isn't sure yet I'm going to get well but he wants to encourage me. Anyway, it's going to be months, and when I think about it I get pretty unhappy. Going home! He doesn't know what he is talking about. I haven't got a home.

"I've had a letter from Reverend Mother. It is the second one I've had from her. I told you that I did not let her know that I'd been sent here. But she found out, from my mother, who apparently didn't want to tell her anything. But when Reverend Mother makes up her mind, you can't stand in her way. I've been writing to Aunt Gertrude as if I had a job here, without saying it is a TB sanatarium. No use making her even more unhappy. Besides, everybody thinks you've got the plague, if they hear you have TB. Well, they do call it a plague, don't they? The great white plague.

"Well, anyway, I didn't tell Reverend Mother I was coming here and when she found out, she wrote to me saying how unkind it was of me not to let her know. She really does seem fed up with me this time and though I answered and tried to explain why I didn't tell her, I had the feeling that her feelings really were hurt this time and that I wouldn't be hearing from her again. But she has written now to say that Aunt Gertrude is failing a good deal and that soon they'll have to arrange for her to be taken care of in a convalescent home. That means probably in somebody's house, somebody who looks after old people under the supervision of the Sisters. It's too bad she just can't reconcile herself to her changed circumstances, but at least she'll be with devout people and the nuns and that will make her happier."

- - -

"I've been thinking about how I could receive letters from you when I leave Miss Harrington's and go home. The only way I can think of is for you to address me at General Delivery at the main post office — you know, the old place with the tower down on the Avenue and Twelfth Street. Address me as A. Hollins. I'll go and look for a letter every few days. I don't want to get Mother started again on the subject of you.

"It's true. People are terribly afraid of TB. I'm not surprised that Reverend Mother had trouble getting information out of your mother. My mother would really hit the warpath if she knew I was even corresponding with you in a TB hospital. There's a neighbor of ours who has a son who has TB. When I first heard all the horrified whispers I thought he'd committed some awful crime. Poor fellow. It's not his fault.

"The days are dragging along so now. When I look out and see all the beautiful spring weather and the flowering things, I get a dreadful ache for you. Can't the doctor hurry things up?"

- - -

"No, he can't and he says fretting and being impatient isn't going to help me. Yes, it is a beautiful spring. You remember how, about now, we'd be getting ready to play tennis — all those lovely summer days together, out under the trees. I can just taste the sandwiches you used to bring along."

- - -

"Well, here I am back home. Nothing seems to have changed except that Mother and I don't seem to have much to talk about. Oh, she talks about family things and we discuss college, but it is as if we're inventing things to say. I'm even glad when she gets started on the subject of Bob, even though I know it makes her unhappy. At least, it is something that absorbs her and keeps her attention off me. Bob seems to be doing very well in New York. You wouldn't know there was an economic depression to read his letters. He is smart in his own way. He doesn't worry about how other people are affected. He really thinks it must be your own fault if you don't succeed — financially, I mean. But what my mother yearns after is being told the details of his personal life — what kind of a place he lives in, the people he meets, the girls he is interested in. And of course Bob would never tell her all that, especially about the girls.

"I'm sending you a parcel of books. You don't have to hide any of them. They're just things that may keep your mind off the way you feel and so on. That's one good thing about being back home. I can go to the bookstores and get you books. I began to feel as if I was living on a desert island at Miss Harrington's."

- - -

151

"Sometime when you are downtown would you get me some sheet music? There is an old piano here in the dining hall. Somebody donated it. Several of the convalescent patients can play instruments, so I thought I could get up a scratch orchestra. It would help me get through the rest of my stay and maybe some other people, too. I feel as though I'll go crazy otherwise. Everybody was thunderstruck when I came out with this suggestion. It is the only time I ever made an attempt to do something with the other people here. The nurses think I must be cured, that I'm turning over a new leaf. I hope the doctor thinks so, too. Send me some old songs and things — and some Mozart and Beethoven just for me."

- - -

"It is really summer now and hot and humid, the way July always is here. I expect it is nicer where you are, out in the country, among the hills. I'm trying to study, to keep my grades up when autumn comes. Miss Harrington has recommended me for scholarships at several women's colleges, but I don't know yet which ones will offer me one. It will be a help for Dad for me to have a scholarship but I feel a little guilty about displacing somebody who needs the financial help more than I do. Of course, a lot of girls nowadays can't use scholarships that are offered them because they can't afford to keep themselves, when the scholarship only pays tuition.

"By the way, I ought to tell you that there are three hundred dollars in the savings account. Two hundred, of course, is what you gave me to hold for you. The rest I've been saving out of my allowance. Mother gives me four dollars a week, but she expects me to buy clothes and books out of that.

"The papers are all full of the general strike in San Francisco and the truckers' strike in Minneapolis. John Dillinger was killed by Federal agents in Chicago when they tried to arrest him. President Roosevelt's New Deal is making a lot of impact. The NRA has drafted a new code for all businesses in the country. Bob says most of the people he knows are furious about what the President is doing. Bob himself doesn't seem upset. I think that is probably because the stock market is getting active again and he can use his talent for making money. Dad says that naturally the well-to-do people are unhappy because you can't make such massive changes in the economy of a country without affecting their pocketbooks. A lot of people, though, seem to be more hopeful than they've been the last few years. Mrs. Roosevelt is remarkable. She wants to set up reforestation camps for women, to give women jobs in emergency conservation work the same as men. She says she doesn't see why emergency funds shouldn't be used to help women as well as men. Even mother rather likes Mrs. Roosevelt. She says she knows Mrs. Roosevelt is a lady but she hates seeing any woman be too aggressive. Women lose their dignity, she says, if they get too aggressive."

152

"If you didn't tell me wnat is going on, I'd be like Rip Van Winkle when I got out of here. They don't have such things as newspapers and there is only one radio, in the dining hall. Most of the people here, if they pay any attention at all to what's going on outside, are solidly for Roosevelt. He's given them a sort of hopefulness — not that it can make much difference in their personal lives. But they all have relatives who are out of work.

"I wonder what I'll be doing when I get out of here.

"I realize how your mother feels about women being ladies. That's Aunt Gertrude's idea, too. Women should accomplish things without being blatant or making themselves conspicuous. But as long as women go on accepting the sort of things men want to give them, things aren't going to be any different. I've been doing a lot of thinking while I've been in this place. I don't do a lot of talking to the women here but I do a lot of listening. I'm not as deaf, dumb and blind as the nurses think I am. I certainly do get discouraged at the rotten deal most women get in life. What makes me especially fed up is the way most of them just accept it all and go on humoring the men, as if men are the most important creatures who could exist. I simply wouldn't have a man on the terms they settle for. Come to think of it, I wouldn't have a man on any terms.

"I've been putting off telling you. Aunt Gertrude died last week. Reverend Mother wrote to tell me and said she did not suffer, just faded away — wouldn't eat or take an interest in anything. It seems strange that that should happen to a big woman like that. You remember how she used to like rich things to eat and all the German cakes and cookies she made at Christmastime. Well, she just forgot the whole business. She left me five hundred dollars and a few family things — some Meissenware china my greatgreat-grandmother brought from Germany and some silver spoons. What do you suppose I'm going to do with them? She lost everything else — had to sell everything for a song just to live. She did leave a little money to the Sisters for looking after her. Reverend Mother is going to keep the five hundred dollars for me till I get out of here. She knows she has to, or my mother would get her hands on it and spend it in a week.

"Anyhow, there's one thing that's a real improvement. I've been learning how to drive an automobile. Joe, the maintenance man who drives one of the pickup trucks here, has shown me how and now they let me drive down to Sykesville to get the mail when he's busy doing something else."

- - -

"It is now settled that I'm going to Goucher College in Baltimore. I had three scholarships offered me but Goucher is the closest and that is what mother wants. It seems to be so important to her to have me within reach. I can't bring myself to fight with her about it. It's a pity, because the other two scholarships were for more money. This one will cover my tuition and class materials only. Dad will have to pay my board and lodging. This is too bad. He sends money every month to his brother's widow. My Uncle Arthur died last spring, Mother says from a broken heart because he lost his business, which he had spent a lifetime building up. I've heard some remarks she and my father have made, that sound as if he committed suicide, how, I don't know. This is another drain on Dad's income.

"Do you have any idea now when you will be able to leave the sanatarium? I'm supposed to report in to Goucher just after Labor Day — that's September 4. Mother, of course, will go with me for the day. I have nightmares about not being able to get your letters."

- - -

"Glory Hallelujah! I've just seen the doctor and he says I'm cured! Andy, just think of it! I haven't dared really believe that they would ever let me out of here for fear that it wouldn't happen. I'm to be discharged at the end of August. Andy! Andy! Andy!"

- - -

"But how are we going to meet, 'Bel? Are you coming back to Washington and on what day? Oh, how I wish we could talk on the telephone at least instead of writing this way! I feel so uneasy."

- - -

"I'm leaving here August 31. That's two weeks from now. You won't be going to Baltimore till after Labor Day. Andy, I don't know when the bus will get to Washington. The people here have told me that the social worker who arranged for me to come here will try to help me get a job. In the meantime, I can go and stay at the Evangeline, at government expense. That's a hostel for girls run by the Salvation Army. It doesn't cost very much. It is located on I Street, across from Franklin Park, at Fourteenth Street. That is where I'll be when I get to Washington. I suppose you can find it in the telephone book, so you can call me.

"I'm so excited I'm leaving things out. Yesterday I had a letter from my mother. She said I would have to make some other living arrangement. I couldn't go back there. I was wondering when she was going to say this. She is scared to death of TB and she doesn't want me around, even if the doctor says I'm completely cured. The counsellor they have here had warned me about that. She said I was going to encounter this sort of response from anyone who knew I had been in a TB sanatarium. People, even members of my own family, would avoid me.

"But there is something more in my mother's attitude. She said in her letter that she had given up the flat. Johnny and Sammy are down in North Carolina with Aunt Pearl. They are going to stay there for the time being, because she is going to

Atlanta to live. She has met a perfectly marvelous man who has asked her to marry him and she is so happy. It must be the man she was seeing before I came here. What I figure out is that she has landed some poor fish who has a good job or some money and she doesn't want me around. She probably hasn't told him anything about Mac. She will have to own up to the boys sooner or later. Perhaps this fellow knows about them already. She probably has told him some fanciful story that puts her in a romantic light.

"So I'm in a mess, as usual. I don't have a place to live and I don't have a job. I'm really scared, Andy, about how I'm going to deal with people when I get back outside. Being here for nine months, with a lot of people who are all in the same boat with me, has undermined my self-confidence. I didn't realize that till the counsellor began warning me about what to expect when I get out on my own again. One thing I know: I'm going to need some money."

* * *

Andrea put the note away in her handbag. That was the safest place for anything she received from 'Bel. Her mother would not come upon it there. She sat in her room for a while, thinking, methodically, dispassionately, about how she was to meet 'Bel. It was some time now since her mother had made any reference to 'Bel. Months ago, in fact. At that time she had asked, greatly wishing to seem casual but betraying her suspicion in every line of her face, "Do you ever hear from Isabel?" Andrea had said, "She has written me several times. She is not in Washington any longer." And her mother had said, "Oh? I suppose her mother has moved away and taken her with her." Andrea had said nothing.

I wish, Andrea thought now, I could do without all this hiding. But even as she thought this, the stronger feeling took possession of her that her bond with 'Bel must remain hidden. Very often she felt that some sort of disaster lay across the path of 'Bel's and her life together, that some sort of trap would close on them, destroying them. She knew that such a deep instinctive fear was something no one else save 'Bel would guess that she would harbor. She knew what she looked like from the outside — a quiet girl, a matter-of-fact sort of person, emotionally low-keyed. Even her mother had been surprised at the strength of her attachment to 'Bel and had attributed it to 'Bel's unsettling influence.

Now she was aware that her dealings with her mother had reached another phase. Her mother had accepted the fact that she was no longer the tractable, docile girl she had hitherto been, without a firm conviction of her own. Her mother recognized her as a person, someone for whom she was still responsible, someone she could still control, but only to a degree. The question of 'Bel had not come up between them all summer. Her mother doubtless thought that 'Bel had left Washington for good and that she had

155

ceased to write, since no letters came from her to the house.

That made it much easier, thought Andrea, for her to go and come without being questioned. It made it possible for her to go to meet 'Bel at the place and time she arranged.

She went first to the bank and drew a hundred dollars from the savings account. Theoretically, the teller should have required her to get her mother's signature. But the bank was a small local branch where she and her parents were known and the teller ignored the requirement. He did make a comment about the size of the withdrawal, but she said easily that she was getting ready to go away to college and needed the money to buy clothes.

From a pay telephone in a drugstore she called the Salvation Army hostel and asked for Miss Essory. There was a long wait while the reception clerk looked through files and then she was told that Miss Essory was not expected to arrive until the evening. So she left her name but no phone number. The message would tell 'Bel that she had received her letter and was prepared to come.

Because she could not say to her mother that she was going out at seven o'clock in the evening. Her new freedom of action did not extend that far. She spent an uneasy afternoon and evening and a sleepless night.

The next morning, as early as seemed feasible, she told her mother she was going to the Library. Whenever she said this, it was tacitly accepted between them that she would be gone the better part of the day. She left the house still in the grip of the sense of remoteness from her surroundings that had held her since the day before, when she knew that 'Bel was once more within her reach.

The woman at the desk at the hostel said, "Number 62" when she asked for 'Bel. The elevator took her to the sixth floor and by the time she stepped out 'Bel stood in front of her. Instinctively they moved towards each other and then stopped. Another woman stood there, waiting to board the elevator. Andrea stepped aside to let her pass and sedately they walked side by side to the door that said 62.   Once inside, for a long moment they clung together. It is really 'Bel, thought Andrea. I feel her heart pounding. I feel her breath, fast and hoarse, against my neck.

"Andy." 'Bel released her and moved away a step or two. Andrea, seeing her clearly for the first time, was astonished. The 'Bel she saw now was a well-filled out woman, not the gangling, half-starved girl she had known for so long. 'Bel wore her hair a little shorter. Her grey eyes looked out with the old directness from under her long lashes. Her smile was the same wide smile that had come so seldom to her face before.

Andrea seized hold of her again, feeling the firm flesh where there had always been prominent ribs. She said with a little laugh, aware that she was half-intimated by this new maturity, " 'Bel, you're so much bigger."

"I'm not fat!"

"No, of course not. But you were always so scrawny. My mother was always talking about it. They gave you enough to eat, anyway."

"Yes. When I began to get better, the country air and the exercise gave me a good appetite, and there was plenty of food. Now I've got to get a job to pay for my meals."

She reached over and grabbed Andrea around the waist again. Andrea, with the habit of disguise, involuntarily drew back.

"What's the matter? Are you afraid of me?" 'Bel stared at her in anger.

"Of course not. It's just habit. You jumped when I touched you first."

"That's just habit, too, I guess. I haven't touched anybody since I saw you last. In a place like that, you get used to staying away from people. But we don't have to be afraid here. The door is locked and no one out there can see us." She pointed out of the window to the green expanse of the park.

They stood together, their arms around each other, looking out of the window.

"It's been so long, 'Bel."

"If you think so, how about me? I used to think sometimes you couldn't go on loving me, not the way I love you. Because there were so many things you had and I only had you."

" 'Bel, you couldn't really doubt me."

"You get funny ideas when you're marooned like that, away from everybody and everything, among a lot of people you don't know and can't talk to. Nobody there had any idea what I really was, what I was really feeling, how I was longing for you. If they had known, they would have ostracized me. They would have said I was perverted. The funny thing is some of the women really did develop soft feelings for some of the other women. Several times some woman or other would try to be extra friendly with me. But, you know, Andy, they hadn't any idea what they wanted. They'd talk a lot about the men. There's a superstition that TB makes men more lustful. Well, I think maybe some of the women reacted that way, too, but nobody would ever mention such a thing. There's this business of women not wanting sex, unless they're nymphomaniacs and then they are a menace to everyone. The women would pretend that it was just the men who were anxious to meet them down at the canteen, when as a matter of fact they'd all think about the same thing."

" 'Bel, I've been very lonely for you. You must know that."

"Andy, sometimes, when I first went there, I'd be kind of beside myself, wanting you. Doing it to myself didn't really help. I got so unhappy thinking about you — I suppose, when I first got there, I didn't think I was ever going to get out. I certainly didn't think I'd be there months and months. I thought it would be all over much sooner. And then I began to realize that it might go on for a long time, that I might be in there for years. There are some people there who never really get well, enough to be released, but who don't die, either. I began to think maybe I would be one of those, never get out, never see you again, that after a while you'd be bound to grow away from me, since you would be living in the real world. I used to read and reread and reread your letters. I got so I began to read all kinds of meanings into what you said, things I know you never meant. If you didn't say 'my dearest, my darling' as often as you usually did, I thought that meant you were getting cold —"

" 'Bel, that couldn't be!"

"I know. Now I know. It sounds like nonsense now. Kiss me again, Andy. I'm not dangerous any more."

They caught each other in a frantic grip. Then simultaneously they began to take each other's clothes off. To Andrea, 'Bel's purposeful hands brought a deep relaxation. She shivered as 'Bel's fingers ran down her spine, over her bottom. Under her own hands she could feel 'Bel's firm muscles tense, her skin grow taut.

For a moment they stood naked facing each other, a strange shyness suddenly posessing them. The long months of separation stood between them, full of the fantasies each had conjured up in the effort to quell the ache of loneliness. Obliquely they eyed each other, gazing at each other's body. How strong and tall and straight she is, thought Andrea, eyeing 'Bel's broad shoulders and small, inviting breasts, flat stomach, prominent hipbones, long, firm thighs. She felt the weight of 'Bel's gaze on her own body, feasting on the sight of her own full breasts with their upright nipples, her small waist, the silky curly hair at her pubis.

Then they did look fully into each other's eyes and with a sigh moved into each other's embrace. The full impact of 'Bel flooded Andrea. Even in the concentrated longing of her nights alone when 'Bel was far away she had not been able to recapture the strength, the warmth, the aliveness of 'Bel's body against her own, the thrust of 'Bel herself into her own consciousness.

They lay down on the bed turned towards one another. She felt 'Bel's eager fingers searching between her legs, felt her own desire leap forward to meet that eagerness, overflow. How pale, how barren, how shallow had been the effect of her own efforts, alone without 'Bel, to assuage the hot fire that the remembered image of 'Bel had conjured up. As the concentric circles of feeling died down, she marveled at the completeness of release that 'Bel's caresses brought her. Still clasped in 'Bel's arms, she sank, she wallowed in the sea of 'Bel's love.

She lay looking up into 'Bel's eyes, as 'Bel raised herself on one elbow and looked down at her. Their faces were close together. They could feel each other's breath.

Andrea said, "Sometimes I would be so overcome with thinking about you that I'd come just by myself in bed, in the dark, as if I was trying to find you, reach you by main force."

"I could never do that. I thought I was drying up. Oh, Andy, try me, quick!"

She felt 'Bel's body throbbing under her touch. 'Bel's tender pink membranes swam with moisture. Almost instantly 'Bel's body arched against her, 'Bel's strong arms clutched her in a grip that felt like steel. Once, twice, three times 'Bel came to a climax, scarcely relaxing between each wave of consummated desire.

They lay together, limp, panting a little.

" 'I don't think you have to worry about that now." Andrea's voice was a little shaky.

'Bel rolled over on her back and looked at the ceiling. 'I used to think sometimes that I had imagined you and what you did to me. I couldn't imagine anyone else that close to me. I know, it sounds like nonsense now. Hug me again, Andy. Just hold me."

They rolled together again in the bed and after a while sleep overtook them.

When Andrea drifted awake it was with a sense of luxury. The underlying anxiety of the long months of separation had dissolved. She knew at once that 'Bel lay close beside her. She was surprised at having slept so soundly, without dreams that she could remember.

'Bel stirred, made a little moaning noise and opened her eyes. Andrea, looking down into them, saw a fleeting distress.

"What's the matter?"

'Bel sat up without speaking and looked around the room.

"You're here, 'Bel, with me."

"Yes. I'm not out there anymore. I can't believe it."

She drew her knees up and clasped her arms around them and laid her head on them. "I've been wanting this so much, wanting to be able to leave there and come and be with you. I couldn't think of anything else. And when the time began to get short, I began to think of all the things that could go wrong and prevent me. The doctor was going to say that he'd made a mistake, I wasn't cured. I couldn't leave. And if I managed to get away, then you wouldn't be here. Your mother would have taken you away somewhere. Or she wouldn't let you see me and you didn't really love me. You were just being kind to me while I was sick and now that I was well and was coming back, you'd avoid me, you wouldn't want to be saddled with me and all my problems —"

" 'Bel, what nonsense! How could I love you any more than I do?"

'Bel gave her a long look. "You do love me, don't you, Andy?"

" 'Bel, 'Bel."

They clasped each other and kissed. 'Bel said, "When you're off by yourself that way you begin to doubt things. You begin to wonder if you've been deceiving yourself. How could anyone go on loving you when you're so far away, when you never saw her or talked to her?"

"You didn't stop loving me, did you?"

"Oh, Andy, I loved you more every day!"

"So why should you think that I'd stop loving you?"

"I guess it was silly. I am not a very lucky person, Andy. I could not believe my luck in finding you and having you love me. That's why I got so apprehensive when it came time to leave. I kept thinking of all the disasters that could happen to me — if the bus had an accident, if something happened to you. And if after all I got here and you did get my letter and you were able to come and meet me here and stay with me for a while and we were able to make love, then —"

As 'Bel's pause lengthened Andrea asked impatiently, "Then what?"

She saw the old sly smile on 'Bel's face, the mischievous light in her eyes. "I'd be checked in or you'd be checked in."

Andrea burst into a laugh. "We'd have done it anyway, silly."

"I don't think you would have wanted to, Miss Fussy."

They grinned at each other and then 'Bel said, "As a matter of fact, I suppose what put that idea into my head was that I had some cramps on the way here. Just nervousness, I guess."

"Well, you see, none of all that happened."

'Bel swung her long legs off the bed. She was about to stand up when Andrea's cry stopped her.

" 'Bel!"

She turned in surprise to look at Andrea and followed her gaze to the small red stain on the bedsheet. Hysterically, uncontrollably they burst into wild laughter.

* * *

'Bel said, pulling on her stockings, "The trouble is, I don't know where to begin. I do know I've got to get a job right away."

"I thought the people at the sanatarium had given you some leads."

"They told me about some of the new government programs for young people. They said there would be help for women as well as men. But, Andy, I want to go to college. I'm behind already. I've lost a whole year."

"How about the money Aunt Gertrude left you?"

"I've thought about that. If I pick the right place, that can pay my tuition, and then I could get a job to cover my board and lodging. The counsellor was talking to me about the University of Maryland. She said that the Federal Government is giving grants to colleges to pay students who work on projects for them."

"Why, 'Bel, that sounds fine!"

"Yes, but I don't know how to go about all that."

Andrea watched her downcast face as she brooded for a while. She yearned to be able to say, "I can get my father to help you. He probably knows all about those new government programs. He has some young interns working on government grants in his laboratory now." But she knew it was impossible. It was impossible for her to admit at home that she and 'Bel were in touch with each other again.

'Bel said, "The first thing I've got to do is see Reverend Mother and ask her when I can have the money."

"You don't think she will help you get a scholarship? Has she really changed her mind?

"Do you mean, has she really washed her hands of me? No, not exactly. She isn't as eager to help me as she used to be. She lets me know that she has reservations about me now, that she finds a lot in me to disapprove of. But if I asked her, she would' help me."

"Well, then —?"

'Bel was combing her hair. "Don't you see, Andy, I'd have to go to a Catholic school. I'd have to toe the line as a good little Catholic girl. It would be the Convent all over again."

"Would that be so bad?"

'Bel switched around to look her in the eye. "Don't you see what that would mean? It would be the end of us."

"Would it have to be?"

"Yes. I'm not that much of a hypocrite. I used to think I could be one thing on the outside and another on the inside. But I can't any more. It's not even just that, Andy. I can't accept the idea that what you mean to me is sinful, that what we've just done together is a mortal sin that will destroy my soul. That is what Reverend Mother would think if she knew about it. If I go back into her fold, I'd have to convince myself that she was right and that all the people I was among are right. I would have to obey without questioning. Andy, I'll always question. It's built into me and it seems to me that God must have made me that way. And He must have made you for me to love and to love me."

She grew more vehement as she spoke. Andrea saw the familiar frown on her face, the angry brilliance of her eyes. 'Bel, she thought, was never handsomer than when she was aroused like this. 'Bel's glance took in for a brief moment the little half smile on Andrea's face.

"Don't grin at me like that! This isn't something funny!"

"I'm not laughing at you!"

"You think I'm just talking! You do think I just get off on these tangents. You think I've learned how to be sly and underhanded and pretend anything I need to, to get what I want. Andy, I used to do that sort of thing. I can't any more. Don't you see —"

"I don't think anything of the kind! 'Bel, I wasn't grinning at *you*! I wasn't really thinking about what you were saying. I was just looking at you and thinking how handsome you are now and how I love you —"

"You're just saying that to get out of it! What if I do accept help

161

from Reverend Mother and go off and be a good Catholic and leave you to go to hell by yourself, just so long as I save my own soul —"

Anger flamed in Andrea's face. "Are you threatening me? If that's what you'd prefer, by all means go and do it!"

They faced each other, panting, glaring at each other in fury. They spoke at the same time.

"I'm tired of being told I don't understand, that I haven't a moral value to my name, that you have so much more to give up for me than I have for you —"

"You never understand what it means to be caught in between things the way I am, trying to believe something I've been taught, something I don't want to believe, not knowing if I'm really wrong when I think I'm right, whether I ought to get out of your life before I mess it up the way I mess up my own —"

They both stopped and the anger in their faces turned into horrified fear. Andrea put her hand on 'Bel's arm.

" 'Bel, I didn't mean —"

'Bel stood rigid and speechless.

" 'Bel, please, we can't quarrel now."

'Bel's eyes had filled with tears. "Andy, I'm in such a quandary. Maybe your mother is right. I shouldn't let you stay involved with me. You should go on and live the kind of life she wants you to. I can't be just a friend. I'd have to cut away altogether."

Some of her anger returned to Andrea. "No one, not even Mother, can tell me what I ought to do. 'Bel, if you leave me, I'll never believe in anyone or anything again. You're everything to me, 'Bel. if you think there is something more important than the two of us, you will shatter something that can never be remade in me. What kind of life can I live without you? You say, the kind my mother wants me to live. I suppose you mean for me to go and be like Deedee, marry a man and have children. That is what she'd say if you asked her. But what she really wants is for me to stay by her side for the rest of her life. She thinks that books and abstract ideas can supply anything I need, that I haven't got the kind of emotional needs that would demand anything else. 'Bel, I'd dry up like a sponge without water. I can't be just me, in isolation. 'Bel, you're the only one who will ever break my solitude. If Mother only could understand. She'd have me for life, if she'd allow me to have you. I would never desert her. And I'd stay alive because of you."

She knew she had spoken more vehemently than even 'Bel had ever heard before. 'Bel stood looking at her with wide eyes.

" 'Bel, I've never thought you selfish. I've loved you for a lot of things — because you don't count the cost of things, because you do such reckless things just to prove yourself, because you're always reaching for something bigger than you are. But chiefly I love you because you're you. Don't you understand what you mean to me?"

'Bel's head had dropped and her shoulders sagged. "Sometimes, when I'm away from you, I begin to think you can't really love me, that you just want to be kind and don't know how to extricate yourself without being hardhearted."

Andrea said impatiently, " 'Bel, you've just been away from me too long. You've been brooding there in the sanatarium. Let's forget all that. What we've got to think of is how you're going to go to college. First of all, you've got to go and see Reverend Mother about Aunt Gertrude's money."

'Bel was gnawing her lip. "I've got to tell her that I must be on my own. She'll know what that means. I'm deserting my faith. That's how she will see it." She looked up at Andrea with a sudden return of spirit. "But I'm not! I haven't lost my faith in God. I still believe there are things I must do and things I must not. But I can't believe that God would deny me the one thing in life that makes everything else worthwhile. I don't believe that it is wicked for me to love you. I couldn't love you the way I do if I didn't believe it was right!"

Andrea gave a little sigh. "I don't know anything about a life of self-denial. I don't think that's the way anyone should go. It seems to me it is placing too great a value on yourself — taking it upon yourself to cast away the riches you've been given, instead of using them to a good end. But I realize that many religious people don't feel that way — nuns, for instance. Oh, I know. They are supposed to give up worldly things for the more important things to come hereafter. But if you don't feel that way — you don't feel that way, do you, 'Bel? Sometimes I wonder, because you can be so intense, you can be so single-minded."

'Bel said slowly, "I've wondered sometimes if it wouldn't be a lot easier. It would resolve everything for me. I wouldn't have to be always questioning myself. It would be so much easier than struggling along by myself. I would just have to accept what I am told I must believe."

In the small silence that followed Andrea said, " 'Bel?"

" I couldn't do it, Andy." 'Bel's voice was now firm. "I know it is a mirage. I would not be any more settled than I am now. And I'd die, somehow — I mean, within myself — something in me would have to die, if I gave you up. I would not be me anymore. I don't think God demands that."

"Well, then, you'll just have to tell Reverend Mother."

'Bel nodded thoughtfully. "There are a lot of things I can't accept any more. I'm just not obedient enough. I've got to think things out my own way. So I'll have to tell her I don't want to go to a Catholic college and that means no scholarship, at least as far as she is concerned."

"You'll have to use Aunt Gertrude's money, then."

'Bel hesitated before she spoke. "If she will give it to me. You know, I'm a minor. She could hold onto it till I'm of age. And she might think that's what she ought to do."

"Well, we'll just have to find somewhere you can go and get a big enough scholarship to cover everything. But remember, 'Bel, I'll be in Baltimore and I know that my mother expects me to come home every weekend."

"Then it's got to be somewhere nearby."

"I can help you, 'Bel. I'm going to get a bigger allowance. I've brought you a hundred dollars now."

"I'm going to need that, Andy, right now."

* * *

It was almost dark by the time Andrea got home and her mother commented on the fact.

"You must be careful, Andrea, when you are in Baltimore. I don't want you to be out alone after dark. I've been assured that the College doesn't permit its students to be out in the evenings unless there is a play or a concert to which a group of you will go, or you have special permission. That means if you go out for an engagement of your own, you must let them know where you are going and with whom, and you must be back by a certain hour."

Andrea, who had read carefully the printed admonitions that the College sent new students, nodded. In some way she would have to find loopholes in this new net her mother had cast over her.

The next day was Friday and as her mother pointed out, the last day they could go shopping for the last minute things she would need. They toured the downtown stores, examining satin-lined envelopes to hold her stockings, garter belts for evening wear, sewing kits, the things for her dressingtable. Her basic wardrobe had already been acquired. Her mother had seen to that. In spite of her absent thoughts, Andrea noted her mother's attention to these more frivolous things. Obviously her mother was intent upon providing her with the things that among the girls she was going to live with were considered desirable and important.

They lunched in the tea room of one of the big department stores, eating chicken salad in french pastry cups, surrounded by middle-aged or elderly women, some accompanied by daughters likewise on their way to boarding school or college. What was 'Bel doing now, she wondered? Had she had her interview with Reverend Mother or was she still waiting, on tenterhooks, in the Convent parlor?

She tried to be attentive, to think of things to talk about, to respond promptly to her mother's comments. But her mother noticed her preoccupation, caught her gazing absentmindedly out of the big plate glass window at the people in the street below.

"Dear, are you apprehensive about Goucher? Are you worried about something?"

Andrea brought her gaze abruptly back to their table. She met her mother's eyes, as blue as her own, and saw the slight frown on her face.

"Oh, no! Oh, of course, I'm a little excited. I don't know just

164

what to expect. You know, they said I was to have a roommate. I wonder what she will be like."

"Yes, there are some new things you'll have to get used to. But Miss Harrington's, probably, was a good experience for you in that way. You got used to living with girls your own age. There is one thing, though, that concerns me a little. You know, Andrea, you will be more on your own. I realize that you are going to mingle with some girls who are much bolder than you are, who are more used to going with young men. You will have to use your own judgment, dear. And do remember what I have always told you, that if you don't respect yourself, no one else will. That is especially true as regards young men. If you allow a man to treat you without respect, or act so that other people will think that you do, you will lose their respect, too. It is all too easy for a girl to lose her reputation in dealing with men. You've never been placed in any situation where you had to think much about this. But do remember that now you will have to foresee situations for yourself. I'll not be there to point them out to you."

"Yes, Mother."

"Do be careful about the people you associate with. I know a lot is said nowadays about young women having greater freedom. I'm glad to see some of it. I am glad that girls can choose when and if they marry or want to follow some career. Getting married isn't everything. In the past few women had a choice. But you do. You have a wonderful future ahead of you, if you want a career. Your father and I are very proud of you. So take care and don't get yourself involved in some situation that would spoil everything, something you would regret in the future."

She can't, thought Andrea, she just can't, come out and say to me in so many words, Don't go getting involved with the first man that comes along. I suppose if I did and got pregnant, she'd see me through. I know she would. She would never desert me or turn me out of the house. But I'd shatter something for her if I did.

Aloud Andrea said, "I don't think you'd need worry about that sort of thing, Mother. You know, most of the girls at Miss Harrington's couldn't think of anything else but it didn't bother me. Don't worry about me."

The thought of 'Bel crossed her mind. She glanced at her mother out of the corner of her eye, but her mother had reached for her handbag and was looking at the check the waitress had handed her.

It was the next day, at a moment when she was absorbed in her own thoughts, that her mother suddenly said, "Andrea, did you draw a hundred dollars out of your savings account last Wednesday?"

Andrea looked up to see that her mother held a letter in her hand. The postman had dropped the mail through the slot in the front door just a few minutes before.

She felt cold with apprehension as she said, "Why, yes. The teller said I could, that he knew me and it was all right."

"Well, I don't mind you doing that. But Mr. Connelly, the vice-president at this branch, has written to say that they need my signature for their records. However, I'm very surprised. What did you want the money for?"

"Oh, some books and records I wanted to take with me. I really didn't think you'd object, Mother."

"I can't imagine what you would spend a hundred dollars on. That's a large amount of money. Andrea, you mustn't be extravagant. Even with your scholarship this is a great burden for your father."

And you've been very generous with me, thought Andrea, remembering the shopping expeditions to buy her an outfit. Anything within reason I wanted you'd get me.

"I'm sorry, Mother. I guess all this has rather gone to my head." She smiled, hoping to cajole her mother. As a little girl she had always succeeded in winning her mother's forgiveness by cuddling up to her. It made her a little sick now to find herself still able to do this, to cover a deceit she had never practiced as a child.

III
1934-1935

In the middle of the following week Andrea and her mother took the train for Baltimore. There had been no further opportunity to meet 'Bel. So as they went through the formalities of getting her registered and settled with her things in her room, she fretted. On the surface she practiced maintaining a bland surface. She had learned this at Miss Harrington's and it stood her in good stead now. Her mother noticed nothing except the nervousness that naturally came from embarking on a new venture. She sighed with relief when the train from New York came into the station and her mother boarded for the trip back to Washington. There was a group of girls arriving on it, obviously headed for Goucher, and their commotion covered her last few minutes with her mother.

For the first day or so she was too occupied with the establishment of a routine to have much time for wondering about 'Bel, except at night with the lights out. Her new roommate was from another part of the country and too excited at first with the novelty of her surroundings to pay much attention to Andrea.

She had had to leave the problem of communication to 'Bel. 'Bel knew where she was. Presumably 'Bel would write. Each day she dropped in twice, once in the morning and again in the afternoon, to the office where mail was received. There was no letter from 'Bel before she had to leave on Friday evening to catch the train for Washington.

She spent a fretful weekend at home. She tried to keep up a cheerful manner with her parents, to answer with enthusiasm her father's questions about her teachers and the methods they used and her mother's chiefly unspoken inquiries about the new social world into which she had stepped. By Saturday evening she was suffering from a mixture of exhaustion and frustration. She suspected that her mother saw through her efforts to hide the unhappiness that lay underneath. She was grateful that she said nothing. Probably she interpreted it as the strain of coping with new demands and expected it to pass as Andrea grew more used to her new life.

There was a note from 'Bel on Monday morning. It said simply, "Can you meet me at the Enoch Pratt Library at noon on Tuesday, near the front door? I'll be there. If you don't come, I'll know you couldn't."

Andrea thought quickly of her class schedule. If she sat at the

167

back of the classroom, she could escape before the period was quite over. It was Miss Pierson's class on mediaeval history and Miss Pierson paid little attention to the students who were not vitally interested in the subject.

When she got to the library she saw 'Bel standing at the bottom of the steps. 'Bel saw her at the same time. Soberly they walked to meet each other. There was no one on the street close enough to see the light in 'Bel's eyes nor notice Andrea's breathless eagerness.

"Gosh! I was wondering if you could make it. At least they don't keep you locked up in the daytime."

"No. I'm supposed to eat in the dining room but perhaps I won't be missed. It's only lunchtime. They'll probably not notice. We're all supposed to be present for dinner."

"I've got a lot to tell you."

"Well, where can we go? We can't talk in the library."

Andrea saw a funny smile appear on 'Bel's face. 'Bel pointed. "See that?"

An old model-T Ford stood at the curb near them. Andrea stared. "Is that yours?"

"Yes. I bought it for twenty-five dollars. I had to spend some money on tires. If it won't start, I have to crank it. You know, I've learned how to service it. You needn't be afraid to ride in it."

'Bel's gaiety reached Andrea. "Where can we go?"

"Out to Druid Hill Park. It will only take a few minutes and no one will see us there."

They found an empty stretch of road in the Park and 'Bel pulled over to the curb. Then 'Bel said, ·

I'm going to the University of Maryland. I was a little late enrolling but I can make it up. My first year's tuition is paid."

"Did you get Aunt Gertrude's money?"

"No. Her estate has to be probated. But Reverend Mother persuaded the lawyers to advance enough money for my tuition. She was reluctant but she did it. I have to earn my board and lodging. I'm living in the dormitory and paying my rent by working in the Registrar's Office. I can get my meals by working in the cafeteria. I've got to get some other jobs to earn money to put away. I could do typing for people if I had a typewriter."

"We'd better buy you one, 'Bel."

"All right. Where's the cash?" She was grinning as she held out her hand.

A fleeting memory of her mother's questioning about the hundred dollars went through Andrea's mind. "I'll get it. How much would you need?"

"I guess I could find a secondhand one for fifteen dollars. But there is something else, Andy. We've got to work out how we are going to communicate. I can drive here to Baltimore from College Park in less than an hour. But I have to know where I can meet you."

"And when, 'Bel. I don't have very much unsupervised time. Oh, it isn't as bad as Miss Harrington's. There they never let you out of their sight. But I can't be cutting classes too often or be absent from the campus for hours at a time. It would be noticed if I did that regularly."

They were both thoughtfully silent. Finally Andrea sighed. "We'll just have to pick our opportunities, 'Bel."

'Bel looked at her sidewise. "You don't think your mother would let me come home with you on weekends sometimes?"

"It's not a question of her letting you. I haven't spoken of you for more than a year now. I don't want her to know that I still see you. She hasn't forgotten you, but she doesn't mention you. I want her to go on thinking I've outgrown you."

'Bel laughed, and then asked seriously, "Do you think she knew what we did back there, when I used to come to your house?"

"I think she recognized what she saw but she didn't acknowledge it. She just decided to put a stop to it."

"Just like that." Andrea heard the note of bitterness in 'Bel's voice. "People don't give any importance to the way girls feel about one another, do they? They say it is a phase. If they are kind, they say it is a normal stage in growing up. I've been reading Freud. According to him, we've failed to mature. We're stuck in childhood."

"Is that what you believe?"

"Of course not. I don't feel like a child when I love you. Perhaps some girls do have crushes when they're growing up and then forget about them later on. And some women go on having crushes, like schoolgirls. But that's not you and me. Is it? Or one of these days are you going to say to me, this is all over. It's been nice while it lasted, but I'm going to get married and have children."

'Bel's eyes were dancing as she spoke but the anger in Andrea's face stopped her.

Andrea burst out. " 'Bel, I won't put up with you talking like that any more. Why do you needle me that way? If one of us is going to give up the other, it won't be me. It's you who have the real doubts."

"You mean, because I've agonized over whether I'm losing my immortal soul? You needn't worry about that any more. If I've got an immortal soul, you own it. Andy, I'm just trying to be funny. We're in such an awful hole. We can't see each other, talk to each other when we want to, tell anybody we love each other, because somebody is always watching us. What I really want to know is, does your mother really suspect us or does she simply not like me? If she doesn't really know, we could just act like good friends. You're bound to get to know other girls at Goucher. I could just be one of those you take home with you for a visit occasionally."

Andrea shook her head. "I don't know about Mother. She is so

169

suspicious that sometimes I wonder if she ever felt something like this for another girl when she was young. She is certain you're bad for me. She thinks I'm easily deceived and could be led into some mortal danger without knowing it. She thinks you're a very clever girl but your morals have been ruined. She'd do anything to keep you away from me. I won't risk it, 'Bel."

"I see. I'm the rotten apple that will spoil the barrel. I suppose sometime or other we'll be able to do what we want, but it won't be for a while. You've got to be older."

"I'm seventeen."

"That's four years before you're of age."

"Yes."

* * *

Without the old car they wondered what they would have done. With it they managed to meet several times a week, away from the College. Their meetings were brief. Andrea, careful not to call attention to herself by any unusual behavior, did not stay out long enough to be missed. 'Bel, with three or four jobs besides the two that earned her board and lodging, had few opportunities to spend more than one or two idle hours. There were a good many nooks and corners of Baltimore, they found, where they would not be seen and recognized. Wrapped in their own private world, they hugged to themselves these moments of privacy.

Thanksgiving was almost upon them when they realized that it meant a separation of a week.

"I'm not going anywhere. Dad isn't feeling well and Mother says we'll stay home. What are you doing, 'Bel? Doesn't everybody leave where you are?"

"Oh, they won't lock me out of the dormitory. But I'll have to scrounge my food. Unless I go and visit Aunt Pearl in North Carolina."

"Do you mean that seriously?"

'Bel shrugged. "I don't know. I didn't think of it till just now."

"Well, why would you? Your mother is not there, is she?"

"No. She's in Atlanta. I guess it is because I had a letter from Aunt Pearl the other day. She wrote to me because she just had to complain about my mother to somebody. She said that Ethel Mae — that's what she calls my mother — had come to get the boys to take them to Atlanta, where she is now living as Mrs. Lemuel Watkins, the wife of a prosperous local businessman. That's Aunt Pearl's description. She knows my mother is ashamed of her — always has been, except when she was down and out and need Aunt Pearl as a refuge."

"She's taken the boys?"

"Aunt Pearl says that my mother told her that her new husband wants to adopt them. He's considerably older than she is and he hasn't any children of his own, though he's a widower. That's a lucky break for the kids. He seems to be a kind man — a little stupid when it comes to a woman like my mother. I wonder what would happen if I turned up in Atlanta and introduced myself."

The trace of malice in her voice caught Andrea's ear. "You wouldn't really do that, 'Bel. Do you mean that your mother hasn't told him about you?"

"I'm sure she hasn't. Aunt Pearl went on about that at some length. My mother wants to bury all that part of her life — my father and me. She has fabricated a new past for herself. Probably she has made out that she is younger than she really is. She has probably told him that she is just an innocent little thing who was taken in by a man who deserted her. Well, that's Mac, of course. I wonder how she explained Mac's disappearance. I wouldn't put it past her to have told him that Mac married her under false pretences, that she found out he was already married. How could she own up to me, under those circumstances?"

"You think she would deliberately invent all that?"

"Wouldn't she? My mother can tell lies more easily than the truth. Life is always more colorful the way she tells it. I guess she started out telling him a pack of lies and then when she saw she had him seriously interested she had to invent some more for consistency. Aunt Pearl is fed up with her."

"She ought to know your mother by now. She is her older sister, isn't she?"

"By twenty years. Aunt Pearl really brought my mother up. That's what galls her now — my mother's ingratitude. You see, Aunt Pearl wants me to come and see her because she wants somebody to sympathize with her. She tells me how cruel it is of my mother to deny me, her legitimate child, and claim her bastards in my place. She ends up by quoting the Bible — Aunt Pearl is fond of quoting the Bible, it seems to give her real satisfaction: Knowest thou not that the triumphing of the wicked is short and the joy of the hypocrite but for a moment? I think King Lear is more appropriate: Sharper than a serpent's tooth it is to have a thankless child. But Aunt Pearl doesn't read Shakespeare."

"Oh dear, 'Bel!"

"Yes, oh dear. You know the kind of family I have, Andy. No, I'm not going to visit Aunt Pearl. I can stand my own miseries but I can't face listening to hers for several days on end." 'Bel paused for a moment and then added, "I'll just try to forget the whole bunch of them."

* * *

Andrea, getting dressed in the morning, was conscious of the other girl's eyes on her back. During their first two months of sharing a room, Andrea had maintained a certain reserve, avoiding any sort of intimacy, not even telling Carola much about her parents. Andrea, covertly scrutinizing the other girl, recognized

171

her as shy and nervous. Carola was almost eighteen but this was the first time she had ever been away from home. She was a moderately pretty girl, with brown eyes and fine dark hair and a skin that still broke out once a month just before her period. She did not confess this fact to Andrea, who observed it for herself. The first few nights she spent at Goucher Andrea could hear her crying softly in bed, homesick. She did not make friends easily and Andrea early saw the symptoms: she would try to cling to Andrea, as her shield and mentor.

Undoubtedly Carola was the clinging type, the kind of girl who accepted without question the demands of her parents, the school regulations, the dictates of anyone who appeared to be in authority. I suppose, thought Andrea, in due couse she will marry, hopefully a man who would prove a safe refuge from the world's problems. One afternoon, when they were alone in their room, Carola had burst out into a petulant complaint, of having to be there, of having to study subjects she found no interest in, of having to live among a lot of strangers.

"Why did you come to college, then?" Andrea asked.

It was her family's idea, said Carola. Oh, she supposed she would like it all right, when she got used to it. Her parents wanted her to have a wider background before she got married. It was really her aunt's idea. She had an aunt who ran her own business — a store that specialized in babies' things. The aunt thought a few years in an Eastern college would give her more self-confidence.

"Maybe she is right," Carola admitted. "I ought to be grateful. But just now I'm miserable."

"Oh, you'll get over that. How about joining the glee club? Do you like music? There is a lot of music here in Baltimore."

"I've had piano lessons. I could try. Are you going to join?"

Andrea shook her head. "I'm a listener, not a player."

Carefully she steered Carola away into activities she herself did not join in. In the few hours they spent awake together in their own room she imitated Carola's physical modesty. She never initiated any talk on personal subjects. If Carola repeated gossip about girls who evaded the college regulations — who found ways to go out with boys alone, who risked their reputations by being interested in sex — she listened but did not respond. Carola quickly got used to her reticence and took it for granted. If she had problems of her own, she brought them to Andrea. In spite of herself, Andrea realized wrily, Carola has found a rock on which to rest when the lively waters of college life swirled around her.

Once or twice she took Carola home for a weekend. Her mother fitted up the little back room again as a guest bedroom. Without openly acknowledging this even to herself, Andrea knew that she had seized this opportunity to create a smokescreen for herself and 'Bel. She was amused by her mother's opinion of Carola.

"She is a very nice girl, Andrea. I'm glad you have someone

like that to share your room. I did worry that you might find yourself sharing with someone who was too interested in boys. She seems very well behaved. I do wonder, though, why she wants to go to college. Her parents are well-to-do, aren't they? That's probably the reason."

Lately Andrea had caught Carola watching her, noticing when she came into the room with a letter in her hand, commenting when she returned after a few stolen hours with 'Bel. I'm going to have to be more careful, thought Andrea. I've just assumed she had too many things to do that kept her interested so that she wouldn't notice what I'm doing.

Now, with real stealth she turned around as she buttoned her blouse and looked at Carola sidelong.

Carola said, "Are you going to the movies tonight? There's a bunch of us going to see Edward Robinson and Mary Astor in *The Little Giant*."

Andrea shook her head. "No. There's a student string quartet recital at the Peabody."

"Who's going with you?"

"I don't know. Nobody, I guess."

"You know you are not supposed to go out after dark by yourself."

"I don't think I'll be by myself and besides, the Peabody Institute is just a couple of blocks away."

Carola did not say anything else, but Andrea, finishing her dressing, carried with her to breakfast the feel of danger. It had been a mistake for her to discount Carola's opportunities to observe the details of her daily life. It behooved her to find out, if she could, how much Carola had learned from watching her.

She was going to the recital, of course, because of 'Bel. The string quartet was a scratch group made up of young musicians who had obtained grants from the federal government to continue musical training and the Peabody had lent its auditorium. 'Bel had found out she was eligible for this program and tonight she would be the pianist. After the recital they would have an hour together before 'Bel drove back to College Park.

Andrea was late getting to the auditorium and slipped as unobtrusively as she could into a back row seat. The light on the stage showed her 'Bel completely absorbed in the Mozart G Minor quartet. Another girl was playing the violin and two young men were the violist and 'cellist. Andrea's eyes dwelt on 'Bel's face with love, as absorbed in her contemplation as 'Bel was in the music.

Afterwards, when the evening's rapture had begun to fade, 'Bel noticed her preoccupation.

"What's the matter, Andy?"

"Nothing, really."

"That means you really are worrying about something."

"Yes."

173

'Bel cocked an eye at her sidewise. They stood together in a corner of the reception room, a little away from the table of refreshments that had been provided for the musicians and their friends. They were surrounded by people talking volubly about music.

"Why don't I drive you back to Goucher?"

"No!"

"Well, you don't have to be so positive. What's up, Andy?"

"I'm uneasy about people watching us."

"You always are."

"I have to be. You know it."

"Oh, all right! Don't be so touchy. What's bothering you now?"

Andrea, irritated, saw the light of the happiness generated by the music still in her face and softened. "It's Carola, my roommate. I think she has noticed that I seem to be always going to meet somebody who is not at Goucher."

"Dear me. I shouldn't think she'd suspect you of having a sweetheart on the premises."

"Shut up!"

Her angry eyes sobered 'Bel. "What do you want to do, then?"

"Nothing, I suppose. I'll just have to find out how much she has noticed. And we shouldn't meet like this, so close to the College. It was just chance that there was no one here tonight that knew me."

"You know, there's no law that says you can't have friends who don't go to Goucher. And you know also that there are town girls who go there as day students."

" 'Bel, I've told you. It's because you're so different from anybody else. People can't avoid noticing you."

"How am I so different? Is it written all over my face that I'm from the other side of the tracks, that —"

"Now, don't get your back up. No. You're not the kind of person people ignore. I've tried to pretend I'm as ordinary as possible. But if I'm seen with you, everybody will want to know who you are. It will get around the college, Carola will hear about it and she'll tell my mother. Don't you see? It is a simple as that."

"You shouldn't have taken her home with you. I don't like that anyway."

"Well, she is too far from home to see her family often. I did it so that my mother would think I'm just making a lot of ordinary friends."

"It has probably just reminded her of me. All right, where do we meet and when, next time?"

"It has to be in the daytime and away from around here. Carola can't follow me around all day."

"Are you allowed to use the library at Johns Hopkins, at Homewood? I am. I'm boning up for my biology midterm. I can be there in the afternoons. Maybe you can be there at the same time."

* * *

174

The chilly late Saturday afternoon was grey and still. They stood on the ramparts of Fort McHenry and stared at the colorless December sky and the expanse of dark harbor water. Christmas was upon them and the prospect of two weeks' separation.

"Where are you going to be, 'Bel? Don't they close up the dormitory? Anyway, it won't be heated."

"Yes, but I've made an arrangement with the Botany Department. They've got greenhouses that have to be maintained even if everybody has gone home. I'm going to be the nursemaid for their tropical darlings and they'll let me sleep in a room in the superintendent's house. They've never had a girl do this before but I convinced them. Last year they had a boy from the Agricultural School and he passed out on bootleg hooch one cold night and the greenhouse froze."

"Will I be able to reach you?"

"You think you'll be able to telephone?"

"Whenever I can get away from the house. I suppose it is a long distance call to College Park but it can't cost very much."

"There's a telephone in the office next to the main greenhouse. I can do my studying there."

"All right. I'll try."

They fell back into their silent gazing. Then 'Bel said, "I can't help remembering Aunt Gertrude when it comes to Christmas. She always brought out all those sentimental German ornaments. You remember what a big Christmas tree she always had and all those elaborate balls and stars? And the big Christmas triptik that stood on the mantel all through Advent, with a door or a window to open for each day until Christmas."

Andrea took hold of her hand. "Never mind, 'Bel. One day we'll not be separated like this. You'll have all the Christmas trees you want."

'Bel's laugh broke in the middle. "I don't want a Christmas tree! That's a lot of nonsense. It was always so sentimental and — ugh! I can't find a word for it, unless it's stuffy, hidebound, making a fetish out of an illusion. That's what tradition chiefly is. No, I'm just reminded of Aunt Gertrude and how she meant to be kind. She never understood me or what I wanted and she would have disowned me if she knew half of it. But she was a kind old thing."

"I know, 'Bel. I do wish you didn't have to be off by yourself like this at Christmas, just the same."

"Oh, I'll be all right! I'll spend my time reading up on Karl Marx and dialectical materialism. That's my assignment for political history. 'The history of all hitherto existing societies is the history of class struggle.' Nobody says anything about women struggling. Andy, do you realize that women are practically invisible in history? Oh, I know, there are a few exceptions — Helen of Troy, Eleanor of Aquitaine, Joan of Arc and Queen Elizabeth. Whoever hears of anybody else? You just can't make me believe

175

that women have never been anything but handmaidens to men. There must have been women with talents and ideas down through the ages but nobody ever gave them a chance. You know, you can't argue about this even now with most people."

"My parents don't think that way. There must be other enlightened people in the world."

"Oh, I suppose there must, or else the world would grind to a halt. You know, it's twice as hard for me to get a job as it is for a boy my age. When I apply for one — unless it's something like being a waitress — they say there're so many men out of work, they are not hiring women. Women apparently don't have to eat or have some mysterious way of providing for themselves — by battening on a man, I suppose they'd say. And of course they ignore the fact that women very often have children and everybody knows the men just walk out and leave when the going gets tough. You know, Andy, I'd like to join one of these labor groups that are protesting our economic system. I feel like a fool just going along taking all this nonsense at face value."

Andrea tightened her hold on 'Bel's hand. "Not now, 'Bel. Not now. Please finish college first. You've got enough obstacles to overcome without going after windmills. Promise me, 'Bel, you won't jeopardize what you've achieved so far."

"Little Miss Cautious." But 'Bel's tone was fond as she put her other hand over Andrea's.

In fact, they saw nothing of each other until almost the middle of January. The old car, 'Bel told Andrea when they talked on the phone as soon as Andrea was back in Baltimore, had given up the ghost. Without it she was marooned.

"I've got to get another car, Andy. I can't get around to all the jobs I'm doing without it."

"How much do you need?"

"I think I can get a good 1930 Chevrolet for fifty dollars. Somebody here wants to sell it."

"I'll send you a money order. I brought fifty dollars with me. I told mother I didn't like being here penniless when all sorts of little expenses keep cropping up, like books I can't borrow or going with a bunch to the movies."

"That will clean you out."

"Not quite. I've got ten dollars left over from a Christmas present."

"All right. I'll see if I can make the deal."

A week later they arranged to meet on the Hopkins campus. Andrea, standing in the lee of the library building, saw the car come slowly along the narrow drive and ran to meet it.

"How do you like it?" 'Bel was grinning with pleasure.

Andrea glanced around at the interior of the sedan. "It has a lot more room and the seats are softer."

"And it won't leave me sitting on Route 1 out in the country in the middle of the night."

Andrea stared at her. " 'Bel, what have you got on?"

"Not exactly the attire for calling on a young lady at Goucher, is it?" 'Bel's eyes sparkled as she looked at Andrea. "Overalls and boots. I was working in the greenhouses and I didn't have time to change before coming to meet you. I didn't think you'd pretend you didn't know me. I've told you, they've kept me on as odd job man. I get my room and breakfast and some pocket money. I like it better than office work."

"You're not back in the dormitory?"

"No. Part of the job is getting up at night and checking the heat gauges. You've no idea how pampered some of those little botanical darlings are. They're running experiments on several plants. I'm learning a lot I never knew."

"That doesn't leave you much time for sleep."

"Oh, I get enough. Who wants to spend time sleeping, anyway?"

It was a terrible winter, through January and well into February. Often 'Bel was prevented from driving the distance between College Park and Baltimore by snow and ice on the road. When she did come she wore her overalls under her winter coat and the rubber boots. They were a good deal warmer than a dress and stockings, she told Andrea. In the dark cold evenings they went to the movies, seeking in the stuffy warmth a place where they could be together out of sight of other people.

"This is costing you something, Andy." They were sitting in the lobby of the theater after the early show, squeezing out of the evening the last few minutes of companionship.

"I'd rather spend the money this way."

"But you said you had only ten dollars left after you paid for the car."

"No. Something else occurred to me. I told Mother that I'd like to keep the fifty dollars as an emergency fund, so would she continue my allowance. She said she thought that was a good idea. So in theory that fifty dollars is in my drawer in my room under my stockings. 'Bel, I'm worried about you driving back so late. It's so cold, down to zero. You could have trouble with the car."

"Not as long as it starts."

"Do you have any money with you?"

"About five dollars. Enough for extra gas or something like that. Besides, remember, I bought a heater for the car and it works fine."

"Yes, I know. But can't you be suffocated if the car is closed up?"

"Good grief! Only if there's something wrong with the manifold. Andy, you're getting to be a regular Calamity Jane. Nothing is going to happen to me. Now you've got me jittery about the car. Let's go and see if it will start."

177

They left the theater and walked down the side street to where the car stood under a street lamp. Andrea stood jigging up and down to keep herself from freezing while 'Bel unlocked the car door.

'Bel laughed and leaned forward impulsively to kiss her. Andrea's gaze, beyond 'Bel's shoulder, lit upon several people coming in a group to the corner of the street, where they stood talking and gesticulating.

'Bel," she said urgently, "get into the car, quick!"

With only a slight hesitation 'Bel obeyed. Andrea jumped in after her.

"What's that all about?"

"A bunch of girls from Goucher must have been in that movie. They're trying to get a cab now."

"So what do we do?"

"Just sit here for a while. I think Carola was one of them"

"She couldn't have seen us."

"I don't know. They were all looking for a cab. Probably she wouldn't recognize me at that distance. She wouldn't expect to see me with anyone in your outfit." Andrea looked down at 'Bel's overalls, visible in the light from the streetlamp that came through the windshield.

"Now, don't worry about it!" 'Bel's voice was annoyed. "Have they got a cab?"

"Yes, they've gone."

"All right, then. I'm going to see if the motor will turn over." The car started without difficulty. They sat in it for a while longer, until Andrea said, "It's almost nine thirty. I'll have trouble getting in after ten o'clock."

"I'll take you to the corner, Andy. Nobody is going to see you getting out of the car there."

When they reached the corner of the street where the blank brick wall of the College cut off the view of the surrounding houses, they kissed and 'Bel got out of the car with Andrea. She stood beside it and watched Andrea walk down the length of the snowy block and up the school steps.

In the weeks that followed, from February into March, the weather at last grew milder and several times they were able to meet and drive to some country spot for an hour or so's visit. But Andrea noticed that 'Bel was unable to shake off the bad cold she had caught during the severe weather and that she was lethargic, always about to drop off to sleep.

It was a mild afternoon with a watery sun and they were sitting by the dam at Ellicott Mills. This time 'Bel had fallen asleep, her head on Andrea's shoulder. Andrea, conscious of the precious weight, sat still, thinking. She had not told 'Bel the consequences of that last evening out at the movies. The next day she had had a summons to the Dean's office. At once alarmed she had entered warily and confronted the woman who sat behind the desk. The Dean had been very mild in her manner, as if she mistrusted the situation she had to deal with. She had been informed, she said, that Andrea was making a habit of breaking the College rules concerning absence from the premises. It had been reported to her that Andrea often went out alone during the day without explaining the reason or saying where she was going. But especially bad was the fact that she went out in the evenings more often than the rules allowed and that on frequent occasions she did not return before lights out. These rules, the Dean pointed out, were meant for the benefit of the students. They were there to study and prepare themselves for a degree. If they allowed too many distractions, they could not maintain the standard of excellence required of them. Especially was this true of a scholarship student.

Andrea said, "My grades haven't suffered. Nobody has complained of either my classroom work or my term papers."

"That may be true," said the Dean. "But it is my duty to see that it does not happen. No student can maintain a high average without diligence. Then you don't deny that you have been out often in infraction of the rules?"

Andrea, casting about in her mind for an excuse, said no. But very often she went to the Enoch Pratt and to Hopkins to study in the library. She did not always remember to say where she was going. She was not wasting her time.

"But that does not account for those evening absences, Andrea. I'm going to be frank with you, because you don't strike me as being the sort of girl who is careless either with your work or about your reputation. It has been suggested to me that you have been seeing a man on these evening absences. Now, don't get upset. Of course, this information comes to me at third hand, so I don't give it much value. However, since we feel responsible to your parents while you are under our supervision, I must warn you that this is a serious matter. I mean, it is a serious matter that such a rumor should circulate about you."

"It's not true." Andrea stared directly at the Dean.

The Dean shrugged. "I'm quite willing to accept your denial. I did not think you were the kind of girl who would do that sort of thing. However, I must warn you that you must not go out again in the evening, unless you go with someone else from the College or with a group. I realize that we do have town girls here as day students and no doubt some of you make friends who have families living in Baltimore." She paused as if to see whether Andrea would accept this suggested explanation. But Andrea had not responded and the interview came to an end.

Now, sitting in the car with 'Bel asleep on her shoulder, her mind went once more over the question of the source of the Dean's information. Immediately the glimpse of the group of girls stand-

179

ing at the street corner gesturing for a cab came up before her. Carola had been one of them. Carola was the one girl in the best position to notice her comings and goings. She had underestimated the degree of Carola's interest in her affairs. They were friendly, companionable, as much so as Andrea had dared allow, hypersensitive as she was to the emotional yearning under the surface of Carola's amiability. Her mother had commented more than once on Carola's devotion. "You must not let her get too attached to you, Andrea. It would not be kind." Was Carola the shadow of 'Bel in her mother's mind, she wondered?

But Andrea found herself drawing back from the idea of treachery on Carola's part. It was a pretty dreadful thing, to accuse you of doing something deceitful, of informing on you out of malice. Could it be possible that Carola, resentful of the definite limits that Andrea placed on their intimacy, had revenged herself that way? Sometimes, in the days following the interview, Andrea had been convinced that Carola was guilty. But when she next saw Carola, the girl's apparent good temper made her doubt again. After all, there had been several girls in that group.

And whether it was Carola or another girl, how many times had she been seen with 'Bel? The business about it being a man — that was obvious. 'Bel was tall and in overalls and boots, seen at a distance and in a poor light, could be mistaken for a young man. She did not want to tell 'Bel about this. She would have to worry through the problem by herself.

'Bel woke and sat up. "How long have I been asleep?"

"Half an hour, maybe."

"What a waste of time! Why didn't you wake me up?"

"If you don't get enough sleep at night, you've got to make it up some other time. 'Bel, you've got to give up that job. You can't stand this business of getting up every three hours to check the gauges."

'Bel yawned. "You overlook the fact that they pay me ten dollars a month to do it."

"You'll just have to earn ten dollars some other way."

"That's more easily said than done. Besides, I doubt that they'd keep me as odd-job man in the greenhouses if I said I wouldn't do the night duty. And that job is twenty-five dollars a month for a couple of hours a day."

Andrea was silent for a few moments.

"What are you thinking about now?"

" 'Bel, you know, my parents give me twenty-five dollars a month as an allowance."

"Yes, I know. You're a filthy plutocrat. Do you realize that girls work in Woolworth's for fifteen dollars a week, ten hours a day? And they think they're lucky to have jobs."

"Don't get on your soapbox. The fact that I get twenty-five dollars a month allowance doesn't affect them one way or another. As far as I know, my parents don't own stock in Woolworth's. But

180

pay attention, 'Bel. If I give you half my allowance, you can go back to sleeping in the dormitory and get some other jobs typing and tutoring."

"I hate to give up the money. And how are you going to manage? Your mother is going to find out you're not doing or buying the things you're supposed to use your allowance for."

"She doesn't have to find out. We'll just not go to the movies or spend money other ways. There're ways."

"I don't like the idea. I don't like using so much of your money."

"It's our money."

"It's your parents'."

"It's mine after they give it to me."

"I still don't want to take it."

" 'Bel, if you keep on working at night like this, you'll be sick. You must not get so that you have to go back to the sanatarium." She hesitated to say it, knowing 'Bel to be very sensitive on the subject. She had kept the threat as a last resort.

'Bel flared up. "I'm completely cured. They said so. I'm not going to have a relapse."

"You can get sick again."

"Only if I pick up TB again from somebody who's got it."

"And how do you know you won't, if you're run down and have no resistance?"

'Bel was silent, glowering out at the Patapsco River flowing silently by them in its gorge.

" 'Bel, don't make things harder."

As if she had heard some new note in the tone of Andrea's voice, 'Bel turned quickly to look at her. "Is there something wrong, Andy?"

"No. I just get so tired of always having to disguise what I'm doing — always pretending about something or other. It would be wonderful if I could just be me."

'Bel's mouth tightened. "All right. I'll give up the greenhouse job."

"Then you can give up wearing those overalls and boots."

"Don't you like them?"

"Do you?"

"Yes. For two reasons. One, they're comfortable. Two, it saves me a lot of trouble with men. You know, at first, the men on the work force made a lot of jokes about me. They tried to catch me in odd corners and force themselves against me. They wouldn't try rape — at least, they didn't get that far. I'm pretty strong and I can run and I'm quick at noticing when I'm in a dangerous spot, without witnesses. You know, they're the kind of fellows that think a girl like me is asking for it. But after the novelty wore off they left me alone. They forgot I was a girl and it was the overalls and boots that did it. And it worked with other men, too, when I was driving home at night and had to stop for gas. They thought I was a boy.

181

Didn't give me a second look."

"Please be careful, 'Bel."

In place of the greenhouse job 'Bel found some tutoring to do. There were refugees beginning to arrive in Baltimore, she told Andrea, professional and intellectual people escaping from Hitler and the Nazis. Most of them knew English but some of them knew it only as a written language, not as a live tongue. She had been recommended as a coach by some friends she had made at Hopkins.

"They're interesting people, Andy. They like to talk about ideas and music and psychology, what makes human beings act the way they do. I think it is pretty dreadful that such people should be driven out of their homes and denied the means of earning their living, just because they're Jewish or are opposed to totalitarianism. And worse than that, even — be imprisoned and killed for their beliefs or just because they had Jewish ancestors."

"I think Hitler and his crew will rue the day. Dad says they're driving all the best brains out of Germany."

'There's one woman I'm coaching, she is the wife of a professor in the University of Berlin. She is much younger than he is. She has been trained in the social sciences. She is very intelligent — not doctrinaire like a lot of them." 'Bel paused for a moment. "Andy, that could have been my situation — I mean, if my father's people hadn't left Germany way back yonder."

"What do you mean, 'Bel?"

"She is only one-eighth Jewish. One of her greatgrandparents was a Jew. That makes her an outcast in her own country. I'm very glad Aunt Gertrude is no longer living. She'd be so unhappy. You know, Andy, the Great War was a bad time for her. There was all that nonsense about not playing Beethoven's music, for instance. And all those atrocity stories — Aunt Gertrude used to cry over them even years later, when I got old enough to understand what she was talking about. As if a war, any kind of a war, isn't an atrocity in itself. But now — It makes me sick, Andy, to look at the newsreels showing all those grinning young men dressed up in armbands and shiny boots, burning books in bonfires or painting swastikas on synagogues and beating people in the streets."

"Of course, 'Bel. There is something dreadful in just witnessing somebody else's humiliation, especially when it's done with physical violence. But what do you mean, 'Bel, when you say you could have been this German woman?"

"I guess I never told you. I suppose it's one of the things I kept buried under my Catholicism. Aunt Gertrude's mother — my greatgrandmother — was a Jewess. She was a convert to Catholicism. She joined the church to marry my greatgrandfather. It cost her her share of the family inheritance. So I'm like Frau Gutermann. She says there are a lot of Germans with Jewish ancestors who succeed in hiding the fact. But her husband is Jewish and she does not intend to desert him. That's another thing, Andy. This business of applauding somebody for putting some abstract non-sense like racial pride or religious dogma ahead of all other commitments, to yourself or someone you love. That's just the sort of thing men think up, to justify the things they do, like going to war. You know I am a pacifist. I'm against war. It never solves anything. It merely wrecks human lives. Armies and battles are just games for little boys who never grow up. But I am beginning to wonder about letting fascism take over the world."

" 'Bel, you're all wound up. Have you been arguing with somebody?"

"Oh, there is a bunch of us in my year in college who get into arguments every time we're in the same room — mostly the political science majors and some of the pre-law-school students. We've got all varieties. Some even call themselves reds — communists. I think they are pretty callow. I don't think they know what the real thing is. They've been going off to join picket lines at some of the strikes — in Pittsburgh and New York. I feel like joining them sometimes. But I don't have even enough time to do all the studying I should."

"Well, you forget that sort of thing for the time being. You could find yourself in jail or in the hospital."

"Yes. But people do have to learn that the world needs changes. Do you know that there are some people who are calling Mrs. Roosevelt a communist because she wants to start a program for young people? She doesn't think we're all loafers, just a lot of undisciplined idlers who could get jobs if we tried. Therefore, she is a communist. I don't know where people get such ideas anyhow. Everybody I know is trying to do at least two or three things just to be able to eat and go to school."

* * *

When Easter came Carola, after vacillating for some time, suddenly decided that she would go home for the holiday, after all, as her parents expected.

So on Saturday Andrea found herself alone on the streetcar riding home from Union Station. She was a self-composed young woman, her blonde hair caught back from her face in a clasp, her clear blue eyes gazing steadily about at her surroundings. The day had turned suddenly warm and she had taken off her jacket and held it folded neatly on her lap. Her white blouse accented her fresh youthfulness. She was aware of the glances of the other passengers. She was used to that sort of attention. Her transparent skin and delicate coloring always drew people's eyes. She ignored the glances. The thought flashed through her mind, I'm Mother's true daughter. One doesn't notice strangers.

'Bel had said to her once more, "You still don't want to try and see if your mother will accept me?". Andrea had said No. No, her mother would reject 'Bel again and this time more completely than before. Because this time it would be altogether apparent to her

183

what Andrea and 'Bel were to each other. This time there could not be the easy excuse that they were children, uncertain nubile girls groping their way into maturity. It was all bound up, thought Andrea, in her mother's attitude towards sexual desire. Her mother had made it clear to her that the sexual act was disgusting. As far as a woman was concerned, it was an act of submission to the male appetite and could be made endurable only as a means to satisfy a husband or obtain children. That a woman should seek pleasure in sexual indulgence was a shameful thing not to be tolerated. If she felt so, then to let her know that physical ecstasy was part of the bond between 'Bel and herself would be to invite disaster. Her mother would never accept that. And Andrea was mortally afraid that her mother's sixth sense would instantly penetrate any disguise she and 'Bel might contrive.

What did her mother really think about love? Had it always to be something disembodied, never given physical expression? That could not be true. Andrea knew that she loved her husband. Between her father and mother there was a complete bond. And her mother had never been stingy in showing her love for her children. What came from her mother to Andrea herself was something especially strong, a pure, all-enveloping love. You couldn't mistake love when it came to you that way, even if it threatened to overwhelm you.

The streetcar reached her stop and she picked up her small suitcase and got off. The walk to the house was short. She was conscious of a deep regret, that on these occasions when she came home, she could not look forward to an unclouded happiness in seeing her mother. The fact raised the sense of guilt in her to a familiar pitch. She had been given the great gift of being treasured, of security in the steadfastness of her mother's love. Her present state seemed a double disloyalty.

Her first surprise on entering the house was the stillness, the stillness of an empty house. Where was her mother? The idea that her mother would not be there awaiting her had not occurred to her. All the conversational gambits she had prepared suddenly fell to the ground and she was left bewildered.

Her eye lit on the white paper propped on the telephone stand. She snatched it up and read: "Dear, 'I've just had a phone call from Bland. She says I must come to luncheon with her in Alexandria. Our cousins from Charleston are here and since their visit will be brief, this will be the only occasion we can all meet. Bland is coming to get me in her car and will be here at eleven o'clock. That means that I shall probably have already left by the time you arrive. There are things in the ice-box for you and your father. I shall be back sometime in the middle of the afternoon."

Andrea carried the note and her suitcase up to her room, still too disconcerted to order her thoughts. Her home-loving mother, who never went anywhere without elaborate preparations, to pick up at a moment's notice and go to lunch. Of course, it was Cousin Bland, the cousin with whom her mother had grown up and gone to school with, who had always been in the place of a fond sister. She knew from her mother's letters that Cousin Bland's husband had been elected to the House of Representatives from their district in Virginia. He had been one of those swept into office by the Democratic landslide that had brought Roosevelt to the White House. There had been a great to-ing and fro-ing between her mother and Cousin Bland about finding a suitable house and furnishing it in a manner that accorded with their Virginian notions of grace and hospitability.

As she grew used to the surprise of her mother's absence, Andrea began to enjoy the situation. A certain freedom, a certain lightness in the air had taken the place of the subdued, anxiety-ridden suspense in which she had approached this Easter break.

After a while she heard the front door open and close and went to the stairhead to call to her father. At lunch together they talked about her mother's absence. It was as intriguing to him, Andrea saw, as it was to her, but not so surprising. Her mother, it seemed, had several times lately had unexpected engagements with Cousin Bland. Her mother was always, of course, home to dinner. A chief tenet of her life as a wife was that her husband's creature comforts must not be neglected, that she should not be absent when he returned home at the end of the day.

"Bland certainly peps her up," he said, as Andrea served him the chicken salad. "For that matter, I expect Bland is making more of a stir in Congressional circles than her husband is."

Andrea saw him smile to himself at the thought of the bustling little woman who was his wife's cousin and the dry, saturnine man who was her husband.

"Mother is enjoying it all?"

"Oh, certainly. She hasn't had this much excitement and entertainment for some time."

"Then I'm glad."

Her father gave her an understanding glance. "She's been unhappy about a number of things lately. She can't reconcile herself to Bob's assertion of independence. I tell her it's only reasonable that he should have gone off to pursue his own life. But she misses him. And she misses you, Andrea. I'm glad you're closer enough to come home often."

Andrea, with a pang, said, "Yes."

On Easter Monday Andrea got off the streetcar in front of the White House. There were crowds of children carrying gaily painted baskets waiting at the gates with their mothers to be allowed into the grounds for the Easter egg rolling. Andrea walked around the iron-fenced park to the White Lot behind. The Chevrolet sedan was parked close to the Zero Milestone. 'Bel stood beside it, leaning against the hood. She wore a pair of light brown baggy trousers and

185

a long-sleeved shirt, with a leather jacket and a scarf.

Andrea said, "Where did you get that outfit?"

"Don't you like it? If Amelia Earhart can wear it, I don't see why I can't."

"Well, you're not Amelia Earhart, for one thing."

"And what's the other?"

"It makes people look at you."

"Then they'll just have to look at me. Let's get in the car and then you won't be embarrassed by being seen with me."

They got into the car and 'Bel said, "Your mother seems to be too busy to notice what you're doing. That's fine for us. I'm glad we don't have Carola on our hands."

"Yes. But Mother is going to want me in tow for some of these affairs of Cousin Bland's. She has to show me off. That's an important sort of thing in their world."

'Bel started up the motor. "Let's forget them for a while. Let's go out in the country."

They drove out Sixteenth Street into the Maryland countryside, following the winding road between broad fields and stretches of woodland. They finally reached a spot where there was a grassy place off the road under a big maple tree. 'Bel drew off the paving and stopped the car. They looked at each other and smiled. 'Bel put her arms around Andrea and kissed her.

"This is the most privacy we've had for some time."

Andrea kissed her back. "Yes."

They sat close together and drank in the happy serenity that came to them in the mild breeze, fragrant with the sunlight dreaming on the meadow beyond the fringe of trees and undergrowth. Insects hummed in the underbrush and there was a sudden fluttering of the wings of a mockingbird building a nest. From the fields around came the calls of kildeer, meadow larks and bobwhites.

"It's going to be summer soon," said 'Bel.

"Are you going to summer school?"

"I want to. If I'm going to graduate in three years I have to make up credits. You know, I spend so much time on jobs I can't carry a full schedule of courses. I'm wondering if I ought to get a full-time job during the summer and save some money, instead."

"What kind of a job?"

"Anything I can get that pays more than my board and lodging."

" 'Bel, you shouldn't waste your time doing something that won't help with your college work."

"Well, what do you think I'm thinking like this for, except to save up money for college next year? Oh, I know. You think I'm going to work in a roadhouse again. The fact remains that it isn't easy to get a job if you haven't got experience and you can't get experience if you haven't got a job. Being a waitress is the only kind of experience I can show, except these odd jobs I've been working at all winter."

"But not in a roadhouse."

"The tips are bigger."

"It's too dangerous, even though we don't have Prohibition any more. There's too much drinking and fighting. There are stories in the newspapers all the time."

"All right. No roadhouses."

They sat for a long time, sometimes talking, sometimes silent, aware of each other, of each other's being, of each other's body, with yearning. Occasionally a car passed on the road — a farmer in an old Ford who paid no attention to them, a newer car with several people in it whose heads turned to stare at them.

Finally 'Bell said, "Andy, I'm hungry. I've found a place we can go and get a sandwich."

'Bel knew all the byways of this part of the world and she drove to a roadside tavern in a small town nearby, which was nothing more than a collection of delapidated buildings. Well Digging, said a sign on one. A gas station housed in an old barn with one pump in front of it carried the name Hodgins' Corner.

The tavern was full of men when they reached it. Lunchtime, 'Bel explained. 'Bell led Andrea to the slot machines in one corner and they fed dimes into it till they were rewarded by the sudden clatter of a shower of coins. "They've hit the jackpot!" a male voice exclaimed and for a brief moment Andrea was conscious of the stares of many eyes. But the men's scrutiny was brief and she realized that in this setting 'Bel's clothing called less attention than her own. When a table was vacated in a corner they walked across to it. The stout woman wearing a gingham dress, who stood behind the counter filling orders and taking money, followed them with her eyes, obviously noting the style and quality of Andrea's flannel skirt and jacket. Her gaze lingered on them until she turned away to attend to the elderly black man in overalls who waited patiently for the sandwich he would take somewhere else to eat.

Andrea was glad to sit down so that the table and the subdued light of the corner would shield her. 'Bel fetched them sandwiches and a bottle of beer to drink between them. As she sat down, Andrea murmured, "Don't they know you're a minor?" 'Bel murmured back, "Who's to tell them? She didn't ask me. Do you like beer, Andy?"

"I've only had it a couple of times, with Dad. Mother thinks drinking beer is not ladylike."

'Bel suppressed a laugh and poured the beer.

* * *

187

Carola was already back in their room when Andrea returned to Baltimore. One glance told Andrea that she was in a complaining mood. Nevertheless Andrea asked,

"Did you enjoy Easter?"

"No. I wish I could have stayed with you."

Oh, dear, thought Andrea, and tried to turn the conversation to something else. But Carola's mood had settled in. She told Andrea that she might as well not have gone home. Her parents were preoccupied with her younger sister. Her younger sister liked boys and could think of nothing else. Her parents said she was too young. There had been a constant family wrangle on the subject.

"I would have had a much better time with you, Andrea. Your mother is always so nice to me."

"Well, I think this time you'd have found her absentminded, too. She is very busy now with her Cousin Bland, whose husband is in Congress." Andrea was able to keep the conversation going about Cousin Bland and congressional Washington for some time. But presently, after a long pause, Carola said,

"If your mother is so busy, that ought to give you more time for your private life."

It was the slyness in her tone of voice that caused Andrea to switch around and demand indignantly, "What do you mean by that?"

Her first glimpse of Carola's face showed her the malicious smile on the other girl's face. But this changed to an expression of alarm.

"Oh, you know what I mean, Andrea. You don't tell everybody everything you do. I don't." Underneath the alarm Andrea saw Carola's feeling of satisfaction. For once she had gained Andrea's full attention.

"What is there to tell?" Andrea demanded. "What kind of a private life do you think I have?"

Carola began to look offended. "Well, if you don't know what a lot of the girls have been talking about, that's too bad."

"What have they been talking about?"

"You're out a lot, away from College by yourself. You don't go with the rest of us much. It's only once in a blue moon that you join the bull sessions in some of the girls' rooms. You don't say anything about the men you are interested in —"

"That's a lot of stuff! When I'm not here I'm at the Pratt or at Hopkins. I've got a lot of work to do to keep up my average. I'm here on a scholarship and my father and mother would never forgive me if I didn't keep it up."

"Oh, yes, I know. You're really brainy. We all know that and we also know you can keep up your average with one hand tied behind your back. But even if you're mesmerized by books, we think there's somebody else and he isn't in a book."

188

"Who is *we?*"

"Oh, the girls in our class —"

"A little clique of your friends, you mean. Carola, I thought you were my friend. You've told me so often enough. I wouldn't say you are, if you talk about me behind my back like that."

Her reproach seemed to reach Carola. "I don't talk about you. But I can't keep the others from talking about you. And they're always asking me questions. They think I ought to know."

"There isn't anything for you to know. Why don't you tell them that? And why don't you tell them to shut up?"

"Oh, I think it is a good thing that I listen to them. Otherwise, you'd never find out."

"I don't want to find out. Do you think I give a damn what they say?

She realized she had been betrayed into imitating 'Bel. Carola's eyes grew a little wider at the expletive.

"Maybe not. But you are being foolish." Carola paused as Andrea turned away in an effort to control her temper. Presently she said in a troubled voice, " 'Drea, you really ought to know that they're convinced that you're involved with some man that your parents don't approve of. That's why you sneak out, so you can meet him when nobody is noticing. 'Drea, listen to me. I don't have to tell you that sort of talk is going to ruin your reputation. Nice girls don't do that sort of thing. You remember what happened to Ursula Bondi. She got mixed up with that Jewish fellow and even if she's married now, she still gets talked about. Nobody really wants to know her."

Andrea stood still, with her back turned to Carola. Horrified as she was by what she heard, nevertheless she felt a sense of relief, as if there had been something worse that she expected. And so there was. Apparently nobody suspected that it was 'Bel she was involved with. But a man? The interview with the Dean came back to her. Someone had seen her with 'Bel when 'Bel was wearing her greenhouse clothes. But had it been Carola herself?

She turned to look at the other girl. But Carola now looked merely vexed, at her apparent failure to hold Andrea's attention.

"All I can say, Carola, is that your friends certainly don't have much to occupy themselves with, if all they do is gossip about me." She was trying to throw up a smokescreen and she guessed that Carola half-suspected the fact.

"All the same, I think you'd better do something to stop them," Carola said petulantly.

"And what do you suggest — that I call a meeting and announce that, contrary to what they think, I'm not running around with Mr. X?"

Carola sniffed. "You can be funny if you like. What I guess you'd better do is not keep going off by yourself. That's what they watch."

The next time they met, Andrea told 'Bel about it.

"So that's what you've been so skittish about. Why didn't you tell me back then, when you saw the Dean?"

"I just didn't want to."

"What are you going to do about it now?"

"For one thing, I've go to be friendlier to Carola and that bothers me."

'Bel silently raised her eyebrows.

"You know why. She hangs onto me like — like a limpet, I think the phrase is. She has a real crush on me, 'Bel, and if I don't treat her as coldly as possible, she would be all over me."

"The fatal fascination of Miss Hollingsworth."

"Oh, shut up. I am going to have to be chummier — go around with her more. The trouble is the other girls are going to laugh."

"So long as you don't miss your dates with Mr. X. So I'm Mr. X. That's why you said we'd have to stop going out in the evenings."

"Yes. I was out of bounds."

It turned out as Andrea predicted. Her greater availability to Carola produced an immediate response. Carola was noticeably more cheerful. Andrea made a point, when they went out on a class outing, or a visit to the art gallery, or to an afternoon matinee, to pair off with Carola. She took Carola home with her more often on weekends.

"I'm not sure," Andrea told 'Bel, "whether I'm not jumping from the frying pan into the fire. I know everybody is talking about me and Carola now."

"As long as she doesn't get hysterics or kiss you in public, that's all right. They'll just laugh."

The college year came to an end. Carola wept as she packed her belongings. Andrea, irritated and conscience-stricken at the sight of her tears falling on the clothes as she folded them into her trunks, tried to be casual without being hard-hearted.

"Don't cry, Carola. We'll probably be roommates next year."

Carola stopped what she was doing and raised pleading, tear-filled eyes. "But, 'Drea, it's three months! Don't you realize it?"

"Of course I do, Caro, and I'm going to miss you. But there's nothing we can do about it. You'll find plenty to keep you busy at home."

But Carola wailed, "Oh, 'Drea, I'm miserable. Please love me a little bit."

Reluctantly and yet anxious not to show her reluctance, Andrea put her arms around her and kissed her. It was the first time she had made such a spontaneous gesture and Carola responded by clutching her in a deathlike grip. Andrea patted her and spoke gently. After all, Carola was a pretty girl, an attractive girl. If only her emotional needs had been fastened on someone else!

When she had soothed Carola into a quieter grieving, she

190

returned to making automatic responses while her mind ran on with her own thoughts. She hoped Carola's infatuation was just that, an infatuation that would pass. Carola's well-to-do parents obviously showered every luxury on her. Yet she was in a sense forlorn. She lacked the initiative to seek her own satisfactions in life. She needed a prop, a stay, someone deeply interested in her and ready to give her the support necessary so that she would not merely remain passive, enduring whatever befell her. I'm not for her, thought Andrea. She'll probably get a husband one of these days, somebody her parents will pick out for her.

But in the meantime it was awkward, this dodging. Obviously Carola knew nothing of the fulfilment of love with another person. Sometimes she clumsily sought to hug Andrea, pet her. Andrea made a careful response, stiff with fear that by some gesture she would betray a greater sophistication. She had soon discovered that Carola's concept of sexual pleasure was the same as that of most girls of her strict religious background. It was grounded chiefly in her ignorance of her own body. Dutifully she responded to the teaching of her elders in sublimating the sexual urge into a romantic ideal, bodiless. Andrea thought, with a touch of grimness, I could live with Carola for fifty years and we'd never come closer to each other than two clothed bodies, modestly hidden from one another.

She roused herself from her musing and tried to pay more attention to Carola.

When she got home and was settling in for the summer, she mentioned Carola to her mother. Her mother listened sympathetically.

"Yes, I can see that she has become very attached to you, Andrea. She must be rather lonely. And she is a sweet girl."

"That's the trouble, Mother. She never takes the initiative. Some of the teachers have talked to her about that. She could make better grades if she would speak up more."

"Well, I'm sure you have been very good for her, Andrea. Of course, one must always be a little careful with someone like that, not to let her overstep the bounds. Not that she'd mean to. It is a normal phase for girls to be fond of each other — rather a preparation for later life when they are wives and mothers."

Andrea said nothing further. There was something strange here, she thought. Mother can be indulgent of Carola. I'm sure her true opinion is that Carola is a little goose. Obviously, I can't be in danger from a little goose. Whereas 'Bel was a real danger, a danger that had to be stamped out before it got out of hand.

'Bel had got a job for the summer with a government committee that was sorting old records for storage in the new National Archives when the new building was completed downtown on the site of the old Center Market. She was going to be rich, she told Andrea, with a salary of a hundred dollars a month. They met

191

frequently for lunch, in fine weather eating sandwiches on a bench on the Mall under the tall elm trees.

In the middle of June Andrea had a letter from Carola. Carola's mother and aunt were going to Europe for six weeks and taking Carola with them. Would Andrea come too?

When she read the letter she put it down, already thinking of the phrases she would use in saying No. But when her mother came home and opened the letters waiting for her on the telephone stand, she found one from Carola's mother. Carola, it said had talked so much about Andrea and how much she wished they could be together on this first trip abroad. Would Andrea's parents allow her to join them? Since this might be financially burdensome to them Carola's mother offered to pay for Andrea's passage and expenses abroad.

Andrea watched the surprise on her mother's face. "Well, this is really extraordinary. Had you any idea of this, Andrea?"

"Carola wrote me and asked me if I would go."

Andrea watched her mother becoming used to the idea. She had expected her at once to say it was impossible. Her mother was very touchy on the subject of accepting money from other people.

But her mother said tentatively, "It would be a wonderful opportunity for you. I've never been to Europe. I should like you to have the chance. Carola's people are perfectly trustworthy and cultivated. Going that way with well-to-do people you will travel in a much better way than would be possible otherwise. However, we cannot allow them to pay your expenses. Your father will see to that."

"But Mother, Dad can't possibly afford it!"

"Oh, I think he may feel that he can. He would always be ready to make sacrifices for you, darling."

"Yes, but I don't want him to. They are just asking me because Carola doesn't want to be with just her mother and her aunt. She wants somebody her own age, who'll lead her around to what she really wants to see and do."

"Well, naturally. I realize she hasn't much initiative. Wouldn't you like to go abroad, Andrea?"

Under her mother's scrutiny Andrea was silent. Of course, who wouldn't, she thought. But the idea of being miles across the ocean from 'Bel —

Her mother said briskly, "Well, I'll discuss it with your father. I'm sure he will be in favor of it."

* * *

"So now," Andrea said to 'Bel, "what am I going to do? Mother is bound and determined that I'm going to Europe with Carola."

'Bel munched her sandwich. "Looks like you're going."

"I can say I won't go."

192

"And fight a war with your mother for the rest of the summer?"

" 'Bel, don't you realize? I'll have to share a cabin and hotel rooms with Carola. I won't be able to get out of her sight. It will be a hundred times worse than college."

"Yes, I realize all that. But you will get to go to England and France. You'll just have to handle Carola. What's the odds, Andy? All we can do for the rest of the summer is sit on this bench for half an hour a day. When you get back to Baltimore we can have more time together."

"You're pretty cool about my being away for six weeks. I suppose, if you had the chance, you wouldn't think twice about it."

"Now, don't get your feelings hurt. Andy. We're a couple of prisoners in this situation. You won't face your parents. So there's nothing we can do."

"I've told you a hundred times: What good would it do for me to face my parents? I'm a minor. They can still control what I do."

"You can run away. We can go somewhere else and make our own way."

" 'Bel, that's ridiculous. You know it is. I've got to finish my education and so do you. We don't want to live like a couple of fugitives, without decent jobs, just hand to mouth."

"We'd make our own way," said 'Bel stubbornly.

" 'Bel, sometimes you're just as childish as you can be. You know that isn't anything more than a pipe dream. If I leave home, my parents can have me picked up by the police and brought back. Do you think for a moment that my mother would rest till she had me back? And do you realize how miserable my life would be after that? You haven't got anybody to account to."

'Bel shrugged. "We're back where we always are. You won't take a chance."

Andrea's anger boiled. "Take a chance for what? You know as well as I do that that is no solution for us. You're lucky. You haven't anybody to stop you from doing anything you like. Do you want to take off right now, wash your hands of me?"

"You mean, there's nobody who gives a hoot about me."

"Except me and apparently you don't care about that."

"Now don't start on that."

"How many times must I tell you that I'm doing the only thing I can so that we can see each other at all? If my mother knew I was meeting you, she'd find some way to put a stop to it."

"What could she do? Lock you up?"

"She'd find out where you were and tell you what she thought of you and how you're ruining my life. I don't think you'd come out of that very well."

"Oh, all right: Go to Europe with your little soul mate, tag along where she wants her dear, darling 'Drea to go—"

For a moment Andrea was silent with rage. She jumped up from the bench. "If that's the way you feel about it, good bye. I've

193

had enough of this."

'Bel jumped up to grab her arm. "Andy, I didn't mean that! I was just goaded into it. Please, Andy."

The people on the benches nearby were staring at them. Instantly aware of the fact they began to walk down the path together as if nothing was amiss. After a while the enforced appearance of composure cooled their anger and resentment. The old feeling of unity surrounded by menace reasserted itself. They stood on the street corner, saying goodbye with a cool indifference to cover their murmured endearments.

When the time came Carola and her mother and aunt came to Washington to meet the Hollingsworths. They were cheerful, confident women, contented with themselves and their outlook on life. Andrea observed her mother measuring them up, deciding that they were indeed safe guardians.

On the voyage over Andrea spent as much time as she could reading or walking on the promenade deck. In the evenings she and Carola joined the dancing in the main saloon, picking their partners under the watchful eyes of the two women. When the two of them were alone in their cabin she chiefly listened while Carola talked. Carola seemed content with this degree of closeness. It did not occur to her, Andrea surmised, that there was more to friendship than this cosy intimacy.

The pattern was set for the rest of the trip. Each evening she wrote to 'Bel at her boarding house near the Capitol. In London and Paris she inquired at the American Express for 'Bel's letters when she went to pick up her mother's. Invariably Carola was with her. She was never really able to shake Carola off. She was conscious of Carola watching curiously, noting the fact that when she got letters she always opened the one from her mother but that 'Bel's she simply put unopened in her handbag. She told 'Bel, at least there is always a little privacy in the bathroom.

Their six weeks abroad had run up into the last week in August, with barely time left to get ready for the new college year. Hurriedly Andrea told her mother all the details of the trip home, as they went on shopping expeditions for new clothes. Her mother was still much involved with Cousin Bland, anxious to show her off as the grown daughter newly returned from a trip to Europe. But a day came when she was able to escape and go and find 'Bel.

'Bel had told her in her last letter that her summer job had ended, that there would be a week when she would stay in the boarding house room before returning to College Park.

"I'll hang around waiting for you, Andy," she said.

Andrea found the old tall red brick house behind the Library of Congress. The front door was open and she went in and climbed the stairs to the first landing. There was no one about. She stood hesitating. 'Bel had mentioned in her letters that she lived on the second floor, with a window that looked over the small oblong of back garden. With the impatience that had been gathering in her in the course of the trip home and the days since her arrival back in Washington, Andrea stepped over to the furthest door and knocked.

It opened immediately and 'Bel stood there, silhouetted against the light from the window. Without a word she stepped back to let Andrea come in. For a moment they simply stood looking at each other. Then sweeping aside the wall of physical separation that had stood between them for so many days they stepped forward and seized each other.

For the next hour their communication was almost silent. A sort of hunger drove them on to undress each other and lie on the bed pressed close together. Without the need to speak they told each other of the long absence, the unappeasable longing that had gnawed at them for the previous week, when they knew each other to be within a few minutes's space away. Their lovemaking seemed incidental to some larger groping and joining. Andrea, flooded by the overwhelming ecstasy that 'Bel's fingers released, felt free at last of the nagging temptation that was not a temptation in Carola's constant presence. Her own fingers sought with powerful eagerness the tender moist folds of 'Bel's most intimate region. She felt 'Bel's answering eagerness to be invaded by her, felt herself drowning in the joy of 'Bel's crushing embrace.

After a while they lay spent, side by side, looking at the ceiling. Still there was no need to talk. They both recognized something: the six weeks' separation had carried them a giant step further into a mature realization of each other as part of themselves. Their usual worlds, their usual associations, their usual intimates had fallen farther away, stood now far away outside their own charmed circle. The Greeks, thought Andrea, considered the circle the symbol of perfection, for it had no beginning and no end. So it was with herself and 'Bel. They were no longer children. They had left something behind.

'Bel said, "I have to go back to College Park tomorrow."

"I have to register Monday morning at Goucher."

"You can telephone me at the dorm. I'll be on the desk there for the first day."

When she got back home Andrea had difficulty in responding properly to her mother's remarks. She was still enveloped in the remoteness, she was still immersed in the warm sensuousness of the world she had left in 'Bel's room. Her detached manner roused her mother's surprised suspicion.

"Where have you been, Andrea? You're not paying much attention to what I'm saying."

Trying to shake off her lassitude Andrea answered, "Oh, at the Library. I thought I'd better get a little start on going back to studying."

Her mother eyed her for a moment longer. She sees a difference, too, thought Andrea.

* * *

Carola was late returning to college. She had somehow, on the trip home, picked up mumps, which she had never had as a child. Andrea, glad of the respite, was also unable to find opportunities to meet 'Bel.

"I've got to help all these freshmen find their way around here," 'Bel had told her on the phone. "It's part of my job here on the dorm desk. The place is a madhouse. There are more new students here than there have ever been before. Yes, that seems to be our luck. When you're in the clear, I'm tied up and vice versa. I don't wish that poor girl any bad luck, but maybe she'll have complications and have to stay home longer."

Carola missed the dance held to welcome the new girls at Goucher, in the newly decorated Recreation Hall. Andrea, telling her mother about it, said the College had come a long way since its early years when none of the students were permitted male visitors and dancing and card playing were forbidden.

Her mother made a deprecating sound. "Well, of course, Andrea, in the 1880s even the idea of a college education for young women was considered radical. It took considerable enlightenment for a conservative religious denomination to undertake to provide such a thing."

"So," said Andrea, teasing, "they shut the girls up in a nunnery with watchdogs to keep out the wolves."

"Well, I suppose most of the girls accepted it as normal. Women have a great deal more freedom than they did when I was your age. I was not allowed to go out of the house without hat and gloves. You don't realize the extent of your freedom. Who are the young men who are invited to this dance?"

"Oh, they're friends of some of the girls and I suppose some brothers and cousins, especially of the day girls from Baltimore City — boys from St. John's in Annapolis and Notre Dame and Loyola and even some from Hopkins — the older men. You needn't worry, mother. We don't have chaperones but there is plenty of surveillance. Usually some of the girls — the city girls especially — go with their escorts off the campus after the dance for more fun, but it is always in a group."

"I hope you're careful, Andrea, especially if there is drinking."

"Some of the older girls say it is easier' now since we don't have Prohibition anymore. It seems at first some of the boys didn't know how to behave, without speakeasies and hip flasks. But don't worry, mother, I don't let boys get ideas."

Andrea had no chance even to talk to 'Bel during the days just before the dance. 'Bel had said that as soon as she could work out her schedule she would call. But she had not called. Getting dressed for the dance Andrea was aware of a sense of annoyance. She put on the long-skirted dress and pinned on the small bouquet her mother had sent for her shoulder. How much more enjoyable it would be if she could spend the evening with 'Bel — if, in fact, they could go somewhere they could dance together. She wondered if any such place existed. She knew that there were places in the world — either very innocent or very sophisticated ones — where women dancing together aroused no comment. But not in her particular sphere.

Still thinking about this she left her room and joined a number of girls headed for the Recreation Hall.

"Hello, Andrea," said one of them, "We've got a really good band tonight — not just an ensemble from one of the hotels."

"They call themselves The Cossacks and they're nifty — real rhythm," said another girl.

"How did you manage to get them?" Andrea's question was asked mainly as a matter of conversation. The girls she was talking to were members of the Student Council and it did not do to ignore them.

"We convinced the Dean it was all right to hire them. They're all boys working their way through college. That was a great point with her. The Dean's all right."

Andrea nodded. The group she had attached herself to had reached the Recreation Hall. A row of heads turned as the stag line saw them enter. Here we go, thought Andrea, saying Yes to the young man who asked her for the first dance. While he talked she looked towards the band seated on a low platform at the other end of the room, tuning their instruments. Obviously to act out their name they wore loose Russian blouses and baggy trousers tucked into boots. Her interest was caught by what one of the girls had said about the band, that they were boys who had thought of this means of earning money in order to stay in college. 'Bel would be interested in that.

The band launched into the first number, *Betty Co-Ed*, which Rudy Vallee had already made a hit. Yes, thought Andrea. It's true. The band is very good. Her partner was a good dancer and she enjoyed the dance. With scarcely a pause the band went on into *It Don't Mean A Thing If It Ain't Got Rhythm*. Andrea's partner yielded to another boy who cut in.

By the time the band stopped with another abrupt clash of cymbals most of the dancers were thirsty. There were bowls of punch on the refreshment tables. Andrea eyed them warily. Undoubtedly the school authorities believed the punch to be made exclusively of fruit juice but she had been warned that sometimes the male guests surreptitiously emptied flasks into it. She accepted a small glass from the last of her partners. He was a short, sturdy fellow with closecropped hair who was, he said, on the boxing team of his college. She listened to him patiently while he talked about his track record, his marksmanship. He reminded her of her bro-

197

ther Bob, as Bob used to be at his age. He was enthusiastic about the band. It was as good as any of the name bands, he said.

"Do you mind if I go and talk to the fellows?" he asked.

"Of course not," said Andrea, pleased at being free of him. She looked over at the band. They had left the band platform and had gathered behind the end of the table on which one of the punch bowls sat. They had been invited to slake their thirst. Andrea stepped closer to the table to set down her glass. Her gaze was on what she was doing, finding a spot free for the glass in her hand. Another hand came into her line of vision. Amazed she stared for a moment before raising her eyes. Then she looked up, seeing first the Russian blouse and then 'Bel's face, grinning at her.

She gasped softly. "What are you doing here?"

"Playing the tenor saxophone. Next intermission can you go outside for a breath of air?"

"Yes."

The next group of fox trots and waltzes seemed interminable to Andrea, though now her ear was attuned to catch the sound of the tenor saxophone. Of course 'Bel could play any instrument. She had a natural talent. The saxophone seemed to be speaking to her now, in the middle of the crowded dance floor.

When the intermission came she escaped from her current partner with a murmured excuse which he took for granted meant she wanted the powder room. Instead she found her way through the throng to the big door that stood open to the mild night. Several couples were visible as anonymous figures in the diffused moonlight. She stepped into the shadow cast by a big bush and waited.

A slight sound behind her told her 'Bel had found her way out there.

'Bel said, without waiting for her to speak, "I know. You're upset. You don't want me anywhere near here. It just happened, Andy. Somebody asked me if I'd like to play with them. It was one of the boys who knew I need money. He knew I could play the saxophone."

"I'd have liked a little warning."

"How could I warn you? The band didn't get the offer till a couple of days ago. I've played with some of the boys over at Peabody, in chamber music. There is more money in this sort of thing. It's good of them to let me have a chance like this. I cut my hair a little shorter. There's no reason for anybody to think I'm not just another of the fellows."

"But still it's dangerous, 'Bel."

"We can't always be safe, Andy."

"You don't have to push our luck."

"One day there's going to be a showdown."

A slight shudder went through Andrea. 'Bel was aware of it.

"All right, Andy. I don't suppose we'll ever play here again. The band is a temporary thing — just a stopgap. How about being near the door when this show closes up? I've got the car down the side street."

"I'll try."

The rest of the evening went by in a sort of dream. The lights, the band music, her dance partners, the throng around her all had a touch of unreality. The sound of the tenor saxophone was the most real element. She tried to keep her preoccupation within bounds. She felt a tremendous relief when the band played *Good Night Ladies*, and began to pack up their instruments. They had come in a bus and under cover of the milling about of the girls and their guests and the members of the band, Andrea slipped away down the street. As she reached the corner a girl's voice called after her, "Come with us, Andrea," but reckless at last she turned the corner out of the girl's sight without replying.

* * *

Carola returned in the midst of the postmortems of the dance and the other parties that took place shortly thereafter. There was a good deal of suppressed excitement in the air, a compound of the remembered freedom of the summer plus the suddenly recognized responsibilities of the new school year, catalyzed in the euphoria of the evening of the dance. A sense of having been left out, of having been cheated of a major event in the corporate life of the college weighed on Carola.

The third afternoon after her return Andrea came back to their room to find her sitting alone and idle, sunk in what was obviously a self-absorbed misery.

"What's the matter, Carola?"

"Oh, I seem to miss out on everything."

"What do you mean?"

"I had to go and get those silly mumps and I wasn't here for the beginning of school. Now everybody is already 'way ahead of me."

"You'll catch up in no time, Carola."

"But I wasn't here when everybody else came back. I missed the dance. I don't know what's going on, nobody tells me —"

"Oh, the dance. Well, that's a pity. It was a good dance. But cheer up. We'll have more of them now that we've got the new Recreation Hall."

Andrea was determined to be cheerful but Carola lapsed into a dogged silence. Andrea turned away to her own concerns. All at once Carola said, " 'Drea, I've missed you so while I was sick."

Dear God, thought Andrea, guiltily aware that she had written Carola only one letter. She said, pusillanimously, "I didn't think you'd be away so long."

"I don't think you really cared."

Andrea recognized in Carola's voice the tone that meant that she intended to quarrel. "I did, Carola, but I was pretty busy, and as

I said, I didn't know you'd be laid up for so long. I was expecting you every day."

"I hear you enjoyed the dance pretty well."

"So would you have. It was wonderful."

"Especially afterwards, I guess, when you went off with somebody on your own."

Andrea turned slowly around. "Where did you hear that?"

"Oh, some of the girls. They all saw you."

The girl who called after me, thought Andrea. The moment on the dark street came back to her. Carola may have been late in getting back to school but she had lost no time in catching up with the gossip.

Andrea tried to be casual, turning away again. "I don't see what is wrong with that. Everybody else went out after the dance."

"Yes, but they all went in a bunch. You went off by yourself. There was somebody waiting for you. You know, I'll bet your mother doesn't know you're running around with some man."

"It isn't so."

"Everybody thinks it is."

"And I suppose you can't wait to tell my mother. I didn't think you were a little sneak, Carola."

"But what were you doing, then?"

"It's none of your business, nor anybody else's."

She might temporarily silence Carola, but she knew she could not stop such gossip. Carola's resentful mood lasted. Andrea, in an attempt to mollify her, made it a point to suggest that they go together to the art classes at the Walters' Gallery and offered to join her in shopping expeditions in the downtown stores. Gradually Carola became less sulky but she still was quick to complain whenever Andrea was absent for any length of time without saying where she had been.

She was especially fussy about weekends. She had come to feel that whenever Andrea went home for the weekend she could take it for granted that she was invited to go along. But Andrea did not go home on weekends as often as she had. The presidential campaign year of 1936 was coming up and her mother's attention was completely absorbed by Cousin Bland and the fortunes of the Democratic Party in Virginia. Mrs. Hollingsworth was new to such close association with politics and politicians and to her the unfolding of political events was enthralling. Her enthusiasm overflowed in her letters to Andrea. She had met Frances Perkins — Madame Perkins, the Secretary of Labor, the first woman to be appointed to the President's Cabinet. She had heard Mrs. Roosevelt talk about the problems of young people who could not find work. The national Youth Administration would be the answer, Mrs. Roosevelt said.

"Andrea, she likes nonconformity in young people with the courage to pursue their ideals. And she is convinced that young women must have a say in things. Cousin Bland is a little upset by her. Bland is conservative, as you know, and Mrs. Roosevelt's views, especially about Negroes, make her uneasy. I wish you could be free to come with me to some of these affairs, though I realize that nothing is more important than your schooling."

'Bel said, "Your mother is certainly wide awake, Andy. What does your father say about all this?"

"I think he is a little surprised and amused. He never thought of Mother as a political firebrand. But he encourages her. He just doesn't think that there is enough fundamental change being made. But, after all, you can't expect politicians to bring about Utopia. They are too afraid of what they think their constituents will do."

"You know, I like your Dad. He isn't afraid of thinking about change."

"No, he's not afraid of change. But he's pessimistic about the human race and he's getting worse. He asks about you, sometimes, 'Bel, when my mother isn't present."

One weekend in November Mrs. Hollingsworth went to New York. It was to be a big party of them, she explained to Andrea. Cousin Bland's husband was going to a Democratic Party rally and she was excited by this prospect of seeing political action at first hand. But, she said, Bob warned her that he could not introduce her to his friends. They were all rabid on the subject of That Man in the White House. In any case, she would be too busy with Bland to have time for other social events.

"Dad is staying home, of course," Andrea told 'Bel. "He hates anything like that. But he doesn't expect me home. He is immersed in a series of experiments in the laboratory and he won't take a minute away from them."

'Bel's eyes began to shine as she listened. "That's our chance, then."

"Our chance?"

"Yes. I've been thinking. Why don't we go away on the weekend ourselves — just anywhere?"

Andrea's eyes grew speculative. "I could say I was going home, couldn't I? Nobody would know the difference — unless something happens and they have to try and find me."

"Oh, damn it! Why do you always have to think about disasters?"

"Don't get upset. I'll take a chance. But Carola is going to sulk when I say I'm not taking her home with me."

"Tell her you're going with your mother."

"No, not that. She would be sure to mention it to Mother sometime in the future. That would let the cat out of the bag. I'll say something about Dad. She is always afraid of Dad."

Saturday morning Andrea took the train to Washington as usual. The forty minutes ride had become as familiar to her as the old streetcar trip to high school had been. There were several girls who might also be going to Washington for the weekend, so she had arranged with 'Bel that she would board the train, in case any of them were present. Then at Laurel, where the train made a routine stop, she would get off, hopeful no one would see her. She had been lucky with Carola. Carola's aunt was on the way to New York and had stopped in Baltimore to visit with her niece. Carola had been furious but she could not blame it on Andrea.

'Bel's car was parked behind the train station. As soon as Andrea got in, 'Bel started the motor.

"I guess we'd better stay this side of the Bay," 'Bel said. "The ferry takes too long."

Andrea agreed. "I've got to be sure to be in tomorrow at the usual time. Mother might call me. She thinks I'm staying in Baltimore. If she does, I hope nobody says I'm supposed to be in Washington.

It was a mild day, without sun. Their drive as they backtracked towards Baltimore and the Bay was along county roads with little traffic. They would avoid Annapolis. They did not want to go anywhere where a stray encounter might bring them face to face with someone who would recognize Andrea.

The quietness of the day seemed to mute their tongues. It was not yet winter but the trees were bare and the fields were full of old cornstalks or lay stripped. Both of them were aware of a suspension of thought and feeling. It was only after they had stopped for lunch at a roadside tavern and were back once more in the car that they wanted to talk.

"I haven't told you," said 'Bel. "I have a chance at a full scholarship for next year."

"Where?"

"That's the hitch. Wellesley. But I might as well go to China."

Andrea did not answer.

"Of course, it is not certain yet. It depends on how I do this year."

"You can't turn down anything really worthwhile."

"But I can't go a million miles away, either."

"There are trains between here and New England."

"And train tickets cost money. I don't suppose the scholarship would include a sum for commuter travel to Baltimore."

"Don't try to be funny."

They were both silent for a while.

Then 'Bel said, "Let's forget it. I don't want to spoil this windfall."

Their conversation continued to be desultory, held down by the welter of thoughts in the mind of each. That's the trouble, thought Andrea. There was so much they said to each other silently while they were separate that it all became unwieldy when they were at last together again.

When it got late in the afternoon 'Bel suggested that they find a place to spend the night. There were several little towns they went through, sleepy places that nevertheless expected a few travelers, because on the lawns of some of the old rambling houses they saw signs that said "Guests". Stopping at one of these they asked for a room. The elderly woman who came to the door nodded and let them in.

Andrea observed that before she answered the woman's eyes surveyed 'Bel deliberately from head to foot. 'Bel's hair was still shorter than usual, she wore her leather jacket and pants and boots. The woman transferred her scrutiny to Andrea, noting the good quality woolen skirt, the expensive cardigan, the cashmire wool jacket.

In the end she said two dollars for the night and fifty cents apiece for dinner. 'Bel had brought a small case with night things and they went upstairs to the big bedroom with a view over the river. They sat in the musty warmth, happy in their joined solitude.

They did very little talking.

"We're never by ourselves, even when we're alone. I have the feeling that you never forget your mother for a moment."

"Yes, I do. I had then, till you mentioned her."

"It's two years before we can act for ourselves, without your mother. Even then, will you really leave home?"

"That's too far away for me to think about now."

"Would you really abandon me, if your mother required it?"

"How could I? I would die. I seem to die when we're apart for too long."

— —

"Women are afraid, afraid to admit they love each other."

"With good reason. Women can be read out of society very easily."

"Women don't have very good weapons to fight with."

— —

"It can't be complete — love can't be complete, if you can't do this with someone you love — in bed, like this, naked against you."

"I never understood platonic relationships."

"They are false — between lovers. Imagine, not to feel you there, like this, warm and soft."

"They are false — to the core. Because the desire is there and it is denied and festers. How else —"

"Sweet 'Bel. Oh, 'Bel!"

Then Andrea was aware only of the ecstasy of having 'Bel's head between her legs and feeling the soft urging of 'Bel's tongue on the little bud of her desire, awakening the concentric circles of delight.

— —

About six o'clock they both awoke and remembering where they were, dressed quickly to go downstairs to dinner. Supper was an early meal in a place like this, 'Bel reminded Andrea. They ate it at a small table, alone in the big old diningroom, ham and spoonbread and collard greens. Afterwards they sat for a little while, for politeness sake, with the old woman who invited them into her own sittingroom and talked sedately about things that would not reveal where they were from or why they were there.

At last they went to bed, to sleep and wake and make love, in the conspiratorial dark, disturbed only by the creaking night sounds in the stillness of the old house. Andrea, drifting off finally, thought, whatever the future held, it had to be made of herself and 'Bel together. Their oneness was something that had a life of its own.

* * *

Several times after that, during the remainder of November and through December, they were able to salvage a few weekends, never going to the same place twice. Andrea was not as fortunate on these later occasions in having a ready-made excuse for not taking Carola with her to Washington. Carola sulked. Andrea tried to overcome this by paying more attention to her during the weekdays. She was aware of the humorous comments of the other girls, giggling behind their backs. Carola seemed oblivious of this surveillance.

At Thanksgiving she took Carola home with her. 'Bel did not accept her decision easily.

"God damn it, Andy! I'm sure her mother wants her to come home. Why did you invite her?"

"Because I can't stand all the pouting I'd get when the Thanksgiving break is over."

"You're soft. All you have to say is, No, you can't come home with me."

"You don't have to room with her, 'Bel. If I do this now, I can get out of it at Christmas. We'll be in the clear then."

"We'd better be," said 'Bel grimly.

When Christmas came 'Bel stayed in the dormitory.

"There isn't any heat. But I'll just be sleeping there. In the daytime I'll be in the Registrar's Office. I've got a job filing records. You can call me on the phone there."

Cousin Bland had gone back to Norfolk for the holidays and Andrea's mother was less preoccupied with things outside her home. Nevertheless, she did not object when Andrea said that she wanted to join a group of young people who were going to spend Christmas Eve at the Washington Cathedral, for a performance of Verdi's Manzoni Requiem.

The Saturday before Andrea had called 'Bel at College Park.

There was always a moment's suspense while she heard the phone ring in the deserted office, waiting to see if 'Bel would answer. They had arranged to meet at the end of the Tenleytown car line and 'Bel had driven them to the Dalecarlia Reservoir where they could walk in solitude for an hour or so in the chilly gloom of the wintry afternoon. They supposed other people were about but they saw no one in the monotone landscape, among the bare trees whose branches showed black against the grey sky. They held hands as they walked along.

"I didn't actually tell her that the group was from Goucher, but that is what she thinks," said Andrea.

They walked along in silence. Then Andrea said, "I'm going to have to be home earlier than the rest of them want to break up. Mother has agreed to my going but she's going to be sitting up for me. How are we going to arrange that, 'Bel?"

"I suppose we could ask one of the boys to take you to your door. I can wait in the car out of sight."

"She probably is going to ask me ahead of time about how I am going to get there and get home."

"Well, then, I'll ask Jerry Silverstein if he'll pick you up and deliver you back. He's a smooth operator. He'll know just what to say to your mother. He's at Peabody on a scholarship. One of these days he is going to be a famous violinist. He says so and I believe him."

"Does he —?" Andrea hesitated and 'Bel said, "Does he have to know why we're asking him to do this? I'll tell him that your parents want to be sure you have a reliable male escort. After all, the affair is going to be from eleven o'clock at night till the wee hours of Christmas Day. And there is going to be an enormous crowd. That sounds reasonable. If Jerry wonders about anything else, he won't say anything. He's a good guy."

So when her mother asked her about the details of the evening she said that a boy from the Peabody Institute in Baltimore had invited her to go with him. She had met him at a dance at Goucher, which was true. She noticed that her mother's eyebrows twitched a little at the Jewish surname but she said at once, "The Jews seem to produce so many extraordinary musicians."

Andrea told herself that there was no reason why she should feel so oppressed by a sense of guilt. Her mother's concern was that she be protected and safe. She would be as protected and safe as under any more fully disclosed arrangement. Nevertheless, during the first hour while she stood in the constantly thickening crowd in the partially finished nave of the great church, she found it difficult to enter into the spirit of comraderie that existed between 'Bel and the group of girls and young men. It was not until the music began that her preoccupation left her. The soaring sound of the organ, the thrilling orchestration of the voices, ringing in the high arches, finally banished her thoughts of herself. This exalta-

205

tion lasted until they all emerged into the cold night air, caught in the stream of people that flowed out onto the steps of the South Transept, and were greeted by the brilliant stars in the great expanse of sky above the city spread out below.

* * *

Carola was already in their room when Andrea got back to Goucher. She was in a gay, talkative mood and Andrea was able to keep her own side of the conversation to brief sentences.

In the midst of her chatter Carola came close to her and put her arm through Andrea's. "I missed you so much, 'Drea."

"Why, from what you've been telling me, it sounds as if you had a pretty good time, Carola."

"Yes, but it would have been so much better if you'd been there with me."

Andrea tried gently to extricate herself from Carola's embrace. "Oh, I doubt it. Besides, you know my mother would never consent to my being away from home at Christmas."

Carola began to pout a little. "You're always so matter of fact. Don't you ever miss me?"

"Oh, yes, of course."

Carola dropped her arm and moved away. "What did you do during the holidays, 'Drea?"

"The usual things. We always have a pretty quiet time, unless Deedee and the children come to visit. You know my parents don't go in much for entertaining."

"But what did you do?"

"To tell you the truth, I spent most of my time at the Library of Congress. I'm working on a paper about Eleanor of Aquitaine."

Carola made a face.

Immersed in her own concerns, Andrea paid little attention to Carola for several days. Then it began to dawn on her that the other girl's euphoric mood had vanished, that each day Carola became more and more sulky. Several times she came upon her surreptitiously crying. In exasperation she thought, Now what is the matter? She made efforts to cheer Carola up. She sacrificed some of the time she would normally have spent studying in trying to talk to her about things that should have interested both of them, simply sitting with her. But Carola rejected these overtures. For the first time Andrea saw that she was not merely pouting, feeling neglected or unhappy. There was sullenness in her mood now. She turned her head away when Andrea spoke to her and answered only in monosyllables. And this mood intensified as the days passed.

In fact, her malaise affected everything she did. Quite often she failed to appear for meals. She began to look pale and puffy-eyed. At night Andrea could hear her sniffling softly as if she were

206

trying to suppress sobs. Several of their classmates made remarks to Andrea about her, which Andrea tried to turn off casually.

Carola's classroom work began to suffer. Her grades, never more than average, began to slide to the bottom of the scale. She was sent for a few days to the infirmary after she broke down in class and cried hysterically when the instructor rebuked her.

It was then that Andrea returned to their room to find the portentous yellow envelope that meant a summons to the Dean's office.

The Dean appraised her deliberately.

"Andrea, you know, of course, that Carola has had a nervous breakdown. She is in the infirmary now. I'm afraid that we shall be forced to send her home for the rest of this semester."

Andrea tried to keep her composure under the Dean's scrutiny. "I didn't know it was that bad. Did she break down again, in class? I was not there."

"Yes. You surely must have been aware that Carola has been suffering under some sort of nervous strain. What I have called you here for is to ask you whether you can explain what is troubling her. You room with her. I understand that you have become very close friends with her."

Andrea nodded. "I went abroad with her and her mother last year. She goes home with me quite often for weekends, since she is so far from her own home."

"Yes, I understand that. Therefore, I should think you might be able to throw some light on what is the matter. Does she have any problem at home?"

"Oh, no!"

"Her parents give every indication of being devoted to her. So her unhappiness must stem from something here, in her school life. That disturbs me very much."

"I don't know what to say. Carola was very cheerful when she came back from the Christmas break. It is only since she has been back that she has been so unhappy."

"Hasn't she said anything to you?"

"No. I have asked what is the matter, but she won't answer me. When I tried to visit her in the infirmary, she told me to go away."

"Then is it something she blames you for?"

"If it is, I don't understand what it could be."

The Dean said in a voice that showed she knew she was treading on delicate ground, "You know, of course, Andrea, that the most reasonable explanation is that Carola is unhappy over an emotional involvement with someone. Have you any idea who such a person could be?"

Andrea looked down at her hands in her lap. Of course I know what you're asking me, she shought, what you want me to say. You've heard the gossip among the other girls, that Carola has a crush on me and that we're very chummy. Now I've done something that Carola doesn't like and Carola has gone into a decline over it.

Andrea said carefully, "We've been very good friends. But she has not told me why she is so unhappy. I haven't changed, but she acts now as if she didn't want to be friends. I don't know why. I don't know what I have done to make her unhappy."

"Then you do think it is something that you've done?"

"I don't know. She blames me for something. At least, I suppose that is what is the matter. But I don't know what it is."

"Have you asked her?"

Andrea hesitated. "Not in so many words."

"I see. Well, this is all very unfortunate. I had thought that perhaps Carola has imagined that she was in love with some boy she has met here — someone her parents don't know or don't approve of. That couldn't be the case, could it?"

"I don't know of any boys she goes with. She has never mentioned any to me."

"I'm sure she would have, if that were the case. It does not look as if we shall get to the bottom of the matter unless Carola decides to tell us. This is not the sort of situation I like to see develop among us."

The Dean was looking steadily at Andrea as she said this. But at least, I'm dismissed, thought Andrea thankfully. That parting phrase indicated a certain sympathy for someone caught up in such an emotional mess unwillingly. But she also thinks I'm a pretty cold fish.

Within a couple of days Carola's mother came to fetch her home. She spent the intervening days in the infirmary and Andrea was glad of the respite. She was also thankful that she was away from the College at the time Mrs. Giles arrived and that the Dean, anxious to keep everything out of sight, had arranged that Carola be ready for instant departure. In the few days that followed there was no sign of any ripple in the smooth surface of College life. Andrea, however, was acutely aware of the talk among the other girls behind her back. She wondered if the Dean was aware of it, too.

In spite of her guilty feeling, Andrea could not stifle the sense of relief that Carola's absence gave her. Even if she was now notorious among her classmates, she had at least the room to herself, for complete privacy. Now when she went out to meet 'Bel she needed no elaborate excuse to avoid Carola's company.

'Bel said, "Just the same, I wonder what it was that precipitated all this."

"I suppose it was just the inevitable climax. She was always trying to pin me down, get me to say I loved her as much as she loved me. But she didn't have any idea what she meant by it. She's still just as innocent as a child. Oh, 'Bel, what can you do in a case like that?"

"Nothing, I suppose. But there's no point in your feeling guilty. You didn't seduce her. If she'd had a grain of sense, she would have known that you were otherwise committed."

"No. She wouldn't. I'm glad she didn't, anyhow. She would never have left off till she found out who it was. 'Bel, you know, a person can't decide who he or she is going to fall in love with. It's not a matter of calculation. But why did it have to be me, for Carola?"

'Bel grinned at her. "You really want me to answer that? Because you're irresistible, tantalizing, desirable. You caught me, didn't you?"

"Oh, shut up!"

Carola had been gone a week and it was Saturday again. The forty-minute train ride to Washington was again the normal thing. This time Andrea felt a certain rebelliousness. Her mother was no longer as involved with Cousin Bland as she had been before Christmas. Or perhaps it was simply that Cousin Bland was slightly less active in political affairs. In any case, Mrs. Hollingsworth had indicated that she expected Andrea to be home more often for weekends. The comparative freedom of the past months had spoiled Andrea. She was conscious of wanting 'Bel, to the exclusion of this tedious trip to an equally tedious weekend. Then a shaft of guilty feeling went through her. After all, her mother did have a claim.

She was still preoccupied with her own thoughts when she arrived at the house. The remembrance of 'Bel was strongly with her. Bemused she used her latchkey to let herself in. As she stepped into the house sounds came from the kitchen that told her that her mother was home. But her mother did not call out at the sound of the front door. This little, half-realized fact made her at once wary. She walked down beyond the stairs and into the kitchen.

Her mother, standing in the middle of the room, seemed to be awaiting her. An invisible wall prevented her from going to her to kiss her as she usually did.

In place of her usual greeting her mother said sharply, "Oh, you've got home."

Trying to be natural Andrea said, "Yes, the train was on time, for once."

Her mother sat down at the kitchen table and pointed to the other chair. "Sit down, Andrea. I must have an explanation from you."

Andrea saw then that there was a letter lying on the table, several sheets of heavy linen paper covered with an untidy handwriting.

"I've just had a letter from Carola's mother."

Catching her breath Andrea said, "Has she got worse?"

"She is under a doctor's care. He says she must have treatment in order to get over this unfortunate infatuation. I am greatly

209

distressed about this, Andrea. It is one thing for a young girl to become fond — perhaps overfond — of another. It is another for her infatuation to be carried to such an extreme as this. You should have realized that you had to discourage her, even at the expense of seeming unkind."

"I told you all about this, Mother. I told the Dean. I did try to keep her from getting so overwrought about — about me —"

"Yes, but you did not tell me the rest of it."

"The rest of it?"

Mrs. Hollingsworth picked up the letter. "Carola's mother says: 'The doctor told me that I must make every effort to get her to tell me everything, all the details, so that we shall be able to reason her out of this despair. I have succeeded — my little girl is an obedient child and she has been very frank with me. I am appalled at what she told me. She says she was always happy with Andrea, that Andrea was like a real sister to her. But during the last year she has noticed that Andrea was no longer open with her, that Andrea was getting quite unfriendly. At first she could not understand this but she has discovered that the reason is that Andrea is having an affair with a man. She says there have been rumors among the other girls about this for some time but that she did not believe it until she got back to College after this last Christmas vacation. Then the girls told her that ever since the beginning of this school year Andrea has been spending the weekends with this man, when she was supposed to have been with you. Carola has been unhappy that Andrea did not take her home with her as she had done in the past but now she understood why. I know you will be dismayed at hearing this but I feel it is my duty to tell you about it so that you will be able to save your daughter from the consequences of her reckless behavior. I would never have believed it of Andrea except for the fact that Carola is certainly in no state to have invented such a tale."

Mrs. Hollingsworth put the letter down. "This is incredible. I cannot believe it, Andrea."

"You do not need to. It's not true." Even in her own ears her voice sounded very cold.

Andrea saw the expression of her mother's face lighten, as if she was eager to embrace the least excuse. "Do you mean that Carola has after all imagined this? Of course, a girl in such an overwrought state can very well convince herself of something fabricated by her own imagination. Is that the explanation?"

"I don't know." Andrea was unable to face her mother.

Her mother was exasperated. "Andrea, answer me directly. Is there any truth in what Carola says?"

Andrea answered wildly. "No. Caro has always been jealous. She is always watching me. I don't know what she has imagined — I mean, what is the basis of what she has imagined. The Dean asked me if I knew what had upset her. I told her I didn't know —"

"The Dean? The Dean has questioned you about this? You've not said anything to me about it. Has this tale been going around the school?"

"No, no! That's not what I mean. The Dean wanted to know if I had any explanation for Caro's behavior. She knows the other girls talk about Caro and me —"

"Carola and you?"

"Well, yes — you know, Caro was always hanging around my neck — you know, Mother, that was why I wasn't so eager to go abroad with them — I've told you Caro is too — emotional —"

"Yes, so you have." Under her thoughtful gaze, Andrea wondered. Is she thinking about 'Bel? Is she remembering 'Bel? Does she think I just naturally get myself into such situations? She must not find out about 'Bel now.

When she did not speak, her mother said, "Then you think perhaps Carola has invented this tale in order to hurt you, to get revenge because she thinks you have slighted her?"

"Oh, not quite that way. Don't blame her, Mother. She is so upset she doesn't know what she is doing."

"No, no. I don't wish to be unkind to the girl. But certainly she cannot be allowed to spread malicious tales, even if they are simply the creation of her own misguided feelings. I must reply to Mrs. Giles' letter. I shall tell her as tactfully as possible that her daughter's imagination has got out of hand."

With a little sigh of relief Andrea watched her mother's attention stray from herself. Once or twice more during the weekend her mother opened the subject again. But for the most part she seemed preoccupied in considering what she should say to Carola's mother.

The next time they met Andrea said to 'Bel, "It's not over. Mother never lets go of something like this. She is going to try to get to the bottom of it regardless of what I say. I dread going home next weekend."

"Don't go. Invent something."

"That's easy to say. If I tell her I'm not coming home next weekend, she is likely to order me to do so. She would be angry and suspicious."

"She seems to be willing enough to believe your theory that Carola's imagination has run wild."

"That's because she can't really believe that I would have an affair with a man. She doesn't think of me as sophisticated enough. She really doesn't believe I can be a liar and deceiver. As I am."

'Bel contemplated her grim face. "Now, don't get into that mood. You are not really wicked, you know. What else could you do — if you don't come out and tell her about me?"

Andrea's head dropped. "Oh, 'Bel, what a mess I'm in!"

The next Saturday Andrea approached the door of her parents' house reluctantly. She had not heard from her mother during the week. This in itself meant nothing special. But often her mother

211

did write her a note during the week and she would have felt more at ease if one had been in the mailbox for her. In her anxiety she had taken an earlier train than usual. When she let herself into the house she thought she felt a charged atmosphere and rebuked herself, saying she imagined it.

But one glimpse of her mother's face told her her intuition had been right. Mrs. Hollingsworth was washing the breakfast dishes. Dad must just have left, though Andrea.

Seeing her, her mother said, "I've had another letter from Mrs. Giles. Read it."

She thrust the closely written sheets at Andrea. Unwillingly Andrea read the letter.

"I realize that you find it hard to believe that your daughter has been acting this way. But I know my own child and I am sure that she is telling the truth. I have questioned her again, as much as I can without getting her too upset. She says she always knew that Andrea must have been interested in someone else. Andrea was often out quite late at night. In fact, at one point she was reproved for this by the Dean and told that she must conform more to the College regulations, which, as you know, are quite liberal. Caro tells me that it was common knowledge among the other girls that Andrea was involved with someone who never came openly to the dances and other social events. Several of the girls caught glimpses of him. From what I gather, Andrea must have been very secretive. She has not made any close friends except with Caro. Her association with Caro has been a disaster for my child, who has always been trusting and truthful."

Andrea, unable to go on reading, looked up at her mother. Her mother's eyes were dark with anger, her face pale and her lips in a tight line.

"Who is this man? And how far have you gone with him?"

Andrea did not answer. Her legs were trembling and she sat down on the nearest chair. She was suddenly terribly afraid of her mother, who hovered over her in menace.

"Is he the young Jew who came here last Christmas Eve, to take you to the Cathedral?"

Andrea shook her head.

"Then who is he?"

Her mother's hand gripped her shoulder, the fingers digging painfully into her flesh. She tried to speak and did not succeed.

"You will tell me who this man is and what you've done with him! I never thought I would have a daughter who would do such a shameful thing, who would have so little self-respect as to make herself any man's tool. I thought you the soul of honor, that I could depend on you, that I did not need to watch or suspect you of bad behavior, that you would never hide things from me."

Andrea, her head on her arms on the table, heard her mother's words fall on her as so many shafts. She had never before experienced this sense of helplessness, this inability to defend herself. She was everything her mother was saying. She had indeed for a long time been a liar, a cheat, an unworthy daughter. In any time of serious trouble before in her life, her mother had been available for shelter, for comfort. There was no shelter or comfort now. She could not hide from her own sense of self-betrayal. She had flouted all the tenets on which she had been brought up.

Her mother's voice penetrated again into her awareness. "I shall tell your father. He must know what you've been doing."

Andrea sat up and cried out, "Oh, no! Please don't tell Dad!"

She and her mother exchanged a long, violent stare. Her mother turned abruptly away. No, she won't tell Dad, at least not now, thought Andrea. It is still between the two of us.

For a while her mother had nothing more to say and Andrea retreated upstairs into her own room. She sat there in a state of apprehension, waiting for her mother to seek her out, until her father came home. She tried her best to act as if nothing was wrong, when she went downstairs to greet him. Her mother was silent most of the evening, but her father did not seem to notice.

They were alone together briefly in the kitchen just before dinner. Her mother said, as if she had spent the intervening time debating with herself, "If you will not tell me who it is you're involved with, I shall take all the steps I can to find out for myself. I forbid you to have anything more to do with him. If you do not obey me, I shall inform the Dean that I want your privileges restricted, that you are not to be allowed away from the College by yourself for any reason, at any time."

Andrea burst out, "Mother, it is not what you think. Caro *is* mistaken, in spite of what her mother says."

"But you don't deny that you have been seeing someone, only that you are not —" she obviously found it hard to say the phrase "— you're not having an affair with him? Very well, but I don't intend to allow you to see anyone you do not bring to this house. He must be disreputable — or unworthy, if you act this way about it."

They both heard her father stir in the diningroom and fell silent by tacit agreement.

Her mother made no further attempt to talk to her before she returned to Baltimore. But she traveled back with a heavy burden of reproach.

'Bel awaited her at the train station. It had been agreed between them that she would always park the car down the street, so that if there were other girls returning by the same train, they would not see Andrea join her.

'Bel, watching her emerge from the station, thought, I'd know her anywhere, just by the way she walks — that sedate, unhurried, self-possessed walk. She looks so elegant, you'd never guess at this distance that she's only eighteen.

As Andrea came close enough, she saw her face. Good grief!

What's gone wrong now? It must be something more about Carola.

Andrea, still walking deliberately, reached the corner and in the same unhurried fashion, looked behind her. She's looking to see if any of the other girls got off with her and have noticed her, thought 'Bel. This damned business of always being on the watch.

"What's up, Andy?" she asked, impatiently, reaching over to open the car door.

Andrea did not answer as she got in and closed the door after her.

"Well, what is it? Don't just sit there like a statue. Say something."

Andrea glanced nervously back along the street. "Let's go somewhere else."

'Bel drove out Charles Street to Druid Hill Park and parked in a deserted bypath. Spring had come and the trees were clothed in the fuzzy green cloud of new leaves.

Andrea said, "Mother has had another letter from Mrs. Giles. She says Carola is telling the truth, not imagining things. I am running around with a man and everybody at Goucher knows it."

"Your mother believes that?"

"I told her it wasn't so. She has the idea now that I'm seeing somebody — somebody unsuitable — but that I'm not yet going to bed with him."

God, thought 'Bel, I never realized how much like her mother she can look when she gets that grim expression on her face. "What did you tell her?"

"Nothing."

"Nothing?" She looks like the end of the world. "You must have said something."

"She said she was going to tell Dad about it but she didn't. This is something between the two of us. She is going to let it stay that way for now."

"What do you mean by that?"

"I mean — Mother doesn't care if I don't do what Deedee did — get married to a proper kind of husband and have children. She doesn't think every woman has to get married, if she doesn't want to. But if I don't do that, then I must be celibate, a woman who finds her satisfactions in herself and her work. She has the idea that this is the worthier thing to do anyway and she was really happy to think that's what I wanted. She thought she was providing me with the means and encouragement to achieve that kind of life. You see, don't you, what a shock this is to her — the idea that I'm not only carrying on a sordid affair — that's the way she would think of it, sordid — but that I have been deliberately deceiving her, when everybody else has known about it all along."

'Bel's tone was dry. "You draw her to the life."

Andrea suddenly looked at her. Her eyes blazed and her face reddened. "You've never known what it is to have someone who has always been wrapped up in you, somebody you can't bear to disappoint, somebody whose happiness you can't destroy by doing things she hates —"

"You needn't rub it in. I'm fully aware there's nobody who gives a damn about me."

'Bel saw Andrea droop at once. Damn it, I should have kept my mouth shut. She's having a hard enough time without my sniveling about myself.

" 'Bel, I don't mean it that way. It is simply that I can't make you realize what I am up against with my mother. I'm not dealing with a stranger, somebody I can just walk away from."

"Did she make you promise anything?"

"Not promise. But she is threatening to go to the Dean about me if I don't stop seeing this — person."

"Then are you going to stop seeing — this person?"

" 'Bel."

"Well, then what are you going to do? You've denied that you're having an affair with a man, but you haven't given her any explanation of what you are doing. So she will continue to suspect the worst."

"If there are no more rumors, I think we can live the thing down. I know she still wonders if Carola hasn't invented some of this."

"Then I suppose we'll have to be real cagey. I'll always wear a dress when I'm going to meet you somewhere." 'Bel made her tone purposely light but she saw no answering smile on Andrea's face.

"That will scarcely help. I don't want you recognized. I don't want you seen. If the rumor gets back to Mother that I'm always going around with a girl who is not at Goucher, she will immediately be suspicious. If she should find out it is you —"

"Why on earth don't you settle the whole thing by telling her it is me?"

Andrea drew a long breath. "I'll never make you understand. 'Bel, do you want us separated for the next two or three years? I mean really separated, so that I could never see you at all? That is what it would mean if my mother discovers that it is you I have been having my affair with and not only that, I have been systematically deceiving her about it? It would look pretty bad, wouldn't it, back to when she shipped me off to Miss Harrington's. I tell you she would stop at nothing to separate us for good. I would not doubt that she would take me out of Goucher and send me somewhere else —"

"I'd follow you. You know that."

"And what a mess it would all be. 'Bel, I can't do it. We must wait till I can tell her that I am old enough to act for myself, till she realizes that I'm no longer a child to be controlled and disciplined. Oh, 'Bel, how can I let her know that I have been deceiving her, that I have been lying to her, that I have betrayed her trust in me,

215

that I have been living one sort of life on the surface and another out of sight. She would disown me. I'd no longer be her daughter. I love my mother, 'Bel."

She put her face down on 'Bel's shoulder. So that's it, thought 'Bel. She can't break that bond.

* * *

Carola did not come back to College. But, thought Andrea, I don't believe she was the one who really spied on me. It was some of the other girls, some of the more sophisticated ones, on the alert for sexual alliances. Carola was too docile, too obedient in what she had been taught, to look for anything so rebellious, so unthinkable, as a girl who followed her own desires in conflict with the rules imposed on her by those in authority.

Carola's absence made it easier for her to arrange meetings with 'Bel. Carola was not there to observe her comings and goings from their room. The other girls did not have quite that intimacy of observation. Whether they would notice if she came and went at odd hours would depend on the accident of the moment.

But the weekends with her mother were a penance she could not avoid.

- - -

"Have you seen this man since you were home last?"
"No."
"What have you done, then?"
"I tell you, mother, I am not involved with a man."
Her mother stared at her as if to read beyond her words.

- - -

"Do you mean to say that you have not been in touch with him?"
"Mother, there is no man I'm involved with."
"Andrea, don't infuriate me! If you are not involved with someone, why have all these rumors been created? Who is this person you're rumored to go around with?"
"It's all a mistake."
"If that is the case, why can't you be more candid with me?"

- - -

"Andrea, I'm exasperated with this subterfuge. You must tell me the truth. You must answer me. Tell me at least who this man is, and why it is that you feel it necessary to hide your association with him. He must have a reason for acting clandestinely. You're only just eighteen. This has been going on for more than a year. He must be very reprehensible to take advantage of a young girl like this."
Andrea did not answer.

- - -

216

"You will force me to go to the Dean and ask her to restrict your freedom of movement. I never imagined that the day would come when I could no longer trust you, when I would have to ask the help of strangers in controlling you."

"Mother, you must not do that! You cannot do that!"

"I must and I can, if you do not give me the full details. Is this man married? That seems to me the most likely explanation. And he has not told you so. You're too innocent to realize what may lie behind appearances. Of course he would not tell you. He would invent other reasons."

"Oh, Mother, this is impossible! Won't you believe me when I tell you there is no man? He is the fabrication of somebody's imagination."

"Do you mean Carola?"

"No, I don't. At least, I don't think so."

"She says she heard it from the other girls. And her mother still insists that she is telling the truth. How can I believe you if you don't give me a complete explanation?"

- - -

They fought this battle through April and May. Andrea, desperate, found it harder and harder to concentrate on her school work. For the first time in her life, her academic grades fell. The Dean, alarmed, sent for her.

"Andrea, of course, your work is still acceptable. But we're used to better than average with you. And it is obvious that your health is suffering. There must be some problem that is worrying you. Can you tell me what it is?"

Andrea shook her head.

"I'm sorry you feel like that. It often helps to speak of one's troubles to someone who is trustworthy. Hasn't your mother noticed?"

"Yes."

"Ah, then, I'm relieved. Sometimes young people try to handle situations they have no experience with, without seeking help. But if your mother is aware of your problem—"

- - -

'Bel said, "You might have told her that your mother is your problem."

"It's not a laughing matter."

"I didn't say it was. You do look like the wrath of God, you know. Andy, sooner or later you're going to have to tell her. This situation can't go on much longer, even if you are just as stubborn as she is. What are you thinking about now?"

"Something that happened in the Dean's Office."

"What?"

"Just after she dismissed me and I was about to go out of the room, she suddenly stopped me and asked, "Is your problem in any way connected with Carola?"

"Well, I'll be blessed! That's the closest she has come to mentioning it, isn't it? What did you say?"

"Of course I said No. What else would I say?"

"Have you heard anything more about Carola?"

"No. Her mother is in a huff now with my mother and doesn't write any more, thank heavens. But you know, 'Bel, Carola had them all scared. They thought she would commit suicide at one point. Oh, 'Bel! If that had happened —"

"Well, it hasn't. What went wrong between your mother and Mrs. Giles?"

"Mother evidently told her plainly that she was sure this was all a figment of Carola's overwrought imagination, that Carola wasn't in any shape to be believed. Mrs. Giles didn't like that."

"Well, your mother is standing up for you, anyway."

"Oh, she'll always do that, as far as other people are concerned."

* * *

The time came down to the final exams. Andrea, struggling to keep up in her studies, began to feel as if she were trying to keep her footing in shifting sand. Her conflict with her mother preyed on her mind even when she immersed herself in her textbooks and term papers. Any moment of leisure was instantly taken up entirely with what her mother had said, her mother's obvious distress, the feeling of guilt that overwhelmed her when she contemplated the long course of subterfuge and half-truths she had used to hide her relationship with 'Bel.

It would be impossible, she thought, even to convince her mother what 'Bel meant to her. She could not cut herself off from 'Bel. She loved 'Bel. It was such a simple statement to express so much. 'Bel was part of her. She herself was part of 'Bel. It was hopeless to tell her mother this. She would not be believed. Whatever she said would be dismissed as a schoolgirl's infatuation, or a perversion, an abomination, something in either case to be instantly eradicated.

Since she had remained alone in the room she had shared with Carola, no one noticed that she sat up far into the night. She dreaded going to bed, for at once all her inner debate came back into her mind and sleep was lost.

The end of May came, with the year-end exams over but the results not yet known. It was the last Friday and many of the younger girls had left for home or were packed ready to go. Andrea felt at sea in the emptiness of the afternoon. Commencement for the senior class was a week away. She could come back for that. There were no more classes to serve as a bulwark against solitude, no more term papers to defend her against thought.

Now she sat at the window of her room and gazed absently out into the warm afternoon. There were two hours before she could meet 'Bel. Except for 'Bel she could just as well have taken the morning train to Washington. Her trunk was already on its way there. If her mother had known that she had no more school commitments, that was what she would have done. But she had told her mother that there were one or two things she needed to do, another conference with one of her teachers about summertime study.

She thought, one more subterfuge to add to all the rest. She felt terribly tired and unequal to the prospect of the next three months. Her mother had made no secret of the fact that she was eagerly anticipating the summer, when Andrea would be firmly under her surveillance.

'Bel said, when they met in a sandwich shop on the edge of the Hopkins campus, "Andy, you look pretty washed out."

Andrea nodded absently.

"You're real down about going home."

"You know what it it means, 'Bel."

"That your mother is not going to let you out of her sight. Couldn't you get a job, to get out of the house?"

"I think she is going to say that I don't need a job, that I'd better rest up. She has already told me that we are going to visit Deedee in Cincinnati some time this summer. Deedee's husband is being sent to Europe on his firm's business."

"What's he going to do? Hitler and the French are pretty close to war. And the Italians are building up their airbases, now that they have Ethiopia and Somaliland."

"I don't know. I suppose businessmen have their own ways of looking at things."

"Well, jolly for you, any way."

"What are you going to do, 'Bel?"

"I haven't made up my mind yet."

"You want that job in New York, don't you?"

"I don't want to be that far away. I guess I'll try for a government summer job in Washington."

"The New York job means a lot more."

'Bel looked at Andrea's downcast face. "What are you trying to do, drive me away?"

" 'Bel, don't start that. I can't stand it."

"Well, don't cry here. I wish to God you'd bring it all out in the open."

Andrea looked up at her. "Perhaps I'll do just that."

'Bel, in sudden fright at the look on her face, said hastily, "Andy, watch your step. You know what your mother is like."

"I think it is too late."

'Bel's alarm drained away to uneasiness. "You mean, she suspects it now?"

"What? About you? No, you're something that happened three years ago. She may not even have thought of you since."

"Are you sure of that?"

"No, I'm not sure. I can never be sure of something like that with Mother. But she has not mentioned you."

'Bel watched her as she slowly finished her sandwich. They got up and left to drive to the train station.

As Andrea mounted the train steps, 'Bel pleaded, "See if you can call me and tell me what is happening."

"Oh, 'Bel, if I can!"

* * *

The day after she got home her mother announced that they were going to Cincinnati in a week's time, to spend at least a month. Deedee's husband's trip abroad had been hastened by political events.

Andrea was so shocked she could not speak.

Her mother said complacently, "It will do you good to be in new surroundings."

Andrea found her voice. "But, Mother, I've only just got home! Besides, what about Dad?"

Ordinarily her mother would never have arranged to go away and leave her father to fend for himself for so long a time.

Her mother said, "You're not looking well, Andrea. Your father commented on it last night. I told him that you've been studying too hard. You need a change of scene. He agreed with me."

There was an undercurrent of steel in her mother's voice. She is giving me notice, thought Andrea.

In a panic she tried to think of a way to reach 'Bel. If she could go out somewhere she could try to call her. The pretext occurred to her: she would go to the drugstore to get sanitary napkins. In the drugstore she hurried to the pay booth. Thank goodness it was empty. But when she completed her call to the Registrar's Office, there was no answer. In despair she listened to the phone ringing, finally, reluctantly, hanging up. 'Bel had left. But she remembered that 'Bel said she would stop in at the Office a few times to pick up mail. Andrea bought a pad of paper and a package of envelopes. 'Bel had had at their last meeting, no idea where she would be living through the summer. As long as Andrea was at home they had a means of communicating. I'll type the envelope, 'Bel had said, and your mother won't get suspicious about my handwriting. But now —

She scribbled a note to 'Bel, thrust it into the envelope and bought a stamp for it. She was aware that she was praying as she did so. A prayer, she suddenly thought. To whom? To some divine power, certainly. There was no temporal agency that could help them. 'Bel would be astonished when she told her.

In the following week she went with her mother downtown to

shop and the question arose whether Andrea had enough money to pay for presents for Deedee's babies.

"How much do you have, Andrea?"

She was forced to admit that she had nothing. She heard her mother's sharp intake of breath.

"And what have you spent all your allowance on? You don't have any new clothes. You haven't had free time to go to concerts and the theater, so you have told me."

Andrea tried to be vague. "I don't know, Mother. I don't pay much attention to money. And sometimes I go out with girls who go to expensive places."

She expected her mother to come out with a direct question: Do you give your money to him? But her mother turned away with a little gesture of disgust.

The day before they took the train to Cincinnati she received a letter in an envelope with a typed address. In the corner was printed "McAdams Typographical Service" and her mother handed it to her without a second glance. Her heart was still beating fast when she carried it upstairs to her room.

'Bel said, "Damn, blast and hell! You can write to me but how am I to write to you? You gave me your sister's address but that's worse than useless. If you start getting letters there, your mother is really going up in smoke. I suppose I can send letters to General Delivery at the main post office. But will you be able to go there and get them or are you under house arrest? I'll try that. I'll write you once a week and post it on Sunday."

On the train Andrea wondered what her mother had said to Deedee about her. There was a wide range of subjects on which her mother was very candid with Deedee. But her mother had a way sometimes of being candid without mentioning the heart of a problem. Her mother had probably said Andrea had been studying too hard and needed a change. Perhaps her mother had even said something about Carola and Carola's breakdown. But had she said anything about the disreputable man who was seducing her?

I'll soon know, Andrea thought, as the train pulled into the station and they both waved from the window to the smartly dressed young matron awaiting them on the platform. When they had embraced, Deedee's eyes ran quickly over Andrea from head to foot. All she said, however, was, "You've lost weight, 'Drea. Wish I could get rid of a few pounds."

Deedee's house was a big, sprawling place in an old suburb that was still prosperous. How, Andrea wondered, do I find my way downtown? She had glimpsed the main post office as they left the train station in Deedee's car. I suppose if I say I want to go to the Public Library, that will sound normal, and it must be near the post office.

She bided her time for several days while her mother and sister caught up with the endless recital of family history that

221

always occupied them after a separation. As usual, Deedee paid little attention to her. To Deedee she was still the baby of the family, whose interests and doings were too juvenile to require attention.

So she was surprised one afternoon, when they were alone together, to hear Deedee say, "You're still wrapped up in him, 'Drea?"

Andrea looked up to meet her sharply inquisitive eyes. Deedee went on, "You don't have to tell me. You've been off in a cloud ever since you got here. Mother says that's the way you've been for several months now. You haven't said a thing since you got here."

Andrea blurted out, "But I never do, when you and Mother are talking."

Deedee threw her head back and laughed loudly. "No, that's certainly true! You never do. But you don't usually go around in a fog. Oh, I know, you're just like Dad—the absentminded professor. But 'Drea, you certainly have Mother in a stew—her good little darling who never gave her a moment's anxiety."

Andrea, uncomfortable, looked away.

"Drea, to tell you the truth, I never thought you'd do something like this. I never thought you'd get interested enough in anybody to act this way about them. Who is he, really? Is he a musician? Mother said something about a Jewish boy you went out with at Christmas time, a violinist."

Andrea still did not answer. She was troubled by her sister's curiosity. As a young child, when Deedee was a sixteen-year-old, she had been vaguely aware that Deedee liked boys, that she was always surrounded by boys, that boys were always coming to the house in pursuit of her. She also had been vaguely conscious of the fact that Deedee sometimes did things surreptitiously behind her mother's back, but that she engaged in these undercover activities gaily, with a sense of fun, with no sense of guilt. To Deedee it was a game to be enjoyed by those like herself who were bold enough, confident enough, sure that she would come out the winner. Deedee never seemed to worry that she might hurt her mother. And her mother had always seemed so mild, whenever she discovered Deedee in some subterfuge, so ready to accept Deedee for what she was, so uncondemning.

Deedee went on talking. "Mother says she discovered that you went off with him on weekends. 'Drea, did you really? I'd never have had the guts to do that. You were taking an awful chance. There is such a thing as getting pregnant. You know enough to realize that, don't you?"

Andrea looked at her again, appalled. In a way she had understood that as one of the reasons for her mother's concern, yet she had never really thought about it. It seemed so remote from the reality of herself and 'Bel. Of course Deedee would think of it. But it had nothing to do with herself.

Deedee was still talking. "But, seriously, 'Drea, you shouldn't let anybody get you so deeply involved. Of course, any girl likes to have a private life, but it isn't worth it to ruin your reputation. That's easy to do, you know. You can lose it and never really get it back again. You've seen it happen with other girls. I remember when I was still in school there was a girl who had to have an abortion. They hushed it up and afterwards she married a solid fellow, somebody from a good family. But even now there is a sort of cloud over her. I used to go out with her on double dates. She was an exciting sort of person. But I never let Mother know, not even afterwards. You have to remember, 'Drea, that Mother doesn't see things just the way we do. She is an older generation and, in a way, you have to protect her."

Andrea felt herself shrinking into herself. She did not want to be made Deedee's confidante. She did not want Deedee's advice. She said in annoyance, "It's not true."

Deedee was so surprised she simply stared for a minute before saying, "You mean, Mother is off the track? Well, what in God's name put the idea into her head? She is absolutely convinced that you've been having an affair. She just hopes she put a stop to it before you went to bed with the guy. I wonder —"

Andrea was conscious of Deedee's hard stare. "Are you?"

"Am I what?"

"Are you still a virgin?"

Andrea felt the blood rushing into her cheeks. She stared back at Deedee angrily. Deedee suddenly turned away to hide a little smile. "You'd better not let Mother know, you'd really upset her for life. I've been wondering since you got here. You've changed, you know, 'Drea. Are you still seeing him?"

Andrea said angrily, "I don't want to talk about it."

Deedee was offended. "You'd better talk to me instead of Mother, you know."

"I've told Mother. I don't want to talk about it."

Her mother coming into the room saved her from more questions. She escaped upstairs.

In a day or so she said she would like to go to the Public Library and Deedee gave her directions how to get there. Her mother seemed blandly indifferent and merely nodded when she said where she was going. Sitting in the streetcar on the way downtown Andrea felt short-tempered and unhappy. Of course her mother's sudden relaxation of vigilance came from the fact that she believed she had removed Andrea to a city far from any possibility of pursuit by the shadowy enemy. The old sense of guilt rose to the surface as she found the main post office and asked for letters directed to A. Hollins. There were two.

'Bel said in the first one: "There's really no point to my writing you so soon. You can't possibly come and get it for a while after you arrive there. But I can't help it, Andy. I'm pretty miserable with

223

you so far way. I've started my new job. It's all right. Gets pretty boring sometimes but in any case it pays my board and lodging."

In the second, she said: "I wish to God I knew whether you're getting these letters. It's like putting them into a bottle in the sea. Do write to me as soon as you get this."

Andrea took a writing pad out of her school briefcase and began writing a letter, standing at the tall desk in the post office.

* * *

A month later they were back home. Her father, Andrea guessed, had made some mild protest about her mother's prolonged absence. Throughout the long train trip she had striven to control the restlessness that possessed her. She knew her mother was covertly watching her. She had not had time to write to 'Bel and warn her of their return. She would have to await the first opportunity to leave the house by herself.

But her mother forestalled her. Just after breakfast her mother said, "Andrea, I hope by now there is no more question of your continuing the association that has caused us so much trouble. You are obviously still very unhappy." She paused for a moment and then said in a voice tight with emotion, "My darling, I would never willingly make you unhappy. You must know that. But I cannot stand aside and let you ruin your life by succumbing to the influence of someone who cannot have your wellbeing at heart. Believe me, these last few months have been dreadful for me, perhaps more dreadful than for you, though you probably cannot realize that. I have hated to set a watch on you, to treat you as a child I could not trust. Andrea, can you tell me now, truthfully, that this affair is over, that you will not keep up this association, that in the future I can go back to trusting you, depending upon you?"

The pleading in her mother's voice pierced Andrea. Oh, God, she thought. I can stand anything but this. She sat perfectly still. Underneath her outer quiet, in the center of her being, she felt a faint stir of recklessness. She wondered if it was merely the measure of her exhaustion. In spite of the guilty self-reproach that her mother's appeal had aroused in her, a harder feeling told her that her mother was close to winning the war between them. Her mother had worn her down to the point of giving up the struggle. But the warning was swamped by the rising rebellion in her heart. She suddenly had no more patience for disguising the truth about 'Bel. 'Bel's question, Why, Why, Why? had taken root in her mind. She told herself that she had stifled her natural openness, her native honesty at first to preserve the means of staying in touch with 'Bel. Then the feeling had grown that she must save her mother from the disappointment and pain of knowing something she could not face. The very strength of her mother's horrified rejection that she had a lover had driven her to redouble her efforts to hide the truth. The last months' tug-of-war had increased this fear of avowal to such a degree that it had absorbed all other considerations. Her mind had run in a groove. If her mother felt so bitterly fearful of a male lover, how would she feel if she knew that it was 'Bel who was the menace?

The menace. There it was again, the underlying terror of the situation, which came out spontaneously in the imagery of conflict, peril, unknown horrors.

She became aware that her mother had been silent while she pursued this painful line of thought. She looked up to meet her mother's eyes, fixed on her in an unwavering gaze.

She spoke slowly. "Mother, I am not—I have never been interested in a man. There is someone I love, someone I shall always love beyond anyone else. It is pointless for me to deny it."

"What are you talking about?" Her mother's voice was suddenly furious, her eyes blazed with anger.

"I love a girl, a girl like myself."

"This is ridiculous! Andrea, don't mock me. I warn you I will not tolerate insolence. And don't tell me lies—and such a stupid lie."

"Mother, I'm not lying. It is a girl, not a man."

Still breathing heavily, her mother snapped, "How can you possibly talk such nonsense at a time like this? Andrea, you seem to have lost all sense of the seriousness of your behavior. You are in love with a girl! That is something a child might say. You keep reminding me that you are nearly a grown woman. Yet you can say such a silly thing when I am trying to talk to you as a grown woman. You cannot be so childish. You do not suppose for one moment that you can deceive me, that you can cover up what you are really doing by telling me such a story!"

Andrea sighed hopelessly. At the sound her mother looked at her keenly, without speaking. Then she demanded, "Who is this girl?"

Looking up Andrea saw that a new thought had come into her mother's mind. Her mother demanded again, "Is it Carola?"

Andrea returned her gaze. "No. I have never deceived you about Carola. It is 'Bel—it is 'Bel I love."

For a brief instant her mother's puzzlement showed on her face. Then her anger returned. "Do you mean Isabel Essory?"

"Yes." Involuntarily Andrea looked away. The sound of 'Bel's name seemed to be something that loomed tangibly in the air between them, something that held a universe of unknown things.

For a long time the room was quiet, except for the hurried ticking of the kitchen clock. Andrea, still afraid to look up, waited for the sound of her mother's voice.

When it came it seemed muffled, as if by an upwelling of emotion. "It has been several years since I told you that you must not see her again. You are in touch with her again?"

225

"I have been in touch with her always."

She could hear the quick intake of her mother's breath. "So all this time you have lied to me, you have gone behind my back, you have deliberately disobeyed me."

Oh, if only I could say to her, Andrea mourned desperately, I could not give up 'Bel. 'Bel was my life. 'Bel is still my life. She has been my life since I met her. You've never understood. If you understood now, you would reject it.

Aloud Andrea managed to say, "Yes, I have."

"And you feel no shame about it, no remorse!"

With sudden boldness Andrea looked up to face her. Oh, Mother, she thought, don't you see what kind of toll it has taken of me, how I've been burdened with guilt at the disguise you've forced me to live under?

Aloud she said, "I haven't any excuse, Mother, except that I could not tell you. You did not allow me to try and explain to you about 'Bel. You rejected her as my friend."

Her mother interrupted. "Certainly I did and I will again. If you are serious in what you are telling me now, I am appalled at the state you are in. Obviously you do not understand the dreadful things you have done, in allowing these horrible rumors to circulate about you in Baltimore, sacrificing your reputation for such a chimera. Don't you realize that what you say you feel about this girl is something that cannot be accepted, something that cannot even be spoken of among ordinary people? Or is it just a silly infatuation? Yes, that is what it must be. You've simply not outgrown your dependence on this girl. What happened with Carola should have shown you how silly and disrupting that sort of thing can be. I cannot imagine what this girl means by encouraging you. She has always been more sophisticated than you. She has not lived your sheltered life. She knows perfectly well what she is doing and she must be doing it for her own advantage. Of course, that is it. She has used you, she is using you now. You have given her your money, haven't you?"

"Mother, that is not true. Yes, I've lent 'Bel money. She has a very hard time trying to get an education. Everything is given to me. I must share it with her."

"Oh, indeed!" Her mother's tone was icy.

"Mother, don't talk like that! I love 'Bel. She loves me."

"Be quiet! You shall listen to me. Isabel is someone who is determined to feather her own nest. She is a girl who has nothing but her own wits and ambition to use. She has known from the beginning that she can use you, that you're too innocent to see what she really wants. I thought that surely you had learned that when she tried to entrap Bob. Now she has you so besotted that you do not understand what she has led you into. And she does not care that she is ruining you. It does not matter to her that she has led you into a bypath of life from which you can never escape, while she

226

will seek the first opportunity to go on to something else. She will discard you, Andrea, when you are no longer useful to her."

Andrea put her hands over her ears. Her mother demanded, "How far has she taken you? How deeply are you involved?"

The different, quiet tone of her mother's voice penetrated to Andrea and she dropped her hands. " 'Bel is mine, the same way I am hers. You cannot separate us, even if you make it impossible for me to see her."

She looked up directly at her mother and saw that the anger in her eyes was fading. In its place was dismay and fear. Andrea, seeing this, felt the weight of domination between them shifting to herself. It had never occurred to her that her mother should be frightened.

But frightened of what? "Mother, I love 'Bel. We are part of each other, as much as you and Dad. You would not allow anyone to come between you and Dad."

Her mother's face was white and strained. "You don't know what you are talking about. Don't speak of your father and me in the same breath as this—connection of yours." She stopped and her anger seemed to drain away further. Half-pleading, she said, "Andrea, you cannot continue in this association. Even if Isabel is as sincere as you are, which I do not believe possible. I must make you understand what you are doing to yourselves, what havoc you are making with your futures. Don't you see that you are putting yourself in a box, cutting yourself off from the normal current of life?"

The telephone ringing startled them both. After a stunned instant her mother hurried to the phone. From the first words her mother spoke, Andrea knew it was Cousin Bland and that if her mother did not peremptorily cut her off, the conversation would go on for a long time. For some minutes she continued to sit at the kitchen table, aware of the tumult in herself and at the same time hearing in her mother's voice the tone of captive distraction as Cousin Bland talked on.

All at once she felt an irresistible urge to leave where she was, to go and find 'Bel. Impelled by it, she ran past her mother up the stairs to her own room to find her handbag and back downstairs again and out of the house—as if, in fact, she thought with a sudden shaft of wry humor, the devil himself was after her. She ran all the way to the car stop, half-expecting her mother to call after her.

She phoned 'Bel from the first pay phone she could find. They met in the government cafeteria in the building where 'Bel was working.

'Bel said, as they put their food trays down on a small table in a corner. "What's up, Andy? You look as if something pretty awful has happened?"

Andrea sat down and was still for a while, waiting for the turmoil of her feelings and her headlong flight from the house to quiet down. 'Bel reached over to cover her hand with her own. "It's something pretty bad."

Andrea looked at her in tragic dismay. "Mother knows all about us."

"It's a bit overdue, isn't it?"

The calm, half-ironic tone of 'Bel's voice brought Andrea back to herself. "Yes, of course. But now it is done."

"Well, then, at least the air will be clearer."

"It isn't as simple as that."

"She still won't have me?"

"No."

"So we proceed without her blessing."

Andrea did not answer. 'Bel spooned soup into her mouth and then said, "Has she laid down some more prohibitions?"

"We did not get that far."

"Didn't get that far? Did she throw you out of the house? Glory hallelujah! We're free!"

Andrea automatically glanced around to see if 'Bel's exclamation had called anyone's attention. She shook her head. "No. Things aren't any different, except that now she knows who it is I am involved with. She knows it is you. But don't you see? She is hurt now because not only have I got myself into a worse fix than an affair with a man, I've been deceiving her for a long time."

'Bel ate a couple more spoonfuls of soup. "Then the thing to do is for you to take me home with you and we'll both talk to her."

Andrea sighed in despair. " 'Bel, you don't—you won't understand. You cannot talk to her. She will not talk to you. She refuses to believe that our attachment to each other is anything but a delusion. Either you are victimizing me or we're both benighted."

'Bel's glance was disbelieving. "Let's try and see. I'll take the afternoon off. I'm getting paid by the hour. I'll blow four hours' wages on a try." A sudden thought seemed to occur to 'Bel. "Does she know you've been giving me money?"

"Yes."

"I see."

In the end 'Bel persuaded Andrea. When they entered the Hollingsworth house, Andrea nervously motioned for her to stay in the hall while she went to look for her mother. The kitchen was deserted, so she climbed the stairs. The door to her parents' room was open and her mother called out, "Is that you, Andrea? Where have you been?"

Andrea stood in the doorway. "I went downtown. I went to see 'Bel."

Her mother was sitting by the window, some knitting in her hands. She put it down and was ominously still.

"Mother, I do not want to lie to you. I never have wanted to. I would much rather have been able to tell you about 'Bel, all the time."

"There was nothing to prevent you."

"You would not have allowed me to see her, to write to her, to help her when she was alone and needed help."

"She had her own family."

"Her mother deserted her, went away and left her alone."

"You are quite right, that I would not have allowed you to continue to associate with her, whatever her misfortunes. It is you I have to think of. I sent you to Miss Harrington's school in order to save you from a friendship I knew to be harmful. I'm sorry Isabel had difficulties. I would have helped her, if it had been in my power to do so. But my first duty is as your mother. You should not have left this morning while I was talking to Bland."

"I'm sorry. I couldn't help it. I had to see 'Bel. I haven't seen her for a month."

"Nor will you hereafter."

Once again Andrea felt herself overwhelmed by helplessness. She said, 'Bel has come with me. She is downstairs."

Mrs. Hollingsworth got up quickly. "You must ask her to leave."

"Mother, I can't!"

"Then I shall." She stepped past Andrea and went down the stairs, Andrea trailing after her.

'Bel stood in the middle of the hall, tall and slouching easily in her short-sleeved summer dress. A memory of 'Bel three years before, in the house as her algebra tutor, swept over Andrea. She wondered if her mother had the same impression.

'Bel turned at the sound of steps and stood looking down at Mrs. Hollingsworth. "How do you do, Mrs. Hollingsworth. I'm Isabel Essory. Do you remember me?"

Andrea saw that whatever her mother had expected 'Bel to say, it was not this. Her mother said stiffly, "How do you do? Yes, I remember you."

Andrea listened tensely while 'Bel said with an astonishingly calm boldness, "I remember your kindness to me, when I used to come to your house. It meant quite a lot to me when you and Mr. Hollingsworth befriended me. I hope you will let Andrea continue to be my friend."

Andrea watched her with shining eyes. Brave, forthright 'Bel! She had the poise of a woman much older than she was. Andrea saw that her mother was disconcerted by 'Bel. She doubtless remembered 'Bel as an awkward girl who sought to cover her unease with a certain bravado. Now she stood looking up at 'Bel with tightly closed lips and angry eyes.

Because she was silent, 'Bel was encouraged to go on. "Andy tells me that you know all about how we've stayed friends all these years. You have not liked that. But Andy means a lot to me, Mrs. Hollingsworth, more than anyone or anything in the world. I'm sorry if anything I have done has made you angry at me. Please don't blame Andy for anything. She was only trying to help me."

With a sense of doom Andrea kept her eyes on her mother. Her mother's face grew harder. 'Bel's every word plainly made her more adamant and yet 'Bel did not see this. Andrea saw 'Bel's confidence grow with the older woman's silence. She wanted to reach out frantically and warn her.

All at once Mrs. Hollingsworth said, cutting 'Bel short, "You are not welcome in this house. I have forbidden Andrea to associate with you further. This time I mean to see that she obeys me."

The color rose darkly in 'Bel's neck and face. Her grey eyes seemed to darken, as they did when she was angry. Her lips moved as if she was about to retort. Then she turned her eyes suddenly on Andrea and closed her mouth. Picking up her handbag she turned abruptly away, opened the front door and ran down the steps. Andrea ran to the door to watch her striding down the street.

Through the storm inside her she heard her mother say, "You heard what I said."

She turned to face her mother, the rage in her heart urging her irresistibly to upbraid her. But the sight of her mother's face stopped her short. The realization flooded over her that for her mother to have said the words, "You are not welcome in this house," was such a blow as she might have received from an enemy's weapon. Her mother was very pale and for a moment Andrea thought she would lose the strength to stand. She jumped to her side, but her mother made an impatient gesture and sank down on the chair by the telephone.

Presently her mother said, "Andrea, don't you understand what you and this girl are doing? Don't you see why I must forbid you to associate with her?"

Andrea, alarmed, saw her mother's lips trembling and realized that she was on the verge of tears. She had rarely seen her mother weep and the sight unnerved her. She knelt down beside her and put her arms around her.

"Mother, please, I don't want to hurt you."

"Then why don't you accept what I say?"

Andrea drew back involuntarily. "Because I know that 'Bel and I love each other. No one can come between us, no one, no matter how long we are separated. Mother, believe me, you can make me obey you while I am under age. But as soon as I can I will join 'Bel."

Her mother drew herself out of Andrea's arms and stood up. Without saying anything further she went upstairs. For the next few hours they dwelt in the house together without speaking. Andrea, restless with the thought of 'Bel, of 'Bel's frame of mind, with the almost intolerable longing to go and seek 'Bel, wandered from room to room. Finally, shortly before the time when her father was due to come home, she went to find her mother.

She said, more abruptly than she meant, "Mother, I can't

simply cut myself off from 'Bel like this. I must go and see her."

Her mother said bitterly, "I recognize the fact that you are defying me. I do not wish to hear that girl's name mentioned again. If you go to her now, it will be the last time you see her with my permission."

For a moment Andrea did not answer. There was a sort of knell in her mother's voice. At the same time rebellion swelled in her heart. Reluctantly she said, "Yes. I will tell 'Bel. I'll—I don't know when I'll be back."

She left the house before they had any more to say.

* * *

She found 'Bel at the address 'Bel had given her.

'Bel, whitefaced and grim with the anger that still seethed in her, was silent when she let her in. Andrea tried to hug her. 'Bel stood rigid, her crossed arms held tightly against her body. Andrea stepped back.

" 'Bel, I knew it would not work. You do not realize how Mother feels. I wish you had believed me."

"I thought your mother did like me. But she hates me. She hates me because she thinks I have taken you away from her."

"She would never recognize that, 'Bel."

"But that is what it is, Andy. Even if you married, married a man, you'd still be her little daughter. But she can't see that with me."

"She says, 'Bel, that if I see you any more, it will not be with her permission. Till I'm of age, I'll be defying her."

"You could always leave, you know, just walk out. You're eighteen years old. You're not a child. She should not expect to treat you as one."

"You know I cannot do that. I've told you before. If I ran away and hid, she and Dad would never rest till they found me."

"You don't have to run away and hide. What can they do to you? They couldn't make you come home, really, Andy. What would they do—keep you under lock and key?"

"I don't know what they would do. I'll be nineteen next April. Next June I graduate. I've kept my side of the bargain."

"I don't give a damn about all that. If you left now, we could manage on our own. It would just take longer. Are you afraid of not living in the kind of luxury you've always had? Does that mean more to you than being with me?"

"Oh, 'Bel."

Her gesture of deprecation caught 'Bel on the raw. Violently she lashed out. "All right. If that's the way you want it, goodbye. Evidently, I've been mistaken all along about your real feelings. What the devil have you been doing all this time, if you can't walk out now and take your chance with me?"

" 'Bel, I love you. You know you're not talking straight. How

231

can I do that now? My mother knows I love you. I've told her and she believes me, even if she pretends she doesn't. From now on I don't have to lie and cheat. She knows I am going on seeing you, even without her permission —"

"Yes, you've fixed it all up for yourself. But what about me? I'm supposed to go on being somebody who's loathsome, some sort of an evil influence—You don't give a damn about my feelings!"

Again Andrea tried to put her arms around her, but this time 'Bel flung her off. "You can't it have both ways. Make up your mind."

After a long moment Andrea said coolly, "All right. I have. If you can't last it out this way, I'll leave you alone. Mother is right. It is just a passing thing. We'll both recover."

The quietness of her voice brought 'Bel around to face her. "Andy —" Dismay was in her face but her arms hung nerveless at her sides.

Andrea softened. " 'Bel, don't be so angry, please. I know it is hard on you. But I've always counted on you. I've always thought I could put up with anything because you've always been there when I needed you." She thrust her arm through 'Bel's and clung closely to her. " 'Bel, please."

'Bel turned to take her in her arms. They stood embraced for a long time, while Andrea's rare tears soaked through the cloth of 'Bel's dress and 'Bel murmured in her ear.

After a while they sat down on the bed. In a sober voice 'Bel said, "You mean then that we'll just not be seeing each other the way we've been doing."

"I expect so. It will be difficult."

"Then I guess the thing for me to do is to write and tell them at Bryn Mawr that I'm applying for a scholarship, if one is still available. I can go to New York now and see if I can get a real job for the rest of the summer. I'm just wasting my time here."

" 'Bel, you should have done that earlier. It's because of me that you haven't done as well as you could have, getting through college."

"Now, don't start that. As long as there was any chance we'd be together, I wouldn't give a hoot in hell for what I might have been doing." 'Bel paused for a moment, at another thought. "Andy, what about your Dad?"

"What about him?"

"Will your mother talk to him about us?"

"I'm quite sure she won't. There are things she feels she has to protect him from. This is one of them. Besides, she hasn't given up on me yet. She won't want to admit to him that she has." Andrea was thoughtful for a moment. "Dad is the real reason I can't just walk out now. He has his heart set on my graduating next June. He is very proud of the fact that I've got through college in three years. He's already looking forward to sending me to graduate school."

232

"God! We'll never come to an end of it, Andy! Are you always going to find a reason why we can't be independent?"

Andrea sighed. " 'Bel, don't go looking for trouble in the future. What we've got to do is deal with this now."

'Bel gave her a long look but did not pursue the matter. Instead she said, "Are we going to be able to write to each other?"

"Yes, of course. Especially after I'm back in Baltimore."

"You're pretty cool about it all." There was the remnant of resentment in 'Bel's voice.

Andrea answered her only with a half-sad look. The last of 'Bel's anger left her. They sat for a long time silent, contemplating the unknown territory stretching out ahead of them like a desert.

IV
1936-1938

In was not quite the desert they anticipated.

In September Bob was married to the daughter of one of the senior partners of his firm. Andrea went to New York with her parents for the wedding. She wrote ahead of time to 'Bel, and one afternoon she was able to leave the hotel so that they could meet in Penn Station, where 'Bel got off the train from Bryn Mawr and where they spent a couple of hours in the midst of the constant boil of people.

A few times after that Andrea went to New York by herself. Her new sister-in-law was a quieter girl than Deedee and more her own age. They did not develop any closeness. Instead they fell into a degree of easy familiarity tinged with formality. She doesn't really want to know me, thought Andrea. She doesn't really feel at home with Bob's family, but she is too polite to show it.

Sandra did not seem to mind that when Andrea come to spend a weekend she did not mingle with Sandra's friends. Bob obviously did not care what she did. They neither seemed to notice that she was seldom in the apartment nor had any curiosity about where she went or what she did. She went to New York only when she could arrange to meet 'Bel. They would meet in Pennsylvania Station and spend several hours walking about the streets of Manhattan, going to the Metropolitan Museum or having a meal in an inexpensive restaurant.

At Goucher Andrea's life had settled into a much calmer routine. She heard indirectly that Carola's mother had sent Carola to a college in another part of the country. Her new roommate was a German girl, the daughter of Jewish refugees, and between them a certain comradery existed.

Finally, thought Andrea wrily, I am alone with my books. Most of the time she maintained an inner control, dwelling on the pleasures of learning, seeking the emotional release of listening to music. But occasionally her control slipped and for some solitary hours she struggled with a voiceless rage, a demand for 'Bel that disrupted her outward calm and sent her out to walk for hours until some semblance of peace returned.

She was amused, in a detached way, by the fact that this new sedateness of hers won the approval of the head of her house and the other teachers. Their air of benevolence seemed to indicate that they had chosen to forget any bad reports held against her in the past, as if she had emerged from a time of trial and was now successfully placed on the path she should follow. But Andrea was aware that the reputation she had made in her first two years still flourished among her fellow students.

Lisa, her new roommate, said, "The girls talk about you. What was this great mystery—this great affair of a man?"

Lisa was a pudgy girl who wore her dark hair in a straight bang across her forehead. Her humorous, twinkling eyes were disconcertingly direct. Andrea had grown used to her bluntness. She had said to Andrea that she was surprised that the American girls she lived amongst were so squeamish and lady-like.

"There was no great affair of a man."

"Then what is it they talk about? Don't you know that they giggle and say half-things and tell the new girls that you are dangerous?"

"Dangerous!" Andrea's astonishment was genuine.

"Oh, no. It seems you have a secret private life, you were almost expelled because of a love affair, another girl—the girl who used to live with you in this room—had a nervous breakdown over you. That is the sort of thing they say."

"Do they really? You're exaggerating."

Lisa's eyes opened wide in satisfaction. "Ah, so it is true? You confess it! I hear it in the coldness of your voice."

"I don't confess anything. Lisa, you just want to pry."

"Pry? What does that mean? Oh, I want to know about you, inside! Well, that would be interesting. You're much more interest-ing, Andrea, than the girls who talk about you. Do you suppose that is what they call dangerous? You are not such a child. So if it was not a man —?"

"No, it was not a man," said Andrea firmly and turned away from the conversation.

Her consistent silence, maintained in order to give the impres-sion of indifference, did not prevent Lisa from probing. At first she tried, irritated, to shut her up. Then she became used to the foreign girl's provocation. Lisa was always good humored when she asked personal questions or passed along the gossip she overheard. She thinks it's a game, thought Andrea, a battle of wits, and she wins if I lose my temper and say something nasty.

After their sparring had gone on for a while she began to like Lisa. She even considered inviting her to go home with her on the weekend. The thought for a moment caused her spirits to brighten at the prospect of having someone else present to lighten the gloom of her visits home. Second thoughts dispelled the impulse. The remembrance of the uneasy silence between her mother and her-self came back to her. And Lisa's uninhibited questions and blunt remarks would disconcert her mother, probably offend her, cer-tainly comfirm the suspicions that lay beneath the surface.

                                    * * *

'Bel put down the Labor Department report and sat for a while
staring out of the window. Her mind refused to absorb the statis-
tics, the significance of the graphs. Spring had not come yet but an
uncontrollable restlessness surged in her. She supposed she had
reached a saturation point. She could no longer shut Andy out of
her mind. Or at least the active contemplation of her, because
awareness of Andy lay as a solid underpinning to all her consciousness.

It was a good thing that all winter she had been overwhelm-
ingly busy, with her classroom work, her studying, the extracur-
ricular activities she took on and the labor union problems in
which she was immersed. Nearly every weekend she went to New
York, to join a picket line, attend a strategy meeting of women on
strike against the garment industry, or a rally to drum up funds.
She had thrown herself into it all with a burning conviction that
social injustice had to be faced. Thank goodness, I've got the energy
for it, she thought.

She wrote to Andrea: "Andy, I've got to get into it. Women
have got to fight to protect themselves, to make men give them an
equal share of the world. No man— no employer, no government
administration made up only of men—is going to give women an
even chance. Even in the WPA jobs women don't get equal treatment. It's harder for them to get jobs and they're always the first
fired when there are cutbacks. It's insane, this idea that most
women work for the fun of it, that they're a menace because they
take jobs away from men who have families to support. Suppose
you had several kids and worked fifty hours a week for fifteen
dollars. Or worked in a sweatshop till you got too sick and were
fired? You know, women got the vote when I was two years old and
nothing much has happened since. It's all got to be changed."

The bonus for herself had been the fact that she did not have
time and energy left to brood over her situation with Andy. These
miserable few hours—not more than a handful of weekends in the
whole winter—that they had spent trying to talk to each other in
the din of Manhattan!

Like the last Sunday morning. They had enjoyed the eerie
desolation of the deserted streets of lower Manhattan. They had
ended up in the back pews of Trinity Church, after the morning
service. Their thoughts had seemed to go to one another in the
emptiness of the big church, colored by the light through the tall
painted window. Glancing at Andy, she had thought, everybody
who looks at you wants to get closer. There is something about you
that makes people want you—I suppose, because at the same time,
you let them know you're unattainable, you're untouchable, you're
off somewhere, but infinitely desirable. Don't look at me that way.
I can't kiss you here, in the light of stained glass windows full of
saints, under the eyes of that verger or whatever he is, doing

something with the candles on the altar. If I only could —

It's that black look you've had ever since the big scene with your mother. You're holding back all the time and the strain is beginning to tell. Three more months to go and I've a terrible feeling that you're not going to be able to break loose even then. Are you going home that final time and tell your parents that you're moving out for good, with me? You're going to tell me you can't, you can't break their hearts.

That's it, drop your head. The old lady coming down the aisle, who has just finished her prayers, thinks you're a good girl who has come in here to seek comfort in petitions to God. And who am I, I wonder, in here with all these same appurtenances of religion that I'm used to—the hushed quiet, the tall reredos, the rows of empty pews that speak of sedate Sunday congregations—all except the incense and the holy water basin and the votive candles and the Holy Mother and the dead bleeding Christ?

" 'Bel, what is the matter?" Andrea's urgent whisper roused her.

She could not speak. Instead she slid to her knees onto the prayer cushion and dropped her head on her clasped hands. She could feel Andy beside her, still speaking to her in the wordless fashion of so much of their communing. What can I say to her, what can I say to explain myself, even to myself? God must be there, I know that in my bones, in the depth of my soul, and I know that God would not deny me Andy. There is nothing that can make any struggle worthwhile, nothing that can reconcile me to any evil, save me from any despair, except the existence of Andy. Without her nothing has any value, no riches, no success. The day is without the sun, the night without the moon and stars. And myself a husk.

She had raised herself back up onto the seat and answered Andrea's whispered concern. "It's all right. It just gets to me sometimes."

*　*　*

The end of May finally came. Andrea, gazing out of the window of the room she shared with Lisa, felt a curious lassitude. Everything she had been doing for the last three years had finally come to an end and there was a strange lack of climax. She had finished college. She had her degree. She had listened with detachment to the exhortations of the commencement speakers. The only feeling she really had was that the daily and weekly habits she had acquired in three winters, the minutiae of life that had become second nature to her, had stopped.

Looking down out of the window her eyes registered the sight of the red brick wall where the sun shone on the luxurious green of the shrubbery. No one stood in the walk there. The deserted spot seemed symbolic in her mind of her state of the moment— motionless in an empty space, the past fallen away and the future featureless.

237

As she thought this someone came into her view. It was Lisa, plodding along in the clumsy manner that was characteristic of her. Andrea roused. There was something after all that she would feel the break with. She would miss Lisa's daily company. She leaned out of the window to wave back at Lisa, standing below and shouting something up to her which she could not understand.

She had learned a lot about Lisa. There were times when the tragic circumstances of Lisa's life overflowed in her, when Lisa wept and lamented with an abandon that at first embarrassed Andrea. When Lisa burst out into loud sobs and half-German imprecations, she could be distinctly heard in the other rooms in their corridor. The other girls twitted Andrea. What was she doing to her roommate to make her so noisy. Did she beat her, mistreat her? They were joking, yet underneath the laughter Andrea was aware of a group memory, a group reference to the days when Carola was her roommate.

And though they might make fun, for Lisa it was real tragedy. She told Andrea that her parents had finally escaped from Cologne, in the middle of 1936, when Hitler's revived army had invaded the Rhineland, breaking the Treaty of Versailles. It had been her father's third or fourth move in an effort to save some of his property from the Nazis. It was only because his had been a commission merchant's business, dealing internationally, that he had been able to save anything and to take his family out of reach of the Nazis. He was trying to rebuild his business life in New York. That was why he had sent Lisa to Goucher, to give her a fresh start in this new country. But Lisa's mother's family—Lisa's grandmother, her aunts, her cousins—some of them had been scooped up and taken God knew where. The rest were so scattered that they had also been lost sight of.

Whenever Lisa returned from a weekend with her family she was tearful, easily upset by any bad news on the radio concerning events in Germany. Obviously Lisa was a barometer of her own mother's feelings of betrayal, rejection, persecution.

But most of the time Lisa had been a cheery, quick-witted companion who stirred Andrea out of her own depression. Lisa often made her laugh in spite of herself. So when Lisa was sad or querulous or frantic with the grief her mother bestowed on her, Andrea did her best to comfort, to console, to dry her tears.

Yes, she would miss Lisa. Lisa herself had once or twice lately exclaimed suddenly at the fact that Andrea would be leaving for good when May came. Lisa had come to Goucher with credit for study in German schools but she had yet another year to complete before she would graduate.

At these times she would burst out, "Oh, liebchen, I am so sad at parting with you!" sentimentally shedding a few tears.

"But Lisa, we'll write to one another. You can come and visit me. I will show you Washington."

These moments of unhappiness had been brief and in a few seconds Lisa was laughing again at the good natured jibes they traded with one another.

Andrea's thoughts were interrupted by sounds from the corridor. She recognized Lisa's voice among others. Lisa must have come into the house. Andrea opened her door and looked out. The corridor was lined with trunks and boxes ready to be taken away by the porter. A group of girls stood a little way away, Lisa in their midst. They turned their heads at the sound of Andrea's door.

With a bound Lisa was suddenly upon her, clutching her in her short, strong arms, weeping on her shoulder.

"Ah, liebchen! The trunks! They make it so real! You are leaving! You are going away from me forever!" Lisa lapsed into a torrent of German Andrea could not follow.

Andrea tried vigorously to dislodge her, to loosen her grip. But Lisa only increased the strength of her hold. Andrea, acutely aware of the fascinated stares of the girls down the corridor, tried again desperately to free herself.

"Listen, Lisa! Let go of me! You're making me a joke!" she hissed into Lisa's ear.

But if Lisa understood her, she did not leave go. At last, seeing that she must accept the situation, Andrea pulled her into their room and shut the door.

Almost at once Lisa let go of her and began to mop her tears. She began to speak more softly but still in German.

Andrea said peremptorily, "If you want me to understand you, you'll have to speak English."

Lisa suddenly smiled. It's like the sun coming out, thought Andrea, watching the other girl's broad face. It's impossible to be cross with her.

Lisa's tears were gone. She crooned, "I mustn't be so naughty now, must I, when we are about to part. I mustn't give you bad moments to remember me by. Ah, liebchen, I shall be very unhappy when you have gone away."

"Oh, you'll get over it," Andrea said crossly. "In the meantime, you've given those girls something more to gossip about. You remember what kind of a reputation I have."

Lisa laughed out loud. Her eyes were merry. "We must keep it shined up! How dull it will be when you are not here! You must write to me and tell me all about the clever things you will be doing."

"And you write to me, Lisa," said Andrea, kissing her.

Lisa grabbed her and kissed her again and again.

* * *

June passed in a slow, sweet warmth. 'Bel's letters came infrequently. Andrea was sure that her mother recognized the handwriting on the envelope but she said nothing. They both tried

239

to keep up a normal flow of talk but Andrea's spirits were too low for her to regain her usual resilience as her energy returned with quiet and rest at home after the strain of the last semester at Goucher. She knew her mother noticed this and was worried, casting her sidelong glances when she thought Andrea absorbed in herself.

Then when July came her mother said one morning, as they sat alone in the kitchen after breakfast, "Andrea, wouldn't you be better off if you had something to do?"

Andrea looked up, surprised.

"You've always been so occupied with your studies. I think you need something to do. Of course, you were pretty tired when you first came home. But you are over that now."

She thinks I'm brooding, thought Andrea, and it would be just as well to give me something for my idle hands. "Why, I suppose I could get some sort of job."

"That is what I had in mind. Cousin Bland has come up with an idea that I think you might find interesting."

Ah, so she and Cousin Bland have been discussing my state, thought Andrea. "What on earth would she come up with?"

"Well, she heard about this from Professor Howell, of the University of Virginia. He is in some way connected with Bland's husband. He is looking for some young person—of course, he thought of a young man, but Bland says there is no reason why she couldn't convince him that you would be just right for the job."

"Well, what is it?"

It was the sort of job her mother would approve of, thought Andrea. General Abernethy's widow, said Cousin Bland, had died during the spring, leaving her Georgetown house full of papers and trophies that had to be sorted and classified before they could be turned over to the Government, as he had intended. The General himself had died twenty years before, at a great age. He had fought in the Civil War as a Confederate officer, had been an Indian fighter in the Federal army in the West thereafter, had ended his active career in the Spanish American War, had been a military observer for the United States in China during the Boxer Rebellion. Obviously the accumulated memorabilia of his life would be a treasure for the government archives.

Of course, said Cousin Bland, Professor Howell could not be expected to spend the hours of a working day sorting and sifting this material. A woman had been hired a month ago, a librarian from one of the middlewestern universities who was reputed to be an authority on official documents. She needed an assistant. Cousin Bland, on hearing this, had immediately thought of Andrea. Of course, she realized that Andrea had thoughts of going on to graduate school but in the meantime —

"It was very kind of Cousin Bland to speak for you, dear," said Andrea's mother. "I've talked to your father about it. I've convinced him that I really think you need to take a year off from studying, for the sake of your health. And yet this job would keep you in touch with scholarly things. He has agreed, though he does make jokes about the military mind."

Andrea gave a little laugh. "I can hear him."

"Do you like the idea?"

Andrea shrugged. "It will, as you say, give me something to do."

Her mother gave her a long worried look. But she went on. "One thing I don't quite like about it. It seems that Miss Schwenk — that is the librarian — wants whoever gets the position to live in the house with her. The terms of her contract are that she must live there as curator and she does not want to be alone. That I can understand. But I don't like the idea of your having to live somewhere else in Washington when your home is here."

For the first time Andrea's interest was really caught. "Well, why not, Mother? Georgetown is only a step away."

Yet it would mean the feeling of freedom. The thought lit a little spark in her. She suddenly was aware that her mother was still looking at her and that this fact had registered with her. Afraid that she had hurt her mother and ashamed that she had, she relapsed into the lassitude that had held her captive since she had left Goucher.

The house in Georgetown was tall and narrow, with a curving iron stairway up to the first floor entrance and a deep areaway with steps that led to the door of the English basement. There must be a hundred like it, thought Andrea, approaching it down the sidewalk of uneven bricks. She paused for a moment at the break in the low wall that guarded the areaway. Was she to use the downstairs door or the one up the flight of iron steps? Did the new curator live downstairs or up? There was space in the areaway to park a car but it was empty. Finally she walked up the steps and rang the bell.

It was several minutes before the door was opened by a woman who said at once, "Oh, you must be Andrea Hollingsworth! Come in, Andrea."

She stepped back into the narrow vestibule. She was a little taller than Andrea and wore her dark hair cut in a smooth, short bob. Long earrings dangled from her small ears. She had a high-bridged nose and a narrow chin. A good looking woman, thought Andrea, in her thirties.

"I'm Daphne Schwenk. Professor Howell told me that you would be coming for an interview this morning. Come and sit down here and we'll go over the job details."

The entry led directly into the long room that filled the depth of the old house. Tall windows at the other end looked out onto a brick-paved terrace and beyond that a narrow garden surrounded by high walls. A big sofa was set at right angles to the windows. Behind it was a full-length portrait in oils of General Abernethy in a bemedalled uniform. The walls of the room were lined with small, flat glass cases filled with objects.

Miss Schwenk, noticing Andrea's gaze about the room, said with a laugh, "It's a museum, isn't it? Mrs. Abernethy, I'm told, had a great reverence for her husband's memory."

The faint echo of derision in her voice told Andrea, more than her accent, that Miss Schwenk was encountering for the first time the Southerner's ritualistic regard for family and status.

"In any case, she seems to have preserved everything, absolutely everything. But there is no order in the mass of material. Everything is here but higgledy-piggledy. That's my job—to sort and classify and catalog. Do you think you've got the patience to help me? I don't expect you to have any training or experience in this sort of thing. I told Professor Howell that I would really prefer someone I could instruct. But you must have patience."

"I think so," Andrea murmured.

"You've just graduated from Goucher, haven't you? An English major? Well, that ought to be a good groundwork. I suppose you've been told the other details—your salary and so forth?"

Sitting beside Andrea on the sofa she paused and gave her a long, sharp stare. A moment's surprise showed in her eyes when Andrea shook her head.

"No, Cousin Bland just told Mother she thought it would be a good job for me."

"Cousin Bland? Oh, I see! Mrs. Robins. She is related to Professor Howell, isn't she? Well, the salary is seventy-five dollars a month. Not bad for a girl just out of college. But an important feature is that whoever takes the job has to live here with me. Naturally, I'm a little choosy about who that will be. You look as if you'd be a good housemate."

For the first time a slight smile appeared on her face.

"That's all right with me. Of course, my home is here in Washington. My parents' house is on Rittenhouse Street, just off Sixteenth. My mother wonders why it is necessary for me to come and live here when it would be so easy for me to come and go by streetcar."

The smile vanished from Miss Schwenk's face. "It's absolutely necessary. I will not live here by myself. I told Professor Howell that. He agreed that it would be a requirement of the job."

Andrea looked at her curiously. There was a trace of fanaticism in the way she spoke. Why?

"It's all right. I can come and stay here as long as you want me to."

"Then it's settled. Can you come tomorrow?"

* * *

'Bel called her that night from New York. Alarmed, she went to answer when her mother said it was long distance for her. 'Bel

242

had purposely written sparingly—long letters that made fat envelopes, but mailed only once or twice in a week. For her to call by phone —

'Bel said, "Andy, I've just found out what I have to be doing the next month or so. I wanted to let you know right away. I get so tired of having to write it all down."

"Well, what is it?"

"Well, what's the matter? You sound as if you're mad about something."

"No, I'm not. Go on and tell me."

"In the first place, there is this report I said I would do, on the garment workers' strike. Then there is a job they want me to do that will take at least a month. I suppose it doesn't really matter. I couldn't see much of you if I was in Washington. What are you going to do?"

"Did you get my last letter?"

"Yes. You said your mother had told you about a job for the summer, cataloguing books or something."

"You might read my letters more carefully. I said Cousin Bland had recommended me for a job as assistant to a librarian who is going to catalogue the Abernethy papers. You've read about them in the newspaper."

"Well, I suppose I have, whatever they are. Will you get the job?"

"I've got it!"

"Good for you! Have you met the librarian?"

"I saw her this afternoon. She said I have the right kind of background for the job. But I have to live there in the Abernethy house with her."

'Bel's voice was suddenly belligerant. "Why?"

"She says she is afraid to stay there alone."

"What's the matter? Does she think the house is haunted? Has somebody told her Georgetown is full of haunted houses?"

"I haven't the slightest idea."

"Damn it! Here is the golden opportunity. You're living away from home and I could see you every day and I'm tied up here and can't come to Washington."

"I thought of that."

"Oh, did you? You don't seem very much upset about it, Miss Prune."

"You know I am. It's not just for the summer, 'Bel. I'm taking a year off before going to graduate school. I don't know how long the job will last."

"What are you doing that for?"

"It's supposed to be a good idea, so I won't get stale."

"You mean your mother thinks so. Andy, are you all right? Damn it! I wish I could see you and see if you're all right."

"Don't get ideas. No. I'm all right."

243

"You're certainly loquacious. I suppose your mother is right there, hovering around. She answered the phone, didn't she?"

"Yes."

"And she knew my voice and didn't give me a chance to say anything."

"I guess so."

"How about giving me the address of the Abernethy house? It's on N Street, isn't it?"

"Yes, but I can't do that now. I'll tell you the next time I write."

"Oh, I see. You don't want your mother to know that you've told me where I can find you. God, Andy, when are we going to stop all this?"

"I don't know."

"Well, don't sound so miserable. Your mother has made a nervous wreck out of you. I suppose she sees that now. Andy, I miss you."

"Yes."

When she put down the phone and went back into the living room where her father sat reading, she was aware of her mother's frowning glance.

"That was Isabel."

"Yes."

"Is she in Washington?"

"No. In New York."

"You have seen her there, haven't you?"

"A few times."

"By arrangement?"

" 'Bel was in New York quite a lot this past winter. She has been working with the people who organized the garment workers' strike. Since she was there anyway, we used to have lunch together sometimes."

Her mother did not reply.

The next day Andrea took a suitcase with her when she went to the house in Georgetown. Miss Schwenk—Daphne, she had been instructed to call her Daphne and she practiced this now to herself—had given her a key and she let herself in. She stepped into the stillness of the closed-up house and stood for a moment looking around at the glass cases, the ceremonially arranged furniture, the General's portrait. She thought suddenly of 'Bel's Aunt Gertrude in the apartment on Washington Circle. That had been a sort of museum too but not as dead-seeming as this one. But perhaps that was because Aunt Gertrude, a living woman, had been in it. Perhaps while the General's widow had been alive this house —

The sound of soft footsteps on the stairs interrupted her. Miss Schwenk—Daphne—put her head around the door. "Oh, it's you! You're early."

Andrea saw then that Daphne was not dressed, that she wore a filmy negligee over silk pajamas.

"Are you an early riser? Well, that's fortunate. I regret to say that I'm not. But that must mean that you're not a night person. I'm not at my best till after lunch. Don't mind if I'm short-tempered in the morning. You've brought a suitcase? So the first thing will be to show you your room. It's near to mine on the third floor. You had better learn the layout of the house. You see here, this staircase goes right from the basement to the top floor, so that you don't have to go through any of the rooms on any of the floors."

Andrea followed her into the enclosed stairwell. At each floor there was a small landing and on each landing a piece of old furniture, a small table with a glass top to display old letters and documents, a little bookcase with solemn, calf-bound volumes, old prints and photographs on the walls, only visible when the lights were on. At the first landing Daphne led the way into the big room that occupied the whole center portion of the house, with a round window that overlooked the street at one end and windows at the back overlooking the garden. This, said Daphne, was the old drawingroom of the house. It was even larger than the room downstairs because a slice had been taken from that to make a modern kitchen.

"Imagine, Andrea, the kitchen was once down in the basement and everything had to come up on a dumbwaiter. The bedrooms are up this next flight of stairs. You see, there are three. I'm using the one in front. There's a modern bathroom here. This middle one has been turned into a workroom for us. I thought you wouldn't mind being in here, at the back."

She opened a door to display a small room with one window overlooking the garden and another that faced the white-painted brick wall of the next door house across a narrow airspace, just wide enough to allow for a fire escape. Daphne's eyes went immediately to this window, Andrea noticed.

"I wish there were some iron bars at that window," she said, as if this was a thought that came to her automatically. "But the fire department won't allow that. Will it make you nervous?"

"Why no." Andrea looked at her in surprise.

"Because, you know, it makes a very easy access for anybody who wants to break in and your bed is right in the path."

"I'm not nervous. I don't think this is a dangerous neighborhood. I went to high school close by."

"Of course, you're accustomed to it and therefore it would not seem dangerous to you. But times change. I'm used to living where one should think of such things. Though they can happen anywhere."

She must have an obsession about it, thought Andrea.

She was shown the basement. Down here, said Daphne, they kept their stationery supplies and the file cabinets for certain material.

"There's no space, of course, up in that room where we're going to work. So we have to store things down here. It means going up and down stairs a lot. I really wonder how Mrs. Abernethy managed. She lived here well into her eighties, you know, though I believe she spent her last days in a home for army officers' widows."

"That's the door into the areaway, isn't it?"

"Yes, but there is an iron grill on it, you see, and also on the entrance to the furnace room, so I don't worry about them. And that little room there was for a maid, I suppose. It has a window into the areaway but that has bars on it. There is a lavatory and a basin in the corner and there is still a bed there."

Andrea glanced briefly at the small iron bedstead and the cotton ticking mattress. There was a colored woman, said Daphne, who came twice a week to clean, but she did not spend the night.

"I try to have guests on Tuesdays and Sundays, so that she'll be here the next day to clean up the kitchen. Though she is good about coming when I need her. She knows how to wait on the table. Now you know your way about. Let's go back to the workroom. You can have a look at some of the things I've been sorting. I'll go and dress."

Daphne had lived in the house for a couple of weeks, but she had not spent the night there alone. She had been able to find friends to come and stay with her. Otherwise she went to a hotel. Professor Howell had arranged for the extra expense to be taken care of.

"Now I can really settle down to the job, since you are here. There is a lot of tedium to this sort of thing, of course, but there are moments when you'll find it interesting and entertaining."

Daphne, Andrea discovered, really did not like to get up early. Also she often went away for several hours at a time, to consult people at the Library of Congress or the War Department. To Andrea these hours to herself were luxurious. The quiet old house, the strange collection of memorabilia, some of the pieces of ancient furniture, intrigued her. She found herself spending hours reading accounts of Indian fighting in the West, or of journeys into the interior of China. The General had a pompous, self-important way of expressing himself but he also had had a natural curiosity about the places he had visited and the people he had found there.

In the middle of the week Daphne gave a dinner party and for the first time Andrea saw her in the setting in which she was most attractive. In their intervening moments of conversation Andrea had learned that a principal reason for her taking this job was that she had wanted to come to Washington. She was originally from Michigan but she had spent most of her working life in New England and New York. She had a fund of anecdotes about well-known people and her own professional experiences which she transmuted into amusing tales, some of them close enough to scandal to add spice to dinner table talk. Washington and Washington society seemed to stimulate her to her best efforts. Her vivacity seemed to peak when she had filled a room with people eating and drinking.

That part of the job, thought Andrea, is not going to be dull. And she is really intelligent. Daphne had instantly learned to dissemble her first reactions to some of the people she met in official Washington. She quickly grasped the degrees of association among them. The second time she heard of Cousin Bland there was only a polite alertness in her manner. Cousin Bland, she had learned, was the wife of a Congressman from Virginia.

"I must meet your mother, Andrea. They are related, aren't they?"

"Yes, but Mother is not a political person."

"And your father? Perhaps your parents would like to come the next time we give a dinner." Daphne had quickly picked up the habit of saying "we" about the social functions she arranged. She is really very amiable, thought Andrea.

"Dad never goes to dinner parties and Mother does not go out in the evenings without him."

"Oh, I see."

The first weekend came and she had her first skirmish with Daphne.

"But my mother insists that I come home for Saturday and Sunday," said Andrea. "I mentioned this, Daphne."

"You know I cannot be here by myself. I meant that you could go home on weekends when I'm away or have someone to stay here with me." Daphne's expression was mulish.

"But, Daphne, it is only for Saturday night. I can come back on Sunday evening."

"I just can't stand being here by myself at night."

"But why, Daphne? It really isn't dangerous. Lots of women live by themselves in this neighborhood."

Daphne snapped, "They probably haven't been raped."

Andrea stared. "Do you mean you have been?"

Daphne was chewing her lip. "My roommate in college was—by a sex maniac who slashed off her breasts and left her so damaged she lost her mind. It could have been me. It happened right on the campus. I had to identify her in the hospital —" She stopped speaking, overcome by the recollection.

Andrea, aghast, murmured, "I'm sorry, Daphne." There did not seem to be anything else she could say. She got up impulsively from her chair and went across the room to put a comforting arm around Daphne's shoulders. "I'll talk to Mother again, Daphne."

Daphne cast her an anguished look. "I've got to do something. I'll see if I can find someone to come and visit me on weekends sometimes. But stay with me this time, Andrea."

"Yes, I will."

In the end they agreed that Andrea would stay whenever Daphne failed to find a friend who could come and visit on Saturday night.

Andrea was alone in the workroom the first time 'Bel called from New York.

'Bel said, "Oh, hi! I haven't had a chance to call before this."

"It's been long enough."

"Well, I'm making progress. Perhaps it won't be too long before I can come down to stay."

"What are you going to do down here?"

"I don't know. I'll get a job of some sort."

"You ought to stay up there and do something that will contribute to next year's college."

"I thought you were complaining just now that you didn't hear often enough from me."

"Yes, I know. But 'Bel, you haven't finished college yet."

"You don't have to rub it in, just because you are Miss Speedy."

" 'Bel, stop being funny. This is serious. You've got to graduate.

"Well, Bryn Mawr isn't the only college in the world. I can go somewhere closer."

"I'd rather you stuck it out there."

"A couple of hundred miles away? What's the matter. Have you found somebody more interesting?"

There was dead silence at Andrea's end of the line.

"Andy, Andy, don't get mad." There was alarm in 'Bel's voice. "I didn't mean anything."

"Well, don't say things like that, then."

There was a pause before 'Bel said, "I guess I had better come down there sure enough and stay. This has gone on too long. We can't stand it, not any more. Damn graduating."

" 'Bel."

"What?"

"I've got to be with you. I can't stand this separation any more. But I shouldn't tell you that. I shouldn't interfere with what you're doing. What you're doing will make all the difference in the future —"

"So we sacrifice the present to the future. We've had enough of that, Andy. As soon as I have this job off my hands, I'm coming down. I'm coming down to stay and your mother is not going to stand in the way this time."

" 'Bel, you mustn't —"

"For God's sake, don't start crying. I'm too far away."

After that they talked frequently on the telephone, brief calls because 'Bel's money was short. I can pay for them, said Andrea. Keep the money till I get there, said 'Bel.

Sometimes 'Bel's calls came while Daphne was there. Andrea

was conscious of Daphne's quick, curious glances, though she pretended to go on with her work. Finally, one day she said, as Andrea hung up, "You must have a very assiduous friend in New York."

"Yes. It's someone I've known for a long time."

"He must be quite devoted."

He, thought Andrea. Idly she considered whether or not she would enlighten Daphne. I've got the habit, she thought, of not telling more than I absolutely have to. Half-truths. How silly.

But when she looked up, ready to explain to Daphne, she saw that Daphne had turned away to the letter file she held in her hands. There was a little smirk on her face. Andrea said nothing.

* * *

Daphne had said merely that Timothy McGuire was a civilian official in the Army Department. She had met him when she had first come to Washington in the spring, and for a while, before Andrea had come to live with her, he had come to the house quite often. But ever since last May, when Hitler's planes had begun dropping bombs on Spanish cities—in support of the Fascists in the civil war, they said; as practice runs for a larger war, McGuire said—he had been working night and day. When Daphne talked about him, about his dedication to duty, his great sense of responsibility, his extreme cautiousness if he was asked any probing questions by the other guests who came to her parties, Andrea was chiefly interested in Daphne's own manner. She wants him, she thought. And he is a bachelor, probably a little older than she is. And I don't think he is interested in getting married. He probably is used to fending off women like Daphne. But he likes the attention. He knows she is delighted to have him come here whenever he wants. She'll put aside any other engagement for him without even letting him know that is what she is doing. Poor Daphne.

He had begun to come frequently to the house. Daphne was usually on the alert to welcome him, but this time it was Andrea who was at the front door. He was a tall, thin man, in a well-cut dark suit. He got out of his car, a new Packard that he had parked in front of the house. Andrea, watching from the top of the iron steps, saw him reach back to pull out a large black briefcase. He must be in Army intelligence, she guessed, or something even more secret. Certainly he was an attractive man. He had a long jaw, black hair, heavy black eyebrows and there was often a sardonic smile on his face.

He came up the steps now, carrying the briefcase, which he held up for Andrea's notice.

"Where can I put this?" he asked.

Andrea glanced about. They stood together in the small entry, with the babble of voices in the room beyond as an accompaniment to their interchange.

"Why, we can put it in here." She opened the door of a cupboard in one wall of the entry. In the wintertime it was used for visitor's wraps and boots. "Do we need to lock it? Perhaps I can find a key."

McGuire considered it. "I imagine this is safe enough, if no one else has observed that we put it in there." He handed the briefcase to her and she put it on the single shelf and closed the door.

They went on up to the drawingroom, where an argument was going on about the defeat in Congress of the bill to reorganize the Supreme Court. McGuire's entrance distracted the disputants. Daphne got up from her chair to greet him. She shouldn't flutter, thought Andrea. She's not the fluttering type and he is critical.

A young man—a law clerk to one of the justices, Andrea had been told—immediately began to talk about the latest spy stories. "It seems pretty easy for foreign agents to infiltrate us," he said to McGuire.

Andrea glanced at McGuire. He undoubtedly was annoyed. He disliked any reference, no matter how oblique, to his official status. He made a fetish of the secrecy of his activities, Daphne said. Now he blandly ignored the young man and began to talk to Andrea.

"You weren't here the last time I came," he said.

Andrea, surprised, since he rarely said more than How do you do and Good bye to her, replied, "That was last Saturday afternoon. I usually go home on the weekends."

"Home?"

"My parents' house. They live in Washington."

More guests were arriving, until the gathering had become typical of Daphne's parties, talkative, crowded, with little knots of people arguing, laughing, honing their social gifts. In the midst of it Andrea found McGuire at her side again, a half-filled glass of gingerale in his hand. She knew he never drank alcohol, at least in public.

"So you're not here with Daphne all the time."

"I'm only away on Saturday night. My mother likes me to be home for a while on the weekend. I'm afraid it inconveniences Daphne sometimes."

He looked at her with raised eyebrows.

"She objects to being left alone at night."

"Ah! Does she take the Georgetown ghost stories that seriously?"

"Oh, no. She is afraid of something more substantial— intruders."

"Georgetown is very well policed." But it was obvious that his mind was not on the subject of Daphne's fears. He went on talking, light, careless phrases, with no meaning beyond that of making her aware that she had aroused his interest. Here it is again, thought Andrea. It dismayed her, this dealing with a man. Ever since she had been old enough to encounter this sort of interest in a man she had experienced a feeling of awkwardness, an unwillingness to play the part imposed upon her, this irritation at having to spar around sexual overtures. When she told 'Bel about such occasions, 'Bel grew cross and said why didn't she just tell him whoever he was, to go to hell. But she could not do that, least of all with McGuire. His intentions were plain but nebulous. It was his way of dealing with women. He expected women to find him attractive and he liked to play at responding to them. What do I say to him? Andrea wondered. How do I let him know that I'm not interested, without hurting his feelings?

Her long silence had intrigued him. "You've just graduated from Goucher, haven't you?"

"Yes."

"And now you are handmaiden to Daphne. That won't last long, will it?"

"I don't know."

"You'll be getting married." He was smiling at her. "Aren't you engaged?"

Suppose I said Yes, thought Andrea. She found it almost irresistible to say Yes, but in the end prudence held her back. Instead, she said, answering him obliquely, "Eventually I am going to graduate school."

"Ah, the joys of the intellectual life."

She could not tell whether his softly spoken comment was meant to be sympathetic or satirical. It was his usual manner and when she overheard him conversing with Daphne, she had the uncomfortable feeling that he was secretly laughing at her obvious eagerness to respond to his overtures. But perhaps this was not so and he really did mean the devious compliments he so often made.

He was the last guest to leave that evening and when she came back from seeing him out of the front door, Daphne was moving around the drawingroom gathering up ashtrays. She did not answer when Andrea made a casual comment about the evening. Throughout the rest of the time before they separated for the night Daphne gave very short answers to anything she had to say. By the time she went to bed it was obvious to her: Daphne was sulky because of the attention McGuire had paid to her.

The next morning the air seemed to have cleared and they were back on their usual friendly basis. But whenever thereafter McGuire came to the house, which he did frequently, Andrea sought to avoid him. She did not altogether succeed and after each of his visits Daphne was again short tempered, casting half-angry glances at her and pursing her lips.

At the beginning of August McGuire gave a dinner party. This Daphne explained, was something he did every so often, as a means of keeping up his end of the social game. He had an apartment on the top floor of a new building that overlooked the river, lying far below. It was a novelty to most of his friends and everybody stood gathered on the balcony admiring the pattern of lights amidst the black spaces of the river banks until the mosquitoes drove them inside. She and Daphne had come together and she expected as a matter of course that they would go home together. The evening wore on and Daphne, exhilarated by the drinks and the wine, was gay and talkative, somtimes overwhelming McGuire himself when he was telling anecdotes. At these interruptions he smiled at her, as if amused at this unusual ebullience. His smile seemed to check Daphne. In response to it she became almost incoherent, as if overcome by the sun of his presence. Andrea, embarrassed for her, glanced covertly around to see if anyone else had noticed.

By degrees everyone else left and she and Daphne were alone with him. Andrea was as self-effacing as she could be, trying to pretend she was not really present, while Daphne grew more animated, with a sort of feverish sparkle to her eyes. Oh, dear, thought Andrea, if I could only leave! At last, in desperation she said, "Daphne, don't you think we ought to ask Tim to call us a cab?"

Daphne, as if suddenly aware of her presence, said crossly, "Well, I don't know! Is it that late?"

She wants me away from here as much as I want to be, thought Andrea. But before she could speak McGuire said, "Don't worry. Of course, I'll take you home whenever you want to leave. But I hope not soon."

Nevertheless, Daphne's exuberance seemed to be checked and after a few minutes she said, in a resigned voice, "I expect you're right, Andrea, we'd better go."

Andrea, sorry that her happiness had so suddenly evaporated, thought, She is sobering up. Daphne still chattered on, as they stood in the small vestibule of the apartment, while McGuire handed them into the light wraps that was all they needed in the sultry August night. She walked abruptly out of the apartment when he opened the door, down the corridor to the elevator. Andrea, about to follow her, felt McGuire's hand on her upper arm, his fingers gently kneading the soft flesh.

"Couldn't you stay?" he murmured. He smiled down into her eyes.

"No, I'm sorry." She spoke more shortly than she intended to, in an agony of misgiving that Daphne would look back.

"Some other time, then?" he persisted. He was still smiling but in his eyes was the beginning of resentment.

Desperately Andrea blurted out, "It's true, you know. I am engaged."

He dropped her arm and she saw his mouth at once form a tight, angry line. They both walked out of the apartment down the corridor to join Daphne, who stood watching them approach.

When he left them on their doorstep and waited while Daphne unlocked the door, he was brief in saying good night. Daphne stood for a moment to watch him return to his car and then followed Andrea into the house. Standing in the entry, without taking off her wrap, she said, 252

"You can't leave him alone, can you?"

Andrea saw that her face was flushed and her eyes burned.

"What do you mean?"

"Don't try to look so innocent. Well, I'll tell you, I don't think he is interested in schoolgirls."

"Daphne, what are you talking about?"

"It's disgusting—a silly girl like you, without an iota of experience, making a fool of yourself over a man like him."

Andrea felt the blood rising in her own face. Does she really believe that? she wondered. Is she so blind she can't see what it really is? "I haven't been doing anything."

"Oh, no? Every time he comes here you've been hanging around his neck, monopolizing the conversation, trying to keep everybody else from talking to him. And now this evening—it's disgusting. Do you think I didn't see you hanging back there, smarming all over him?"

"Daphne, be sensible. It's not me. He's the one —"

Daphne screamed at her, "How can you be so conceited? Do you think he'd look at you twice, if you weren't always underfoot? You think you are so fascinating, don't you? You think because you have some boy as crude as yourself following you around that you can catch a man like Tim?"

"Daphne, you're all wrong. Listen to me —"

Andrea broke off when Daphne made a strange sound and turned away from her to walk across the room. Why, she's crying! "Daphne, I'm sorry if you're unhappy about him. But I haven't done anything. You've told me yourself he doesn't like women to get too interested in him. And I'm not the least bit interested, honestly I'm not."

Daphne's tears were in her voice. "Oh, no, you're just too magnanimous, aren't you? You think you've caught him, so you can be just so condescending —"

"Daphne, stop talking nonsense!" Andrea was astonished at the tone of command in her own voice. She had never before spoken like that to someone obviously older than herself. But the tone in her voice seemed to break down the last reserve in Daphne, who burst openly into sobs. Good God! thought Andrea. She must really be in love with him. I don't think he cares anything about her. He just likes coming here and being made a lot of. He must know she is foolish over him.

For a while there was only the sound of Daphne's crying. Andrea, overcome with embarrassment, could not decide whether to leave the room or to stay and try to comfort Daphne. Her indecision held her still, wishing that she could be transported bodily out of Daphne's presence, yet full of pity for the genuine anguish that had reduced Daphne to such abject misery.

Presently, when Daphne began to wipe away her tears, Andrea ventured, "What do you want me to do, Daphne? Shall I stay upstairs when he comes?"

Daphne's swollen eyes flashed angrily. "Oh, no, indeed! Do you think I'm such an object of pity that I'd ask you to do that? And do you think that I really believe that you haven't been trying to get his attention, just to show you can? After all, it's pretty flattering for a man like that to make such a fuss over a girl as young as you are."

That's it, thought Andrea. I'm young. That's what attracts him. But I can't say that to her. It would only make her madder. She is always telling me how he prefers mature women, women like herself.

Andrea sighed with relief when Daphne walked out of the room and climbed the stairs to her own bedroom.

* * *

For once Andrea was glad to be spending the weekend at home. There was a letter from 'Bel. "I've finished up here now, thank goodness, Andy, and I'm coming down to Washington as soon as I can get things arranged. I'll give you a ring when I know for certain when."

She looked up from reading the letter to see her mother's eyes fixed on her. Her mother had recognized 'Bel's handwriting on the envelope. Andrea waited, steeling herself, for her mother to say something. But her mother did not. Perhaps everything had been said between them already—the eternal dialogue, the echo of so much that had been voiced or had been understood: "You won't let me go, you won't just accept the fact that 'Bel is part of me and I'm part of her"; "You don't give a thought to me. You don't care if you destroy my happiness and your father's. You've become so hardened that you think nothing of flaunting this infatuation of yours. You're as governed by that girl as if you were still a child."

For a while Andrea dreaded the thought of a whole weekend under the weight of her mother's disapproval permeating the whole atmosphere. But her mother seemed to turn away from further silent warfare. Andrea watched her covertly. Her mother did not look as old as she was. She was as slim as Andrea herself and her dark hair showed very little grey. But now there seemed to be a certain relaxation in the natural tautness of her posture, a casual droop to her shoulders. If she would only, thought Andrea, soften a little towards me.

On Sunday afternoon the house in Georgetown was empty when she arrived there and she waited apprehensively for Daphne's return from New York. When Daphne did appear there was stiffness between them but after a few hours it became obvious that the episode of Friday evening was to be buried between them. As the days went by the awkwardness grew less and on the surface they seemed to return to their normal companionship. The fact that McGuire did not come to visit was a help. Daphne did not mention him but her increasing cheerfulness made Andrea suspect that she had met him elsewhere.

'Bel called one afternoon while they sat together in the workroom, sorting files.

"This is it, Andy. Friday. For God's sake, be there! Even if you are not nursemaid. Is she going away?"

"I don't know. I'll be here."

"You'd better."

When she put down the phone she glanced at Daphne. Daphne was smiling.

"Your friend again?"

"Yes."

"When is he coming down here? These long distance engagements aren't very good."

"No."

Daphne, as if aware that she had not answered her question, asked, "Does your mother know about him? He seems to call you here all the time."

"Yes, she does."

"And she doesn't approve. Well, they say the course of true love never runs smooth."

She is enjoying this, thought Andrea. Wait till she meets 'Bel.

The next day Daphne told her that she was going to be away again, this time to spend both Saturday and Sunday with people who had an estate near Middleburg, at the foot of the Blue Ridge. She was excited. She liked to ride, she told Andrea, and it was a long time since she had been on a horse. In her enthusiasm Andrea caught a glimpse of another possibility, that McGuire also was spending the weekend in Middleburg. When the chauffeured car came to fetch her, Daphne ran from the house full of gaiety.

"I'll see you Monday, Andrea. You can spend Sunday night with your mother. She'll be glad of that, won't she?"

"Yes," said Andrea, and stood for a while at the top of the iron steps, watching the car go down the street. Poor Daphne. Her cheerfulness, her optimism had returned with whatever promise there might be in the weekend. I hope she is not disappointed. And remembering McGuire, she was full of misgiving.

The street lamps began to glimmer among the big elm trees, still pale in the lingering August dusk. There was no one in sight and the quietness had settled back as the sound of the car ceased. At this hour even the traffic on Wisconsin Avenue was desultory. Andrea went back into the house. She sat down under General Abernethy's portrait and switched on a lamp to read while she waited for 'Bel.

Each sound from the quiet street caught her ear, but the footsteps or the sound of a car went on past the house. She had no idea how 'Bel would arrive. In 'Bel's voice on the telephone she had picked up the suppressed chuckle that meant that 'Bel had something new up her sleeve. Oh, 'Bel, come!

The hoarse sound of a motorcycle coming slowly down the street struck muted through the closed front windows of the house. The sound wound down to a labored putt-putt, seemed to come nearer, echoing against the wall of the areaway. Andrea got up and went out again on the landing of the steps. Looking down she saw a motorcycle within the wall, a motorcycle with a sidecar and at first thought it was a policeman and wondered why. The back of the tall figure of the cyclist was turned towards her.

"What do you want? she demanded. "This is private property."

The tall figure turned at her voice and looked up at her, with 'Bel's grey eyes and wide grin.

"You the owner?" Bel asked, impudently, climbing the stairs.

Andrea retreated into the house, pulling 'Bel towards her by the front of her jacket. They stood for a breathless moment, face to face, staring into each other's eyes. Then they clasped each other close, everything else forgotten for a long moment.

When they released each other, Andrea said, running her hand over the leather jacket, "What are you doing in that outfit?"

"Riding a motorcycle. Good thing it isn't as hot as it has been. Didn't you see it, didn't you hear it, that shining monster down there?" 'Bel pointed out of the still open front door. "I guess it will be safe there, won't it—safer than on the street, anyway."

She stripped off the jacket and flung it and her helmet onto the narrow bench that stood in the vestibule. Andrea picked them up without a word. "What's the matter? Are they going to contaminate something?"

"You can't leave them there. I'll take them up to my room."

'Bel glanced around the drawingroom. "That's right. You're living in a museum, didn't you say? God! What's that? Oh, the General, of course." She suddenly turned back to Andrea. "Are we alone now?"

Andrea nodded. "Daphne left early. She won't be back till Monday morning."

"Andy! Then we've got the whole weekend!"

"Except for Saturday night. My mother does not know that Daphne will be away tonight and Sunday night. But she expects me home tomorrow night. I didn't want to let on anything unusual was happening."

'Bel caught her in her arms again. "Oh, Andy! Let's forget about other people for now."

Andrea put her arms around her neck. "How long have you been riding, 'Bel?"

"Oh, since about noon. I don't want to ride Route 1 again for a while. Oh, yes, I'm quite aware that it is dangerous. But I got here and I'm hungry. Do you have anything to eat in this museum?"

They went to the kitchen and while 'Bel stared out of the window over the garden, Andrea made sandwiches. They went out on the terrace to eat them. The garden was in darkness but there was a faint glow of light reflected from the street lamps. They sat close together on the single cushioned bench.

"What are you going to do, 'Bel?"

"Wait it out until you can say goodbye to the ancestral halls."

"You can't do that."

"Why not?"

"You'll waste too much time."

"You mean it's going to take that long? You're twenty-one a year from next April."

"It's not as simple as that."

In the darkness 'Bel traced the outline of Andrea's jaw. "I'm pretty fed up with being put off, Andy."

"I'm not putting you off. There's nothing magical about my being twenty-one."

"Your birthday is magical. You'll be twenty-one and free — as free as air."

"Not really. Everything will be there just the same."

"But then you could move out. You could come and live with me."

Andrea did not answer for a moment. Then she said, "When the time comes, 'Bel, I'll do it. But the time has to come."

'Bel sighed into her ear. "All right. But I'm going to stay here, right by you, till you make up your mind."

" 'Bel, you're tired. Let's go to bed."

The bed in Andrea's room was a little narrow for two, but they clung close together and did not mind it. Even in the sultriness of the August night the warmth of each other's body was a benediction, a solace, the miraculous end to the long separation. They made love with the length of their bodies pressed close, their mouths together, their hands moving over the soft flesh, seeking reassurance of this reunion. 'Bel fell asleep quickly, overcome by fatigue. Andrea remained awake for a while, stroking her, fondling her, murmuring into her dreaming ear.

In the morning they breakfasted in conjugal ease, sitting in the kitchen.

"What kind of a job are you going to get, 'Bel?" asked Andrea, passing her the jar of marmalade.

"I'm going to be a bonded messenger. That's the main reason for the Harley-Davidson out there. Isn't it a beauty? It's not brand new but it's been nicely kept."

"It must have cost a lot even so."

"Yes. I spent most of the money I saved."

"Then how are you going to get the bond?"

'Bel gave her a sheepish smile. "Borrow it from you. I'll bet you're wealthy now. Where do you keep it — under your mattress?"

"Don't be ridiculous. Mother doesn't pay any more attention to my bank account. But I've got some here, in the drawer of my bureau. I thought you might need some. Daphne doesn't know it is there. She'd have a fit. She'd think we would be broken into by a robber with x-ray eyes."

"Is she that much of a nervous nellie? She sounds neurotic, from what you told me."

"Well, she has had a pretty bad experience." Andrea stopped, finding herself reluctant to embody the tragedy by airing it in words.

But 'Bel's attention was not really on Daphne. "All right, then. I can go this afternoon and get the job. It's a company that has an office downtown."

"Will they hire you?"

"Why not?"

"You're a girl."

'Bel glanced down at her long legs clad in riding breeches and leather boots. "I guess I can overcome that objection."

"They'll know you're a girl, just the same."

"I didn't aim to deceive them, just convince them that I can do the job as well as any dumb male who applies."

"What would you have to do on this job?"

"Carry confidential papers about from here to there. From what I'm told, this company has a contract with several federal agencies, especially for emergency messenger service."

"That means you'll be working all kinds of hours and going all kinds of weird places. Oh, 'Bel! Couldn't you think of something more normal?"

"Nothing that would pay as well. Besides, I think I'd enjoy this, for a while. It's different from anything I've done before."

Andrea sighed and got off her stool. "All right. Help me clear up the dishes. This is Saturday, you know. Will this office be open?"

"Oh, yes. I told you, they operate on a twenty-four hour basis seven days a week."

"So I probably won't see as much of you as I did when you were at Bryn Mawr."

"Now don't be such a sourpuss. Besides —"

"Besides what?" Andrea demanded, noticing 'Bel's glance about the kitchen and into the room beyond.

"I've got to live somewhere. This is a pretty big house. Wouldn't there be somewhere where I could sleep here? That bed in your room is a little narrow, but —"

"I've thought about that already. But there is Daphne to take into account. I don't know how she'd take to the idea."

"I'd be around — one more person to keep the burglars away."

"We'll have to ask her when she gets back on Monday."

"When are you going to your mother's?"

"After lunch. And I'll be back tomorrow afternoon."

'Bel caught her around the waist. "Kiss me again, Andy. I can't believe you're within reach."

When she could, Andrea said, "You can sleep in my room tonight. You wouldn't be going to work till Monday, would you?"

"I guess not."

* * *

Saturday afternoon and evening and Sunday morning passed on leaden feet. Andrea hoped that her mother did not notice her more than usual absentmindedness. How early, she wondered, could she leave to go back to Georgetown without arousing comment?

Finally she escaped and by five o'clock had reached the Georgetown house. Surprised, she heard voices as she opened the front door. One of them was certainly 'Bel's and the other sounded like Daphne's. She glanced out to the terrace and saw them both seated out there, Daphne perched on the edge of the cushioned bench, 'Bel slouched in one of the armchairs, her legs crossed, her arms hanging over the chair arms, a glass of scotch in one hand.

Daphne gasped and jumped around as Andrea came across the room towards them. Her glass of scotch was on the little iron table beside her. The late afternoon sun, reflected from the wall of the house next door, caught the plume of smoke from her cigarette.

Daphne said with nervous eagerness, "I know. I'm back sooner than you expected. My hostess had an emergency in her family and had to cut the weekend short. I was very startled to find your friend here. You did not tell me you expected her."

Andrea sent a little secret smile in 'Bel's direction. That crude boy who is following me around, she remembered. She said smoothly, "I had no chance to tell you that 'Bel was staying here overnight."

"Oh, it's quite all right, quite all right! I don't mean you to think I object." She stubbed out her cigarette and then sought frantically for another.

Good heavens! thought Andrea. What has happened to her? Is something wrong about McGuire? "I'm sorry about your weekend, Daphne."

"Oh, that's all right! I don't think it is anything very bad. And I've been enjoying talking to your friend. She has been telling me about her job. What an unusual thing to do!"

Andrea glanced in 'Bel's direction again. "Do you have it?"

'Bel nodded. "I talked them into hiring me. I guess they think I'm a better security risk than most of their applicants. But I need somewhere to live. I'd like to persuade Daphne to let me stay here."

"But there is no room! We have to use that third room upstairs as a place to work. That's why Andrea has to have that little room at the back."

'Bel said, "Well, I have been down in the basement. You've got a maid's room down there, with a bed in it. I could use that and I wouldn't be in your way. It's even got its own entry."

259

"Oh, but Isabel, that's hardly fit for anyone to live in!"

"I've lived in worse. There is nothing wrong with it. I can sleep upstairs when Andy isn't here. Wouldn't you like that?" 'Bel was smiling as she asked Daphne the question. "You wouldn't have to worry so much about being alone at night. You wouldn't have to arrange for someone else to come and be here."

"Except," Andrea struck in, "you're likely to be out working at night sometimes, even on the weekend."

'Bel shrugged and did not respond.

Daphne drew another long nervous drag on her ciagrette. "But, Andrea, don't you think it's rather a poor place for her? It was only meant for the maid to spend an occasional night here."

"That's up to 'Bel. If she doesn't mind —"

"We can try it, if you really want to, Isabel." Daphne laughed uncertainly. "I expect the neighbors will wonder why we've got a man living in the basement."

Andrea, suddenly angry, retorted, "That's stupid."

'Bel said drily, "It might be just as well if they did think so, for Daphne's peace of mind."

Daphne laughed again, her nervous, jerking laugh. "Oh, I'm sure they'll soon realize their mistake." She took a quick swallow of her drink, then looked at Andrea. "You might have told me that your friend who was always calling you from New York was a girl."

Her frantic nervousness seemed to be quickly subsiding and as it did so her normal love of teasing came to the surface. But this time there was perhaps some malice, thought Andrea. She wants to pay me back for McGuire.

"You didn't really give me a chance, Daphne," said Andrea blandly.

'Bel, who had been watching them, suddenly drew her legs in and stood up. "Why don't we go and see about the room? Do you have some bedclothes for me, Andy?"

"I expect we can find some." Andrea glanced at Daphne.

"Of course. In the closet next to the workroom," said Daphne, also getting up. "Well, I think I'll go and straighten my room while you take Isabel downstairs."

Downstairs in the maid's room Andrea said, "This mattress is musty," as she and 'Bel turned it.

"I can get a new one tomorrow. Besides, as soon as she goes to bed tonight, I'll come upstairs."

"Tell me what happened. Something did. She was like a cat that's been locked up in a closet."

"Something did, all right. After you left yesterday I went downtown to that office and told them they ought to hire me. They objected because I'm a girl but after arguing some they decided to try me. In fact, what I think it is is that the men there just don't think I can do the job, that I'll get scared or something and beg off. But they want to have fun out of seeing me fail. You know how it is.

260

Anyhow, they said I could try it for a couple of weeks. After that interview, I didn't know what to do with myself, so I went to the movies and saw a rerun of *Man of Arran*. You remember it, Andy? We saw it in Baltimore — all about the people planting potatoes on the seaside terraces, in seaweed and sand, and the basking sharks swimming by —"

"Yes, yes. But what happened, 'Bel?"

"Why, I came back here and everything was so quiet and peaceful. I got myself something to eat and then I went up to your room and got into your bed and went to sleep — such a sound, restful sleep, as if you were there with me. I guess I thought you were, really."

"And then what happened?"

"I must have really slept. I know I woke up once and it was just daylight and I went back to sleep. And then all at once some noise woke me and when I opened my eyes it was broad daylight. I listened for a while and I heard somebody closing the front door. All I could think of was that it was you, that you'd come back earlier than you expected. But it didn't sound just like you. Somebody was puttering around downstairs and I didn't think you'd do that. I just didn't think of Daphne at all. The idea didn't cross my mind. So I put on my clothes. I didn't like the idea of confronting some stranger naked."

"But it was Daphne."

"I heard whoever it was coming up the stairs and I waited to give them time to reach the landing. Then I opened the door of your room. I was braced for trouble and what did I see? This woman staring at me as if I was the devil himself. She began to scream. God, I've never heard such shrieking in my life. When I went towards her to tell her it was all right, it was just me, a friend of yours, she let out one last screech and collapsed on the floor, just out like a light. Good God, Andy! What is the matter with her?"

'Bel heard the intake of Andrea's breath. "Oh, poor thing!"

"Poor thing, why? What's the explanation, Andy?"

"She is terrified of being raped. Her roommate in college was raped and mutilated. Daphne has never got over it. This is terrible, 'Bel. I would not have frightened her like that for anything."

"Well, you couldn't know she was coming back today."

"Yes, but perhaps I should have made more of an effort to tell her about you — We just haven't been getting along very well, 'Bel. I can see what happened. She thought she was in the house alone and then you walk out of my room and she thinks you're a man who has climbed in up that fire escape. Her mind dwells on all sorts of dangers. That fire escape, for instance. She says she doesn't see how I can sleep in that room, with it in my window."

"Well, it's too bad I scared her so. Of course, I didn't have any idea of something like that. I got some cold water and bathed her face and revived her. She came around pretty quickly. Now that you've told me, I can see why she had that awful look of fear in her eyes when she opened them. It gave me a turn, really. She pulled away from me and I thought she was going to start screaming again, so I began talking, saying something nonsensical like, are you all right. But she began pushing me away in a frantic sort of way, yelling, "Get away! Leave me alone. Don't touch me!' I thought she'd have the whole neighborhood in an uproar. But these old houses have pretty thick walls and they're lived in by people who don't expect to hear cries for help from next door. Anyway, it finally dawned on me that she thought I was a man. Of course she thought I was about to rape her. I disabused her of that idea. Then she stopped screaming and cried for a bit. When she began to quiet down I said why didn't we go downstairs and have a drink. You came in a little while after that."

"So that was what it was."

'Bel studied her thoughtful face. "Did you think it was something else?"

'I thought it was something to do with McGuire."

"Who is he?"

"I'll have to tell you all about him."

But now 'Bel was smiling at her and taking her in her arms. "But not just now. Just think, Andy, we've got a place to be by ourselves. Who cares if it is in the basement. Nobody will know anything about us."

"Umm-mm," Andrea said dubiously into her neck.

* * *

It was a sort of demi-paradise. Whenever they could, on a Saturday or Sunday, when 'Bel was not working and Andrea could avoid going home, 'Bel drove the motorcycle out into the country, with Andrea in the sidecar. Even as the warmth of summer began to ebb there were lots of days when they could get away where nobody was at all likely to see them. They began to forget the long dry months of separation. These precious hours and those in bed together when they were alone in the house or Daphne was asleep, were a dream of bliss, what they had thought about incessantly when three hundred miles had separated them. After all, thought Andrea, Mother can not know how often Daphne goes away. She must expect that as the work gets more demanding Daphne must stay in Georgetown and then I must stay with Daphne.

The only comment her mother made was to inquire once, in a petulant tone, "Doesn't Miss Schwenk have a friend who can come and stay with her more often?" Because Andrea had explained to her the source of Daphne's fear of being alone in the house at night and her mother had been both shocked and sympathetic. Andrea had answered, "Oh, yes, but the friend she depends on hasn't been able to do that lately."

Her mother's complaint was not the only thing that added to

her uneasiness. She wondered just how much Daphne did guess about 'Bel and herself. Often, when 'Bel came home after dark, wheeling the motorcycle into the areaway as quietly as possible, Andrea lay in bed, her ears straining for some sound from Daphne's room that would tell her whether Daphne was also aware of 'Bel's return. There was never such a sound and that fact in itself made Andrea suspect a carefully silent Daphne, watchful in the dark.

There had been no sign of McGuire since 'Bel's arrival and Andrea mentioned this to 'Bel.

'Bel said, "There you go again about McGuire. Who the devil is McGuire?"

"She's in love with him."

"Don't tell me!"

"Don't poke fun, 'Bel. She really is. And he couldn't care less about her. Daphne is a nice woman. All she wants is a chance to spend her life waiting on him, smoothing all his troubles away. Oh, 'Bel, I am sorry for her, because he'll never think of her as anything except a convenient refuge when he wants entertainment."

"Tell me more about him," said 'Bel and Andrea obeyed, giving her an account of the evening at McGuire's apartment.

"You never said anything about this to me before," 'Bel said accusingly, when she had finished.

"You were too far way. You'd have gone off half-cocked. We'd have had a fight, about something I don't think is worth fighting about."

"Well, what does McGuire do?"

"He does something mysterious in the Department of the Army. He always comes here with a briefcase he wants tucked away out of sight. He gets mad if anybody tries to talk to him about his job, but I think he'd be upset if everybody didn't act as if he was involved with top secrets. He flatters Daphne by acting as if this is one safe spot where he won't be in danger of being spied on. Daphne takes him very seriously. She seems to feel she is his guardian angel or something like that."

"Does he know I'm living here?"

"No, of course not. He hasn't been here since you came. I don't think Daphne writes to him. I gather from her that he makes these sudden disappearances and nobody knows where he is."

"What do you suppose he's going to say when he finds out I've moved in? Do you know what happened yesterday, while you were out? The woman next door met Daphne on the street out front and asked her who it was rode the motorcycle and what was he doing here. I heard them talking but they didn't see me. Daphne said I rented a room in the basement. The woman said, That's a funny arrangement — two women in the house and a man in the base-ment, Daphne just giggled, but she didn't tell the woman who I was. The woman still thinks I'm a man."

Andrea shrugged. "Either that's her sense of humor or she has some idea of letting it be thought that we have somebody here who can protect us from intruders. You know her preoccupation with that."

September came and there was still no sign of McGuire. Daphne said cryptically that he was probably out of the country. The newspapers were full of the dismemberment of Czechoslovakia and the growing storm of antisemitism in Germany. There was probably a connection, thought Andrea.

There was a marked difference in Daphne's manner while he was gone. She had become relaxed and cheerful. It was as if she really had forgotten the evening of the quarrel between herself and Andrea.

It was obvious that 'Bel intrigued her. Sometimes when Andrea came back to the house from a trip to the Library or to a government archive, she found 'Bel seated in the drawingroom or on the terrace with Daphne. 'Bel's irregular working day, sometimes beginning in the afternoon and going on into the night, made it easy for Daphne to invite her upstairs. Whenever this was the case Daphne, so busy as a rule, so preoccupied with the responsibilities of her task, laid aside her work and spent hours chatting with 'Bel, bantering with 'Bel, probing 'Bel's life history. At first Andrea gave no importance to this attention. 'Bel was always interesting to talk to and certainly the General's memorabilia must grow tedious at times. But after a while she began to see a purpose in Daphne's behavior. At times she would catch Daphne looking at her as she came in to find them together, a cruel little smile on her face.

One afternoon when this was more obvious than usual Andrea suddenly recognized what she saw: Daphne was taking her revenge for McGuire.

She said sulkily to 'Bel when they were alone, "You're spending a lot of time with Daphne these days."

'Bel's extra sensitivity at once caught the tone in her voice. "She gets bored with the General. And I have to pass the time somehow when you're not here."

"Does it have to be with Daphne?"

'Bel looked at her. "Andy, you've never been jealous before."

"Haven't I? What do you know about it? You've been in New York for months. How do I know what you've been doing — whether you were even thinking about me?"

She heard the note of hysteria in her own voice and saw that 'Bel did, too. I'm acting like a jackass, she thought.

'Bel came close to her. "Andy, Andy. You know I don't think about anybody but you. You're on edge all the time now. Damn your —"

She broke off abruptly and Andrea knew that she had been going to say "your mother" There was a vast resentment in 'Bel

264

that sometimes surfaced at moments like this. Andrea felt immediately deflated. Whenever the tight rein she kept on herself broke this way and she relieved the tension by attacking 'Bel, this let-down followed, this feeling of hopelessness, of the pointlessness of rebellion.

'Bel's arms were around her. "Andy, I love just you. How could anybody else mean anything to me?"

One last burst of anger seized Andrea. "Why do you play up to her? You act sometimes as if I wasn't in the room."

"That's not true. We're always pretending, aren't we, in front of everybody. Daphne is not an exception. In fact, if you ask me, I think Daphne knows all about us. She's no fool."

No, Daphne was no fool, thought Andrea. This could not be the first woman-situation Daphne had experimented with. Somewhere and sometime Daphne had learned the malicious pleasure of playing with someone like 'Bel — open, unwary 'Bel — creating discord between lovers.

It was all very well for 'Bel to be offhand. In spite of herself, 'Bel enjoyed the pseudo-flattery with which Daphne showered her. 'Bel could not be cruel. She could not retaliate. Daphne spent hours catechizing 'Bel about her experiences, laughing uproariously when 'Bel, responding to her provocation, told anecdotes about the funnier side of life in the labor troubles in New York.

Andrea complained, in moments of despondency. "It makes me sick to watch her — and you."

"Andy, don't be silly. She isn't really interested in me. She is just trying to get your goat. She has noticed that you get upset, so she does it just for that."

"I think she is getting soft on you."

'Bel, stretched out in the bed beside her, laughed into the pillow. "What a thought! She thinks I'm a freak. I bet she makes jokes about me to the people who come to her cocktail parties. The missing link who lives in the basement."

"She never mentions you. And I hope she never does."

"Well, I've got to be careful. I want to stay here, Andy — like this, in bed with you. I don't want to make her mad, so that she doesn't want me here."

Then one afternoon in October Andrea's mother and Cousin Bland came to the house. It was not the day of one of Daphne's cocktail parties but she was always prepared for guests. This was the first time that Cousin Bland had come to observe the classification of the Abernethy papers. Professor Howell, she explained, was always singing the praises of Miss Schwenck and the efficient job she was doing. Daphne smiled, the epitome of grace. Under the constant flow of Cousin Bland's talk, Andrea watched her mother's careful examination of her surroundings.

She knew her mother was not very interested in General Abernethy What she chiefly wants to know, thought Andrea, is how I fit into all this. Fortunately the basement was not on the tour of the house. Andrea waited anxiously for Daphne to make mention of 'Bel. It would be like her, thought Andrea, to say something just to see whether Mother knows about her. But Daphne said nothing.

Daphne offered tea or sherry or something stronger and Cousin Bland, with the practice of a dedicated party-goer, at once sat down in the drawingroom and went on talking about her recollections of Mrs. Abernethy. There was another ring at the doorbell and Andrea went to answer. McGuire stood on the doorstep.

He greeted her as if the episode at his apartment had not taken place. He handed her his briefcase and waited while she put it away in the cupboard. Daphne's quick ear had picked up the sound of his voice at once. She came eagerly out to join them and bring him into the drawingroom.

It amused Andrea to watch as the two older women carefully and unobtrusively assessed him. She could not tell whether McGuire realized that he was under scrutiny. He was his usual blandly mysterious self.

After half an hour Cousin Bland announced that she and Andrea's mother must be going. Daphne, with sudden bright eagerness, said why didn't she go with her mother and spend the evening at home? Andrea, understanding her intent to be alone with McGuire and knowing that 'Bel had left for work in the middle of the afternoon and would be gone into the night, said, Yes, she would.

Cousin Bland took them to the house in Rittenhouse Street in her own car and hurried off. She was due at an evening party, she said.

Andrea's mother said, as the two of them went into the kitchen, "Miss Schwenk is a very attractive young woman. Who is Mr. McGuire?"

"He is a civilian with the Army. That is all I know about him. Daphne says he has a very responsible job."

"I thought he paid rather a lot of attention to you."

"Oh, he doesn't come there to see me. He is Daphne's friend. I think she would like to marry him."

"He did not strike me as being the marrying kind. I am glad you are not attracted to him. You are not, are you?"

She doesn't like him, thought Andrea. "I've told you, Mother, he is Daphne's friend."

"That does not always signify — that he should come to see her but is interested in you. I am sure Bland and I had the same impression of him."

They worked together at getting dinner, without much conversation. Andrea was sure that her mother had noticed that during the last two months there had been no letters from 'Bel and

266

no phone calls. That could mean only one thing, that 'Bel was in Washington. Her mother surely could not think that she had ceased to communicate with 'Bel. But her mother had not spoken of this. It was one more thing that lay unvoiced between them.

* * *

Now that McGuire had come back Daphne was again tense. Her manner towards Andrea hardened. When McGuire came to the house she watched him intently. When he was not there her thoughts obviously were absorbed in him, so that she often did not hear when Andrea asked a question about their work and had to repeat herself. She doesn't see him at all as he is, thought Andrea. She reads all kinds of things into the least little attention he pays her. She is bound to be disappointed one of these days.

Andrea's concern prompted her, once or twice, to make a mild criticism of McGuire, to point out some of his foibles. But Daphne sprang to his defense fiercely.

"Andrea, you are altogether too critical of people. I've noticed that. If people don't suit you, you're too quick to find fault with them. That's a habit you ought to correct."

Andrea, startled, went to reply but stopped. If Daphne, who delighted in witty and sharp-tongued comments on her guests, thought her hypercritical —! Well, there was no use quarreling with Daphne, she would not be warned. A passionate love had closed her eyes to McGuire, the mortal.

McGuire's return made another difference. While he had been gone there had been few opportunities for Andrea and 'Bel to go off by themselves into their special world. Andrea had tried to arrange for evenings out, when 'Bel was free. But Daphne had objected strenuously. She needed Andrea, she said, to help when she had guests. And they might be out too late after dark and she became frightened.

With McGuire's return she relaxed her protests. She scarcely noticed when Andrea left the house.

"She wants him to herself," Andrea told 'Bel. "She doesn't want me around."

"That's fine with me," said 'Bel.

" 'Bel, he isn't interested in me now. You know, he's an unforgiving type and he won't forget what happened at his apartment that evening."

"But Daphne isn't sexy."

"I don't think I am either."

"You mean, you're both bookish types. But there's a difference. Poor idiot. He doesn't know the opposition he is up against."

'Bel noticed the difference McGuire's presence made in another way. Daphne forgot her. 'Bel never came upstairs when she heard the sounds of people in the house. But when there were no

267

visitors she breezed into any room in which Andrea and Daphne were or Daphne alone and began the cheerful banter that she enjoyed. But now Daphne did not respond, or only with a quip or two, her mind obviously elsewhere. 'Bel was offended. Thin-skinned 'Bel, thought Andrea, instantly aware of anyone's manner towards her, suspicious of any falling away in someone's attention and sympathy, ready to see in the change criticism of herself. Andrea, watching her, saw her eyes stay fixed on Daphne, resentment ready to turn to dislike. Daphne was oblivious to the scrutiny.

One night, in Andrea's bed, 'Bel said, "He has her mesmerized, doesn't he?"

"Yes."

"He was here today, wasn't he?"

"Yes. How did you know?"

"I was leaving for work this afternoon when he arrived."

"Did he see you?"

"Unless he was blind. I came out of the basement while he was standing at the front door, looking down at me. He was very interested, until Daphne opened the door and fell all over him."

"I wonder what she told him."

"About me?"

"Yes. He's always curious about people."

"I suppose that's part of his job."

"I guess so."

A little before Thanksgiving McGuire disappeared again for a while. Daphne's interest in her own household returned. She was cheerful and fell back into joking with 'Bel. She even suggested that 'Bel go with her to New York to spend the Thanksgiving holiday. But 'Bel, with a glance towards Andrea, said she could not go. It was part of the terms of her job that she should be available for emergencies on holidays.

Afterwards Andrea said, "Of course, if you could get off, 'Bel, you might as well. I'm going to have to spend the whole weekend with my mother."

"Oh, I'll just hole up here, Andy, and wait for you. Perhaps you can get back before Daphne and we'll have the house to ourselves."

Which they were able to do.

* * *

Christmas came and went and McGuire returned with the New Year, while the Christmas lights still shone in the front windows of houses across the street. This time there was a sort of excitement in Daphne's manner and Andrea wondered whether he had unbent to the extent of telling her more of his doings. Andrea had acquired the habit of noting the events recorded in the newspapers as clues to what he might be engaged with. Italy, she remembered, had withdrawn from the League of Nations early in

December. The Japanese were consolidating their position as the chief power in the Far East. War was inevitably coming, said 'Bel, who had joined the Women's League for Peace and Freedom.

One evening late in January, when Daphne's cocktail party was just beginning to break up, Andrea went to answer the doorbell and found McGuire on the doorstep. For the first time he had someone with him, a stolid-looking blonde man who nodded to her when McGuire introduced her. Then with his usual urbanity McGuire handed her his briefcase and waited with a smile on his face while she put it away in the cupboard. He is playing up to the new man, thought Andrea. There were several people with Daphne in the drawingroom and they all knew McGuire. They looked with curiosity to see who the man was he had brought with him.

That was another of McGuire's little foibles, thought Andrea. Without really changing his manner or saying anything out of the ordinary, he succeeded in giving a subtle emphasis to what he was doing. The man with him must be someone of importance, though Andrea did not recognize his name as one she had seen in the newspapers. He must be someone with an even more mysterious importance than McGuire's own. Andrea saw McGuire look smiling into Daphne's eyes as he introduced him. She saw the sudden flush of pleasure in Daphne's face. Evidently Daphne understood some hidden significance in this. Andrea knew that she got an inordinate delight in the feeling that her parties sometimes served as a stage for the mingling of the great in Washington society. So McGuire had brought her a new prize and with his touch of the sardonic, had offered it to her as he would have a bouquet of flowers. If Daphne would only not lose her poise so, Andrea complained to herself.

The party went on beyond its allotted time, as Daphne's parties often did. Once or twice in the course of the evening Andrea went to the lower floor to the kitchen, to help the maid fetch ice and sandwiches. She listened each time for some sound that would tell her whether 'Bel had come home. Her ears were always quick to pick up the muffled putt-putt of the motorcycle being wheeled into the areaway. If she missed that, a faint sound of music would tell her that 'Bel was lying fully dressed on the bed in the maid's room, reading with the radio on. But all she heard were the voices on the floor above and Edna the maid moving about in the kitchen.

The last time she went downstairs, just as she started back up the stairs, she was stopped by the ringing of the front doorbell. When she opened it she saw 'Bel standing there in the light over the door. 'Bel had on her leather jacket and helmet and winter boots.

'Bel was grinning at her astonishment. In her gloved hand she held a brown leather case. "This is for McGuire," she said but did not release her hold on it as Andrea automatically reached for it. "Sorry. I have to give it to him. No substitutes. You'll have to bring him down here. I don't want to go up there."

Curious, Andrea asked, "How did you know he was here?"

"I didn't. This was sent to his office and the guard there said to bring it here. Evidently he is never out of touch."

McGuire, when Andrea brought him downstairs, merely glanced at the tall figure standing in the obscurity of the vestibule.

"Sign here," 'Bel said, thrusting a pencil and pad at him. When he had done so, 'Bel unlocked the case and handed him the large envelope that lay inside it.

McGuire made no effort to open the envelope. Instead he said, "My briefcase, please, Andrea," and she got it for him out of the cupboard. Absorbed in his own thoughts, McGuire seemed suddenly to realize that 'Bel still stood there. He looked at her, frowning.

"What are you waiting for?" he asked.

"Give me back the pad, please," said 'Bel.

He thrust it at her impatiently. She took it and stepped out of the door. Andrea, glancing out, saw her run down the steps and disappear under them into the basement entry. Turning back to McGuire she saw that he also was watching. Then he opened the briefcase, thrust the envelope inside and handed it back to her.

He said, "I've been waiting for this. I don't have to deal with it just now. Put it back, will you?"

Andrea put the briefcase back in the cupboard. He stood waiting for her to go up the stairs ahead of him, but she said she had to speak to Edna in the kitchen. When she heard him answering Daphne's questions she ran down the stairs to the basement.

"'Bel said, "What's the pitch, about the briefcase?"

"He always brings it with him and has me put it in the cupboard."

"What's that for — window dressing?"

"I don't know. Daphne is very flattered. She thinks he has such confidence in her that he can relax here in this house."

Andrea lingered in the basement until they heard the sound of voices coming downstairs. Then she went up to meet Daphne and the others as they reached the front door.

Daphne was very talkative when the maid had left and they were alone. She was still keyed up, talking rapidly and aimlessly over a wide range of subjects. Suddenly she asked,

"Why did Tim go downstairs? I heard the doorbell. He didn't tell me when he came back upstairs. I suppose he did not want to speak of it in front of the others."

"A messenger brought an envelope for him. It was to be delivered to him and no one else."

"A messenger?"

"Well, it was 'Bel, in fact."

"Isabel? That's funny."

"It's not funny at all. You know she works for a special messenger service." 270

"But it's funny that it should be Isabel!"

"A coincidence, I suppose. The company she works for does a lot of top secret work for the government."

But Daphne had already left the subject. "You know, Tim must have a fascinating life. What a lot of thrilling stories he could tell if he did not have to be so discreet."

"Yes." Resigned, Andrea listened to the long praise of McGuire. Poor Daphne. Did he really place a special value on her? Or was she simply someone he liked to spend some of his leisure with, somebody he could dazzle? Daphne did not go to bed with him. That Andrea was sure of. Daphne had been brought up to think no man would respect her if she gave in to him. But she wanted desperately to marry and to marry him.

Daphne was oblivious of Andrea's yawns. It was after eleven o'clock when the phone rang. Daphne ran to answer it. Andrea heard her exclamations: "But, Tim, I've no idea! Are you sure? Yes, certainly, come around. We are still up."

She turned away from the phone, frowning in distress. "He has lost an important document. Andrea, you did say it was Isabel who brought that envelope to him?"

"Yes. What of it?"

"Something is missing. He's coming here to talk to us."

Within minutes they heard the sound of his car in the deserted street. Daphne was at the door as he came up the steps. The man who had been with him earlier in the evening was right behind him.

Under the overhead light in the vestibule McGuire's face was grim. He began at once, "Andrea, you remember the envelope that fellow brought me? You saw me put it in my briefcase. He did, too."

Daphne broke in. "But what is it, Tim? What is the matter?"

"A large envelope was delivered to me here earlier this evening. I was expecting it. I knew what it contained. So I did not open it but put it immediately into my briefcase. Then when I returned to my office I examined its contents and something is missing. Someone must have tampered with —"

Andrea broke in, unwisely, "It certainly was not the messenger."

McGuire glared at her. "How can you be so sure? What do you —"

Andrea was suddenly aware of the stolid man standing behind McGuire. It was obvious to her that McGuire's suppressed panic was fueled by his presence. He said now, "Perhaps, Tim, you had better explain just what is missing."

McGuire replied, "The envelope that was sent to me was one of those large inter-office envelopes closed by a string clasp. Inside it was a smaller sealed envelope, among some other papers. They were all classified materials, but that smaller envelope is vital. You remember, Andrea, that the messenger brought it in a locked case, which he unlocked in my presence. It is the sealed envelope that is missing."

He had gone to his office, thought Andrea. McGuire had taken his companion back to his office with him. The diligent, unsleeping civil servant. It must have been a blow to find a vital document missing, under the eyes of such a witness.

McGuire's companion was looking at the door to the cupboard. "There is no lock on it," he said.

McGuire said crisply, "This was one place where I did not think such a precaution necessary. Until this evening, only Andrea and I knew my briefcase was in there." When the other remained silent he snapped, "Yes, I know what you're thinking. Are there any safe places?"

Daphne burst out, "Oh, Tim! Nobody here would do such a thing!"

McGuire said, "Nevertheless, I'll have to question that messenger. Isn't he the fellow who is living in your basement?"

Andrea noticed the slightest twitch in the stolid man's blond eyebrows. Daphne said breathlessly, "Oh, of course! Andrea, will you see if she is there and bring her here?"

McGuire, absorbed in himself, paid no attention to the "she" and "her". Andrea saw the blond man's eyebrows twitch again.

The light was on in the basement room as Andrea went down the stairs. It shone as a crack across the basement floor. When she opened the door she saw 'Bel lying in the bed, naked under the bedclothes. She sat up and swung her feet to the floor.

"What's all the commotion, Andy?"

"That fellow" flashed through Andrea's mind as she looked at 'Bel's long legs, small breasts, white skin, tuft of silky hair. "McGuire. He says something is missing from that envelope you brought him this evening."

'Bel got up from the bed, glowering. "Then it was missing when I got it." She reached for her clothes, draped over a nearby chair and quickly put them on.

"He didn't look in the envelope when you gave it to him. I saw that. I think he should have. He should have checked what was in it. He's mad now because he didn't."

"That's not my responsibility," said 'Bel.

The group upstairs had moved into the diningroom and stood together in the middle of the rug under the General's portrait.

McGuire switched around, ready with his attack. But he stopped short. 'Bel wore the same white shirt and riding breeches she had had on earlier, but she wore no helmet or leather jacket. In the glow of the lamps she was unmistakably a woman.

Suddenly uncertain, McGuire demanded, "Are you the messenger who brought me that envelope earlier this evening?" When she said, "Yes, he demanded, "Where did you get it?"

"From the guard at the north door of your office building."

"What did you do with it?"

"I didn't do anything with it. My orders are to have the person making the consignment place it in my carryall and lock it."

"But you can unlock the carryall."

"Of course. Sometimes I have more than one consignment to carry in it."

"Then you could have opened that envelope and taken something out of it."

The other man said, mildly, "It wasn't a sealed envelope. It was only fastened by a string clasp."

'Bel, enraged, ignored him. "What am I supposed to have taken out of it?"

McGuire rasped, "Suppose you tell me."

'Bel exploded. "I did not open the envelope. I took nothing out of it." His angry grin goaded her. "You goddamned sonofabitch, you —"

McGuire cut in. "I've only got your word for it. What's your name? You work for the All Agency Security Messengers? Seems to me it's highly suspicious that they'd hire a woman for this kind of work — a woman masquerading as a man. How many people do you fool?"

Andrea caught hold of 'Bel's arm and pulled her back. Daphne, terrified, tried to intervene. "Oh, Tim! There must be some other explanation!"

"You bet there's an explanation," said McGuire. Then he seemed to become aware of the man with him and, stepping back, made an effort to regain the appearance of calm. "There's an important document that has been removed from the envelope you brought me. I ought to call the police and have you arrested. For reasons I can't elucidate at this moment, I can't do that, not at this time. But you'd better not try to bolt. There's going to be an investigation of this."

'Bel said, "You can go to hell!"

McGuire ignored her and strode towards the front door. The man with him bowed blandly to Daphne and followed him out.

Daphne said, almost in tears, "Oh, Isabel! What is all this?"

"He's made a mistake and he doesn't want to own up to it," said 'Bel.

"Tim would never make a mistake. There must be something you know —"

'Bel yelled at her, "You can take your goddamn —"

Andrea caught hold of her and dragged her towards the stairs. "Come on, 'Bel! Don't start yelling at Daphne. She doesn't know anything about it."

Downstairs in 'Bel's room, Andrea said, "This is a mess."

'Bel said, "I could tear him apart."

"That wouldn't do any good. If you haven't done anything, 'Bel, there's nothing he can do."

273

"What do you mean, IF I haven't done anything?"

"Of course you haven't. I mean, he can't harm you."

"That's what you think. He'll make me lose my job, anyway. If he has me arrested, I'll have a police record. And you've forgotten something else. If I'm fired because of his complaint, I'll lose my bond. That's five hundred dollars down the drain. What do you mean, he can't harm me?"

"I'll be glad if you have to get another job. I never liked you doing this work."

"How am I going to get another job if I've got his accusations against my record and I can't prove anything? Do you think anybody is going to hire me if they think I'm dishonest — that I'm ready to make a buck by accepting a bribe?"

"Is that what you think McGuire thinks, that somebody paid you to steal that document?"

"What else would he think — unless he thinks I'm a spy myself instead of being a stooge for one."

"A spy?"

"Don't you know what he is? He is in Army Intelligence. He's probably got spies on the brain."

"But, 'Bel, it's ridiculous to think you'd be one."

"It's not ridiculous to McGuire. Why do you think he was threatening me with arrest?"

"Oh, 'Bel, what are we going to do?"

'Bel began to take off her clothes. "Right now I'm going to bed. Are you going to stay here with me?"

"Yes," said Andrea without hesitation.

The phone ringing somewhere else in the house woke Andrea just at daylight. 'Bel, waking also, watched as she got up and put on her clothes. Upstairs she found Daphne already in the kitchen.

"What an awful night, Andrea! I was frightened upstairs by myself."

"You need not have been," said Andrea, shortly. " 'Bel and I were here."

Daphne, pale from sleeplessness, pulled her dressinggown closer around her. "Tim called me half an hour ago. He has been up all night, of course. He said he had questioned the guard, who said the envelope was left with him by another officer in the department — Tim didn't say who it was. The guard didn't know what was in the envelope, of course. Tim says he can't get hold of this other officer till later today. In the meantime he's filed a complaint with that messenger service, and warned them that there may be a warrant out for the messenger later. Oh, Andrea, this is dreadful!"

"He couldn't wait, could he?"

"Andrea, this is top secret material that has been lost. He can't delay. Goodness knows who has got hold of it. Don't you remember the business about the Tuborg spy case that was in all the papers?"

"Daphne, I don't believe in all this stuff. Why would he arrange for anything so important to be brought to him like this? It wasn't so urgent, because he never bothered to look at the papers until he got back to his office. He's just making a show to impress people."

The pink flush came up in Daphne's face at once. "Andrea, you're very wrong. You seem to be incapable of understanding what this situation may mean. I'm sure Tim is not making a needless fuss."

"And in the meantime he's getting 'Bel fired, with a bad name. That's nothing, is it?"

She turned away, not listening to Daphne's justifications. She felt sick at her stomach and refused to eat breakfast. Upstairs they worked in an angry silence, speaking only when a question had to be asked and answered. Whenever the phone rang Daphne picked up the receiver and Andrea sat tensely listening until it was obvious that the call had nothing to do with 'Bel or McGuire.

It was early afternoon when he finally called. Andrea strained to hear what the voice clacking in the receiver said, but she could understand only Daphne's infrequent half-phrases.

"Oh, well, then it's settled! You've found it! Oh, I'm sure they'll understand how it came about — no blame on you."

But McGuire's angry voice on the other end continued. When Daphne finally hung up she sat back limply in her chair. She looked unhappy.

"It's all right, Andrea. Tim has found the missing material. He was able to get in touch with the officer who sent him the envelope. They could not find the missing inner envelope at first. But after ransacking the office they found that a careless clerk had failed to put the sealed envelope in with the rest of the.papers. Oh, my, what a relief! Poor Tim! What a terrible night he has had!"

"What has he done about 'Bel?"

"Isabel? Oh, I don't know. I didn't ask him. He didn't mention her. I suppose he will notify the messenger service."

"You suppose? Daphne, you're so wrapped up in McGuire you can't give a thought to anything else. He's been the cause of a good deal of trouble for somebody else. Don't you see that if he had done what he should have done, examined that envelope when it was brought to him, this wouldn't have happened? At least he would have known then and could have checked with his office before all this business blew up like a balloon?"

Daphne, startled by her vehemence, faltered in her reply. "Surely, Andrea, you realize that Tim has such important considerations to weigh that he can't think of something as minor as a messenger. He does not know Isabel. She's just —"

Andrea, overborne by her own indignation, walked away from her.

A little later she heard the motorcycle and then the slam of the basement entry door. Without a word to Daphne she got up from her desk and went downstairs. She found 'Bel standing in the middle of the maid's room, still clutching the gauntlet gloves she used for driving.

'Bel said, "I've lost the job."

"But McGuire called Daphne and said the sealed envelope was found — it was never lost. Some jackass forgot to put it in with the rest of the papers."

'Bel nodded. "So they told me. But he had already made the complaint and they say they never go on hiring somebody after a complaint has been made, no matter what the outcome." She spoke calmly. "I've got an idea they're glad to get rid of me anyway. They don't want to hire a woman and now that I've shown I can do the job just as well as a man, they've lost interest in waiting for me to break down." She was silent for a moment and then added, "One thing, though. They cancelled the bond and gave me back the money. I was ready to raise Cain about that, but they didn't argue."

"Well, you stay here. You can get another job."

"What about Daphne? She may not want me here."

"Daphne is going to have to accept the fact that you're staying here while I'm on this job."

'Bel gave her a quizzical smile. "Just like that. And how about McGuire coming here?"

"He'll just have to lump it." Andrea was thoughtful for a moment. "I wonder how much more we're likely to see of him."

'Bel looked at her in surprise but did not answer.

* * *

Nevertheless, though she had considered the matter, it was another thing to watch Daphne's disappointment. There was no sign of McGuire. At first his absence was not too remarkable. He had so often in the past vanished for short periods of time. But the weeks kept passing and Daphne obviously looked for him every afternoon.

Daphne made no question of 'Bel staying. Her preoccupation seemed to shut out both Andrea and 'Bel. She even seemed indifferent to whether she was alone in the house, though Andrea doubted that she would remain there overnight without protest.

'Bel got a job selling phonograph records at a new music store that opened on the ground floor of an old house on Wisconsin Avenue, near the carstop where the girls from Annunciation gathered every afternoon. It wasn't much money, she said, but she could listen to all the new releases. Obviously it was a stopgap, till the future became clearer.

So they all three hung in a state of waiting.

'Bel said, "But what is she waiting for?"

"For McGuire to come back."

"Where is he?"

"I've no idea. But even if he is here in Washington, I don't think he's coming back to this house, to see Daphne."

"Why?"

"Because he has been made to look like a fool — he thinks so, at any rate, which amounts to the same thing. I told you he is an unforgiving sort of person. He doesn't want any reminders. So he is off Daphne."

"That's hard on Daphne."

"Yes. It's too bad. Because she doesn't understand that that's the case. She keeps hoping and expecting him to come again. She is always thinking of excuses why he doesn't come to her parties, even if somebody tells her he is in town and asks her if she has seen him. I think she does see him occasionally, at somebody else's house. He doesn't treat her well, because she comes home so unhappy."

"You ought to tell her. Talk straight to her."

"I've tried. She won't believe me. She thinks I'm being malicious or revengeful or something. She is blind to his faults."

A weekend came when spring weather rushed into Washington and the surrounding countryside. Daphne was suddenly ecstatic. She would be away, she told Andrea, from Friday to Monday, with friends — "the Mendozas, you know them, of course," who had invited her to their place on the Severn River near Annapolis. Andrea recognized them. Mrs. Mendoza was an old friend of Daphne's who had married a Latin American diplomat. She had made a determined effort all winter to promote a romance between Daphne and McGuire, who had known her husband for a number of years.

Andrea was troubled at the sight of Daphne's feverish gaiety, the excited anticipation with which Daphne waited for Friday to come. It must mean that Lily Mendoza had told Daphne that McGuire would also be a weekend guest. It was with a sigh of relief that Andrea saw Daphne fly out of the house on Friday morning, relief with a sense of foreboding underlying it.

That Sunday Andrea and 'Bel went for the day up the Potomac, above Great Falls, for a hike through the spring-budding woods. It was well after dark when they returned to the house in Georgetown. Astonished, they gazed up at the sight. Every window was lit, yet there were no cars in the street. When Andrea unlocked the front door and they went in, there was no one on the ground floor and no sound in the rest of the house.

"She must be here," said 'Bel. "She's got every light on."

"But she's not due till tomorrow," Andrea protested.

"This has happened before, don't you remember?"

Andrea went to the stairwell and called, "Daphne, are you up there?"

For a few moments there was no answer and then Daphne's head appeared over the stair-rail of the top floor, dark against the bright light.

277

"Yes, I'm here," she said. "Where have you been?"

"We didn't expect you back till tomorrow."

"Well, I must say, I wasn't happy to get here and find the house empty. It was a good thing it was still daylight." Daphne's tone was petulant and she withdrew her head.

Andrea looked at 'Bel. 'Bel shrugged.

"I quess we'd better turn out some of the lights," said Andrea.

Daphne had closed herself into her bedroom by the time Andrea reached the top floor. Andrea saw no more of her till the next day. And then she had to rely on her own observation to fathom the reason for Daphne's premature return. She thought at first that McGuire had failed to show up for the weekend party. But as time wore on she decided that he had been there and something had taken place between him and Daphne that had brought matters to an end. Daphne's mood was black. She sat for half an hour at a time, frowning into space, inaccessible to even the most routine questions.

Her manner did not change as the days went by. She's not sleeping, thought Andrea, seeing her reddened, pouchy eyes. She paid little attention to her meals, picking at the food in front of her before pushing her plate away.

"She's miserable," Andrea said to 'Bel, as they sat together in the spring sunshine on the terrace while Daphne was out. "He must have told her he doesn't want her, he wants out of their relationship. He's an utterly selfish bastard."

"Good riddance," said 'Bel, plucking a dead leaf from the Virginia creeper that was just sending out new tendrils.

"Not to Daphne," said Andrea.

Then the afternoon came when Daphne, who had been out most of the day, came in with an air of disaster met and conquered. She moved about the workroom for a while, abstracted, obviously keyed up to say something. Andrea sat still, sorting index cards.

At last Daphne stopped abruptly beside her and said, "Andrea."

Andrea looked up.

"I've made up my mind. I have told Professor Howell that I shall not continue with this project. It has been interesting, but I feel it is really a dead-end for me, professionally. I've had a good offer from a large library which I find very attractive, not in Washington. He was distressed but sympathetic. He praised me for what had been done so far."

Andrea spoke after a moment. "I'm sorry you're going, Daphne. I know you're not happy —"

Daphne hurried to cut her short. "That's neither here nor there. The point is that I'm leaving at fairly short notice, in June. He persuaded me to stay till then. He's been so kind I couldn't refuse, though I wish — I wish —"

You could leave right this moment, thought Andrea, and

never set eyes on this house again. But she said nothing and Daphne went on. "I told Professor Howell that you are very capable and can carry on till they find another curator. In fact, if you want me to, I can speak to him about making you my successor —"

"That's kind of you, Daphne, but I don't want it."

Daphne shrugged and turned away. "Well, as you wish," she said and relapsed into her own absorbing thoughts.

In the days that followed Andrea found the details of the job left more and more on her own hands. Daphne seemed to care very little how things went. Often she was away from the house for hours at a time, too restless to sit over the tedious task of sorting and comparing and classifying. Andrea struggled to keep abreast of the daily correspondence, the telephone inquiries that Daphne once had been delighted to encourage.

'Bel said, "Looks as if the boat is sinking under you, Andy, and Daphne's already swimming for shore. Are you sure you don't want the job?"

"Of course I'm sure. Don't you realize that if I stayed on, I'd have to move back home? Mother would see no reason why I should live here. And then where'd we be?"

* * *

April had just begun. The forsythia, the lilac, the first frail translucent leaves on the trees had transformed Washington overnight from winter to spring. Andrea, arriving at her parents' house on a Saturday afternoon, was aware the moment she saw her mother's face that some new disaster was shaping.

For a while her mother said nothing beyond a brief acknowledgement of her presence. They had long since ceased to kiss when they met.

Her mother said, "Bland came to see me yesterday. She has told me the whole story about Miss Schwenk. She was surprised I did not already know it."

Andrea did not answer. The tone of her mother's voice told her that her mother was chagrined and resentful.

"I would have thought that at least you would have confided that in me. If Bland had not told me, I suppose I would have gone on forever in ignorance."

"Mother, I've told you that Daphne is leaving. I told you that when she told me."

"You did not tell me why."

"I don't really know why. Daphne has not told me."

"Don't keep telling me half-lies! Of course I know what she said to Professor Howell. I have wondered ever since you told me she was not going to continue. She did not strike me as being an irresponsible woman, so there must be another reason. Now I know."

279

What *do* you know? Andrea wondered. "What has Cousin Bland told you, Mother?"

"She has told me all about this affair between Miss Schwenk and that man McGuire. She has told me about what happened there one evening back in February when a messenger brought some important papers to him and they were found to be tampered with. You know how gossip spreads here in Washington, about anything that happens in governmental circles. I don't understand everything Bland said and I don't want to. What I do understand is that there has been a lot of intrigue going on there at that house and that you're involved in it."

"Mother, that's not true! Daphne hasn't been having an affair with McGuire. She's in love with him and she wants him to marry her. But he has backed out."

"That's beside the point. I've no concern with her. But the business of the messenger. Bland says the messenger was living in the house. Everyone thought it was a man —"

She stopped in midsentence and Andrea waited in silence for the inevitable.

"It was Isabel, wasn't it?"

Andrea looked up to find her mother's eyes blazing at her. "Yes, it's 'Bel," she said quietly.

"She has been living there in that house with you."

"Yes."

The silence went on for a long time, till Andrea, desperate to break it, said, "Daphne offered to speak to Professor Howell about keeping me as curator."

"He would not have agreed."

"That doesn't matter, because I told her that I intend to go to graduate school next September."

"You can make whatever arrangements you wish. There is still a year before you are of age and till then I am still responsible for you. But this house is no longer your home. Understand that. You must come here from time to time, for your father's sake. I will not have him made miserable by knowing of the type of life you have chosen. But you are no longer my daughter."

Andrea, horrified at the whiteness of her mother's cheeks, reached out to touch her. "Mother, Mother! You can't mean that!"

But her mother moved away swiftly. "Leave me alone! Don't touch me! Don't dare!"

They stared at each other across the abyss that had grown steadily wider between them. I know her now, thought Andrea, in the midst of the fog of misery that enveloped her, better than I would ever have known her if I had stayed her daughter. And she knows me now. We're closer than we have ever been. There are no barriers between us now. She sees into me and I see into her. Oh, Mother!

She turned away and walked out of the house.

* * *

To wear out some of the anguish that possessed her she walked all the way from the carstop on Fourteenth Street to the house in Georgetown. The Saturday afternoon was filled with the sweetness of spring. The mild air promised summer. The people she passed on the street were obviously relaxed with the charm of the day.

When she got to the Georgetown house and opened the front door she was met by silence. The house was closed up and the dead air rang in her ears. Daphne was gone for a long weekend to New York. 'Bel, she supposed, was at work. She took her small suitcase upstairs to her room and then went into the workroom. Something to do with her hands would help. She picked up the pile of unanswered letters Daphne had left on her desk.

She succeeded in part in the effort of concentration. For a few minutes at a time she was able to read with comprehension, weigh the matters concerned. But inexorably her thoughts wandered back to her mother. Her mother's voice over the months came to her, "You are so blinded you cannot see what you are doing with your life. You've let Isabel ruin your life." And her own replies, " 'Bel has done nothing at all. I love 'Bel. She loves me. It's *not* wrong for us to love each other as we do."

She pulled her thoughts back to the letters before her. But soon again she was justifying herself to her mother. "I have not said anything about 'Bel simply because you won't let me. But she exists, even if you want to deny she does, she exists as my other half. She exists and she loves me and she would never do me any harm."

All at once, in the midst of her inner pleading, she heard the faraway sound of a flute. She dropped the letter she was holding and listened. Mozart. It must be 'Bel. 'Bel had come in and had not known that she was sitting here alone upstairs. She jumped up and fled down the stairs. The music of the flute flowed up to her, fluid, effortless, seductive, joyous. 'Bel must have the radio turned up full blast.

But when she reached the basement she realized that it was not the radio. The door of the maid's room was open. She could see the back of 'Bel's head and her hands holding the flute. She stood at the door till suddenly the music stopped and 'Bel turned around, her face radiant.

"Andy! Look! Isn't it a beauty?"

'Bel held the shining instrument out to her. "Somebody came into the shop and wanted to sell it. I told him he could let me have it right away. Now don't get upset. Yes, I spent everything I've saved on it. I haven't a cent left."

She stopped abruptly and looked hard at Andrea. "You've had a fight with your mother."

Andrea's eyes suddenly filled with tears. "I'm — Mother said —"

281

'Bel laid the flute down and came and put her arms around Andrea. "She threw you out."

"She said I could do what I pleased. She said it's not my home anymore. She said I could come back now and then, just so Dad won't be upset.'

"Well, that's nice."

" 'Bel, she disowned me. She said I'm not her daughter any more."

"She can't change a biological fact. But I guess that's not what she is thinking about. Well, all right. We go on from here."

"I said I was going to graduate school next September."

"All right. You go to Hopkins and I'll go back and finish at Bryn Mawr. I can commute from Baltimore."

Then they looked at each other in a kind of amazement.

IN THE GAME by Nikki Baker. 192 pp. A Virginia Kelly
mystery. First in a series.   ISBN 01-56280-004-3 $8.95

AVALON by Mary Jane Jones. 256 pp. A Lesbian Arthurian
romance.   ISBN 0-941483-96-7   9.95

STRANDED by Camarin Grae. 320 pp. Entertaining, riveting
adventure.   ISBN 0-941483-99-1   9.95

THE DAUGHTERS OF ARTEMIS by Lauren Wright Douglas.
240 pp. Third Caitlin Reece mystery.   ISBN 0-941483-95-9   8.95

CLEARWATER by Catherine Ennis. 176 pp. Romantic secrets
of a small Louisiana town.   ISBN 0-941483-65-7   8.95

THE HALLELUJAH MURDERS by Dorothy Tell. 176 pp.
Second Poppy Dillworth mystery.   ISBN 0-941483-88-6   8.95

ZETA BASE by Judith Alguire. 208 pp. Lesbian triangle
on a future Earth.   ISBN 0-941483-94-0   9.95

SECOND CHANCE by Jackie Calhoun. 256 pp. Contemporary
Lesbian lives and loves.   ISBN 0-941483-93-2   9.95

MURDER BY TRADITION by Katherine V. Forrest. 288 pp.
A Kate Delafield Mystery. 4th in a series.   ISBN 0-941483-89-4   18.95

BENEDICTION by Diane Salvatore. 272 pp. Striking,
contemporary romantic novel.   ISBN 0-941483-90-8   9.95

CALLING RAIN by Karen Marie Christa Minns. 240 pp.
Spellbinding, erotic love story   ISBN 0-941483-87-8   9.95

BLACK IRIS by Jeane Harris. 192 pp. Caroline's hidden past . . .
                                               ISBN 0-941483-68-1   8.95

TOUCHWOOD by Karin Kallmaker. 240 pp. Loving, May/
December romance.   ISBN 0-941483-76-2   8.95

BAYOU CITY SECRETS by Deborah Powell. 224 pp. A Hollis
Carpenter mystery. First in a series.   ISBN 0-941483-91-6   8.95

COP OUT by Claire McNab. 208 pp. 4th Det. Insp. Carol Ashton
mystery.   ISBN 0-941483-84-3   8.95

LODESTAR by Phyllis Horn. 224 pp. Romantic, fast-moving
adventure.   ISBN 0-941483-83-5   8.95

THE BEVERLY MALIBU by Katherine V. Forrest. 288 pp. A
Kate Delafield Mystery. 3rd in a series. (HC) ISBN 0-941483-47-9   16.95
                           Paperback   ISBN 0-941483-48-7   9.95

THAT OLD STUDEBAKER by Lee Lynch. 272 pp. Andy's affair
with Regina and her attachment to her beloved car.
ISBN 0-941483-82-7   9.95

PASSION'S LEGACY by Lori Paige. 224 pp. Sarah is swept into
the arms of Augusta Pym in this delightful historical romance.
ISBN 0-941483-81-9   8.95

THE PROVIDENCE FILE by Amanda Kyle Williams. 256 pp.
Second espionage thriller featuring lesbian agent Madison McGuire
ISBN 0-941483-92-4   8.95

I LEFT MY HEART by Jaye Maiman. 320 pp. A Robin Miller
Mystery. First in a series.   ISBN 0-941483-72-X   9.95

THE PRICE OF SALT by Patricia Highsmith (writing as Claire
Morgan). 288 pp. Classic lesbian novel, first issued in 1952 . . .
acknowledged by its author under her own, very famous, name.
ISBN 1-56280-003-5   8.95

SIDE BY SIDE by Isabel Miller. 256 pp. From beloved author of
Patience and Sarah.   ISBN 0-941483-77-0   8.95

SOUTHBOUND by Sheila Ortiz Taylor. 240 pp. Hilarious sequel
to *Faultline.*   ISBN 0-941483-78-9   8.95

STAYING POWER: LONG TERM LESBIAN COUPLES
by Susan E. Johnson. 352 pp. Joys of coupledom.
ISBN 0-941-483-75-4   12.95

SLICK by Camarin Grae. 304 pp. Exotic, erotic adventure.
ISBN 0-941483-74-6   9.95

NINTH LIFE by Lauren Wright Douglas. 256 pp. A Caitlin
Reece mystery. 2nd in a series.   ISBN 0-941483-50-9   8.95

PLAYERS by Robbi Sommers. 192 pp. Sizzling, erotic novel.
ISBN 0-941483-73-8   8.95

MURDER AT RED ROOK RANCH by Dorothy Tell. 224 pp.
First Poppy Dillworth adventure.   ISBN 0-941483-80-0   8.95

LESBIAN SURVIVAL MANUAL by Rhonda Dicksion.
112 pp. Cartoons!   ISBN 0-941483-71-1   8.95

A ROOM FULL OF WOMEN by Elisabeth Nonas. 256 pp.
Contemporary Lesbian lives.   ISBN 0-941483-69-X   8.95

MURDER IS RELATIVE by Karen Saum. 256 pp. The first
Brigid Donovan mystery.   ISBN 0-941483-70-3   8.95

These are just a few of the many Naiad Press titles — we are the oldest and
largest lesbian/feminist publishing company in the world. Please request a
complete catalog. We offer personal service; we encourage and welcome direct
mail orders from individuals who have limited access to bookstores carrying
our publications.